The Pearls and the Crown

Book One

The Pearls

Deborah Chester

ACE BOOKS, NEW YORK

THE BERKLEY PUBLISHING GROUP
Published by the Penguin Group
Penguin Group (USA) Inc.
375 Hudson Street, New York, New York 10014, USA
Penguin Group (Canada), 90 Eglinton Avenue East, Suite 700, Toronto, Ontario M4P 2Y3, Canada
(a division of Pearson Penguin Canada Inc.)
Penguin Books Ltd., 80 Strand, London WC2R 0RL, England
Penguin Group Ireland, 25 St. Stephen's Green, Dublin 2, Ireland (a division of Penguin Books Ltd.)
Penguin Group (Australia), 250 Camberwell Road, Camberwell, Victoria 3124, Australia
(a division of Pearson Australia Group Pty. Ltd.)
Penguin Books India Pvt. Ltd., 11 Community Centre, Panchsheel Park, New Delhi—110 017, India
Penguin Group (NZ), 67 Apollo Drive, Rosedale, North Shore 0632, New Zealand
(a division of Pearson New Zealand Ltd.)
Penguin Books (South Africa) (Pty.) Ltd., 24 Sturdee Avenue, Rosebank, Johannesburg 2196,
South Africa

Penguin Books Ltd., Registered Offices: 80 Strand, London WC2R 0RL, England

This is a work of fiction. Names, characters, places, and incidents either are the product of the author's imagination or are used fictitiously, and any resemblance to actual persons, living or dead, business establishments, events, or locales is entirely coincidental. The publisher does not have any control over and does not assume any responsibility for author or third-party websites or their content.

THE PEARLS

An Ace Book / published by arrangement with the author

PRINTING HISTORY
Ace mass-market edition / December 2007

Copyright © 2007 by Deborah Chester.
Cover art by Matt Stawicki.
Cover design by Judith Lagerman.
Interior text design by Laura K. Corless.

ISBN: 978-0-441-01548-1

ACE
Ace Books are published by The Berkley Publishing Group,
a division of Penguin Group (USA) Inc.,
375 Hudson Street, New York, New York 10014.
ACE and the "A" design are trademarks belonging to Penguin Group (USA) Inc.

PRINTED IN THE UNITED STATES OF AMERICA

10 9 8 7 6 5 4 3 2 1

Chapter 1

In the hot, dusty province of Ulinia, there existed but one road and one pass through the steep and treacherous Jawnuth Mountains. Just below that pass sprawled the bustling crossroads market of Kanidalon, a prosperous town featuring rug warehouses, hostels, customs offices, wagon makers, artifact dealers, and throngs of travelers—mostly pilgrims and merchants. Anything was for sale in Kanidalon; anything could be bought, for sufficient price. Even so, thievery was rife, and the Ninth Legion was stationed there to keep order and protect both the mountain pass and the imperial countinghouse.

Less than a league away from Kanidalon, there stood a sleepy, nameless village well off the beaten path, a village that sheltered many displaced cutthroats and fugitives. Admirably located from a thief's perspective, it was close enough to easily sell to Kanidalon's black market and close enough to the road to rob travelers whenever the soldiers weren't on patrol.

Tucked away in the foothills up a winding, wooded track, the village was hard to find, a place no prudent man entered if he valued his life or his money purse. Yet on a hot, late summer's day, Vordachai, warlord of Ulinia, rode into this den with five-and-twenty of his best warriors.

Burly, bearded, clad in armor, and fisting a stout war mace studded with steel spikes, Lord Vordachai was neither a prudent man nor one that any prudent thief would dare attack. With his armor and saddle leather creaking, his spurs jingling, he rode into the village as though he owned it—which, perhaps, he did—and his dark, beady eyes darted here and there across the motley assembly of incurious villagers that spilled out of doorways to watch him pass. If he noticed that not all the watching faces were those of peasants, if he noticed the lookout concealed among the scrub halfway up the hillside behind the village, or the sudden, chirring rise of a flock of little qualli disturbed from the brush, Lord Vordachai gave no sign.

By birthright and brutal muscle, he ruled this province with a fist of iron. His barons obeyed him; his peasants feared him. And the presence of imperial troops in his largest city chafed him raw.

But it was not imperial business he sought today.

At the village well, he reined up and bellowed for the headman.

A gaunt fellow with a scraggly beard and nervous eyes sidled forth reluctantly. He lifted the end-cloth of his head wrap to his lips and forehead in salute, bowing low. "My gracious lord," he murmured.

By this time, Vordachai's lackey had drawn a wooden pail of water and poured some of it into the warlord's horn-cup. Vordachai drank deep and slung the remainder away, leaving a long, thin damp mark in the dust.

"How many inns and wineshops has this village?" he asked.

The headman hesitated as though he feared to give the wrong answer. "Th-three, my gracious lord."

"Bring their proprietors to me."

* * *

At the opposite end of the village, a rat-faced man in a sleeveless jerkin darted through the idlers cluttering up the inn yard, and ducked into the gloomy taproom of the Maiden's Thigh. Near the room's one window, a group of men with army tattoos on their cheeks and bared arms were daring each other to *drakshera* by vying to see which of them could balance a dagger on the tip of his tongue without splitting it. Roaring with laughter, shouting friendly curses and jeers of encouragement, they bet coins and knucklebones, trinkets and bootlaces, and when one man cut his tongue and stumbled away, spitting blood, howls of amusement rocked the rafters.

In the back corner, alone and well away from this foolery, there sat a tall, broad-shouldered man. Unshaven, ill kempt, his brown tunic stiff and greasy in need of washing, he sat nursing a tankard of ale. Occasionally he lifted it to his lips, but seldom did he take more than a sip, for it was a sour brew the landlord made here, and it stank worse than horse piss. Now he saw that a fly had fallen into the swill, and was still kicking feebly.

The rat-faced man slid up to his table, bobbed his head awkwardly in greeting, and said urgently, "Best to run, great one. The warlord has come. He's at the well now, asking questions."

Shadrael tu Natalloh grimaced at the fly drowning in his ale and set aside his tankard. Over by the window, someone yelped in pain, and another great, laughing shout rose from the others.

Ignoring them, Shadrael fixed his black gaze on the informer. "Is that not what warlords do, Jutak? Ask questions and collect tribute?"

Despite his filthy appearance, his voice was one of culture and education, and on his tongue Ulinian flowed melodically with the accent of the *aziarahd mahal*, the noble class.

"But he is asking for a man named Shadrael," Jutak said, glancing nervously over his shoulder. "Quick! There is still time to run."

"Why should I?"

At that moment, a war mace thudded into the open door of the taproom with such force it splintered the wood and stuck there. The rowdy noise shut off, and the men who had been playing Kiss the Dagger put their bets away and reached for their weapons instead.

"Shadrael!" bellowed a voice as deep as a bull's. "Shadrael, you leper! Are you in this pestilent hole?"

"I am," Shadrael replied in a normal tone. He smiled slightly to himself and slid his tankard in the informer's direction.

The rat-faced man grabbed it up like a prize and scuttled away with it pressed to his thin chest.

Lord Vordachai strode into the taproom, ducking his head beneath the low lintel. He paused a moment, blinking as though trying to adjust his vision to the gloom, but instead of advancing he retreated.

"Come outside!" he yelled. "Faugh! This place smells worse than a pigsty. Come outside and let's talk!"

Before Shadrael could answer, Fomo joined him, fierce-eyed and protective.

"Who is this fool, calling you forth?" he growled softly. His voice was a hoarse ruin. "Do you want us to deal with him?"

"No," Shadrael said, still smiling that cold, sardonic little smile his men knew to be a warning. "At ease."

The military order was a signal. Fomo's head snapped up. He drew in a deep breath, narrowing his gaze, but kept silent as Shadrael rose from the table, kicked aside a stool, and strolled from the taproom.

Outside, the noonday sun shone hot and bright. Shadrael found it painful, for no longer did he live under the veil of the shadow god's protection. Still, he bore the discomfort without even a wince, just as a seasoned campaigner might march on despite being hampered by a festering heel blister.

The idlers in the inn yard had scattered away. The warlord's men, half of them still mounted, the rest standing next to their horses, blocked the open gate. Shadrael heard them muttering to each other over the fact that he cast no shadow. There'd been a time when their nervousness would have amused him, but he was well past the point of taking pride in scaring a few provincial warriors or the village children.

Vordachai had planted himself in the center of the yard, his fists on his hips, his armor plates reflecting the blazing sunshine like steel mirrors. His shadow darkened the ground at his feet, marking him as unmistakably human and still in possession of his soul.

Perhaps, Shadrael thought, Vordachai was trying to look impressive, standing armored in the heat this way. He was more likely to tempt Gault to strike him with apoplexy.

Vordachai beckoned impatiently, but Shadrael walked without haste across the hot, dusty inn yard away from the warlord, moving with the panther grace of a born warrior. Early in his military career, Shadrael had passed into army legend by daring to take the Kiss of Eternity—the deadliest version of all games of *shul-drakshera*—which few men risked and even fewer survived. It was why he no longer cast a shadow on a sunny day, why he possessed no soul. It had transformed him into one of the fiercest, most ruthless *donare* sworn into Emperor Kostimon's service, a warrior without equal. And even now, unshaven, his hair grown out and falling in his eyes, wearing neither armor nor sword, his boot soles so worn through that the hot dirt burned his feet, he crossed the yard with a swagger that drew every eye to him.

He eased himself deep within the shade of an enormous tree growing next to the wall. The shade it cast was thin and dappled, its dusty leaves stirring from a hot breeze, but it provided enough respite from the sun for Shadrael to focus his full attention on his scowling visitor. Bracing his shoulder against the tree, Shadrael tucked his thumbs nonchalantly in his belt, and waited.

Vordachai beckoned again, but Shadrael did not move. After a moment, Vordachai strode over, kicking up little clouds of dust with each step, his spurs jingling loudly as he scattered a flock of clucking chickens before him.

Puffing a little, his face beaded with perspiration above his dusty beard, he glowered at Shadrael. "You've given me a great deal of trouble, finding you. I searched out Kanidalon before I came here."

Shadrael shrugged. "Aren't you hot, in all that plate armor? Better have your man loosen your buckles or you'll have blisters bursting before nightfall."

"I need no help with my armor."

"Are you at war with someone?"

"None of your jokes, knave! There's little time, and I am in great need of you."

A laugh broke from Shadrael. With a growl, Vordachai closed in on him, but Shadrael was quicker. He evaded the warlord's lunge, whipped out his needle-tipped dagger, and placed the point right in Vordachai's armpit where his armor did not reach. One quick, hard thrust, and the dagger would pierce something vital.

Vordachai froze, breathing heavily, his small eyes narrowing to slits.

"My lord!" Shouting in alarm, the warriors broke into a run toward them.

"Even as I am now, I'm still faster than you," Shadrael said softly, keeping one eye on Vordchai's men. "Call off your dogs, brother."

"It's all right!" Vordachai bellowed.

"They're still coming," Shadrael said, pressing the dagger just a little harder through the padded cloth of Vordachai's undertunic.

Vordachai winced. "Damn you!"

"I wonder if you'll be able to yell as loud when you have only one lung. Call them off."

Vordachai's color deepened, but he shouted, "Chaiblin, halt! I'm all right! Stay back, you whoresons!"

His men stopped halfway across the inn yard, brandishing their weapons and looking unsure. Behind them, Shadrael's men had gathered in the inn's doorway, muttering to themselves.

"If we're going to have a fight, my men against yours," Shadrael said conversationally, "shall we bet on who wins?"

Vordachai rolled his eyes. "In Gault's name, then, drop your weapon. They won't back off until you release me."

"And I won't drop my weapon until they back away," Shadrael said with a smile. Enjoying himself, he met Vordachai's furious gaze and bared his teeth even more.

"You're bluffing."

"Why should I?"

"You won't kill me."

"Shall we see?" Shadrael pushed in the tip of the dagger, and Vordachai sucked in a sharp breath, his eyes flaring wide with alarm.

"All right. All right! Chaiblin!" he bellowed. "Back away, as I have commanded you!"

Slowly, with obvious reluctance, the warlord's men obeyed him.

"All the way," Shadrael said, still using that light, half-amused tone. "They can stand across the gate again if it pleases them."

"Go!" Vordachai yelled at his men, still glaring a hole through Shadrael. "Satisfied, you cur?"

"It will do," Shadrael said.

Of course, by now Shadrael's men had taken up a position in the gate behind the retreating Ulinians. The warlord and his small force were trapped inside this enclosure, like qualli running into a cage after grain. A roar of mocking laughter went up.

Grinning, Shadrael lowered his dagger and released Vordachai, who stepped hastily away from him, rubbing his armpit and scowling.

"You damned whelp," he grumbled. "You waste valuable time with these stupid games."

"I have all the time in the world to waste," Shadrael said

indifferently. Putting his back to the tree, he flipped his dagger up in the air and caught it as adeptly as a juggler. He started to toss it up again, but Vordachai gripped his wrist, and the dagger went tumbling to the ground at their feet.

"This is important, and urgent," Vordachai said grimly, releasing him. "I need you."

"Am I supposed to be grateful? Am I supposed to be interested?"

"I'll pay you, like the damned mercenary you've become."

Dropping his pretense of foolery, Shadrael straightened. "Then I'm interested. What's your price?"

"Nine hundred ducats."

Startled, Shadrael put his lips together, but he did not whistle. His brother looked dead serious, and that alerted Shadrael because Vordachai was as close-fisted with his gold as a miser in a countinghouse.

"That's a fortune," he said cautiously.

"More than I can spare, but I'll double it if all goes well."

"Eighteen hundred ducats?" Scowling, Shadrael shook his head. "You haven't got it. You should have stopped with the first offer. Now I'll take neither."

"I give you my oath on it," Vordachai said. "Nine hundred when you play your part. Another nine hundred if this business goes as I hope."

Still suspicious, Shadrael tilted his head to one side. "What do you want? Am I to start a war with the Thyrazenes for you?"

"This has nothing to do with those miserable dragon keepers."

"What, then? Come on. You're the one claiming to be in a hurry. What could possibly be worth that much to you?"

Vordachai looked all around, oddly hesitant.

"None can overhear us," Shadrael lied reassuringly. "What's the job?"

"Ride with me, alone, beyond the village," Vordachai said, "and I'll tell you."

Shadrael straightened. "Ride with you into an imperial trap, I suppose. What's the price on my head these days?"

"Damn you! Do you think I've come all this way to betray your pox-ridden hide for a few miserable coppers?" Vordachai shot him a look of hurt. "Is that what we've come to?"

If he'd roared and blustered, Shadrael would have known he was lying. But there was little subtlety about Vordachai, and less guile. Something inside Shadrael relaxed.

"Nine hundred ducats?" he asked.

A hopeful grin split Vordachai's bearded face. "Aye! Nine hundred. Come now, and let's talk."

So they rode out together, Shadrael borrowing the mount of the man called Chaiblin, who glowered and made a big show of removing a second sword from his saddle sheath before handing over the reins.

Shadrael ignored the stirrups, which were too short for him, and wheeled the snorting, uneasy horse out of the inn yard. The animal feared him, and sidled edgily with its back hunched under the saddle as though it meant to either buck with him or bolt. Shadrael held the reins short and tight, pushing his will at the animal to control it, and led his brother up the hillside into a copse of dusty trees above the village.

"Satisfied?" he asked.

Vordachai reined up beside him. "Aye. Now we can speak freely. The upstart's sister is on the road, traveling from New Imperia to Trau—"

"You hunted me up to share court gossip?" Shadrael asked, grinning.

"No! Damn you, listen—"

Shadrael raised his hand. "Enough! I've said I won't lead your armies if you go to war against the emperor. I told you that last year, and the year before. Why can't you get it through your thick skull that I won't—"

"Just hear me out, hotspur."

"You haven't the men to take on thirty legions of imperial force. They will squash you like a bug, Vordachai."

"Don't exaggerate. It wouldn't be thirty legions," Vordachai said. "The time is perfect. He's got the Madruns coming at him again on the north and west, and he'll have to send his mobile forces to reinforce the borders. Maybe, with Gault's help, this damned Ninth Legion will be recalled, and we'll be rid of them."

"So you want me to cause them no trouble for a while." Shadrael grinned. "For nine hundred ducats, done!"

Vordachai scowled. "Don't be a dolt. Gods, the insult of having imperial troops stationed here, as though I cannot govern my own province! I tell you—"

"You delude yourself," Shadrael broke in, aware that he was wasting his breath. His brother's hatred of the new emperor remained fixed and implacable. No amount of reasoning ever seemed to penetrate Vordachai's skull. But Shadrael tried anyway. "Under any circumstances, five to ten mobile legions are going to be held in reserve for petty uprisings like yours."

"Petty! I'll have you know—"

"That's an army of fifty thousand. And how many men can you levy from your barons? Four thousand? Five? Or less than three? Hell's breath, they'll keep the Ninth here precisely because you're a known troublemaker."

Vordachai waved Shadrael's remarks away. "Plague smite them if they do! But even so, I've got a cunning plan. A perfect plan. If it goes well, I won't have to fight at all to win Ulinia's freedom."

"The emperor won't let this province secede," Shadrael said flatly, tired of his brother's political woes. They saw each other once a year, sometimes less, and each time it was the same topic. "Light Bringer has too much to lose. If he lets one province go, others will follow. It will never happen. You're a fool to keep pursuing this."

"I've sworn to my death to do it," Vordachai said with resolution.

"Then unswear your oath! Gods, man, have some sense."

"Oh yes? And have you decided to throw your allegiance to this imposter, this gladiator barbarian who has no more right to rule over me than my groom?" Scowling, Vordachai smashed his fist onto the pommel of his saddle. "You have as big a grievance against him as I. Bigger!"

"I have the sense to accept change I cannot undo," Shadrael said in a cold, dry voice.

Vordachai's beady gaze raked him up and down. "I see how well you're prospering. Gault's mercy, a praetinor cut down to a ragged blackguard robbing the purses of old women. When I think of how you used to—"

"Don't. The past is gone. Forget it."

"I won't forget that Emperor Kostimon promised Ulinia its independence if the Madruns were beaten back. An imperial promise! I sent my best forces to him. I held the pass." Vordachai straightened his spine with pride. "Held it and threw them back. They did not overrun us. They did not pour into the south and take Itieria."

"They did take it," Shadrael murmured. "They sacked Imperia, too, and drove Kostimon right off his throne."

"Not from this direction," Vordachai said fiercely. "I did my part. And what reward have I for my loyalty, for my service and valor? This upstart who will not honor Kostimon's promise."

Kostimon would not have honored it either, Shadrael thought impatiently. He'd heard this refrain countless times. "Without a record of the agreement—"

"A pox on the records! A pox on the clerks who keep them! An emperor's word is law. Or should be. Better than any parchment with wax seals. What is that compared to oath and honor? Eh? I tell you I must have relief, and the upstart gives me none. His taxes are squeezing me dry. I've less than a thousand ducats in my treasury, and he wants half of it in tribute. Half! And all the time his leprous tax collector is bleeding off revenue from every caravan that comes through Kanidalon, and the legion squatted there to see that I get no share of it."

"You're entitled to no kickback from that revenue."

Vordachai raised his hands in the air and bellowed like a baffled bull. "Entitled? What about custom? Eh? Tradition!

Since my father's day and my father's father's day? Banished. Forgotten, as though it never existed. Is this the way to reward loyalty? The upstart grants my petitions no hearing. No relief does he offer. My entreaties are ignored, and I'll have no more of it. Do you hear? No more!"

Despite their distance from the village, Shadrael imagined every rat, spy, opportunist, and informer inhabiting it could hear his brother yelling treason all over the hillside. Calculating how long it would take any eavesdropper to peddle the news in Kanidalon, Shadrael squinted at the scrubby hills around him and figured he and his men had better find new quarters for a while, in case imperial agents turned up on the morrow, asking questions.

"I need your help, brother," Vordachai said, breathing heavily. "I tell you I am desperate, and my people are in sore need."

"There's no deliverance I can bring you or your people."

"They're your people, too. Or have you bled Natalloh blood from your veins and put dust there instead?"

"I have ashes for blood and black char for a heart," Shadrael replied, sneering. "You know that."

"I don't believe it."

"The first thing the army does is pound old allegiances out of a man. My loyalty is to my legion, not my birth province."

"Your legion is dissolved," Vordachai said harshly. "Disgraced and dishonored by the upstart's order, and you along with it. What else have you now but Ulinian soil?"

Shadrael gestured angrily. "Why do you come whining to me with your troubles? Did you call another war council among your barons, only to be turned down? If they won't support you in an uprising, do you think you can hire it done for you?" He uttered a scornful laugh. "You waste your breath here, you and your nine hundred ducats. That amount wouldn't even hire you a cohort of mercenaries."

Vordachai looked hurt. For a moment he sat in silence before he lifted his chin and said with dignity, "My plan will work. Hear it before you gainsay it."

His anger fading, Shadrael swallowed a sigh. It was always the same. Vordachai was obsessed, and he simply wouldn't listen to reason. "What, then?"

Eagerness lit up Vordachai's face, and he crowded his horse closer, putting his head close to Shadrael's. His breath stank of parsum, a fermented paste made from onions and herbs, used to season meat stored too long in brine barrels.

Nostrils flaring, Shadrael leaned back, but Vordachai didn't notice. "The upstart's sister, the Lady Lea, is making a long journey to Trau. And you will abduct her."

Shadrael involuntarily jerked on his reins, sending his horse's head tossing up in protest. "What?"

Vordachai beamed. "Ha-ha! I knew it would surprise you. All these years, you thought I had mere brawn while you had all the brains, but I can be clever, too, little brother. I can be very clever."

Stunned by his stupidity, Shadrael struggled a moment to find voice. "Holding her for ransom," he said slowly, while Vordachai went on grinning in delight. "Her return in exchange for Ulinia's independence?"

"Yes, yes!"

"Are you mad?"

Vordachai threw back his bushy head and bawled with laughter. "Not mad," he choked out, still guffawing. "Brilliant! Brilliant! Now, listen—"

"No. It will start the war you want. The Ninth will lay Ulinia waste. There won't be a town or village standing when they're through. The people you're doing this for— oh yes, the *people*—will be enslaved and sold into hard labor as traitors. Your barons will lose their lands, if not their heads, and the Natalloh flag will be burned. And if you think Bezhalmbra will withstand a siege, think again. They'll starve you out, and sacrifice the lady if they have to, because this won't be about rescuing her. It will be about stamping out treason."

"You—"

"Hear me!" Shadrael said ruthlessly. "I am trained in this. I have dealt with traitors, followed orders to burn them out, kill their servants and even their livestock, tear down their holds, salt their fields, and sell them into slavery down to the merest child. And you, my brother, once you're pried out of your fortress like a river mollusk from its shell, you will be dragged naked through the streets of New Imperia before they gut you and hang pieces of you on the gates."

Vordachai stared at him, and a little moment of silence fell between them while Shadrael's warning hung in the air.

"I—I believe you care," Vordachai said quietly.

Frustration shuddered through Shadrael. He looked away. "Hell's breath, brother, will you not think for once in your life and cool your spleen?"

"Bah!" Vordachai swept his arm in a dismissive gesture. "My barons have been yammering this same message of doom like bleating sheep. I never thought to hear you spouting such gutless drivel."

"It's called good sense."

"Faugh! It's cowardice, nothing more, and a refusal to seize opportunity when it's thrown in our laps. I know the penalties for treason as much as the next man. I'm not going to fight the upstart for what I want. I'm going to outwit him."

Shadrael shot him a look of flat disbelief.

"No, hear me!" Vordachai shook a thick finger in his face. "Why do you think I'm not going to use my own men? Why do you think I want you, a leprous, flea-ridden road bandit, to take on the job? Eh? Eh? Why?"

"Tell me."

"Because they won't know I'm behind it!" Vordachai roared with fresh laughter, wriggling his bulky shoulders with sheer delight.

Shadrael sighed. "The moment you issue the ransom demands you will implicate yourself."

"Who says I'm going to do that?" Vordachai tapped his nose and nodded sagely. "The lady's route does not take her near Ulinia. She won't be taken by Ulinian warriors." He pulled out a roll of parchment and slapped it into

Shadrael's hand. "Here is the map of her intended journey. Imperial roads all the way, a short, direct path straight to Trau. She'll be moving fast in hopes of beating the snows there."

Shadrael unrolled the map reluctantly. "How did you get this?"

"I have my sources in the palace."

It was a crudely drawn map, hastily sketched, with only the names of a few towns scribbled on it, but it provided more than enough information. As long as the lady stayed on imperial roads, Shadrael thought, it would make her progress swifter and his job of ambushing her harder.

"Now," Vordachai said, "the demand for her ransom will be sent by a Thyrazene in my employ, thus laying a false trail straight to that province instead of mine. Eh? And while the upstart is busy crushing those worthless lizard lovers and the eggs of their pox-riddled dragons, laying waste to their province instead of mine, as you so eloquently described it, I shall *rescue* the girl and hand her over to His Imperial damned Majesty. Do you see?" He clapped his hands together in sheer glee. "Ha-ha, yes! Oh yes, I see by your face that you begin to understand me."

Shadrael found himself amazed. It *was* a clever plan. Far more devious and complex than he'd supposed his brother could think up. Which renewed his suspicions.

"Who else knows about this plan?" he asked.

"No one! It came to me in a dream."

"You jest."

"No, I swear it on our father's sword. It came to me, like a gift from the gods, and I have been thinking of it night and day since."

"As soon as the girl is returned to her family, she will betray you."

"Not if she never sees me while she's a prisoner. Not if she isn't imprisoned at Bezhalmbra." Vordachai winked. "She will meet me only as her rescuer."

Shadrael found himself nodding in approval. "How many war councils have you called to discuss this?"

"None! Have I not just said it's known only to you and me? Who could I trust not to go running to the nearest imperial agent to betray me for a price?"

"You think I won't betray you?" Shadrael asked sharply.

"Not when I'm paying you a fortune. Eighteen hundred ducats should ease the shock of being kicked out of the army, eh? Eh?"

Shadrael's temper flared. Sometimes his brother had all the tact of a wild boar.

Vordachai sighed deeply, lost in his dreams. "The Lady Lea is said to be a lovely creature. By all accounts, her beauty rivals that of the empress. And you've seen the empress, haven't you?"

"Once."

Vordachai nodded. "Yes, and I hear that the upstart grants his younger sister her every wish. The people of New Imperia are said to worship her. She's some kind of prophetess, rumored to be as popular as the upstart. He'll pay anything to see her safely returned. His gratitude will be enormous. His generosity infinite. Because without her bewitchment on his subjects he could lose his throne."

"You are the one bewitched and befuddled if you believe that," Shadrael said scornfully. "Who feeds you these tales?"

"My sources in the palace serve me well." Sobering abruptly, Vordachai clamped a hand on Shadrael's arm. "But it all—*everything*—depends on you. You will not fail me, I know."

Scowling, Shadrael pulled away. "Your trust is . . . quite touching."

"Trust? Why shouldn't I trust you?" Vordachai gestured impatiently. "I don't care what you are, what you've been. I know you, and whatever you profess now, you were born a son of this ground. This land is in your heart, blood, and bones, boy! You know you want Ulinian freedom as much as I."

"Freedom," Shadrael whispered bitterly, his thoughts inward and deep. "Oh yes."

"Well, then. It's settled." Vordachai held out his meaty hand. "Are we agreed?"

Drawing his dagger, Shadrael twisted in the saddle and threw his weapon deep into some nearby bushes.

There was a muffled scream, and a scrawny body crashed out of the brush to land sprawling in the dust. Dismounting, Shadrael walked over to the rat-faced informer and toed him onto his back. His dagger protruded from Jutak's chest.

Vordachai stared. "What the—"

Ignoring his brother, Shadrael bent swiftly, touched the informer's throat to make certain he was dead, and pulled out his weapon. It was a shame to lose Jutak, Shadrael thought, but he couldn't afford to let the rat go selling this conversation to imperial agents.

Cleaning his weapon, he walked back over to the horses and mounted.

Vordachai was still staring at the dead man. "Who is that?"

"A spy. Do you know who will command the lady's armed escort?"

"How in the breath of harmony am I supposed to know that? How long do you suppose this man was listening to us? I never heard him follow us here."

"You should have sent for me to meet you, not come bellowing for me in a public inn," Shadrael said.

Gripping his sword hilt, Vordachai glared about in all directions. "Who else might be watching us, spying on us?"

Shadrael smiled a little. "Isn't it late to be asking that question? Who will command her armed escort?"

"I told you I don't know! What can it matter?"

"If I know the commander, I have the advantage on him."

"Better for you if you don't," Vordachai said sharply. "You wouldn't enjoy slaughtering one of your old friends."

Shadrael shrugged.

Vordachai frowned at him, then looked again at the corpse. "I—by Gault, you're damned cool when you kill, aren't you?"

"What of it?"

Vordachai shifted his gaze away from Shadrael's steady one and finally seemed to pull himself together. "She's already two weeks on the road. I could find out who commands her escort, but it will take too long to help you now. I do know that she's got a full squadron of cavalry."

"Not the Imperial Guards? Any predlicates? Regular army?"

"Cavalry."

Annoyed, Shadrael snapped open the map and glared at it. "A fortnight of travel should put her in Chanvez by now. That means she's what? Another two weeks, three perhaps, from the first Trau checkpoint?"

"Probably."

Shadrael crushed the map in his fist. "Why didn't you wait, say, another twenty days to tell me? I have as much hope of catching up with her as—"

"Told you I've been hunting your miserable hide in every rat-infested hole in these mountains," Vordachai said irritably. "If you'd take your home with me, as I've generously offered more than once, you would have been to hand."

Shadrael stared at him hard. "You don't want something like me in your home."

"Uh, no, perhaps not." Vordachai cleared his throat uneasily. "She isn't moving that fast perhaps. A retinue of that size, plenty of attendants, bound to be moving slowly. And anyway, you can catch up with her once she's in Trau."

"Trau is a filthy land, all marsh and bad roads. And I've men to hire and provision." Shadrael pointed at Vordachai's purse. "Hand it over."

Vordachai clamped a thick hand on his money and scowled. "Why, you thief, you won't be paid until the job's done."

"I don't carry an officer's commission these days, and my men don't stay with me from loyalty to the Imperial Seal. Money!"

Grumbling, Vordachai dug out a few coins.

Shadrael scornfully refused to take them. "The whole purse," he said.

"What?" Turning scarlet, Vordachai closed his fist on the coins. "That's an outrage! You haven't more than twenty men here. What—"

"Do you think I'm fool enough to pit twenty bandits against a hundred trained cavalry? Use your head for something besides a helmet stand!" Shadrael said angrily. "If she's as important to the Light Bringer as you say, she'll be well guarded by the best. I'll need at least a company of my own, preferably two."

"Where are you going to scrape up that many men around here?" Vordachai asked, squinting suspiciously. "You dare not recruit in Kanidalon, and I can't give you any of my warriors."

"That's my business." Shadrael pointed at his purse. "Hand it over."

"The cost of hiring a hundred men at—"

"Don't bargain with me, you skinflint. It's a small price to pay for Ulinian freedom, remember?"

Grumbling, Vordachai tossed him the purse. It was heavy, and the coins inside made a satisfying chink when Shadrael hefted it in his hand.

"That's to be considered an advance on the nine hundred, mind," Vordachai said with all the sharpness of a man whose treasury is smaller than his expenses. "And she must be brought safe to me. Unharmed and—and untouched."

Shadrael shot him a black glare, hissing slightly through his teeth, but Vordachai meet his gaze sternly and did not back down.

"Whatever you are is one thing," he said fiercely. "But I know the kind of men you lead. Guard her well, brother. The upstart won't pay for damaged goods."

Shadrael said nothing.

"Then it's settled." Fresh excitement flashed across Vordachai's face, and he held out his hand once more. "Seal our bargain, brother."

Shadrael said nothing, made no move to shake hands.

Turning red, Vordachai allowed his to drop. "I—I suppose it is not safe for me to touch you." Vordachai's voice held a trace of hurt. "The fearsome *donare* of our family, something we never expected."

"If Father did not want what I am, he should not have put me into the army," Shadrael said coldly.

"Well, he got little return for the exorbitant price of your commission," Vordachai retorted. "When you were named praetinor, we thought for certain you would soon be a general and make us all rich. Instead, stripped of honors and discharged, that's you. Knocked down to a common thief."

"Which you now need," Shadrael replied tonelessly. "Urgently."

"Aye, so I do." Vordachai eyed him and shook his head with a sigh. "All these years, and you're still as stiff-rumped and prickly as a—"

"You'd better go," Shadrael said.

"Yes." Vordachai glanced at the dead informer and grimaced. "When next I see you, there will be celebrations and feasting, all the bounty at my disposal offered in your honor."

"Don't feast until the girl is in your stronghold."

"Take her to Muhadim, and tell her nothing." A grin was already spreading across Vordachai's face. "By Gault, I cannot believe this day is at hand. If anyone can bring this off, you can. Until we next meet, Commander."

"Until we next meet," Shadrael responded.

As soon as the warlord had ridden out of sight, ex-Centruin Fomo emerged from the brush, skirted the corpse of Jutak, and came up to Shadrael's stirrup. "Do we let them ride out of here?" he asked hoarsely, his eyes curious in his scarred, battered face. "Do you want them ambushed beyond the creek?"

Shadrael was already thinking of how to best find the men he would need quickly. The dangerous task Vordachai had offered him made Shadrael's heart quicken, as though he were stepping forth to commit an act of *shul-drakshera*.

He liked the chance of striking revenge against the emperor who had stripped him of rank, career, and future regardless of the fact that a man with no soul could not unswear his shadow vows as required.

Abduct the Lady Lea, sister to Caelan the Light Bringer. Shadrael grinned to himself. Young and perhaps innocent. Unaware of what was about to befall her. Oh yes, he would enjoy escorting her into darkness. He would enjoy it very much.

From down the hill, he could hear his brother's voice raised in a bawdy song.

"You fool," he murmured. "I would have done this for no coin at all."

"Commander?" Fomo asked.

Shadrael shot him a glance. "Let the warlord and his men go," he said, and began to issue his instructions swiftly.

Chapter 2

Remaining in the shade of a tree, Shadrael waited impatiently for dusk. In his mind, doubt and determination were mingling together. With the short time available to him, he had but one sure way to summon extra forces, and that was to use magic.

Cut off from the shadow gods, Shadrael could no longer dip from their power, power available to anyone sworn to them, anyone with the talent and courage to take it. Now there was nothing but a dwindling, carefully hoarded reserve of magic left inside him, hoarded the way Vordachai guarded his treasury of gold.

And when it runs out? asked a little voice in the back of Shadrael's mind. *What if it's already gone?*

He shook the little voice away as he might empty a scorpion from his boot.

When the magic ran out, he would be a walking husk of a man, as doomed as the shadow gods themselves.

Until then, he had a job to do, a chance to strike back at Light Bringer, who had shattered his world and future.

Shadrael tilted back his head to gaze at the darkening

sky. Stars were coming out, hanging above him, looking
almost close enough to touch. Standing up, he untied the
horse he'd borrowed and set it free, knowing it would bolt
anyway. Nickering nervously, the animal trotted off into
the gathering shadows.

He stretched up his hand, and murmured a word that
seemed to suck away the air.

Every sound stirring in the brush and scrub—every
singing insect, every scuttling mouse, even the breeze—
went absolutely still and silent.

He spoke the word again, even more softly, and felt the
old power swell inside him in response. A spangle of fire
shot from his fingertips straight up into the air. With it went
a little boom of sound that echoed through the hills and
canyons.

Turning slightly to his left, he shot the signal again, a
flare of multihued light going up and up before it faded in a
cloud of white smoke that hung in the air. The boom echoed
again.

He repeated the signals, one for each direction of the
compass, before he stopped and let his arm drop heavily to
his side. It felt numb from shoulder to fingertips. He could
not even flex it.

Perspiration ran down his body, sheeting his brow and
pooling beneath his clothing. Even so, he felt triumphant.
The summons would reach men from the old cohorts, disbanded men who, like him, had been struck off without
pensions or honor. It would summon other things, as well.
Lurkers, perhaps a few skulks. The use of shadow magic,
increasingly rare, would draw them like a shivering man to
a fire.

Now all he had to do was ready himself and the few men
already at his side. With any luck, they could be on the
march at daybreak, and the others would join them on the
road.

But when Shadrael turned and started down the hill to
the inn, he staggered a little and had to wait a bit before he
descended. He moved carefully, conserving his strength,

closing his mind to the fear that he'd used too much magic, wasted too much of it, and all because he wanted to abduct the lady before she reached Trau.

He wanted no part of that distant marshy province with its cold and snow, if he could avoid it.

Cautiously he made his way, giving the proper signal to the lookout behind the inn. He went through the rear entrance, going upstairs to his room, where he ordered a lackey to bring him hot water. It arrived, eventually, lukewarm instead of hot, and the boy who brought it gave him a sullen, defiant look before slouching away. Downstairs in the taproom came the muffled noise of singing and laughing.

He frowned, well aware that if they were carousing they weren't getting ready to move out. But he did not stop his preparations.

Pouring the water into a basin, he soaped his beard, shaving his face clean with swift expertise. After that, he changed razors and hunched over a scrap of mirror while he cut his hair close to his skull in the army style. No long, romantic locks for an enemy to grab, or to blow in one's eyes during a battle. When he finished, the reflection staring back at him looked like a stranger. He was a tall man, well muscled and fit, his belly lean and his legs strong. He'd kept himself disciplined since his discharge, other than adopting filthy clothes and an unkempt appearance in order to look indistinguishable from the other bandits in the Jawnuth foothills. Now he saw an older face staring back at him, a weary, disillusioned face. Beneath a pair of heavy, formidable brows, his deep-set eyes were as black as Beloth's dead heart.

He dragged out his duff box, a battered old campaign chest that had followed him across the empire and back again. Raising the lid released the smells of oil and camphorda, bringing a host of memories that he grimly shoved away.

He pulled out his armor and began the process of buckling it on. Of course, when he'd been a legion commander he'd had a bafboy to care for his armor and help him, but one of the first lessons an officer learned was how to get into armor unassisted, and Shadrael had not forgotten. He wanted no help tonight. His memories floated too near the surface for him to endure chatter or questions.

The breastplate was heavy, black leather over steel, and custom fitted. He was glad to find that it still fit, after three years put away. In fact, if anything it was a little loose. The weight pressed hard on his shoulders, and he took a moment to remember how to breathe, how to shift his weight in it, how to balance himself. The knowledge, ingrained in him after a lifetime's training, was still there.

The shoulder guards were black plated steel with vicious spikes projecting from the points of each shoulder. They restricted his arm movement somewhat, but since archers had become frequent auxiliaries in the army, it was necessary to wear extra steel to guard his heart from a well-placed arrow.

Belting on his sword, Shadrael loosened it in its scabbard and settled the short, sturdy weapon on his hip. Balancing it on the opposite side was his long, needle-tipped dagger. Ornate of hilt, its pommel stone was a baleful, glowing blood amber, rare to Ulinia, but much prized among army officers with the means to buy one. Blood amber was considered good luck, a protector of sorts. Shadrael hung his throwing blades on their belt hooks, and tucked his small, fang-point axe into his belt at the back, snug against his armor. He tightened his wrist greaves, sliding a tiny throwing knife tighter in its sheath along the inside of his left forearm, then gathered up his heavy gauntlets and helmet with its officer's crest of stiff black horsehair.

His medal of praetinor ad duxa—conferred on him by Emperor Kostimon—hung at his throat, providing the only color besides the eagle insignia of his rank inscribed in gold over his heart and the tiny flash of silver bars beside it to show his victories.

Swiftly he lifted his fingertips to his lips and forehead in salute as he whispered a prayer to the shadow god that could no longer hear him: "Let war come. Let my sword bite deep in thy service. Strengthen me, O Beloth, that I may forget the ties that bind men to men, honor to honor. Help me serve only thee in my quest to shatter the reign of Light Bringer. May thy shadows return forever. Saeta."

Giving himself a curt nod, he kicked down the lid of his campaign chest and strode out with his head high and his ferocity upon him like a mantle.

At the head of the rickety stairs, the inn's lackey almost bumped into him. Yelping in alarm, the boy jumped out of Shadrael's way, staring after him with a face pale and frightened, while making a warding sign with his fingers.

Down in the taproom, there came a fresh roar of laughter and much shouting. No, Shadrael thought, it did not sound as though Fomo had the men ready.

By the time he reached the bottom step and saw the innkeeper gasp at the sight of him and bolt white-faced in the direction of the kitchen, the babble of voices—a few annoyed, but most whooping with wild laughter—rose up in even louder commotion over the sound of snarling and then a shrill, animal cry of pain.

Pausing in the doorway to the taproom, Shadrael saw his men gathered around a gaunt individual named Wilbis, who was holding a cloth sack that twisted and squirmed. A shrill, keening howl came from it again, punctuated by a bark.

"Hold 'im!" someone said eagerly. "Don't let 'im get away from you now!"

Laughter rippled through the group. In the flicker of firelight shining from the enormous hearth, they looked like savages in their long hair-braids and face tattoos. Perhaps a handful had put on armor and sword, their amulets swinging on leather cords from their necks. The rest wore ragged tunics and soft leather footgear designed for stealth. None had so far seen Shadrael in the doorway.

His brows knotted together. If the fools had sold or gambled away their boots and armor, he thought grimly, he would march them until their feet bled and let them curse their stupidity with every burning step.

Wilbis hefted his bundle like he would a sack of tanfroots. "Let's test his *drakshera*, eh?"

Eager shouts rose among the company. Someone produced a rope, and ex-Centruin Fomo—instead of putting a halt to their purpose—slung it over a rafter for them.

In moments they had the dog out of the sack, tied by its hind legs, and hoisted it upside down by the rope. Small and white with a brown head, the dog snarled and snapped, twisting and struggling all the while, as the men danced around it, teasing it and laughing.

Wilbis pulled a knife. "Let's dance for his eyes, eh?"

"Aye! Aye! I'll wager four—"

Shadrael stepped into the taproom. "Let the dog go."

His cold, quiet voice silenced the group. They turned and stared at him, some with mouths agape, others with defiance. Shadrael met them, glare for glare.

Fomo, standing over to one side, cleared his throat. "Line up," he said hoarsely.

Shuffling and coughing, the men scrambled into a ragged line while Shadrael advanced into the room. These brutes were veterans of the Madrun campaigns, blood sworn in the rituals of Faure and Alcua, and as seasoned and tough as soldiers came. They had served him in the now-disbanded Eighth Legion under Emperor Kostimon's banner, and once they had been keen, fearless, and fit, able to march seven leagues a day and fight the next morning.

Now they faced him, ragged and stupid, grown slack and soft from too much ale and not enough hard marching. They had lost that hard-honed edge of alert obedience. Even the few in armor, standing at attention, could not keep their eyes from wandering sideways, as though trying to gauge his reaction. A few were staring frankly, openmouthed, as though they beheld a ghost instead of a legion commander. The rest looked sullen and rebellious, in no mood to serve him or anyone else.

A general atmosphere of guilt, embarrassment, and defiance hung over the room, while the dog swung on its rope, whimpering, and no one obeyed Shadrael's order.

Shadrael raked them with a steely eye, his temper beginning to pulse a little harder. It was said in the army that you never gave the men quarter, for leniency led to independent thinking, independent will, and the eventual decision to disobey. Well, for three years they'd had leniency, and a share of the spoils they stole. And now they did not have to march a third of the way across the empire on his orders. They could sit here and rot their minds and guts in this taproom until their money gave out. He had no military authority over them. He had nothing at all, except his force of will.

Fiercely Shadrael let the silence grow. He did not move, plead, or repeat his order. Not by the merest fraction did he give any indication that he expected less than their obedience and loyalty. If he voiced one word of reasoning, or even asked them to follow him, he would be lost. When he'd put on this armor, he'd made his declaration. The rest was up to them.

In the quiet, Fomo loosened the rope and let the dog drop to the floor. Landing awkwardly because of its tied hind legs, the dog yelped and tried to drag itself upright.

Drawing his small boot knife, Shadrael went to it. At once the dog twisted to face him, raising its hackles and snarling.

"Useless dog," Fomo rasped. Years ago, a Madrun had nearly crushed his throat, damaging his voice permanently and making it hard for him to bawl orders. Another commander would have pensioned him out or demoted him to ranks, but in Shadrael's view, Fomo had been one of the best centruins in the army, as devious as he was efficient. Whatever Shadrael wanted done, Fomo found a way to do it. In the military, such a centruin was a tremendous asset, too valuable to throw away. So he'd kept the man, and Fomo had rewarded his generosity tenfold.

Until now.

"Too small for hunting," Fomo went on, keeping up the inane chatter while his gaze said something else. "Not a good fighter. Belongs nowhere, to no one. No endurance.

No training. Why not let him amuse the men? We caught him easy with a scrap of meat, the little wank."

"Instead of getting ready to move out," Shadrael said, and Fomo dropped his gaze.

"Ain't the army now, Commander," Wilbis said, and the others laughed uneasily.

So there it was, open refusal. Shadrael swiftly seized the dog's neck with his free hand, pinning it while it thrashed and showed its teeth, and sliced through the rope to free its legs. As soon as he released the animal, it sprang up and dashed to the far side of the taproom, where it crawled beneath a chair and peeped out with a low, fierce growl.

The men laughed at it, elbowing each other in scorn. They'd fallen out of line by now.

"Like Centruin says, a proper bit of nothing, it is," Wilbis said, speaking up without permission. "We were going to have a little sport and then eat the scrap. Makes a tasty stew, them little dogs." He shot Shadrael a look of shrewd calculation. "You wouldn't have us set out at dawn on empty stomachs, m'lord."

Some of the others were nodding. They all shuffled their feet, exchanging glances, while Fomo stared coldly into the distance, not bothering to whip them into silence. The centruin—having given his warning to Shadrael—had stepped away from the men. But neither was he at Shadrael's back, and that, too, was a warning.

Gritting his teeth to restrain his temper, Shadrael put his knife back in his boot and slowly straightened. There had been a time when no one questioned anything he said at any time, for any reason, without incurring a flogging. The past, he thought angrily. The damned past.

Shadrael's continued silence seemed to encourage Wilbis, who glanced around at his comrades before shooting Shadrael an insolent grin.

"No, m'lord, we never too keen about marching on empty stomachs. Never too keen about marching at all. No need, is there?" As he spoke, he turned so that his knife was pointed at Shadrael in silent threat. Two other men moved close to Wilbis's back.

Wilbis cocked his head. "Now, if you asked us nice and sweetly to ride out with you on whatever that warlord hired you for, we might consider it, if the price is good. Otherwise—"

Shadrael almost smiled. That was the only warning he gave as he flicked his hand at Wilbis. Red lightning crackled through the air and engulfed the man. Writhing back on his heels, twisting and turning in a futile effort to break free, Wilbis clawed the air and screamed while the others stumbled back from him.

When Shadrael released him, Wilbis crumpled to his knees, twitching and slapping himself with shrill little moans. The air reeked of burned hair and charred wood. A black, smoking gouge marked the floor where Wilbis had been standing. From beneath a table, the little dog howled and shot out of the room with its tail tucked between its legs.

Shadrael waited until Wilbis recovered himself enough to look up. Whatever the man saw in Shadrael's gaze made his eyes bulge with fear.

He lifted his hand in a plea. "No, m'lord Commander. No! Please—"

Shadrael *severed* and saw the man's threads of life reaching out from his head and body toward infinity. Shadrael cut them. In the blink of an eye it was done, and Wilbis lay dead on the floor. As Shadrael turned to the others, the shadows murmured and whispered in his blood, filling his mind with the sweet lust for more killing. He stretched out his hand toward them, toward their fragile threads of life, and felt tempted to slay them all.

Instead, with the last vestige of his willpower, he pulled himself back from madness. He drove the shadows from his mind, and wrenched himself out of *severance*. Even so, it took him a moment to adjust, to regain mastery of his wits.

When he lifted his head, he saw that the men had retreated from him. Most were clutching their amulet bags; a few had their hands on their weapons. Pale and breathing hard, they stared with white-rimmed eyes, aware they could not escape him even if they tried to run.

Shadrael faced them, giving each man a grim stare in turn. "Did you think because the shadow gods are gone, my magic is gone with them?" he asked harshly. "Have you forgotten what I am?"

One man, brawny and hook-nosed, stepped forward with a swift salute. "You are our lord commander. Have mercy on us."

Shadrael flicked a glance at Fomo, who cracked his small whip.

"All of you, to attention!" he rasped.

The men formed a new line with quick obedience. The looks they shot Shadrael now held worry . . . and respect.

His gaze remained icy. He did not value respect gained in such a way. As soon as they forgot tonight's fear, they would have to be disciplined again. He did not want to waste his precious reserves of magic keeping them in line. He would have to stay alert, and outthink them.

"We do not leave at dawn," Shadrael announced. "We march out *now*. Centruin!"

Fomo stepped forward smartly. "Sir!"

"Get the horses and supplies ready. Find these men boots and get them kitted in full gear. I'll—"

A raven flew into the room through the open door, and so strange and unexpected was its appearance that Shadrael broke off in midsentence. The bird was a peculiar ashy gray hue, with a band of white around its neck. Flying straight to Shadrael, it landed on his shoulder.

Although his first instinct was to knock the bird away, something held him still. Behind him, the men were whispering to themselves and clutching their amulets. Even Fomo backed warily away.

The pale raven's claws scratched for purchase on Shadrael's shoulder plate, and the bird pecked in curiosity at the shoulder spike next to it before turning its head and leaning close to Shadrael's ear.

"Harm not my messenger," a voice said in Shadrael's mind. *"Remember that you have issued a call, and I have answered."*

"What are you?" Shadrael asked aloud.

"Come to me. Let us talk."

Frowning, Shadrael strode outside into the dark inn yard, unaware that his men crept cautiously after him.

The raven on his shoulder pecked at his armor, then flew into the night. And before him, a doorway opened in the air, a doorway wreathed in mist, with a pale gray light shining beyond it.

Someone gasped aloud, but Shadrael found himself smiling. "The Hidden Ways," he murmured and walked forward.

A hand plucked at his arm. "Commander, don't!"

Pausing, Shadrael glanced aside at Fomo. The battle-scarred centruin would never show fear, but he was plainly worried.

"Where does it lead?" he asked hoarsely. "What summons you?"

Shadrael gave him a thin smile. "Does it matter? Wait for me."

He stepped into the mist, feeling himself slide from the world he knew into a place of shadow.

Around him lay darkness, impenetrable as though it were solid. Before him stretched a passageway lit by the pale gray light. The mist wreathed around his ankles and flowed forward.

He saw the pale raven with the white band around its throat flying ahead of him.

Without fear, Shadrael followed it.

Chapter 3

It was the first time Shadrael had entered the Hidden Ways since the defeat of the shadow gods. Then the passages through the shadow world had been lit with fires burning the very rock and ground, choking the air with smoke. Now all lay gloom shrouded, still, and very cold. His boots crunched softly on gravel; only when he looked down he saw not pebbles but tiny bits of charred bone. Here and there lay a skeletal hand, twisted claws burned black, or a portion of skull.

Steadily he strode forward, wandering neither left nor right, making no effort to touch anything. A gray light illuminated his path, as dim and immaterial as the dawn. He could see no source for it.

How far he walked, or how much time passed, he knew not. Within the Hidden Ways, time and distance held little meaning. When he came to a small cavern, empty and swept bare, Shadrael saw outlines of demons on the walls. It was as though they'd been hurled against the stone with such force they'd left a permanent impression. He kept walking, leaving the cave and picking his way through rubble that made the footing increasingly treacherous.

Once he inadvertently touched a boulder to steady his balance, and it was so cold it burned his skin.

Thereafter, he moved even more cautiously.

When he came to an open place where the light seemed brighter, showing him an emptiness on all sides, he stopped and waited. The path he'd been following stretched forward as though to infinity. He sensed none of the usual markers ahead of him. To continue meant becoming lost here forever.

The gray raven flew up to him and landed on his shoulder as before. *"Come forward,"* said the voice in his mind.

"No," Shadrael replied. "I have journeyed far enough. Tell me here what you want of me."

"Three more strides."

Frowning, Shadrael counted them off. The raven rode his shoulder until he said, "Three," under his breath, and then the bird flew away, leaving him alone.

Only he wasn't alone. Between one eyeblink and the next, Shadrael saw a man's silhouette appear before him.

Startled, Shadrael stiffened but made no other move. Without turning his head, he sought to determine whether other silhouettes surrounded him, cutting him off from retreat, and saw none.

"Be at peace, Commander," the figure said aloud to him. "I am not your enemy."

The voice sounded familiar, teased his memory. Shadrael frowned, his gaze still flicking here and there alertly. "Name yourself."

"What do names matter in the land of torment?"

It was the line of a poem. Shadrael stifled his sharp intake of breath. "Urmaeor?"

"You remember?"

"Of course."

Memories flooded Shadrael's mind of early days in the service, when he was a raw recruit being honed into a raw young officer. He'd met a slender acolyte in dark robes assisting priests administering the blood bowls and rites of Alcua. Later, in the shocking aftermath of his act of *shuldrakshera*, it had been Urmaeor who had closed the gaping wound of his psyche, Urmaeor who had counseled him and showed him how to channel the power of Beloth without destroying himself. They'd become casual friends, each ambitious to rise to the top of his profession, each successful in gaining promotions. Shadrael had been posted to the Madrun border, and Urmaeor had gone to Imperia to serve in the temples.

Shadrael blinked away the thoughts. "It's been many years, but I have not forgotten your voice, or your love of the Iyna poets."

"Such minor details, despite all that has happened. You are rare."

"So I have been told," Shadrael said with sudden impatience. "Why have you summoned me here?"

Urmaeor spread out his hands. Whispering fires flared hot in Shadrael's veins, bringing alive the agony he'd suppressed since the destruction of the shadows.

Jerking to one side, Shadrael fought not to cry out as he held himself rigid against the pain. Shadow voices murmured to him, in him, around him, all commanding him to walk forward.

He would not take a step.

A force pressed against his back from behind, trying to push him closer to Urmaeor, but Shadrael stiffened his legs, bracing himself against it. The pressure intensified until his body shook and his heart throbbed as though it would burst. Still he held on, refusing to surrender.

Defiantly, he even managed to glare at the shadowy figure standing before him. "You cannot control me," he rasped out, his voice unsteady from his efforts not to scream. "Vindicants stronger than you have tried it."

The whispers inside his head deafened him, the fire racing even hotter through his body, so that he twisted and jerked. Sweat ran in his eyes, and he tasted the coppery bitterness of blood in his mouth. No longer could he draw in air, and his vision wavered, blurring Urmaeor's motionless figure.

But he would not surrender. And although he'd been caught off guard by the swift strength of Urmaeor's power, he managed to *sever*. The fires tormenting him retreated, doused by the icy relief of *severance*. He saw Urmaeor's threads of life, black and withered cords that they were, and reached out for them.

Urmaeor's attack ceased so abruptly that Shadrael staggered. A shimmering wall of energy rose up around the priest, shielding him, and Shadrael dropped out of *severance*.

Winded and spent, aching inside, he dragged in several breaths and wiped the perspiration from his brow. It was tempting to sink to the ground and lie there. Instead, trembling and still short of breath, he found enough pride to straighten.

"Satisfied?" he said angrily.

"My apologies," Urmaeor said in contrition. "Most of the few surviving *donare* I've managed to find have been weak, useless. You seem stronger than ever."

Holding in a bitter laugh, Shadrael spat blood from his mouth instead. "Be damned! You waste my time."

"What else have you, Commander, but time?"

The mocking twist to what he'd said to his brother sent temper sweeping over Shadrael. He spun around to return the way he'd come.

And was met by a wall of darkness obscuring the passageway behind him. He halted, well aware he'd been tricked into venturing beyond the markers. Urmaeor could cloud his senses like this in an eternal game of cat and mouse. Reluctantly, resentfully, he turned back to face the priest.

"Please," Urmaeor said. "I had to test you. Understand that it was the only way to be sure of your remaining capabilities."

"So now you understand me," Shadrael said flatly. "What do you want?"

"My master watches and waits for . . . opportunities,"
Urmaeor said. "A *donare* still able to function, still strong,
still possessing magic . . . this is a rarity he cannot afford
to ignore."

"So you summoned me here and squandered some of that
rare magic so hard to find by forcing me to pass your test."

"You came to our notice when you cast shadow magic to
summon men and *casna* to you. I assure you those you
have summoned will come swiftly in response."

"I never doubted it."

"Ah yes, I see you have retained that unshakable confidence," Urmaeor murmured. "My master wishes to offer
you his help."

"Why?"

"Do we not all serve a common purpose?"

Shadrael was fast losing patience. "Spare me your mys-
tical pronouncements and tell me why I'm here."

"My master—"

"Who is that?"

"The chief priest of the Vindicants."

Disbelief swept Shadrael. "What lie is this? Sein was
destroyed during the Terrors."

"Yes, Lord Sein was lost to us. It is his successor who
wishes to know you. I speak to you on behalf of Lord
Barthel, worthy servant of Beloth That Was and Beloth
That Will Come Again."

"Beloth is gone, destroyed. And we are all of us doomed
to follow our god to perdition."

"To lose protection of the shadows is indeed difficult,"
Urmaeor said sympathetically. "How easy in such times as
these to lose faith."

"Faith!" Shadrael said in scorn. "What would you have
me believe in, priest? What is left but ashes?" He gestured
at the dark wall behind him. "Let me go back."

"You suffer," Urmaeor said as though he hadn't heard
Shadrael's demand. "So do we all, but one such as yourself—
once so close a servant of shadow—what torment you must
endure. I wonder it does not drive you mad."

The aching pain inside Shadrael had not eased. He knew it would stay with him the rest of the night; it might persist for days. But he managed a cold smile. "Who these days is not mad, or close to it?"

"Agreed. Lord Barthel understands your plight, for he also suffered much at first. We feared he might not survive the transition. Perhaps you, having already survived the Kiss of Eternity and its aftermath, drew your strength from that experience. Most *donare* are born as they are. But you were made. The difference is—"

"Who cares?"

"We do. Lord Barthel does. You may feel yourself to be alone, Commander, but you are not. Hear me. When the world was broken by the Light Bringer, Lord Barthel was one of the few in our upper echelon of priests able to reach the Vindicant refuge. We tended him carefully while Sein's first successor perished. The second successor also failed to make the transition, and he, too, died. But Lord Barthel survived, and that's when we realized he'd been chosen to lead us. Since his recovery, he has sent some of us— myself included—to search for those servants of shadow still able to function, still in possession of their powers. To find you here in Ulinia, someone of your caliber and reputation, is surely confirmation that destiny is working to entwine Lord Barthel's path with yours."

"My destiny ended with the arrival of Light Bringer."

"Not so," Urmaeor said earnestly. "Not at all. Your work, your purpose, has just—"

"My work—my purpose, as you call it—is finished. Now I simply exist."

"Summoning an army, however small, is not existing."

Shadrael's brows knotted. He did not speak.

"Bitterness is a dish we all consume," Urmaeor said. "But we are not defeated. The Vindicants are not destroyed, not wiped from the face of the world as Light Bringer intended. Nor are all the Maelites gone. We wait. We watch. We work to bring back the shadows in whatever way we can. My master wants you to join him."

"I'm already hired," Shadrael said.

"By Lord Vordachai?"

Shadrael grew more cautious. "Tell your master I have nothing to contribute to his cause. I'm no priest. I have no prayers to put into the chanting."

Urmaeor hesitated, then spoke in pitch-perfect replication of Shadrael's voice: " 'Let war come. Strengthen me, O Beloth, that I may forget the ties that bind men to men, honor to honor, and serve only thee in my quest to shatter the reign of Light Bringer. May thy shadows return forever.' "

Shadrael had long ago learned not to be shocked by the tricks of Vindicants, but it angered him to know he'd been spied on. He cleared his throat. "A war prayer is habit. Don't read more into it than is there."

"Ah, but my master heard your prayer. It came from your heart, and was not said by rote."

"Has your master nothing better to do than to overhear the private prayers of men?"

"You are willing to sacrifice honor and family ties in order to shatter Light Bringer. Don't trouble to deny you said it. To find such passion, to discover such hatred festering in a wound that will not heal . . . this pleases my master greatly. You are exactly right for our purpose."

"No."

"Yes! You live as a ruined and broken man. Your dreams and ambitions have been destroyed. You wanted to retire as a man of property, with a villa in the hills of Imperia, overlooking the sea. There were to be banquets and feasting every night in your dining hall, nubile dancing girls as scented and soft as the petals of flowers to provide the entertainment, and—"

"A young man's dreams are left in the dust soon enough," Shadrael broke in gruffly. "Let them lie."

"But have they really all left you? Would you not accept a handsome villa in New Imperia if Light Bringer were driven out? Would you not take command of the army this instant if it were offered to you?"

It had been a long time since anyone had read Shadrael's innermost thoughts so easily. He'd lost the habit of shielding his mind, and now he felt exposed, even mocked, by Urmaeor's remarks. Back when he'd been in the army, he'd heard stories of how Lord Sein used to pry into the private thoughts of generals and high-ranking officers for the amusement of Emperor Kostimon. As a legion commander, Shadrael had been subjected to such scrutiny before entering the presence of certain officials. He'd been trained to expect it and submit to it. But the violations he'd borne willingly as an officer were a far cry from what he would tolerate now.

"I do not insult you," Urmaeor said. "I mention these things to persuade you."

Shadrael's hand went to his dagger. "Get out of my head, damn you!"

"Why? You are a man of courage. You would not have dared the Kiss of Eternity otherwise."

"It takes no courage to commit folly."

"Have you lost pride in the ultimate risk? No, Commander. Tell no such lie. Had you no courage, you would not have won the medal you wear at your throat. That you wear it still, despite your public disgrace, is an announcement of how proud you are to bear the illustrious rank of praetinor. Remember that day of triumph. Remember it!"

Shadrael frowned, trying to shut out Urmaeor's voice, but memories were swamping his mind, memories of the day he'd celebrated his greatest military victory with a triumph through the streets of Imperia. The people thronging the avenue had roared out his name. And Kostimon's own hands had hung the medal around his neck. The emperor's yellow eyes had met his, one warrior to another, and the emperor had even smiled.

"A worthy hero, who serves us well," Kostimon had proclaimed him. "Praetinor, behold your people!"

As he spoke, the emperor lifted his hand, and a tide of sound filled the air as the masses cheered and cheered Shadrael's name.

Even now, Shadrael could hear the noise, feel the baking heat. The wind stirred his hair as he bowed to the emperor. How brief that moment of glory had been, yet how satisfying to stand shoulder to shoulder with the emperor, ruler of the world. And as the people cheered, Shadrael's heart had thundered with pride. He'd dared to dream of commanding all thirty legions, ruling the army as Kostimon ruled the empire.

Instead, Light Bringer had swept everything away, broken Shadrael from rank, decommissioned and exiled him. The only thing Light Bringer could not do was take away his membership in the august body of praetinori—a body of men who were members for life—men honored and distinguished publicly, acknowledged and bowed to by every citizen. *Yet who would bow to me?* Shadrael thought.

"Yes," Urmaeor said. "Pride and passion. Strength and courage. Defiance and hatred against your enemies. Yes, Commander. You are exactly what we've sought."

Hatred for Light Bringer swelled inside Shadrael. Aware that the priest was manipulating his emotions, he hardly cared at first. But then he pulled back, closing down the memories and feelings, refusing again to be controlled.

"It's all dust," Shadrael said, pushing away his past. "Dust and tarnish. Useless to me now."

"If you still have pride," Urmaeor said, his voice soft, "you still care. And if you still care, then you will join us."

"The shadow gods cannot be resurrected," Shadrael said harshly. "If that's what your Barthel wants, he's lost in foolish dreams."

"My master is a pragmatist, like you."

"Maybe."

"Our fight is—"

"I have a living to make," Shadrael broke in. "You call me commander, but I'm no imperial officer. Nothing but a mercenary. When I'm free of my current job, perhaps we'll talk again, but not—"

"We are not finished here. Do not try to dismiss me."

"I'll leave when I choose. Even if I have to waste magic

to find my way out. Call up the past all you want, but you won't change the facts of the present. You can dredge up a little army perhaps. You can even strike a few times at villages or burn an imperial arch or two, but the Reformants have taken your temples and ceremonies—"

"Reformants," Urmaeor said with loathing, the first true emotion he'd shown.

Shadrael bared his teeth. "That's right. Face it, priest. Your day is over, just like mine."

Urmaeor lifted one hand, but he did not strike. "Decommissioned or not, you retain the skills of a legion commander," he said in glacial tones. "Your oath to Beloth still binds you to his service, and you are now called to obey that oath."

"When I'm not employed—"

"Lord Vordachai will cheat you of the money he's promised," Urmaeor said. "After you've committed treason for him and abducted the sister of the emperor as he's bidden you, he will not pay you a single ducat more than you carry now."

"Faure's breath, how know you that?"

"Don't be stupid. Can you not see how her abduction serves the Vindicants even better?"

Shadrael understood at once. His hand came off his dagger hilt.

"Yes," Urmaeor said. "Lea E'non is a javelin that can be driven deep into the emperor's flank, to fester, to bring him to his knees. And your hand, Shadrael tu Natalloh, is perhaps the only one strong enough to control that weapon."

An icy tendril of caution curled around Shadrael's spine. The Vindicant spies, he thought, had been busy indeed if they knew of Vordachai's secret plan. He did not deny what Urmaeor was saying. With mind walkers, why bother?

Naturally, he understood that if he agreed to the Vindicant demand, he would be betraying Vordachai, his only brother. *It's only a job,* whispered a voice in his mind. *Serve the one who pays you best.*

But in his heart, he knew it was not that easy.

"Lord Vordachai is an impetuous man," Urmaeor said. "Although we admire his intentions, it would be better for everyone if we Vindicants were to take over the situation. Lady Lea can become a significant political pawn, if that pawn is played with skill."

Crossing his arms over his chest, Shadrael asked, "What will you pay?"

"How long do you think your powers will last? How long can you hoard shadow magic inside you?"

"What does that matter?"

"How long?"

Shadrael frowned. "I have enough to do what I must do."

"Enough to hold the girl helpless while she's your prisoner? She's not without special resources, you know."

Shrugging, Shadrael didn't answer.

"Yes, and then what? When you've finished this task and expended all your magic in doing so, what will be left to you? What will hold back the creeping madness, the internal torment that will only grow more unbearable as you age? I use blood potions as my treatment. You've tried them, and they do not work well for you, do they?"

Shadrael struggled to hold his temper in check. "Urmaeor—"

"You know what is coming," the priest said, "and if you do not, you are deluding yourself."

"Yes, damn you, I know! What would you have from me?" Shadrael snarled. "Shall I mew in fear at the fate that awaits me?"

"My master offers you a way out."

"What?"

"A soul."

Disbelief swept Shadrael. Urmaeor was throwing a cheap lie to him, a bone tossed to a dog.

"*This* is your payment?" he said violently. "Do you think me such a fool to believe you?"

"No one thinks you are a fool, Lord Shadrael."

"Gods! What next will you say? My soul is *gone*. It

can't be recovered." Shadrael glared at him. "Or did you lie about that during my counseling?"

"No. I told you no lie," Urmaeor said in a quiet voice. "There are other souls to be had. Would you mind having one of them instead of your own, as long as you escaped damnation?"

It was like taking a punch in the guts. Shadrael opened his mouth, but could find no words. He felt winded, hollow inside, even a little sick. Could it be possible? he wondered. Yet even as that tiny thread of hope unspooled in his thoughts, cynicism clipped it.

"A new soul?" he said slowly, warily. "This is no Vindicant teaching."

"Things change," Urmaeor replied. "Without the shadow gods to aid us, we must survive as best we can. Share their doom if you wish, or take the escape my master offers you."

"Your master," Shadrael said scornfully. "What is he, who is he, to dispense lives, even souls, as though he is immortal? I believe none of this."

"But you want to believe me. You want to very much."

Breathing hard, Shadrael took a step back. *No,* he thought fiercely, yet there rose in him a yearning so powerful, so overwhelming he could not quell it. How desperately he wanted to undo a moment's mistake, a moment's stupid bravado. Oh, to relive that day when he'd been too young and foolish to know better than to rise to a dare. He'd wanted to impress the men, rough veterans who refused to respect a new junior officer. He'd wanted to prove his valor, to stand out among the other green, untried young decivates, and so he had. The men had feared him after that.

For years, he had simply accepted the situation, accepted it and used it to his advantage. Until the destruction of the shadow gods and the loss of his connection to them, a connection that had kept him vital.

Self-denial, not pride, he told himself. Lying to himself, pretending he did not care, keeping his courage high like a shield when all the time the reality—the desperate, clawing reality—was that he would do anything, *anything* to get his soul back.

And this priest knew it.

"Who offers you the better price?" Urmaeor asked now, extending his hand. "Lord Vordachai's ducats?" Urmaeor held out his other hand. "Or a soul? The choice is yours."

Shadrael frowned. He hadn't believed Vordachai's offer because it had been too high, and he wasn't going to believe Urmaeor's now for the same reason.

"It's not a betrayal of your brother," Urmaeor said persuasively. "Just a better way, politically, of accomplishing the same objective. You do understand that, I'm sure. And eventually, so will Lord Vordachai. Your brother will not be hurt by this. In fact, we may help his cause—"

"Do you think I care about Vordachai's feelings?" Shadrael asked in astonishment.

"The blood ties between Ulinians are said to be strong."

Loosing a hard, bitter laugh, Shadrael shook his head. "You priests," he said contemptuously, "living in your towers, chanting your prayers, carrying out your rituals. It's emptiness, all of it! You have nothing! Nothing!"

"Commander—"

"Have you been banished to the provinces so long you think you're dealing with a peasant?"

"I assure you, Lord Shadrael, that we're fully aware of your lineage and family connections."

"Eighth Legion, damn you! No other family!" Shadrael shouted.

"Yes, of course. Then we're agreed?"

"Sham and trickery. Charlatans without potent magic, thinking you can manipulate lives the way you used to. Well, no more! You're finished, just like the rest of us. Finished!"

"Allow me to—"

Shadrael gestured in disgust. "Not even a ducat for my hire. Instead, you offer me a *soul*. Marvelous. How in Faure's lying name am I supposed to put it back in? Eh? You tell me that."

"Commander Shadrael—"

"Be damned!"

Spinning on his heel, Shadrael faced the blackness yawning before him and spoke a brief, harsh word. It cracked the blackness open, letting gray light spill forth once more to illuminate the passage out.

"Wait!"

Hearing footsteps coming after him, Shadrael angrily quickened his stride. He didn't bother to look back, and after a moment the sound of pursuit faded and stopped. The only noise he heard was the quick crunch of his boots over the bones of the dead.

Chapter 4

Riding in her wheeled litter, closed in by heavy leather curtains lined with silk, and reclining on soft cushions, Lea E'non made one last effort to read from her scroll of poetry, but the jolting was so bad it caused her small overhead lantern to swing wildly from side to side, casting dizzying shadows across the words. Her eyes ached from trying to read in such impossible conditions, and with a sigh she tossed the scroll aside. It made no sense to her why she had to stay out of sight while they traveled through these small towns dotting the banks of the Parnase River, when two weeks ago she'd been allowed to ride her cream-colored gelding along a road lined with cheering villagers.

Imperial politics. She frowned impatiently. "Sit here. Eat this," she muttered aloud. "Ride out of sight. No, today wave to the crowds. Don't smile. Smile with your utmost charm. Be friendly. Be aloof. Bah!"

Flinging open one of the curtains, she peered out and found herself looking at a rock cliff face rising almost from the very edge of the road. Trees grew atop the hill, towering above her. Some of them leaned precariously, with roots exposed where the thin soil had worn away. In places, water was seeping from the stone, dripping down to pool beside the road. The air smelled clean and very cold.

Lea smiled to herself and inhaled deeply, letting her eyes nearly shut. She smelled frost, and woods, and imminent winter.

"Wonderful," she whispered.

At that moment, her conveyance lurched violently, nearly tossing her out on her head. She clutched the frame hard to save herself, and the leather curtain swung down, slapping her in the face. The litter lurched again and stopped.

Around her came the sound of shouts, punctuated by the bitter cursing of her driver.

Lea righted herself, grabbing a cushion just in time to save it from tumbling out into the mud, and opened a curtain on the opposite side.

She saw an enormous bog of mud and cinder where the road should be. Her litter appeared to be stuck in the middle of it. To her right, a cluster of cavalrymen gathered at the edge, talking among themselves with much head shaking and shrugs. More men rode up but didn't dismount. Instead, they called out several joking suggestions and were answered in kind. Deployed from the Household Regiment of cavalry for her protection, the Crimsons looked bright indeed against this gray, sunless day with their short, scarlet cloaks banded in tawncat fur, their shining steel cuirasses and helmets sporting long horsehair plumes, their immaculate black boots, and white gauntlets extending nearly to their elbows. They were also going to be quite useless, Lea told herself, for wading in mud to free her litter.

"Thirbe!" she called.

Her protector came to her at once. "Yes, m'lady?"

"Are we stuck?"

"Aye. Sit tight while the men give this thing a push."

Lea frowned. "No, I—"

But Thirbe closed the curtains and stepped back. Lea was about to push them open again and ask to be lifted out when there came a loud crack of a whip and the snorting of horses. Her driver bawled commands, and the litter shuddered so violently Lea clutched at whatever handhold she could find. But it did not roll forward. Instead, she felt the conveyance sink a little lower, and through the curses of the men she heard a sucking, squelching noise.

They did not give up. More shouts came, and she heard the servants cluster at the back, muttering under their breath as someone directed them to push on command. Again the whip cracked. Again the horses pulled. Again the litter tilted and settled, and did not budge.

When Lea heard the order for a pry pole to be cut from the woods, she pushed open her curtains, noticing they were now liberally splashed with mud.

"Thirbe!"

He picked his way to her, holding up the hem of his cloak. A stocky man grizzled of hair and weathered of face, with a combat-flattened nose and a jaw of iron, Thirbe was formerly of the Twelfth Legion, veteran of four Madrun campaigns under the old emperor, and an ex-predlicate. He possessed all the toughness of boot leather, the quickness and stamina of a man half his age, the cynicism of a gladiator, and the irritable nature of a thirsty man beholding a closed tavern. Right now, his mouth was clamped tight, and beneath the curve of his leather helmet his eyes glittered with ill humor and impatience.

"Aye, m'lady," he said before she could inquire. "It's stuck up to the axles. You'll have to come out of there while they see to it."

Delighted, Lea pulled her pale blue wool cloak around her shoulders, tying the strings swiftly, and held out her hands.

Thirbe scooped her up and carried her to pavement, well out of the way of muddy servants and gawking cavalrymen. Every man who happened to glance in her direction smiled and nodded respectfully. Lea smiled back cheerfully, and no sooner did her red leather boots touch the ground than she was twirling around in excitement.

"What is this place? What a pretty little valley. It looks leagues away from—"

"Aye, leagues from nowhere," Thirbe said bitterly. "Another bright idea from love's winsome dream."

"Thirbe, hush!" Lea glanced around to see if he'd been overheard. "Don't call him that. You will only spread rumors."

"My lady!" called out one of her attendants from a second litter standing near the supply wagons. "Do you require us?"

"No," Lea said with feeling.

Thirbe beckoned to a lackey and said, "Inform Lady Lea's attendants that they are not needed."

As the man bowed and scurried away to deliver the message, Thirbe cleared his throat. "Well, then, the *captain* took some skittish fool notion in his head the moment scouts brought a report of fire in Brondi. He turned off the main road, and now see where we are."

"Fire?" Lea asked, busy staring at the woods to the west and a narrow little valley to the east. A stream bordered the other side of the road, chuckling over rocks and running swift between low banks. She still found it very pretty, and yet a sudden prickle of unease touched her. "What kind of fire?"

"Stupid southlanders," Thirbe muttered with the typical Itierian contempt for any other province and its customs. "Always building with wood instead of stone. Bound to be fires. Nothing sinister about it. No need for that gormless sprat to assume there's a riot."

"Thirbe—"

"Well, there ain't," Thirbe said, exasperated. "He acts fair gutsnapped at times. I don't think anyone's going to attack you, m'lady, with a house fire."

She chuckled despite herself, and pulled up her hood against the cold bite of wind. "Captain Hervan is just being careful."

"Being a damned noddy-knot, for all I can see," Thirbe said. "Pulling us onto this abandoned road with some fool notion of saving time by cutting through yon hills." He pointed to the north.

Lea swung around and stared at a distant purple smudge. "I'm all for a shortcut, anything to reach Trau more quickly."

But Thirbe was scowling, his eyes fierce with resentment. "Ain't quicker to stand here with a wagon stuck in the mud and three-fourths of the available manpower too pretty to heave it out. When imperial roads are abandoned, it's for good reason."

"Is that what this is?" she asked in surprise, looking at the paving stones that were cracked, in places broken enough for weeds to grow there. Tall grass, flattened by a killing frost, sprawled over the crumbling edges, and ahead of them, past the bog where it looked like the stones had been taken up—perhaps stolen—she could see wind-eddied drifts of fallen leaves. "It doesn't look like an imperial road. It's so narrow, and in bad repair."

"The really old roads are narrow," he said. "Gault knows I've ridden over most of them."

"Then do you know this one?"

"No." He made an exasperated sound in the back of his throat while orders rang out and the servants heaved again to free the litter. "We're lost. That's the long and short of it. Lost and on a road gone bad. Darkness will be coming early today, and I'll lay half my wages that it's going to snow."

"Oh yes, there's no doubt of snow," Lea said happily, sniffing the air. "I've missed that most of all."

"Won't miss it when you're halfway through them hills and got sleet freezing the road and nowhere to camp."

Before she could answer, an adjutant came riding up, reining his horse with a flourish and throwing her a salute. "Compliments of the captain, my lady. A tent and fire for your comfort will be set up shortly."

"I want neither, thank you, Barsin."

He was a handsome boy, perhaps her age or a year older, staring down at her with friendly admiration. "It's going to take time to free that litter, my lady."

"Is it?" she asked with such delight that Thirbe shot her a suspicious look.

"Now, there'll be no prowling about," he began, but she waved away his protest as she smiled at Adjutant Barsin.

"Tell Captain Hervan thank you, but I shan't require the tent."

The adjutant saluted again and wheeled his horse away.

Thirbe turned on Lea at once. "Now, what the—"

"I'm tired of being cooped up," Lea said. "I shall ride."

"No, m'lady, that you won't."

She fixed him with a determined eye. "Yes, I shall. Not to explore, but to keep going. If we're to make the best use of this shortcut, we shouldn't waste time sitting about." She clapped her hands, and a lackey came running. "My horse, Wim."

Bowing, the groom darted away to do her bidding before Thirbe could gainsay her command.

"Now, m'lady, you don't—"

"Yes, Thirbe?" she asked, turning her blue eyes on him in wide innocence. "What don't I want to do? Is there a town in this valley unfriendly to my brother's throne? Or some reason why I should not take exercise and breathe fresh air?"

"Catch your death out here in this cold."

Her laughter rang out merrily, causing several people to look in her direction. "Oh, Thirbe, I was born within sight of a glacier. This is merely a mild autumn day, and quite delightful. Come," she said as her gelding Ysandre was led up and the groom held out his hand to help her mount. "Let us continue."

But Thirbe was shaking his head. "We're off the map, off the approved route you were to take," he said stubbornly. "Ain't sensible to keep going."

With the reins in her hand she patted Ysandre's pale shoulder and whispered to him before looking over her shoulder at Thirbe. "Do you have reason to fear bandits on this road? Are you worried about some specific danger?"

Thirbe looked from her to the groom—standing there agog with his mouth slightly open and his eyes wide with

alarm. Lea knew that whatever her protector said would be
spread through the company at once by Wim's gossiping
tongue. Obviously Thirbe realized it, too, for he frowned at
the boy with such quelling ferocity that Wim turned pale.

When Thirbe turned his gaze back to her, she refused to
wilt beneath its scorching blast and simply smiled at him.
"Well?"

"Ain't likely they're going to lurk here. Slim pickings for
any cutthroat lying in wait on this donkey trail. It's just—"

He broke off, pursing his mouth.

Realizing he was honestly troubled and not just grumbling, Lea allowed her amusement to fade.

"What is it, Thirbe?" she asked quietly, taking note of
his restlessness, the alert flick of his gaze here and there,
the way he stood so that his back was never to the woods.
"There's something here you do not like."

"There's *nothing* here I like," he said fiercely, dismissing her groom with a curt gesture.

As soon as Wim hurried away, Thirbe stepped closer to
Lea and lowered his voice. "Nothing I can put my finger
on, but there's an itch between my shoulders. I got the feeling we're being watched."

Lea was all seriousness now. In the three years that
Thirbe had served her, she'd never doubted his instincts or
his professionalism. She trusted him completely. "Should
we turn back?" she asked.

He nodded, to her disappointment, but said, "I'd prefer
it. But we've gone nearly a day this way. If the road hasn't
been cut ahead of us, and so far the scouts don't report
such, then I suppose it's better to keep going than lose another day retracing our steps."

Lea watched him. "I'm not so eager to reach Trau that
I'm willing to abandon common sense. If you have reason
beyond what you've said so far, we'll take the time. If it's
only that you do not like the captain's changing our plans,
then . . ." Letting her voice trail off, she shrugged.

Thirbe said nothing, and after a moment Lea nodded
her head decisively. "Then we continue," she said.

She sent him a look, and he boosted her into the saddle before fetching his mount and joining her farther down the road. Someone called after them, but Lea did not glance back.

"Shall we race away and see how far we can get before they catch up?"

Thirbe didn't bother to answer her nonsense. Sighing, Lea abandoned her impulse to play games and kept Ysandre at a steady walk instead of letting him gallop. He tossed his head and pranced a little, but she didn't relent.

Moments later, the sound of galloping hooves made Ysandre pretend to shy, and they were joined by Captain Hervan and perhaps ten or so cavalrymen.

"Well, Lady Lea!" he called out in his aristocratic baritone. "It seems you have taken command of our party. Are you abandoning us, or leading us onward?"

Lea swallowed a sigh and bestowed a fleeting smile on him. "I am abandoning the litter and continuing our journey on horseback, as is only sensible."

Concern knotted his brow. From the flowing plume of his helmet to the tips of his silver spurs, he was a dazzling creation of all that good looks, fine breeding, wealth, and uniform could provide. No mud splattered the shining perfection of his boots, for he'd been riding at the head of their column all day.

"It's one thing to ride for exercise, Lady Lea, but to travel so for the rest of the day will only fatigue and chill you unnecessarily."

"Why have you created this myth that I am fragile?" Lea asked.

"All the finest ladies are agreeably fragile."

"I will not break, Captain, and I can withstand the cold as well as anyone."

He smiled at her, displaying excellent white teeth beneath a thin, fashionable mustache. "Yes, of course. But why not rest while the servants prepare a fire for you? Getting all the wagons through this mud will take time. You

would perhaps enjoy a meal, and the poet will oblige you,
I'm sure, with his newest song."

Lea had heard the poet-singer rehearsing since morning, between complaints that the cold air was bad for his
voice and requests to please ride in an enclosed litter with
the ladies. Lea was not disposed to listen to any of it again.

She gathered her reins, making Ysandre shift and toss
his head impatiently. "No, thank you."

"Some other diversion? Your priest, perhaps?"

"No." It was useless, Lea knew, to remind him that
Poulso was *not* her priest. Captain Olivel Hervan, despite
his excessive charm served on a platter of flattery, never
listened to anything she said. "I'm going on, Captain," she
said now, firmly. "When the wagons are past this point,
they can catch up. Please inform my ladies that they are
free to ride after me, or remain with the wagons."

"Lady Lea—"

She held up her hand to silence him. "I suggest that in
addition to a pry pole, your men try laying bundles of
sticks across the bog, so that once my litter is free the other
wagons don't stick in the same spot."

"Lady Lea—"

"Come, Thirbe," she said, kicking Ysandre forward.

But the captain's horse moved to block her path, and he
leaned over to grab her reins. "Wait, please."

She jerked her horse to one side, spurring him out of
Hervan's reach. "Never try that again," she said fiercely,
and sent Ysandre cantering up the road.

Chapter 5

She might have won the skirmish, Lea thought some time later, but she wasn't sure it constituted a victory. The initial exhilaration of being outside in the fresh, cold air, riding through this lovely valley had given way to increasing uneasiness as the afternoon wore on.

She could not say exactly what troubled her about the place. The old imperial road wound along the natural contours of land instead of running arrow straight. It followed a stream that flowed shallow and quick between low, flat banks and outcroppings of water-worn limestone. To her right stretched fallow fields, dotted with self-sown saplings and choked with long coarse grass browned and knocked flat by a killing frost.

Strange, Lea thought, that there were no birds here. No flocks of slim, gray-backed chikbeaks flying up in alarm from the undergrowth with that distinct buzzing whir of wings. No marshbirds with gaudy red markings flitting here and there among the weeds, foraging before winter closed in. Plenty of tall, gone-to-seed plumes of fluffy thistle grew along the road's edge, yet where were the tiny

yellow fincos she'd seen elsewhere hanging upside down
and feeding so greedily they barely flew away at the horses'
approach?

The ten cavalrymen riding with her initially had swelled
in number to almost the full squadron of a hundred. Her
ladies had caught up, looking rather flushed and wind-
blown on the placid mares assigned to their use. The musicians were along as well, and one had begun plucking a
lute although he'd yet to find a tune, in Lea's opinion. A
flash of white, crimson, black, and silver went galloping
by, catching her attention. It was Captain Hervan, riding
his large bay horse effortlessly, his short cloak and helmet
plume streaming out behind him. Barsin rode in his wake,
getting splattered for his devotion. Lea saw the pair slow
down at the front of the column and take their usual positions there. Of the wagons there was no sign. According to
Sergeant Kress, who came up to her shortly thereafter at a
sedate and respectful trot, the litter was now safely out of
the mud, but the food wagon proved to be too heavy for the
sticks laid out for it. It had sunk down to the axles and
looked like it might stay there.

Lea exchanged a look with Thirbe. "We'd better hope
we reach an inn by nightfall if we're to have supper," she
said.

He frowned, still looking restless. "Aye, there goes your
gear and grub. Did he leave all the servants behind as
well?"

"They'll catch up," a cavalryman volunteered cheerfully.

Around her, everyone was conversing, completely at
their ease. Lady Fyngie's giggling told Lea that her youn-
gest attendant was flirting with the lute player again. Laughter and chatter filled the air, sometimes ringing through the
valley, and all the while Lea's sense of oppression grew.

She understood now why Thirbe felt as though he was
being watched. She felt it, too, and knew it to be the bad
jaiethquai hanging over this desolate little valley.

No birds. No villages. No barking dogs or running children peeping in shy curiosity from the road hedges. No

curls of smoke from chimneys. Only the sigh of a cold north wind through the trees and frost-burned leaves fluttering to the ground. Aside from the noise of her party, there was no other sign or sound of life here.

The *jaiethquai* seemed so dense and sad that Lea felt as though she'd intruded into someone's grave site. What a sad place, a terrible place, she thought, if not even the wild birds would come to it. She wished she had not come this way either and regretted not turning back when she had the chance.

"Look," Thirbe said, pointing across the stream. "Ruins."

Lea stared hard in that direction. Although it was but midafternoon, the day was growing progressively gloomier, with long, inky shadows already darkening beneath the trees. She saw a few small mounds choked by grass and vines, but no real evidence that any dwellings had once stood. Disappointed, she fingered her necklace of *gli*-emeralds for reassurance, taking care to maintain her inner balance against whatever oppressive forces lingered in this place.

"I don't see them," she said.

"Bound to be more ahead."

She was on the point of asking Thirbe how he knew that if he'd never been here before, but she was interrupted.

"Er, Lady Lea," said a deferential voice. "May I join you for a short while?"

She saw that the priest had ridden up to her. Mounted on a slope-shouldered, nondescript horse, the Reformant was a heavyset man with multiple chins, thick brows, thicker lips, and a large, unfortunate wart on one cheek. He was an extremely ugly man, and although that hardly mattered to Lea, his personality was too colorless to compensate for his looks. Her attendants despised him, making fun of him at every opportunity despite Lea's reproaches. As a result, she felt obliged to compensate for their cruelty by giving him more of her attention than she really wanted to. It was most vexing.

"Poulso," she said now in polite acknowledgment. "Of course you may."

As he rode up beside her left stirrup, Lea shot a look of mute dismay at Thirbe on her right. Her protector waggled his brows without sympathy, as if to say she could have avoided this by remaining inside her litter.

"I thought," Lea said, turning back to the priest, "that you'd elected to stay with the wagons."

Poulso bowed, or attempted to, making an awkward sort of slouch in the saddle. "You have been most kind, most gracious, dear Lady Lea, in granting me the use of the enclosed wagon. Of course, it was a trifle crowded in there among all the chests, and the musicians have been rude about my sitting on one of the panpipperies and breaking it, but I assure you it was a most inadvertent accident and I meant no deliberate harm of their possessions."

"No," she murmured.

"Otherwise, the wagon has been most comfortable, much to my liking. I have stayed quite warm, and my chilblains are better."

"I'm glad."

"My one regret is that you did not see fit to join me in prayer meditations. You would have found it most edifying, Lady Lea. Of course, I am available to assist you in prayer now, if that is convenient."

"No, not now," she said.

She did not subscribe to the Reformant religion, a sort of revised version of the Vindicant doctrine mixed with whatever pre-Vindicant texts scholars had found. Chanting did not edify her or provide spiritual comfort. Nor was she about to seclude herself with Poulso for any reason.

His brown eyes, large and slightly protuberant, rather dewy at the moment with admiration, were staring at her right now, staring and fixed with a rudeness she found disconcerting. Almost all men stared at her, of course, but this was different. She was well aware that her pale golden ringlets and the whiteness of her complexion were considered unusual, even a little exotic, by Itierian standards, and in New Imperia she'd been acclaimed a beauty. Although she wasn't conceited about it, she liked being pretty and enjoyed the admiration, within reason. But carrying on a conversation with someone who stared like a half-wit while breathing heavily through his mouth was less than enjoyable.

"No," she repeated gently now, as he showed no signs of going away. "I have no need of joining your prayers. Is there anything else you wished to say or ask? Because—"

"Oh, er, yes, my lady," he said, blinking and coming out of his daze. "How kind of you to remind me." As he spoke, he fumbled in his purse and handed over a cabochon ruby. "Thank you for letting me examine this jewel that you found yesterday. It is quite fascinating how frequently you discover these, er, treasures. Quite fascinating. What a very sharp eye you must have. I do not know how you do it."

Thirbe choked back a laugh and coughed. Lea resisted glancing at him, knowing she couldn't keep her composure if their eyes met.

"Perhaps you should keep it for further study, Poulso."

Greed flickered in his eyes. He licked his fleshy lips, and his blunt fingers twitched a little. "Oh no, dear Lady Lea. My dear, generous Lady Lea. How kind you are. How ready to bestow favor upon your subjects—"

"I have no subjects," she corrected him sharply. "I do not rule."

One of the cavalrymen riding in front of them glanced back at Poulso with a warning scowl.

Looking alarmed, the priest slouched in another of his awkward bows. "Forgive me. I am clumsy in my mode of expression. I do not wish to offend you, or to speak improperly against His Imperial Majesty, His Supreme Excellency, the emperor who is my most esteemed bene-factor. I meant to say, dear lady, that you rule our hearts, and your admirers are your subjects in—in the sense of—"

"I see," she said, cutting off this nonsense. "You should

keep the ruby. Make sure it's acceptable and contains no magic."

"My dear Lady Lea, I could not possibly accept such a magnificent gift," he protested.

But when she held out the jewel his fat fingers closed over it so avidly his knuckles whitened, and he took great care in securing it away.

"My lady," he said, bowing low. "You would make me a wealthy man, me, a humble servant of Gault—a man sworn to vows of humility and poverty. What am I to say?"

"Sell the stone and use the money to buy more ancient texts for your order's library," she said impatiently, eager to be rid of him. "Repair your temple. Whatever you see fit to do with it. You need not gain personally from this gift."

"I—I see, my dear lady. I shall do as you say. Thank you. And now may I—"

"That is all for now, Poulso. You may leave me."

With a look of disappointment, he obediently reined up his horse and dropped back. Lea could not suppress a sigh of relief. She'd thought he would never go.

"Them little bribes of yours ain't such a good idea," Thirbe said quietly.

She glanced over her shoulder to make certain Poulso was out of earshot. "It got rid of him."

"Aye, but they're getting jealous of each other, wondering when you're going to give out another big jewel and who'll get it."

"Why should it matter?" Lea asked. "When I find the stones, why shouldn't I share?"

"There's a time to be kind, m'lady," Thirbe said gruffly, "and a time to keep things close. Let's get you safely delivered to Trau, and then if you want to bestow gifts, do so at the end of your journey. Eh?" He peered at her from beneath the edge of his helmet. "You understand?"

"Yes. I'll try to remember."

But she frowned as she promised, unhappy about hoarding stones that were simply jewels without any inner *gli.*

Without magical properties, they held little interest for her,
and she did not like to be burdened with too many possessions. That was not the way of balance. Besides, it seemed
wrong to withhold the gifts, no matter what Thirbe said.

"Look, m'lady!" Thirbe said, pointing again. "More ruins! Just like I said there'd be."

This time she had no difficulty seeing them. Lea stared
at foundation stones and fallen walls shrouded in frost-
withered vines. Rubble was strewn in all directions, half-
seen in the dead grass. She saw a large structure standing at
the end of an overgrown field. A barn, she supposed. Its
roof was half-fallen in, its walls skewed. The whole thing
looked as though a puff of wind would send it crashing
down, yet she supposed it had been standing like that for
years. Beyond it, a large town—all in ruins—stretched to
the east.

"What happened here?" she asked in wonder. "This is
no small village."

"Aye, a big town in its day. And this road provided a
pass through the hills to the north. Plenty of traffic and custom through here in the past. If we come to an imperial
arch over the road in a while, we'll know."

"We'll know what?" she asked.

"The name of the place. It'll be chiseled on the base of
the arch, along with the date of construction and Kostimon's Imperial Seal. By rights, that should be struck off
and the Light Bringer's seal chiseled in, but abandoned
roads like this ain't likely to see that kind of attention."

"Imperial towns of this size don't usually lie abandoned," Lea said, still curious. "Was it invaded, torn down?
Swept by fire or plague?"

Thirbe shrugged. "Gone is gone, m'lady. The why don't
matter."

When a sudden clammy feeling rolled over her, she
reined her horse to a sudden halt. The men around her
stopped as well.

"M'lady?" Thirbe asked in concern. "Are you faint?"

She blinked rapidly, forcing back the bad *quai* that had

momentarily overtaken her. "No, I'm . . ." Her voice trailed off as she stared at the ruins. Her gaze was caught by a roofless stone building standing with vacant holes where windows had once been, one rotted shutter still dangling by a bolt. "There's no harmony here. The *jaiethquai* is so very bad. Whatever befell the town—"

"Be at ease there, m'lady," Thirbe broke in, his voice gentler than usual. "A long time back it was. A long time back."

She frowned. "It must have been dreadful. The *quai* . . . everything here is so disturbed . . . tainted. Their souls do not lie easy."

Thirbe cleared his throat in concern. "Whatever ghosts and bad *hoojoo* you're talking about, best we ride through here fast and get on to somewhere better."

"Yes," she said, still feeling shaken. She touched her necklace to draw strength from it. "I agree we'd better go on."

"What's the matter?" asked Captain Hervan, suddenly pushing his horse through the milling cavalrymen. His gaze swept over her, and he frowned. "Great Gault, my lady. How pale you are. You're unwell!"

"No, I—"

Before she could explain, he was off his horse and at her side, pulling her from the saddle without heed for her protests.

"I told you that riding would fatigue you," he said, his arm still around her for support. "Let us rest a bit."

"No!"

But he wasn't listening to her, as usual. He called up a sergeant and issued orders for the horses to be watered and dry rations to be issued.

"I shall share my rations with you, Lady Lea," he said, leading her over to the bank of the stream. "Humble food, of course. But it will revive you marvelously. Just see if it doesn't."

She pulled away from his arm and looked up at him, ready to tell him that she didn't want food or rest. She wanted to ride on as quickly as possible from this dreadful place.

But the others were dismounting, and grooms were running up to take charge of the horses. Ysandre was already being led away to water. The skies darkened, draping low clouds over the hills, and at that moment it began to snow.

Chapter 6

"**Snow**!" Captain Hervan announced. "Shelter for Lady Lea, at once!"

But Lea pulled away from him and lifted her face to the snowflakes spiraling down. The cold kiss of them on her skin cleared away the clamminess she'd been feeling, and she held her necklace in both hands, drawing in its power while she drew in deep breaths of cold air.

"More," she whispered. "More!"

Snow fell heavily now, making a soft, hissing sound as it came down to collect in the folds of her cloak and blanket the ground.

Restored, she smiled, pushing back her hood to let the snow adorn her hair. Holding wide her arms, she twirled around like a child, laughing.

"Isn't it lovely?" she called.

No one answered her.

She stopped twirling and saw everyone staring at her. That's when she realized the heavy snowfall was centered on her alone. Only at her feet was the ground white. Elsewhere, a few sporadic flakes were floating down, nothing more.

The astonishment on people's faces made her laugh. She stepped away from the spot, stamping snow off her boots, and shook out the folds of her cloak.

"Do you dislike snow?" she asked them. "It's just . . . I've missed it so much, you see."

The heavy snowfall in that one spot stopped immediately, as though it had never happened. In her heart, Lea sent swift thanks to the air spirits. They were whimsical and capricious, benign one moment and aloof the next, yet never as hostile and vicious as their cousins the wind spirits. She felt them blow against her, ruffling her curls back from her brow, sensed faintly that they wished she'd lingered inside the circle of snow long enough for them to communicate with her, but it was too late. They were gone.

Thirbe joined her. "All right, m'lady?"

She gave him a radiant smile. "Oh yes."

The others began to relax and move about. Many continued staring at her, but others just shook their heads. A sergeant rapped out orders, and horses were led to the stream.

Lady Vineena, the second of her attendants, ventured up to her with a small curtsy and reached out cautiously to brush snow from Lea's hair.

"It's real," she said in wonder.

"Of course," Lea said. "Why shouldn't it be?"

"But you—did you make it snow harder, just on you?" Vineena asked. Her eyes grew rounder. "Can you control the weather?"

"Not exactly."

"But—"

Lea turned away from her, only to find Hervan blocking her path. His eyes looked dazzled.

"Lady Lea," he said ardently. "Whatever that was . . . your skin, your eyes . . . they're glowing. You're actually radiant. Beautiful. I—I have to tell you how much I—"

"Please," Lea said, and walked away from him swiftly.

He did not follow, much to her relief, and she picked her way over the muddy ground to the stream.

There, she saw the water was starting to turn slushy at

the edges. As she ventured out onto a large, flat rock jutting over the stream, a servant came running up with her drinking cup of Choven silver.

"Shall I fetch you a drink, m'lady?"

Lea took the cup with a gentle smile of thanks. "I'll do it."

Carefully she crouched, tucking her long skirts and pale blue cloak neatly around her legs, and dipped her cup into the water. It tasted pure and sweet, and was cold enough to numb her tongue. Glad to find that none of the poor *quai* hanging about this place had tainted the stream, she sipped with pleasure before refilling her cup.

"Take care you don't fall in," Thirbe said from behind her.

She ignored his warning, ignored also the chatter and movement of people and horses until the marching cadence of booted feet reached her ears. Thirbe spun around, reaching for his sword, but it was only the small group of Cubrian archers who'd been left behind to guard the wagons and had now caught up.

"Looks like maybe the wagons and your litter, m'lady, are past the mud," Thirbe said.

Indifferently Lea turned away. It meant that instead of continuing they would now linger for the wagons to catch up, and she didn't like that idea. They were spending too much time in this strange valley. She didn't know why, exactly, but the instinct inside her to move on was strong.

Just as she was about to rise, a ripple across the flow of water caught her attention. Drawing off her glove, Lea trailed her fingers in the clear water. A face not her reflection glimmered up at her, then vanished. The cool touch of a water spirit glided over her palm.

"Peace to you," Lea thought to it.

"Beware. Beware," the spirit murmured in her mind.

When Lea lifted her hand, she was holding an opal, the symbol of mourning.

Pale and smooth, the stone was shot through with colors of white, gray, pale green, and pink. She admired it, turning it this way and that, wishing the sun would break through the heavy clouds to bring its pretty iridescence to life. Still, it was a sad stone, with a sad meaning, born of the sorrow here.

The warning disturbed her, renewing her uneasiness. She rose to her feet, clutching the opal, and looked around a little wildly.

"Have you found something, Lady Lea?" Fyngie asked, suddenly beside her and looking avidly at Lea's hand. "Another jewel? May I see it? How pretty!"

Distracted, Lea handed it to her, letting Fyngie hold it up and exclaim over it. She made so much noise that she attracted attention.

Lea glanced around and caught a look of intense jealousy on Lady Rinthella's beautiful face before her chief attendant smoothed her expression. Thirbe's warning came back, and Lea found herself annoyed.

There *was* something here, she thought. Something aware that was feeding on people's darker emotions and intensifying them on purpose. She focused a moment, but could not identify it as either a spirit or a living entity. Whatever it was, she did not want more contact with it, she told herself, and shivered.

"Are you growing cold, Lady Lea?" Fyngie asked, dutifully giving back the opal. "Shall I order a fire kindled to warm you? Perhaps we shall stop for the day and make camp. I'm tired and half-frozen. Aren't you?"

Thirbe stepped forward. "This is a right sorry place to camp," he said gruffly. "We've no business to be lingering here."

Fyngie's pale blue eyes widened, and she sent her most winsome smile to Lea. "Oh, please? May we not stop here? It's so pretty. And look at those men trying to walk over the old footbridge. I wonder if they're trying to fall in."

Lea looked at the two laughing young fools in their bright cloaks, teetering on a rickety structure still spanning the stream. Chunks of rotted wood fell into the water, and one man wavered, flailing his arms for balance while the other one hooted with derision. Her gaze, however, shifted past them to the ruins, looking for movement, any evidence of life.

Again, that sense of clammy coldness reached out to her, sinking into her very bones. She gripped her necklace and stepped back. "We should go," she said firmly. "Now."

"I'll convey m'lady's order," Thirbe said at once.

"Oh no," Fyngie protested softly, but Lea ignored her.

Swiftly she returned to the water's edge and crouched there, intending to slip the opal back into the water, but the water spirit did not respond to Lea's call, did not return. She placed the opal on top of the rock where she'd been standing. She had accepted the gift, but respectfully she would not keep it. The *jaiethal* in it was too sad, too strong and dreadful, like a killing breath. It would be foolish to take such sorrow with her, as foolish as befriending a little sand scorpion and keeping it in her pocket.

When she turned to go, she saw no one mounted. A red-faced Thirbe stood near the road, arguing with Sergeant Lor.

"What now?" she asked impatiently. "What delays us?"

"Here, Lady Lea," Vineena said, skipping up to her with the opal. "You dropped this."

"No, she didn't," Fyngie said. "She wants to leave it behind."

"Then may I have it?" Vineena asked, smiling.

"You already have one," Fyngie said.

"Not an opal. It suits me so well. Please, my lady?"

"No," Lea said more sharply than customary. "Leave that where I placed it."

Vineena's eyes widened. "But, my lady, it's valuable. You don't usually leave behind the jewels you—"

"This time is different," Lea said. "Now put it back by the water where you found it."

A pale raven flew over their heads, startling them all. It seemed to come from nowhere, and it flew so close to Lea that she ducked a little. Then it vanished as though swallowed into thin air. She turned around, staring at the trees overhanging the road, but did not see the bird again.

"Must we leave now?" Vineena asked as though nothing had happened. "It's so romantic here. I wish we could explore the ruins. Perhaps some of the men will escort us over there, although I do not think I dare trust that bridge." She sent Fyngie a sly look. "Fyngie might, though, if a certain young adjutant gives her escort."

Fyngie blushed to the roots of her hair, while Rinthella came up to them and quelled both of the young girls with a scornful look. She held out her hand imperiously to Vineena.

"Shame on you for disobeying Lady Lea," she said. "Hand it over at once."

Scowling, Vineena put the opal in her hand. "I'm sorry, my lady," she said to Lea. "I was not disobedient. I was about to do your bidding."

Lea looked at her in disappointment, not at all fooled by the lie. "Oh, Vineena," she said.

"I shall deal with it," Rinthella announced. Turning with a swirl of her skirts, she headed back toward the stream.

Vineena watched her go. "Maybe," she muttered. "And maybe she wants it for herself."

"Why does no one heed my wish to leave?" Lea asked Thirbe. "Why does the groom not bring my horse?"

Her protector was still red in the face, his mouth a thin line of anger. "What do you think? Who countermands your every order?"

She frowned. "Oh, not again."

"Aye, again. And here comes our moon-eyed popinflare now."

"Ah, Lady Lea!" called out Hervan's distinctive light baritone. "Admiring the ruins, I see. Would you care to stroll to them? I'll see you safely across the stream."

He stopped before her, holding his white gauntlets in one hand and standing in a way that best displayed the athletic line of his body. He sent her a charming smile that she did not return.

"I think the ruins are shadow haunted," she said. "Let us continue on without further delay."

"Haunted?" He laughed. "All shadows are gone, Lady Lea."

"Do not patronize me, Captain. Demons may no longer crawl freely about our world, but that does not mean evil is gone. It is time to leave."

"At least wait until the wagons catch up to us," he said persuasively. "No doubt you would be far more comfortable in your litter, especially since the weather is worsening, and—"

"No, thank you. The weather does not trouble me. I shall continue on my horse."

"But, Lady Lea—"

"Groom," Lea said imperiously, beckoning.

Wim led up her gelding in a way that jostled Hervan aside.

"Take care, fellow!" the captain said in annoyance.

Lea swallowed a smile. "Wim, please be more careful."

"Aye, m'lady."

Hervan slapped pale horse hairs from his shoulder. "Well, if you insist, Lady Lea, then I shall escort you to the head of the column. No eating mud for you."

"Thank you."

"She'll be safer in the middle," Thirbe said.

"Oh, but I think we have nothing to fear from bandits on this road," Hervan said airily. He smiled at Lea. "Besides, I know a little of the history of this valley."

"Then can you tell me what happened to the town?" Lea asked.

"Er, no, but when we reach its imperial arch, we'll look for the dates and—"

"Already told her that much," Thirbe broke in.

Annoyance wiped away Hervan's smile. Taller, younger, as glossy and sleek as Thirbe was dour and stocky, the captain looked down his patrician nose with all the arrogance of his class and lineage. "You are the lady's protector, sirrah, nothing more. Keep your place."

"Am," Thirbe said shortly, meeting him glare for glare.

"Better she rides in the middle of the column. You can spin old folk tales once we're through for the day."

Hervan drew in a sharp breath, but before Lea could intervene, Rinthella came up beside her and curtsied. "Is there any service I may perform for you, my lady?" she asked. Her handsome eyes were sparkling, and she looked vivid and lovely in the falling snow. As she spoke to Lea, however, she kept glancing at the captain. "May I fetch you another pair of gloves, Lady Lea? Do you want the musicians to play while you and the captain are conversing?"

"No, thank you," Lea said quickly. "We're leaving."

"Are we?" Rinthella suddenly pointed at the woods. "What is that?"

Both Lea and Thirbe turned, but from the corner of her eye Lea caught the captain and Rinthella exchanging secret smiles. A note passed between them. When Lea faced them, however, both were looking at her attentively, their expressions quite proper.

Disappointed in Rinthella, who was older than she by three years and engaged to marry yet persisted in flirting with any good-looking man in the squadron, Lea despaired of ever seeing her chief attendant behave. With masses of dark hair and haughty eyes, Rinthella was beautiful enough to be paid plenty of compliments without having to seek them, and her penchant for disposable relationships did not bode well for her future marital happiness. As for the captain, Lea found it shocking that he pursued them both. She supposed he and Rinthella thought her too naive and unsophisticated to ever realize the truth. But she perceived that behind their smiling faces they were secretly laughing at how easily they thought they had deceived her.

Raised by the Choven, who courted and married for life, Lea despised these games.

"Rinthella, you may leave me," she said.

Rinthella's dark brows lifted in surprise. Color stained her cheeks as she curtsied very correctly, then flounced away. Hervan watched her go with open appreciation before returning his attention to Lea.

His gaze was warm, showing her equal appreciation.

Astonished, Lea thought, *He has no shame at all*.

"May I assist you, Lady Lea?" he said suavely and snapped his fingers. "Groom! The lady's reins, at once!"

Wim tried to hand the reins to her, but Hervan intervened, taking them and knotting them together as though for a child. Then he cupped her small booted foot in his hands and boosted her lightly into the saddle.

She gave Hervan a cool nod. "Thank you, Captain."

Stepping back, Hervan threw her a cavalry salute and spun on his heel. "Sergeant Taime, mount up the men!"

Taime bawled out commands that were echoed by Lor and the third sergeant down the line, and soon they were riding out. The flag bearer went to the head of the column, and so did Adjutant Barsin, but Hervan angled his horse beside Lea's, crowding Thirbe.

Scarlet with outrage, Thirbe said, "Best leave off paying court to our good lady, Captain, and see to your men."

"The sergeants have things in hand."

"Well, your squint-eyed Sergeant Taime, and Lor, and whosit down the line ain't worth the price of their commissions. We're straggled all over the road, and the column ain't forming up tight like it should."

Hervan gave Thirbe a cold stare and turned to Lea. "Lady Lea, your man-at-arms worries far too much. He's cast his poor spirits over you and made you fear this valley instead of appreciating it. Now he seeks to give me orders. Will you dismiss him from his duties for a while? Perhaps he would enjoy escorting your lovely attendants while I personally attend to your safety."

Lea gasped in affront. "Captain, you go too far! His duty is to remain close to me at all times while you—"

"But how can we enjoy a real conversation with him scowling and muttering as he does?" Hervan asked. "His face could sour milk, and with such an audience how can I find the proper words to express how much I ardently admire you?"

Shocked, Lea reined up her horse so abruptly that Hervan passed her before he wheeled back.

Lea was already gesturing at Thirbe. "To my stirrup," she commanded.

Thirbe obeyed, wearing a grim little smile of satisfaction as he trotted his horse into position before Hervan could block him.

All the while Lea glared at the captain. "You disappoint me, sir. You presume too much, and your behavior is inappropriate."

"To an untried maiden, perhaps," he murmured for her hearing alone. "But not to a woman."

Her brows drew together in consternation.

His eyes were dancing with amusement. "Dear Lady Lea," he went on. "I realize I should not be talking this way while I'm on duty, but my admiration fills my heart to overflowing, and no longer can I avoid telling you so."

"Make a better effort," she said fiercely. "It's improper to speak to me like this."

"Oh, but I am lost to what is proper. My feelings overwhelm me."

"Your feelings are false ones. I—"

She broke off just in time, aware that she could not mention his dalliance with Rinthella without cheapening herself or appearing jealous.

"I know yours," he said, his voice soft and too intimate. "I conspired with Lady Rinthella today. This note?" He pulled out the scrap of folded parchment from the top of his gauntlet and held it up between his fingers. "We planned it to determine whether you do really care for me. Now I am rewarded by your anger, dear lady. I am given hope for the first time."

"I—I—" She could not meet his gaze now. Her anger with him swelled, intensified by his assumption that she was jealous.

"You are shy with me, little one," he said. "You are adorable, and I am your slave."

Her face was on fire. "Stop it!" she whispered. "If the emperor should learn of this—"

"We are half the empire away from the emperor. He can do nothing," Hervan said, grinning. "Let me court you, sweet lady. Let me whisper my adoration into your charming ear and beguile your tender innocence into—"

"Be silent." She felt as though she'd entered a nightmare. "I will not be mocked."

Astonishment widened Hervan's eyes. "Lady Lea, I assure you that I do not—"

"I don't know what you would and would not do," she broke in, distressed. "How dare you talk to me in this way? Exaggerating. Lying."

"Flirting?" he murmured, quirking up one eyebrow.

She shot him a look, fighting the urge to gallop away from him. "There can be only one reason you would dare to court me so improperly, and that is to insult me."

"Never!" Now it was his turn to look shocked. "Dear lady, you misjudge me."

"Do I?"

He had the effrontery to laugh. "Oh yes. If you think true courtship is some ritualized negotiation, you know very little about the way of a man with a maid."

Living at court for three years had taught her enough. She gave him a stony look. "You must fear the emperor would not give his consent to your suit, and so you come at me like this, with the collusion of my attendant, and hope to do what? Gain my affection? Seduce me? Are you that ambitious, Captain?"

He reddened, although a smile played beneath his narrow mustache. "Now who is bold? I admire your spirit, Lady Lea. I admire it very much indeed."

"You may keep your admiration. I want none of it."

Hervan looked at her in wide-eyed innocence that did not fool her for a moment. "You misjudge me, Lady Lea," he said in a very serious tone. "What I've said to you, I mean in earnest."

She met his gaze, clearly, directly, seeing right through his guile. He was the first to look away.

"I think not," she said scornfully. "You flirt with every woman in this party in turn. I give you no leave to do the same with me."

"Plain speaking."

"You force me to it."

Hervan took a lot of trouble to flick a speck of mud off his white gauntlet. "We are not all as clear, honorable, and unlayered as you wish us to be, my lady," he said at last. "A man can admire other women, while loving *one*."

She drew in a sharp breath. "Do you think me jealous of my own attendant?"

"Aren't you?"

He was still trying to manipulate her, she thought, fighting to control her temper. Being provoked into losing inner harmony by such absurdity was another reason why she wanted to leave court forever. "I am not as naive as you believe, Captain," she said. "I understand the ambitions of your family and know exactly why your father sought this assignment for you."

"A long journey is such a perfect opportunity to gain a lady's acquaintance."

She realized nothing she was saying was reaching him. Her mouth tightened.

His smile was sudden and dazzling. "How delightful you are. Such fire and indignation. Such a righteous view of how life should be lived. Your time at court has not seasoned you at all. You remain quite fresh, quite adorable. It's a marvel."

His mockery—delivered so openly this time—hurt. She had nothing else for her defense except the simple honesty he'd just condemned. She could not even shame him.

Frowning, struggling to maintain her composure, she said, "You have my permission to return to your duties."

Hervan's smile grew tight. "Ah yes, the easy way out. As you wish, my lady." Bowing so low that his helmet plume fell forward over his shoulder, he gave her a jaunty little wave and spurred his horse forward to the head of the column, making it cavort and prance as though to display his excellent horsemanship. "Sergeant!" he called out. "Close up the men."

"Aye, sir. Men! Close up ranks!"

"Popinflare," Thirbe muttered, coming up beside her. "Bold as brass and twice as polished."

She stared straight ahead, fighting to hold back tears.

Thirbe's keen gaze watched her face. "Needs his guts reamed for making love to you."

"He wasn't—making love to me," she said unsteadily. "He was hateful!"

Thirbe made a little noise in his throat. "Aye. That's what love is."

She flashed him an astonished look. "No. It can't be. Not like that, so angry and wild. Love is a harmonious union of—"

"Ha! M'lady, you been reading too many scrolls. There's poet's drivel and there's real life." Thirbe cast her a look of appraisal. "Perhaps it's time you knew the difference."

"I—I don't believe you," Lea said, without much assurance. "The Choven are—"

"Begging your pardon, m'lady, but the Choven way ain't ours. Love's sweet dream is dead gone for you—"

"I don't understand what you're saying."

"You do." Thirbe glanced at her and snorted. "Enough."

"But it isn't like that. You heard him. He was horrid."

"Course he was. You ain't meeting him halfway. Ain't even interested. You think a conceited young donkey ass like that is going to take kindly to rejection?" Thirbe laughed in his curt way. "Probably the first wall of indifference he's ever hit. Do him good."

Bewildered, Lea sorted through all that Hervan had said. "Does he really think I'm doing this on purpose, to keep his interest? But I'm not!"

"Don't care a knucklebone for what he thinks. It's you I'm to see about."

"But I don't—"

"Be easy, m'lady," Thirbe said gently. "I know it. If you

did take to that conceited wart I'd have you across my saddle and go galloping back to New Imperia as fast as this horse could run."

"Oh."

Thirbe's keen eyes raked her. "He ain't worth a twig, m'lady. You can do a lot better, and will."

"Do you mean Caelan is negotiating a marriage for me?" she asked, horrified. "But I don't intend to come ba—"

Realizing that she was about to betray her secret plan, she hastily amended her sentence. "I mean, I don't intend to marry."

"You will."

"No, Thirbe," she said with decision.

"Seventeen's a bit young to set your life's track."

"I'm almost eighteen," she said fiercely. "I know what lies ahead of me, and it isn't an arranged marriage to the House of Hervan. Or any other. I've seen no one at court to tempt my heart."

"And you breaking their hearts right and left."

Her laughter rang out. "Oh, Thirbe, what a romantic you are under all those fierce grumbles. I don't—"

Thirbe's gloved hand shot up. "Quiet," he whispered, lifting his head to listen. His gaze went to the hill above them, studying the trees.

She looked up, too, although at this angle she could see very little except craggy rock. Thirbe's expression remained intent, focused. He slowed his horse from its slow trot to a walk, and unbuckled his shield from its saddle strap.

An icy finger of worry touched her spine. "What is it?" she whispered. "What do you hear?"

He kept watching, not even glancing at her. "Heed me well," he said, very softly. "I want you to drop back and gather your ladies. Get over the stream and hide in the ruins."

"But—"

He glared at her fiercely. "Go now."

She knew better than to argue with him, although going into the ruins was the very last thing she wanted to do. For

Thirbe to even consider separating himself from her told her there must be very serious trouble ahead.

Without asking more questions, she tightened her reins and slowed Ysandre obediently.

That's when she heard a sound like running feet. A sound like armor clatter. Movement rippled through the trees ahead, movement that untangled itself from undergrowth and snowfall into man shapes. They came pouring off the hill, out of the trees and thicket, and into the road ahead, blocking the column. Although they uttered no war cry, their intent was unmistakable.

The two cavalrymen directly in front of Lea drew their swords, rising in their stirrups. "Crimsons!" they shouted. "To arms! To arms! We're under attack!"

Chapter 7

Lea's breath caught in her throat. "Thirbe!"

"Go!" he yelled at her. "I'll catch up as I can!"

She backed Ysandre into the middle of the road just as there came an earsplitting volley of screams from above her. Men dropped off the bluff onto the cavalrymen, knocking several of them from their saddles.

One of them came hurtling down atop Thirbe. Lea screamed, but her protector had not been caught unawares. He fended off his attacker with a fierce thrust of his shield, his sword slashing brutally as the man slid past him.

Lea saw blood splash across Thirbe's shield and face. He looked like a madman as he screamed curses and spurred his war-trained horse forward. The horse reared up, striking out with deadly forefeet, and Lea cringed in her saddle, swiftly averting her eyes.

"Bandits!" came another shout. "Crimsons, to arms! Close ranks!"

And from the rear of the column, "Archers, to me!" bellowed a voice in Cubrian.

Although she was aware that Thirbe was fighting to give

her time to flee, Lea was momentarily overwhelmed by the
violence that had erupted so brutally around her. The worst
of the fighting seemed to be at the head of the column, and
she heard Hervan's voice rise shrilly before it was cut off.
A woman screaming in the opposite direction caught her
attention.

Fyngie, she thought in concern, breaking free of her
daze. Wheeling Ysandre around, she kicked her horse into
a canter, veering to avoid a knot of men locked in combat.
A musician on horseback came galloping right at her as
though he meant to run her down. At the last moment he
reined up, his horse sliding on the muddy bank and nearly
pitching him off before galloping on.

Lea kicked her reluctant horse forward, forcing him
through the increasing confusion. She looked everywhere
for her ladies, but did not see them.

Another stern shout in Cubrian rose over the noise. Lea
saw a volley of arrows arc southward into the sky, making
a strange whiffling noise as they flew. And when the arrows
hit attackers at the column rear, cries of death and agony
went up. Already, another volley from the longbows was
firing death into the air.

But Lea had no time to marvel at this new method of
combat. She pressed on, forcing herself not to shrink away
from the brutal emotions and violence as she called over
and over for Rinthella, Vineena, and Fyngie. Again she
heard a woman scream. Looking in that direction, she saw
Fyngie being dragged from her saddle by a pair of laughing men. The girl was pushed back and forth between them
until her cloak was ripped off and her light brown hair fell
from its pins and streamed across her shoulders.

Horrified, Lea screamed, "Fyngie!"

"You can't help her!" Rinthella ran out of the chaos to
grasp Lea's stirrup. Her cloak was torn, and her skirts
smeared with mud. She was clutching something unseen in
one white-knuckled fist. "Where's your protector?"

"Where's Vineena?"

"Don't know! Where's your protector?"

There was no time to answer more questions. Lea kicked her foot from its stirrup and reached down her left hand. "Hurry!" she said. "Climb on behind me."

Rinthella needed no urging. She gripped Lea's hand and sprang up, scrambling fast to settle herself, pillion style, behind the saddle, and encircled Lea's waist with her arms.

"Let's get out of here!" she shouted.

Determined to help Fyngie, Lea instead turned her horse in that direction despite Rinthella's protests. At that moment, Fyngie fell limp in her captors' rough hands, and they tossed her to the ground.

"No!" Lea cried out.

A cavalryman, on foot, backed into Ysandre's side, making the horse shy. His foe lunged forward and Lea saw the tip of a sword project from the cavalryman's back before it was yanked out. The cavalryman fell, rolling over almost under Ysandre's hooves, and the attacker ran at Lea, gripping the long sweep of her skirts and yanking so hard that she nearly went tumbling to the ground.

Rinthella hung on to her, and Lea braced herself, kicking at the man in an effort to break free. As she struggled, a corner of her mind was registering the fact that he wore army-issued armor, the old-fashioned kind of steel breastplate and studded leather straps to protect hips and shoulders. With helmet and short, straight sword, he looked like anything but a bandit. Renegades from some legion, she told herself, even as she reined Ysandre back, making the gelding rear.

There came a rip of cloth, and her attacker lost his hold on her skirts. Overbalanced, he stumbled back. Lea kicked Ysandre hard, sending the horse plunging right into the man and knocking him aside. He went spinning into the path of other fighters, and was stabbed by a blood-streaked Crimson.

Lea didn't look back. Ysandre was spooked now, fighting his bit, wanting to bolt. She gave the horse his head, urging him faster and bending low over his whipping mane while Rinthella clung grimly to her back.

"To the bridge!" Rinthella yelled in her ear. "Hurry!"

Thinking her attendant mad for wanting to use the derelict bridge, Lea didn't bother arguing. Instead, she steered Ysandre directly toward the stream, although the horse broke stride to sling his head and fight her.

A man yelled right behind them. Glancing back, Lea saw him leaping at Ysandre's hindquarters as though he meant to jump astride the horse with them.

She kicked her horse hard in the ribs, and Ysandre shot down the bank and plunged across the water in three great bounds that splashed her boots and the hem of her skirts. Up the opposite bank at an angle they went, Ysandre's hindquarters thrusting hard. They scrambled to the top, and the horse stumbled, nearly pitching Lea forward.

She caught herself just in time to avoid a fall, and was grateful when Ysandre halted, pawing the ground and tossing his head, his flanks heaving. Shoving back her loosened hair and gasping for breath, Lea looked back to see how the battle was going. All she saw was brutal chaos and men dying.

And two of their attackers were coming for her, crossing the stream on foot, their sweaty faces blood-splattered and grim.

"Hurry!" Rinthella said. "They'll tear us to pieces if they catch us!"

Lea urged Ysandre onward, heading for the ruins. Her heart was crying out in despair, but she refused to think about anything other than following Thirbe's orders.

The water spirit's warning flashed through her mind: *Beware, beware, beware*. She'd misunderstood it, and now . . .

Snorting, her gelding dodged around a pile of rubble, stumbling over stones hidden in the tall grass. Lea reined him to a more prudent pace, despite Rinthella's scream for her to go faster.

Desperately Lea looked for somewhere to hide among the broken foundations and short remnants of walls. But unless she dismounted and crawled beneath fallen timbers leaning precariously like spillikins thrown down by a giant's child, she saw nothing that would serve.

"Go *on*," Rinthella urged her. "Oh, hurry, my lady. Hurry!"

"We can stay ahead of those men," Lea said. "Stop wailing and help me find somewhere to hide."

"No," Rinthella gasped. "Don't stop. Keep going. You must keep going."

"Where?" Lea asked in exasperation, resisting the urge to look back again. "Do you see Thirbe coming yet?"

"No." Rinthella moaned with fear. "There are more men crossing the stream and coming after us. In Gault's name, let us run!"

"If this horse breaks a leg, we're lost," Lea said. "Perhaps that old barn at the end of the field . . ."

"They'll see us, no matter where we go," Rinthella said, almost sobbing.

Lea was already aware of that, but she was almost desperate enough to clutch at any straw. Where was Thirbe? she wondered. Without him . . .

She squelched that thought, reminding herself that she wasn't helpless. If necessary, she would call on the element spirits. Meanwhile, she was going to get out of these ruins, where the malevolent *quai* hanging over them was nearly smothering her with fears and doubts, and head for the woods beyond the fields.

Turning Ysandre onto a narrow but fairly clear path through the rubble—perhaps it had once been a street— she dared quicken him to a controlled canter and glanced back in hopes of seeing Thirbe.

The men Rinthella had mentioned were following her, running easily along, as yet too far back to be a threat. Lea frowned at them, however. There was something about their pursuit that puzzled her. They didn't seem to be trying to catch her at all now, just keeping her in sight, or . . . driving her in a certain direction?

Alarm pierced her, but just then she heard the sound of

galloping hoofbeats from the north and smiled in relief.
"Thirbe!"

"It's not!" Rinthella said. "Great Gault, we must run!"

Lea saw a rider clad in legion armor and helmet, his tunic edge the color of fresh blood, a bare sword bright in his
hand. Holding his reins in his teeth and carrying a whip in
his left hand, he raced toward her, his big, scarred warhorse
eating up ground with every stride. The man was close
enough now for Lea to see the snarl on his brutish face and
lethal intent in every line of his body.

Her pursuers on foot cheered him on.

Rinthella's fingers dug into Lea's shoulders as she uttered an animal-like cry of despair.

Lea's own heart was jerking in fear. She could barely
breathe, and it seemed impossible to move. But it was stupid to sit there frozen, no matter how small their chances
had become, and Lea had no intention of giving up. With
Rinthella sobbing into the back of her neck, she turned
Ysandre and kicked him into a reckless gallop, praying he
would not step into a hole and snap a fetlock on this hazardous ground. There was no more time to be prudent.

She forgot her intention of heading for the woods. They
were too far away, and her pursuer's larger horse continued
to gain steadily on Ysandre. She headed instead across the
fields toward the barn, kicking Ysandre every time he
slowed, wishing Hervan hadn't tied her reins together so
she could lash her tiring horse with them. She knew she had
no hope of reaching the barn, much less of hiding inside it,
but she aimed Ysandre for it anyway. Her plan was to get far
enough ahead, far enough to gain just a few extra moments.

The slender gelding gave her his heart and gamely galloped on, although she could hear him groaning now as he
ran. Tears for him ran down her cheeks, but she did not let
him slow. Curling her fingers around her necklace, she
drew on the power of her *gli*-emeralds and sought the air
spirits. It was hard to concentrate with fear thrumming
through her, but she did her best, calling for more snow.

The flakes grew larger, fell faster. Suddenly the snowfall was so fierce and heavy that she could barely see where she was going. She squinted against the sting of driving snow on her face and still would not let the snorting Ysandre slow down. Her slender hope was that his pale coat would blend with the snowfall, allowing her to elude this pursuer.

Ysandre stumbled, snorting, and slowed to a jolting trot despite her kicks.

"We're leaving tracks!" Rinthella said in warning.

Lea hissed in annoyance. She'd forgotten that detail. Again she reached for her necklace and this time drew on the earth spirits, calling for them to melt the snow as it hit the ground. The white accumulation turned to slush, then mud. Ysandre slipped and slowed his gait further.

Praying her simple little plan would work, Lea shoved away her doubts and tried to keep her bearings in the tiny blizzard now blanking out the field and the rickety old barn beyond it. No longer did she hear hooves galloping behind her. Perhaps, she thought, hardly daring to hope . . . Perhaps . . .

A black horse with flaring red nostrils loomed suddenly on her right, cutting her off by rearing up right in front of her.

Ysandre shied back. His hind foot slipped on the wet ground, pitching Lea halfway from the saddle onto his neck. She clung hard to his pale mane, panting with fear, and looked up at a warrior such as she'd never seen before.

He was something from a nightmare, towering above her on the tall black horse. A helmet and jaw guard of steel obscured his face. His cloak was black, flaring out behind him like a cloud of the shadow god. So was his armor black, and his sword. Jagged steel spikes projected from the points of his shoulders, his elbows, and his knees. Through the slits of his visor, his eyes blazed a fiery red, like flames.

Transfixed by the sudden appearance of what seemed to be more demon than man, Lea made the mistake of meeting his gaze, just for the briefest moment.

The world dipped and swirled around her, as though she were slipping *between*, and she saw him only as a shadow, empty of any living light, as bleak and black and horrible as Beloth's spawn. He loomed even larger, seeming to grow as she shrank, and then her vision faded abruptly.

She blinked, finding herself still in the saddle, snow blowing cold and cruel in her face while Rinthella screamed and screamed. Although the snow had cleared her mind of the bad *jaiethquai* she'd encountered earlier, it availed her not at all now. Whatever this man or creature was, wherever he came from, it was not of this place, and her talents were no match for the magic he was using against her.

It was as though an enormous, invisible hand began to squeeze the air from her lungs. She fought to breathe, struggling to control her terrified horse, struggling not to faint, while she tried to reach for her necklace.

"Spirits of . . ."

Her plea for help faded in her throat, unspoken. She could not lift her hand high enough. Her fingertips barely touched the necklace before her hand dropped slackly to her side. Black speckles danced in her vision, and her ears were roaring with thunder. Dropping the reins, she slumped over, heedless of Rinthella desperately shaking her and calling her name.

The black warrior rode forward, reaching out for her, and Lea screamed helplessly in her mind.

"Got you, m'lady!" Thirbe yelled as though from far away.

He galloped up through the falling snow, yelling an old legion war cry, and swung his sword at the torso of the black warrior. His sword caught the black warrior across the back, knocking him forward, and the suffocating hold on Lea vanished.

She choked in a breath, coughing, and pushed herself upright in the saddle. She felt icy cold, a little sick. Her entire body was trembling.

Rinthella gripped the back of her cloak to steady her. "Let's go. Let's go!" she cried.

Half-dazed, Lea could barely hear her for the fury of Thirbe's cursing over the clang and clash of swords. The black warrior had righted himself from Thirbe's initial blow. Now he fought back in silence, defending himself against Thirbe's furious onslaught before he suddenly seized the offensive by landing a blow that split Thirbe's shield and rocked her protector in his saddle.

Lea nearly cried out, but checked herself, backing a frightened Ysandre out of the way as the combat continued. Watching the men, she knew suddenly with a harsh twisting of fear that her protector was no match for this foe. She could see a gold insignia eagle on the black breastplate, saw, too, the muted gleam of an imperial medal at his throat.

Bewilderment filled her. If this man belonged to her brother's army, what mistake, what error was prompting imperial forces to attack them?

Rinthella poked her. "My lady, let's get out of here!"

"I can't abandon him."

Rinthella went on protesting, but Lea stopped listening.

"Commander!" she called out, trying to sound firm although her voice came out weak and shaky. "Stop this assault, in the name of the emperor!"

The warrior's low, evil laugh stopped the rest of what she tried to say. Something in that laugh sent icy prickles of fear through her body. She had the sudden feeling that he knew exactly who she was and that his actions were no mistake. In that instant, her mind reeled with questions: Had there been an uprising? Was Caelan dethroned? Was the army in revolt? She pushed them away. This was not a time for conjecture.

As Thirbe parried another blow clumsily, taking it on his shoulder, she gripped her *gli*-emeralds, calling on the earth spirits with all her strength. The ground shook slightly beneath them, and Ysandre whirled around, snorting, ready to bolt. She reined him hard, barely keeping control of him, and saw the other man with the brutish face block her line of retreat with his scarred warhorse. His eyes were those of a man, not a shadow-sworn demon, but there was no mercy in them. He gave her an evil little grin, saying something she did not understand and pointing his sword at her.

"Gault save us," Rinthella was praying under her breath, but Lea kept her concentration on the earth spirits. They were bringing what she asked for, but slowly, too slowly.

"Please," Lea whispered, desperate that they should respond in time. The ground shook again, causing Ysandre to jump and neigh in fear.

A splintering crash caught her attention in time for her to see Thirbe's damaged shield break. He threw the pieces away, swinging up his sword to parry another hard attack. He was tiring, Lea saw. His face looked strained and grim, but even as he fended off another blow, he succeeded in throwing her a look.

"Run, m'lady!" he shouted. "In Gault's name, run!"

But Lea would not desert him. Letting the second man think he had her hemmed in, she squeezed her necklace harder, making the stones dig into the tender flesh of her palms, while urging the spirits to hurry. And now she heard a distant rumbling. It grew louder while the ground shook steadily, not violently, but trembling with a gathering force that made Ysandre rear. Even the warhorses took fright, and when the black warrior's mount shied back, he missed bringing Thirbe down with what would have probably been a fatal blow.

Swearing, Thirbe charged him, retaliating while he had that momentary advantage. But that wasn't what Lea had in mind.

"Thirbe, disengage combat!" she yelled.

The men continued fighting, her protector ignoring her order.

"Thirbe!" she shouted.

But he grunted suddenly, making an odd, compressed little sound of pain, and slumped partway from the saddle. His sword dropped to the ground. The black warrior rode around him, arrogant in triumph, and raised his weapon for one last blow.

"No!" Lea screamed.

At that moment, the ground rippled and split open like a plowed furrow. It opened beneath the black warrior's mount, and the horse reared up in terror even as Thirbe's horse bolted with him. Thirbe fell from the saddle and hit the ground limply, rolling over and over before he lay unmoving.

"Thirbe!" Lea yelled.

She tried to rein Ysandre out of the way of the running furrow, intending to go to Thirbe's side. Her valiant gelding, fully panicked now, bucked and ran backward with her. Rinthella fell off, landing on her knees in the trampled snow and mud. With all her strength Lea hauled on the reins and managed to circle Ysandre around to go back for her.

"Rinthella!" she shouted. "To me! Quickly!"

But her attendant wasn't listening. "The opal!" she cried, still on her knees and frantically patting the ground. "The opal! I've dropped it, and we need it for luck!"

"Come on!" Lea yelled, kicking Ysandre in Rinthella's direction. "Rinthella, leave it!"

But the scarred soldier was faster. He sent his horse leaping over the split ground to reach Rinthella. The woman screamed and scrambled up to run, but he bent low from the saddle and threw her across his mount's withers. Kicking violently, Rinthella fought him, but he pulled her upright and tore at her bodice, laughing all the while.

Rinthella screamed.

Frantically, Lea called on the earth spirits again. A second furrow raised the dirt, splitting open the ground and running straight at the soldier. His horse reared and plunged back, and Lea turned the furrow to follow him.

"Let her go!" she shouted.

For answer, the centruin pushed Rinthella off his horse so that she fell sprawling across the splitting ground. Her scream of agony horrified Lea, who could not stop the earth spirits in time.

"Rinthella!" she cried.

At that moment she was struck from behind, hard enough

to knock her forward onto Ysandre's neck. The frightened horse dropped his head, and she went sliding off, hitting the ground with a teeth-rattling jolt.

Half-stunned, she had no time to recover before the black warrior had dismounted and was standing over her, his red eyes blazing through his visor. He bent down and ripped the necklace from her throat. The chain cut her flesh, making it sting and bleed, but Lea was too frightened to truly register the pain.

As the necklace was taken from her, that strong connection of hers with the earth spirits, with all *quai* and elements of harmony, snapped, leaving only a weak vestige of what it had been. Disoriented, she sat up, intending to gain her feet and run, but the warrior was too fast for her. He scooped her up in powerful arms and flung her facedown across his horse.

She was nearly fainting. With all her might she struggled to hang on to consciousness. A strange lassitude was creeping through her body. It did not suffocate her this time, but her helplessness scared her so much she found it hard to breathe anyway.

He climbed into the saddle, his knees bumping into her as he settled himself and dug his feet into his stirrups. When he rested his hand lightly on her back, she felt an involuntary *sevaisin* connect them before she fought it off. Revulsion overwhelmed her. She thought for a moment that she might be sick.

"Now," he said in satisfaction. His voice, to her surprise, was refined rather than guttural. He spoke Lingua without a trace of provincial accent. "Fomo! Sound the recall."

Lea heard the blare of a horn. Its shrill call echoed across the valley, carrying a note that seemed to twist painfully inside Lea as though she'd been stabbed by a knife.

Wanting desperately to see how the Crimsons had fared, she pushed against the side of the horse and lifted her head and shoulders. She saw the foot soldiers stop fighting in response to the horn's summons. They left the battle and came running across the stream, threading their way through the ruins at a fast, odd gait that to Lea's eyes did not look entirely natural. She felt chilled and small, her fear so cold and her heart on fire. Choking back a sob, she let her head droop until the sound of shouts made her look up once more.

Those of the Crimsons still able were coming in pursuit. She squinted through the swirling snow, seeing the cavalrymen riding hard in an effort to catch the attackers. She saw their bright cloaks through the falling snow like pinpricks of hope. Courageously they were coming for her with Captain Hervan in the lead. Torn and muddied, he'd lost both cloak and plumed helmet. But he was galloping full tilt, his sword held aloft, his voice yelling war cries like a man demented.

Gratitude swelled inside her. She felt sorry now that she'd been so impatient with him, sorry that she'd wished him a thousand times back in New Imperia and flirting with someone else.

Hurry, please! she thought, wanting to shout it.

Her captor coolly held his position until his men approached and the Crimsons were closing in. The *quai* of death and violence crisscrossed the air, battering her senses. Whether her captor was delaying flight just to taunt the Crimsons or planning some trick, Lea did not know. She vacillated between hope of rescue and fear that she would see all the cavalrymen die before her eyes.

Thirbe, Rinthella, Fyngie . . . so many others slain or wounded—their shocked expressions and cries of agony played again and again through Lea's mind. Grief threatened to overwhelm her, but she pushed it aside for anger—wild, reckless anger, and a desire for revenge.

Lea struggled to resist whatever magic her captor was using to subdue her. Drawing his boot knife, she tried to stab him in the calf, but he was too quick. His gloved hand caught her wrist, crushing it until her fingers went numb. Just as she dropped the knife, he plucked away the small weapon.

"You've fought enough, pretty one," he said to her harshly. "No more trouble from you."

She opened her mouth to defy him, but the centruin gestured for his attention.

"Now, Commander!" he rasped out in a guttural voice. "Now!"

Her captor sheathed his weapons just as his men reached him at a run. They milled around, swearing oaths if they had the breath, and brandishing their swords. Their commander raised his free hand high.

"In the emperor's name!" Hervan bawled, galloping ahead of his men. "Let her go!"

The commander in black armor wheeled his horse around, as though intending to flee. Still holding his hand aloft, he called out three words, three terrible words that should never have been uttered again in this world. Three terrible words known to darkness, shadow, and all things evil, words that should no longer have carried power or force. He spoke them with confidence and authority, like a true believer of Beloth the shadow god.

Spikes of pain hit Lea, making her cry out. She saw a black maw of the shadow world yawning before her.

Horrified, Lea could not believe it, did not want to believe it. Without the power of Beloth, no one was supposed to be strong enough to open even the slightest door into the realm of demons. Yet her captor possessed enough power to fling the Hidden Ways wide open. Who was he? *What* was he? Shocked and disbelieving, she tried to twist herself to look up at him, but his magic still held her all but motionless.

"In the emperor's name, let her go!" Hervan roared. "You will surrender!"

Without answer, the commander led his men into the shadow world. Just inside, however, he reined up and let his men stream inside ahead of him. He was muttering under his breath as though counting, and Lea felt a shudder of effort go through his body.

"Let her go!" Hervan yelled.

"Fomo." The commander spoke quietly, but with force.

The centruin on the scarred horse wheeled his mount around, sword already swinging to meet Hervan's reckless charge at them.

Swords clanged like a thunderclap, and the warhorses thrust hard against each other, bugling in fury of their own. Then Hervan went down, tumbling from his saddle and sprawling on the ground.

A Crimson war cry rose up. Lea saw Sergeant Taime coming at a gallop, his face blood-smeared and frantic. She saw the rest of the Crimsons shouting and spurring their horses faster. Too late, she thought, her heart clutching in despair.

Her captor laughed, low and bleak, and as the grinning centruin spurred his mount through the opening, its hooves crunching over gravel, the commander lowered his hand and spoke a word unfamiliar to Lea. It hurt her to hear it, however, hurt her with the same spikes of pain she'd felt before.

It was as though a veil closed over the world, slowly shutting out the sight of the falling snow, the disorderly halt of charging horses, and the horrified faces of the men entrusted with Lea's safekeeping. Their shouts grew fainter and fainter, until there was only silence, and a black wall shut them from her sight.

The sense of evil lay thick around her in the darkness, and she felt as though she were drowning in it.

Then a pale, unworldly light began to glow before them, illuminating this place they'd entered. It was sickly gray, not true light, and contained nothing life-affirming or wholesome. Glowing dim and small, it left thick pools of gloom where wickedness could lurk unseen. It was light to see by, nothing else. No plant could take nourishment from it. No heart could take hope from it.

Lea trembled, trying hard not to lose her courage completely, and refused to cry. She told herself that she must stay strong, must regain her necklace and find a way to escape as quickly as possible.

Around her, the men were laughing and cheering, slapping each other on the back and raising clenched fists in triumph.

"Mission accomplished, eh, Commander?" the centruin said hoarsely.

"Not quite."

Before Lea could wonder what he meant by that, her captor touched her back.

A clammy wave of weakness sucked her down. She fought it, to no avail. It was like sliding into a bottomless chasm where she heard no more, saw no more of that evil place.

"No!" she whispered, unable to scream.

Then there was only silence and the terrible dark.

Chapter 8

In New Imperia, Bronzidaec hurried along the broad loggia of the inner palace courtyard, keeping well away from the hot sunlight that could betray him, keeping so close to the shadows that his shoulder brushed the wall stones. He pattered along, hurrying, hurrying so fast he panted. His heart thudded rapidly.

Never before had he taken such a risk, not at noontime, not in bright daylight, not among so many people.

The crowds ignored him as they sauntered along in the cool shade that gave them respite from the autumn heat. Their garments fluttered briefly against his arms and face as he pushed past. Now and then, an individual would glance down at him in surprise, perhaps even swat at him in disdain. Dodging, Bronzidaec hurried on.

Even under the loggia's shade he felt exposed. His enchanted disguise was thin at best, and he feared the sun might shine straight through him. The old palace, he thought wrathfully, had been full of crannies and deep shadows, but the new palace was filled with sunlight all day and blazed with candles at night. He loathed it here. He told himself that perhaps Master would be so pleased with his news that Master would release him.

You are a fool to believe it, he thought. A century of bondage stretched before him like an eternity.

But perhaps Master would be pleased. Master *must* be pleased. Bronzidaec had great hopes of being rewarded with more food and permission to sleep on a fine cushion in Master's quarters instead of having to stay in the women's pavilion.

But Master would *not* be pleased if news came to him slowly. Time to hurry, hurry, hurry.

It seemed a very long way to run along this loggia that bridged the women's pavilion to the central portion of the palace, but at last he reached the end of it and hopped over the threshold and under the arm of a guard who glanced at him indifferently. Officials and courtiers wandered about, conversing in low voices. A pair of men in the bright hues of merchants had cornered an official, talking to him earnestly while he shook his head. Farther down the corridor stood a pair of centruins in full armor over their red tunics, their helmets tucked under their arms. The sight of them made Bronzidaec very nervous. A moment later, an elderly man wearing the emblem of praetinor appeared. He was bowed to by minor officials and ushered away with much courtesy. The centruins saluted and fell into step at his heels, and Bronzidaec felt he could breathe again as he watched them go.

Sniffing the air, he searched for Master's scent, and found a trace of it. But just as he started off in that direction, there came the tramping of booted feet, and a tax collector strode into sight, his gaze keen and purposeful. He was followed by servants wheeling a small, stout cart stacked with leather bags of coinage, each labeled and wired shut with the Imperial Seal. A company of predlicates marched with the money, guarding it.

Hastily, Bronzidaec darted out of sight behind a marble column. He waited there until the sound of them faded away. Only then did he venture forth. No one seemed to be paying him any attention. Still, he was shaking as he forced himself onward. His small bare feet pattered across the cold stone floors as he flitted from one column to another. He skirted the huge mosaic laid in the symbol of Gault, making furtive signs of defiance as he went, and followed Master's scent down a long corridor. At the end of it, he dashed through the chancellor's vestibule and on into a small narrow room beyond it, where Master's scent was strongest.

But Master was not here.

Hissing in disappointment, he peered everywhere, running to each corner to be sure. But Master was not here.

Lit by a meager window, the room held a long, stout table of wood much stained by ink and littered with parchments and fingers of sealing wax. Three clerks sat hunched at the table, busy making small black squiggles across large, pale sheets of parchment. Bronzidaec had eaten parchment once and disliked the taste of it. But the ink sent twitches of curiosity through his nostrils. Someday, he would very much like to drink some.

But not now, not today when he'd broken Master's commands and violated every rule to come here. How, he thought angrily, was he to bring Master this important news if Master was not here to receive it? Now he had been disobedient and caused himself much trouble. And all for nothing.

Hesitating near the doorway, he hopped a little to gather his courage, then darted back to the table and stole a piece of sealing wax.

Only one clerk noticed. "Stop that! Give that back!"

Bronzidaec jumped over the threshold and got entangled in some heavy curtains lining the walls of the vestibule.

A huge shadow loomed over him, and a hand closed on his small shoulder, its grip cruel. Emitting a squeak, Bronzidaec twisted and sank his fangs into flesh.

There were few things sweeter than the taste of human blood. In that moment, Bronzidaec was flooded with great delight.

Swearing, the man released him, but by then Bronzidaec

had recognized Master's voice, inhaled Master's scent. Horrified, he pulled himself into a small knot and went to the floor.

"Sorry! Sorry!" he whispered, so frightened by his offense that he could not truly speak.

Master yanked him bodily to his feet. "Stand up, you fool," he muttered in an almost inaudible voice. Anger poured off him in waves, radiating against Bronzidaec, who swallowed hard. "What are you doing here?"

"Must speak. Must tell!"

Master glanced around swiftly. "This won't do—"

"What have you there?" A portly man in a heavy robe of office came up, looking curious. "Someone's *jinja*? Extraordinary."

"Yes, it is," Master said, glaring down at Bronzidaec fiercely. "The wretch has bitten me, too."

"Well, don't suck at it," another man said sharply as Master lifted his finger to his mouth. "They have venom, you know."

"Nonsense," the portly man said, chuckling. "Saeyd, you have a head of leather and wits of wool, believing an old wives' tale like that. Best have the bite seen to, Jafeen, just the same. It can grow sore if neglected."

"I shall," Master said. Ignoring Bronzidaec, he bowed to the other men and exited the vestibule.

Shooed out by a servant, Bronzidaec licked his fangs and followed Master's scent to a dim corner away from the tall windows. Behind a plinth supporting a stone bust, he found a servant's door standing ajar. Skittishly he slid behind it.

Grateful to be enfolded in the gloom, he bumped into Master's bulk, and Master closed the door, plunging them into complete darkness. But Bronzidaec could see in the darkness, much better than he saw in daylight. He sighed happily.

It was a small, cramped space, a landing of sorts with steps leading down inside the thick palace walls.

"You fool!" Master said very softly. "How dare you

seek me out, and at this time of day, when the place is full of every—"

"Master, forgive, forgive!" Bronzidaec said hurriedly, driven to interrupt.

Master's hand swung at him, and Bronzidaec was so rattled that he ducked.

A moment of ominous silence fell over them. "You dare avoid my punishment? You dare—"

"Please listen!" Bronzidaec said, desperate to tell. "I bring news."

Master lowered his hand. "Say it, then, and be quick while I think of how best to flay your miserable hide."

Bronzidaec gulped, but dared not plead for mercy. "I bring news of the lady empress—"

"I know the empress isn't going to Gialta. All our plans and waiting are for nothing. The creature will not leave her husband's side. Bah!" He kicked Bronzidaec. "You bring me nothing but aggravation."

"Wait, Master." Bronzidaec rubbed his aching side. "I have other news. Useful! Useful! The Lady Lea has been taken captive."

"What?"

Groveling on the floor, Bronzidaec dared reach out and grip Master's ankle. "True."

"Are you sure? There's been no news of this at court."

"Very sure, Master."

Master pulled away. "What do I care about her? We wanted the empress, not—"

"There are many ways to achieve the same objective, Master, yes?"

Master kicked him much harder this time, knocking him into the wall. "When I want an imbecile's opinion I'll ask for it. This is useless!"

"But, Master—"

"Get back to the women's pavilion and stay there. And next time wait until I send for you."

Bronzidaec pressed his hot face to the gritty floor. "Yes, Master," he whispered.

"It's the empress you're to watch. Do you understand? The empress and no one else! How many times must I repeat this to you?"

"But—"

"Shut up! Never do this again!"

With another kick, Master whisked himself through the hidden door and left Bronzidaec seething in the darkness, rubbing his sore spots. To console himself, he ate the sealing wax. He did not like it when Master was angry with him, but now he was angry with Master. Master had not listened. Master blamed him for news he did not want. Master did not want the opportunity Bronzidaec had brought him at such risk. No one else in the palace knew about Lady Lea. Master should have been pleased to hear such news first. Master, Bronzidaec thought resentfully, was not a very good spy.

For a while he crouched there, letting his anger grow. It was tempting to go and bite Master again, but that was foolish. It was even more tempting to sneak into Master's private chamber and sick up this sealing wax on his bed. Sealing wax, Bronzidaec decided, was very tasty, but it did not sit easily in his stomach. Yes, he would like very much to sick it up on Master's bed.

But Master would punish him. *I must be more clever,* Bronzidaec told himself. He dared not defy Master openly, dared not risk Master removing the spell and exposing him for what he really was, not here where there would be much woe and death for Bronzidaec. But there were ways, sneaky ways, to harm the new emperor and harm Master, too, Bronzidaec thought. Yawning, he turned around three times, quick, quick, quick, for luck before baring his fangs and hissing to himself.

"I am good spy," he muttered aloud. "I am very good spy. Better spy than Master. I think I should have been made Master and Master into *jinja*."

He hurried, yes, yes, he hurried here and there, busy, busy, busy, until he found Lady Avitria, chief attendant to the empress. She was in the linens room, quietly berating a maidservant.

Tall and slender, with a graceful throat and long, taper-
ing fingers, Lady Avitria had married well and been wid-
owed young, or so the gossip went, leaving her the
advantages of independence, wealth, and high position at
court. Although she was said to have the empress's confidence, there was nothing warm or appealing about her.

She had cornered a Ulinian woman, new to court, new
to service, working in the palace as part of Ulinian annual
tribute. The servant was sullen and quiet, possessing dark,
hostile eyes. She had no friends here. Everyone whispered
that they were Ulinian spies, which they were, but in
Bronzidaec's opinion, very inept and too obvious. Bronzidaec liked the Ulinians, chiefly because they smelled of
spices and a general lack of washing, but also because they
incurred so much suspicion he found it easier to eavesdrop
unnoticed.

"Who assigned you to launder Her Majesty's stoles?"
Lady Avitria was saying angrily. She flung a handful of
brightly colored fabrics at the maidservant. "Look what
you've done to the pleating! A botched mess, which must
be redone immediately. Her Majesty will be dressing for
the banquet shortly, and these must be ready."

"No time," the Ulinian said in very poor Lingua. "Have
other duties. No time."

"You will do as I say, or I'll see you lashed for stealing."

"No steal!"

Avitria gave her a very cold smile. "Will the guards believe me or you if a brooch is reported missing?"

Loathing darkened the Ulinian girl's eyes. She bundled
the stoles together and tossed them across her shoulder. As
she hurried away, Bronzidaec sidled up to Avitria and
hopped for attention.

She flinched. "Get away from me."

"I have news, big news for Empress," he said slyly,
dodging the smack she aimed at his head. "Grant me audience."

"Get away! You have nothing to interest Her Majesty, or
anyone else."

"I do! I have big news. It must be told."

"Palace officials convey news to Her Majesty, not odious little fiends like you."

Stung, he moved closer. "I know where to find sister of Empress."

"Sister?" Lady Avitria's gaze suddenly grew wary. "Lady Bixia? What do you know? Speak quickly!"

"Not Bixia," he said impatiently, shifting back and forth. "Who is Bixia? Lea, Lea, Lea!"

A frown creased Lady Avitria's brow. The two of them glared at each other in silence before she said, very slowly, "Lady Lea is on her way to Trau to officiate over the—"

"Not there," he said slyly, gazing up. "Not there. Not safe. Now I tell Empress."

"You'll tell *me*. Immediately."

The sharp command in Lady Avitria's tone scared him. And she was staring at him hard as though she could see through his disguise. Avitria was dangerous, he told himself. Oh, woe indeed. Revenge was not worth this risk.

Wanting to hide in a cupboard until he was forgotten, he tried to dart away, but she caught him and held him fast by one pointed ear as she shut the door firmly. When he squirmed to pull free, she pinched his ear so hard the pain took his breath.

Released with a shove that made him stumble, he retreated to the far corner of the closet, hissing through his fangs and feeling very sorry for himself. With the door shut, very little light came through a high, tiny window. For once, the gloom and shadows did not reassure him.

"What are you, little creature?" Avitria asked softly, her gaze boring into him. "What are you really? Not a *jinja*. Something . . . else."

"I am *jinja*! Am! Am! I have news, important news. Lady Lea is abducted. She is in danger."

"Oh yes? Are you the go-between, delivering terms of her ransom? Why come to me with such a lie?"

"Tell Empress she is—"

"Silence! If I denounce you for using magic inside the

palace, the priests will stake you in the sunlight at midday. And then, little shadow creature, you will scream and scream as you wither to nothing."

She was staring at him more intensely than before. He felt dizzy, as though the enchantment on him was crumbling. Desperately he clung to it, even as his heart shrank to a cold knot.

Maelite, he thought. *Worse than Master. Maelite is great woe.* The certainty that she was one of those terrible witches grew in his mind and trembled on his small, forked tongue. He wanted to shout the word at her, and yet in horror he held himself silent. As he gazed up into her glittering, fierce eyes, he had the feeling that if he even whispered the word she would kill him. He felt trapped, like a fly on the tongue of a toad.

I am fool, bigger fool than Master, he thought desperately. *I am traitor. Be quiet. Be quiet!* But it was too late to be quiet. Already he had betrayed himself instead of Master. Even if she let him go, he would never be safe, never, never.

"Are you *sure* Lady Lea is in danger?" Avitria asked now. "Who's behind the plot, if there is one?"

At last, the question Bronzidaec wanted. He drew a deep breath. "Question Jafeen."

"Jafeen. Where is he to be found?"

"He is clerk for Chancellor. Clerk! Clerk! Stupid clerk with ink and sealing wax who spies on Empress. Ask him."

Avitria said nothing, and Bronzidaec's words seemed to hang in the air. He found himself panting. *I have done it, made an accusation. Master will hurt me, oh yes, oh yes, Master will hurt me bad . . . unless the guards take him for questioning. Oh, please, let them torture him very hard.*

Heartened by the prospect of Master's legs being so broken he could never kick his servant again, Bronzidaec straightened his small body. He ached to tell this lady everything, but he thought he had said just enough. *Let Master betray the others,* he thought in self-satisfaction. *If they fall, it is not because of me.*

"Jafeen," she said slowly, as though tasting the word on her tongue. She began to laugh. "So Jafeen is behind this supposed plot against Lady Lea. I think you tell me a great lie, creature."

"No, no! No lie! Truth!"

"I think you tell me a great lie to bring harm and suspicion to Jafeen, who is a trusted, loyal servant in my employ."

Bronzidaec stared up at Avitria, seeing the malice dancing in her eyes. A terrible feeling sank through him.

"Or perhaps there really is a plot against Lady Lea," Avitria said as though to herself. She smiled. "Either way, this is the perfect time to take action, while the empress is distracted." Her gaze narrowed on Bronzidaec. "And you will come in very useful."

Panicking, he rushed at her with bared fangs. "No! No! No! I warn Empress. I say she has witch for friend. I tell her—"

Lady Avitria struck him across the face, putting magic into the blow, so that he went reeling back into the wall and slid down it, stunned. A series of shudders went through him, and he wanted to wail aloud.

"Haven't you said enough, little fiend?" she asked softly. "You are done spying. I shall put you to better use."

She advanced on him slowly, slowly. He felt as helpless as a mouse held by the gaze of a cobra, and suddenly he was sick, very sick. The reek of sealing wax overwhelmed his nostrils, and his throat burned. Acute misery washed through his terror, and he wished he had never, never, never come to the palace, no matter how many extra years of servitude it would have meant.

Master is fool, he thought as Lady Avitria bent down to grip his shoulder. *But I am doomed.*

Chapter 9

Olivel Hervan came to with a yelp of pain and the realization that someone's attempt to lift him was causing him intense agony.

"Ow! Kill me or let me lie!" he said, and desperately blinked open his eyes.

"Be easy, sir," Barsin's voice said. "I'm not the enemy."

A sigh escaped Hervan, and he let his hand sag away from his dagger. "Let me be," he said. "Don't move me."

He found himself sitting propped up on the cold, muddy ground, supported, he thought, by his adjutant. Snow was falling on him, and he felt cold to his very bones. He hurt all over, but the worst—a throbbing ache—came from his shoulder. When he tried to put his hand to it, a hot iron of pain branded him. It took all his strength to grit his teeth against screaming.

His adjutant shouted, and several men came running, surrounding him in a circle and staring down with grim faces.

"Here, you," Barsin said. "Give me that blanket. Hold him steady for me."

Men changed places behind Hervan, and then his adjutant—looking filthy and tattered—was kneeling beside him and wrapping the blanket around his legs. It didn't help. Hervan could feel the cold spreading through him, numbing his fingers and toes, rendering his face so stiff he could barely speak.

"Barsin," he began, "put the blanket *under* me, not—" He broke off with a yelp, clutching his elbow and holding it tight against his side as he fought against screaming. Sweat beaded up on his brow.

"You mustn't move, sir," Barsin said. "I think you've broken your collarbone."

"Gods," Hervan said weakly as the agony eased off. He felt quite clammy and spent. "I think you might be right."

Someone gave him smoky mead to drink, and while he waited for it to take numbing effect a minor sword cut on his arm was bandaged.

"Ready, Captain?"

Hervan hesitated and took another deep gulp of the mead before nodding. "Get it over, then."

His cuirass was removed and an awkward sling devised to bind his shoulder. The potent drink might as well have been water for all the effect it had. When the mauling was over, he found himself sweating with pain, sick to his stomach, and ready to stab the next man who came near him.

"Feeling all right, sir?" Barsin asked.

Hervan glared at him. It was, he thought furiously, a damned stupid question, but honor demanded that he keep up a pretense of bravado. The men mustn't see him howling like a peasant.

"I feel like a trussed chicken," he complained. "How in Gault's name could I break my collarbone wearing armor?"

No one answered. Hervan shifted his shoulders experimentally, cautiously. As long as he didn't try to pull his arm from the tight sling that bound his arm in such a way that his fist was jammed in his ear, the bone seemed stable. It was a damned embarrassing injury, nothing to boast about in either the barracks or the palace. Still, he supposed he should be grateful he hadn't lost an arm or an eye. A slight scar or two tended to impress the ladies, but disfigurement would put him right out of the Crimsons for life.

"Do you think you can stand, sir?" Barsin asked worriedly.

"Of course. Put me on my feet, fellows. And for Gault's sake, don't bump my arm!"

Upright, he found himself holding his breath until the freshly stirred pain and nausea subsided to bearable levels. His head felt light and inclined to float a little above his shoulders, but he supposed that was the mead, finally kicking in. Barsin carefully draped a long cloak around him. Gault knew where it had come from, but with his teeth chattering Hervan wasn't going to complain.

A bit wobbly on his feet, he looked around and saw that he was in the middle of the churned-up field where he'd tried to rescue Lady Lea. Of her, there was no sign. He frowned thoughtfully. He remembered seeing her thrown across the warhorse of some brute in black armor, remembered spurring his horse in pursuit, and that was all. The rest of it, until he'd come to flat on his back in the mud and snow, was a blank.

"Uh, Sergeant?" he said.

Barsin's green eyes were watching him as though the adjutant expected him to collapse. "Are you ready for a report, sir?"

"Yes, of course. But where is the—"

"Sergeant Kress is dead, sir. Lor is wounded. Taime is busy seeing to the wounded and organizing a burial detail. Lieutenant Rozer is . . . shall I give the report in his stead?"

"Get on with it," Hervan said wearily. "You're already making the report, Barsin. This is no time to be so damned formal."

Barsin saluted. "Yes, sir. We have seventeen dead and twenty wounded, including yourself. Four men are seriously hurt and may not live through the night."

"And Lady Lea?"

The adjutant blinked at him a moment. "Gone, Captain."

"Gone," he repeated, seeing again in his mind's eye the girl caught up by her abductor and then . . . nothing.

"Yes, Captain. They took her into the . . . you were right there, almost in the maw with them before you were struck down."

The maw of what? Hervan wondered. Seeing the puzzled concern in Barsin's eyes, however, he did not ask. The men had enough problems right now without thinking him incapable of command.

"Captain!"

A short distance away, a man was shouting and waving his arms. Hervan turned in that direction, but as he struggled forward Barsin stopped him.

"Wait here, sir. I'll go."

"What's he found?" Hervan asked, squinting in an effort to see what lay at the man's feet. "What is it? A lady? Great Gault!"

A terrible chasm seemed to open in the pit of Hervan's stomach. Shaking off someone's steadying hand, he forced himself to follow Barsin. He had to see for himself, had to know.

It was not Lea.

The moment he saw the dark hair fanned across the snow, he felt a shudder of relief, followed by sorrow and the terrible sting of anger. "Rinthella," he said softly.

Barsin, who was kneeling beside her, glanced up before slowly drawing a fold of her cloak over her face. Silence fell over all of them. There was not a man among the Crimsons that the beautiful attendant had not flirted with. Bold, vivacious, and great fun, Rinthella had been as available as her dainty mistress was not. Remembering the supple grace of her body and her readiness to receive him anytime, anywhere despite the risks, even because of them, Hervan sighed and bowed his head.

"Why?" Barsin whispered, his voice thick. "Why would they hurt her? What barbarians are these? She is not . . . they've *mangled* her."

"Magic," someone said gruffly, clearing his throat. "Shadow magic."

The cluster of men backed away from Rinthella's body. Clumsily Hervan bent down to take something from that still, slender hand. It was an opal, a large, smooth, milky stone. Its iridescence shimmered as he turned it over in his fingers.

The archer who'd found her drew back with a hiss of indrawn breath. "Bad luck, that."

Ignoring the Cubrian, Hervan straightened carefully with the opal still in his fist. He would keep it, he decided with a frown. Keep it to remind himself of Rinthella, her dark vivid beauty, her unnecessary death.

But how had this all happened? he wondered blankly. This sudden ambush and the aftermath of defeat . . . it was impossible. The Crimsons did not know defeat. Such a thing was completely foreign to the proud tradition of his regiment. The beginnings of shame curled around him, as with it came the sick awareness that he'd let Lady Lea down, let the emperor down, let his regiment down. He'd never failed at anything in his life, wasn't trained for failure. Yet what else was this if not . . . and what should he do next?

Pull yourself together, he thought, turning away from Rinthella's body. *Start issuing orders.* It hardly mattered what kind of orders. The men, he knew, would feel better with something to do.

"Set the scouts to tracking at once," he said. "We must pick up these renegades' trail as soon as possible."

The men standing around him looked so dumbfounded that Hervan stopped talking.

"Well?" he demanded after a moment of silence. "Are you stricken as well as witless? Get to it."

Two of the men saluted, then hesitated and sent Barsin a look of appeal.

"My orders are surely clear enough," Hervan said, wondering if they meant to rebel. Frowning, he turned on his adjutant. "Barsin! Am I not clear enough?"

Barsin hastily wiped all expression from his young face and stood at stiff attention. "Very clear, Captain," he replied crisply. "It's just . . . how will the men carry out your order? I mean—what are they to look for?"

"Tracks, of course. What do you suppose?"

Barsin and the others looked confused, but they all saluted. The men dispersed, leaving Barsin alone at Hervan's side.

"Come, sir," he said in concern. "I think you need shelter and rest. You're in shock, not yourself."

Hervan nodded, liking the idea of sitting down to a warm fire and drowning himself in a flagon of good wine. He started walking back, moving with slow stiffness like an old man. "Have the men pitch camp, and see that those trackers find something before this blasted snow covers everything."

"Sir—"

"Hervan!" roared an irascible voice.

The very sound of it tore across Hervan's frayed nerves. *Why,* he thought with profound irritation, *hadn't Thirbe perished in the fight?* Exchanging a swift look with Barsin, Hervan swallowed a sigh and turned to face the protector.

Thirbe came limping up, begrimed and splattered with blood. His long cloak hung in tatters, and he'd lost both helmet and shield in the fight. Blood from a darkening cut on his forehead still trickled down his face. A great deal more of it had dried into a brown crust on his temple and cheek. His gray eyes held a wild fury. Their expression, plus his filthy face and gray hair sticking up in all directions, made him look nearly demented.

"She's gone," he said without greeting. "Gone into the Hidden Ways and taken captive in the filthy hands of shadow folk. What are you doing about it? Eh? Standing about, wanting the mud cleaned off your white gauntlets and pretty boots, no doubt."

"See here—"

"I told you not to take this road! We could have sat out the trouble at Brondi and gone on when the way was clear.

Stick to the primary roads . . . them was our orders. Now look at the mess we're in. And her in an even bigger mess through your blundering."

His shouting was making Hervan's head ache, but one portion of his comments seemed clear. "You cannot blame me for what's happened."

Thirbe set his jaw. "I can, and I do."

Barsin stepped forward, as fiery as a small gamecock. "Captain Hervan is not responsible for what's happened today. Can't you see he's injured?"

"Son, that makes not a spit's worth of difference to me. He's the commanding officer, and he's made just about every blunder possible today except achieve a total massacre of his men." Thirbe gestured at the detail gathering up the dead. "Half our forces down. Could have butchered the lot of us if they'd wanted."

"We drove them off," Hervan insisted. "With brave valor—"

"Beloth shit! Save your speeches for when you stand before the emperor and explain to *him* how you lost his sister."

Hervan burned to challenge this mouthy old man who refused to keep his place. Only he could barely hold himself up, much less fight a duel.

"Look, you itty-witted whelp," Thirbe went on, "what do you think this was about, eh?"

"Bandits have—"

"The lady. The lady!"

"Well, her beauty is such that fills the eye."

"These weren't common road bandits!" Thirbe roared, making Hervan's head throb harder. "Gods, man, they wore legion armor."

"Renegade soldiers, deserters," Hervan said. "We'll catch up with them soon enough and show them a thing or two."

"Catch up with them how?" Thirbe asked, flinging wide his hands in exasperation. "Have you a way to enter the shadow world? Do you think that priest of ours can open the Hidden Ways?"

Everything grew suddenly too hard for Hervan to understand. Fretfully he looked around and hitched his borrowed cloak tighter about his shoulders. "Shadow worlds . . . what in Gault's name is all this nonsense? You're talking like a fool."

"Wait, Protector," Barsin interjected hurriedly before Thirbe could speak. "The captain needs rest. We mustn't keep him standing any longer in the cold. And your hurts, sir, need attending as well."

Thirbe wiped at the blood on his face. "What matters here is Lady Lea's safety and whether we can pull her back from Beloth's gullet."

"You're mad," Hervan said. "Hidden Ways . . . shadow worlds. All of that is gone, do you hear? Gone!"

"Then what do you call what happened today?" Thirbe asked him. The man's steely gaze pinned Hervan, refusing to let him deny or evade the truth.

If only I could remember, Hervan thought. *But surely . . . surely it wasn't . . .*

"That's impossible," he said angrily. "That clout on your head has broken your wits. The shadows are gone, defeated, vanquished."

"Then tell me what it was, and where they took her."

Hervan shook his head helplessly, wincing as the movement jarred his broken bone. "I can't tell you. I—"

"Can't, or won't, believe it?" Thirbe asked, stepping closer. "Take hold of yourself, man. We all saw it, whether we like it or not."

"But—but *how* could they do something like this?"

"How should I know? The question is how to get her back. If you think that priest can do something, call him forth and have him try."

Part of Hervan wanted to refuse, simply because it was too fantastical, and—more honestly—because Thirbe wished it. Telling himself not to be petty, the captain sent for the priest, who couldn't be found.

"What?" Hervan said in surprise, glaring at the messenger. "Has he been killed?"

"He's not among the dead or wounded, Captain."

Thirbe snorted. "Hiding out, more likely."

"Find him!" Hervan ordered.

A search began, while Hervan went to his tent. Exchanging his muddy clothing for clean was no simple matter, thanks to the way his arm was bound. Clothed at last, he sat shivering by a blazing fire, feeling sick, weary, and tempted to turn everything over to Rozer. But commanding officers did not shirk their duties, he reminded himself. Not with the emperor's sister in jeopardy. Not with Lady Lea's protector pacing about, muttering to himself, with a rag pressed to his bloodied forehead. Why, Hervan asked himself in frustration, couldn't the tiresome man collapse and be carried away? As long as he refused to surrender to his injuries, Hervan could not do so either.

So he sat, aching and feeling wretched, telling himself to think while he had this chance. Only his wits seemed mired in sludge, and he could not come up with a clever solution that was going to salvage his military career, much less advance his ambition to marry the lady and bring his family into alliance with the imperial throne. *Father,* he thought, *is going to be furious.*

Outside his tent came a sudden commotion, with raised, eager voices and the squelch of boots through the mud.

Sergeant Taime ducked inside and saluted. "The priest is found, Captain."

"Bring him inside at once."

"About time," Thirbe said, tossing aside his bloodstained cloth.

The priest came in, his ugly face pinched with cold, his robes soaked and muddy. He held out his hands in supplication. "Praise to Gault that you survived the assault, Captain. My prayers were heard, and I give—"

"Get on with it," Thirbe growled, and Hervan cleared his throat.

"Er, Poulso," he said with some reluctance, feeling a fool. "Well, the thing is, we've need of your special kind of assistance."

"Ah yes, of course. A service of thanksgiving and—"

"No. Not that." Hervan frowned.

"Tell him!" Thirbe said, then turned to the priest and said gruffly, "Lady Lea has been abducted, taken into the Hidden Ways. Will you open them, so we can pursue her?"

The thickset priest stood frozen, his protuberant brown eyes starting from their sockets. His look of alarm told Hervan that he had no inkling of how to perform their request.

"Well?" Hervan asked him anyway.

Poulso ran his tongue across his thick lips as though to moisten them. He started to speak, but his voice squeaked and broke. Clearing his throat, he started over. "Sirs, good sirs, this thing you ask of me is—is—well, it's forbidden. Impossible."

"Her abductor did it."

Poulso glanced around as though he expected *casna* demons to crawl forth from the tent shadows. "Impossible!" he whispered. "Who could draw magic from the shadow side of—"

"Never mind asking who!" Thirbe said. "Will you do it?"

The priest turned his gaze to Hervan in appeal. "My ability to weave magic is ceremonial in nature only. I don't think I could possibly break the great seal set in place by Light Bringer to hold Beloth."

"No one's asking you to do that," Hervan lied. "Just pull open the door, so to speak, so we have a chance to find the lady."

But Poulso was shaking his head, his gaze abstracted. "How can this be?" he whispered as though to himself. "To think that dark magic, shadow magic should still exist, and could be used to such dire purpose. Are you certain?"

"We saw it done," Thirbe said flatly.

The men around them muttered agreement, while Hervan wished he could remember.

Poulso was taken out to the field, pushed along by men carrying torches, and led by Thirbe the indefatigable. Hervan started to go with them, but a wave of giddiness overtook him. By the time he'd fought it back and forced his head to clear, he found himself still sitting close to his tent fire with Barsin anxiously pressing a cup of wine to his lips.

"Ah, that's what I want," he said in appreciation and took the cup.

"You're not at all well," the adjutant said. "The fall you took has shaken you sorely."

Emptying his wine cup to its dregs, Hervan struggled a bit to get out of his camp chair.

"No, sir, please. You're to stay where you are."

"Nonsense. Mustn't look weak to the men."

"No one thinks that, sir."

Hervan made it to his feet and swayed a bit—thanks more to wine than injury. He found a wan smile for his adjutant. "You're a good, loyal fellow," he said, clapping Barsin on the shoulder. "Help me outside."

Leaning on the adjutant, Hervan made his way out into the cold darkness, squinting against the cold wind and wishing himself back in New Imperia, where winters were mild and snow unthinkable. Ahead, he could see a cluster of men and heard shouting. He slowed his steps, aware of Barsin tightening his supportive grip.

In fact, Hervan did not want to hurry. He was afraid that he would find the gateway to the shadow world yawning open before him and demons pouring out to attack the camp.

By the time he reached the group of onlookers, there was a shout, followed by the sound of angry voices and a sharp smack.

"Gault above!" he said involuntarily, reaching for the Choven talisman he'd worn under his clothing since childhood.

"Make way!" Barsin commanded. "Make way for Captain Hervan."

The cavalrymen parted immediately, and Hervan had no choice but to stride through their midst with more confidence than he felt. He found no demon, however. Instead, Poulso lay sprawled on the ground, his robes thrown up to reveal scrawny legs encased in long wool stockings. Thirbe stood over him with clenched fists.

"Sniveling coward!" he was shouting. "What good are you? Answer me that!"

Poulso held his cheek and made no effort to rise. His ugly face was contorted. "This is forbidden magic. Forbidden! Even the scrolls dealing with it have been removed from the library. I am not trained to commit such a vile blasphemy."

"Liar!" Thirbe yelled. "You're a Vindicant—"

"No longer!" Poulso made a hasty gesture. "I reformed my vows, accepted the purging."

"Doesn't mean you can't—"

"My soul would be jeopardized, and I—"

"And what happens to Lady Lea while you're protecting your soul?" Thirbe demanded.

When the priest gave him no answer, Thirbe spun on his heel and came limping over to Hervan.

"Faure's breath, but he's useless," the protector muttered. "And she is lost to us forever."

Chapter 10

$\mathcal{T}he$ men began muttering among themselves, while a pang went through Hervan. *Lost forever.* He did not want to think about Lady Lea, frightened or perhaps hurt, trapped in the clutches of monsters. How could the foul shadows take away someone so lovely, so special? If anyone lived filled with light, it was she. What was happening to the world, if Light Bringer's influence was waning already and the shadows were returning to power?

"Tell me, priest!" he said before he could stop himself. "Does Beloth rise again?"

Thirbe gripped his forearm. "Be quiet, you fool!" he said for Hervan's ears alone. "You'll panic the men if you talk this way."

Hervan pulled free. "And what of you, conjuring up old, forbidden rituals? Priest, give me an answer!"

Poulso rose clumsily to his feet, shaking down his robes into order, breathing heavily. "The shadow god does *not* return," he said firmly, his voice ringing out with assurance. "Have no fear of that."

"Then what supports this magic?"

"I do not know. But—but I *do* know that there have been no dark portents, no signs of the shadow's veil falling over us again." Poulso spread out his thick hands. "Perhaps, well, I do not like to speculate without more study on the question, but perhaps this magic is not very strong. It only seems potent and frightening to us, because we thought never to witness its like again."

His blathering brought back Hervan's headache. "Get to the point!"

"Just because the shadow god is gone, Captain, it does not mean that all evil has been expunged from the world. So many creatures remain, diminished of course, but they are not yet dead or destroyed entirely. It seems to me that a *donare*, yes, a powerful *donare* sworn to shadow might perhaps do something like this."

Hervan tried not to flinch. The murmuring around him grew louder, but he ignored it. It was rumored, Hervan reminded himself, that the emperor was a *donare* also, although never of the shadows. Light Bringer—no matter how amiable his manner at court—remained a formidable warrior supported by Choven magic. He was a god destroyer impossible to lie to and capable of extinguishing a man's life with a word or thought. But the emperor was not here to lead them. *It's not fair,* Hervan thought. *I have no magic to bolster me. I cannot take on a* donare *and win.*

Even as the thoughts ran through his mind, however, he saw a worse alternative in riding back to New Imperia with this terrible news, of kneeling in disgrace before Light Bringer and saying that Lady Lea was lost forever to the shadow realm. Hervan broke out in a light sweat. This would ruin him, ruin his career, and very likely ruin his entire family.

Don't think about it now, he told himself in an effort to stave off panic. Yet he had to think, had to take action. He simply could not fail. Disaster of this magnitude did not happen to the Crimsons, and it certainly did not happen to members of the Hervan family. There had to be *something* he could do.

"A *donare*," he said, pretending to scoff. "We would all lie dead had we faced such a foe."

Thirbe leaned forward. "Saying it was, priest. How can even a *donare* open the Hidden Ways without magic?"

"There is magic," Poulso said. "Magic everywhere, in myriad forms. For example, it crisscrosses this valley now. I feel it. I believe Lady Lea felt it as well. She called it something different. I suppose she—"

"Never mind that!" Thirbe broke in. "If we're up against a *donare*—"

"We're not," Hervan insisted.

Thirbe ignored him. "What can we do about it? You're saying his magic is weakened because of the shadow god?"

"Because the shadow god is gone. Correct," Poulso said. "Those who are shadow sworn live in a diminished state, magically speaking. Many suffer terrible afflictions and illness. Even if he's opened the Hidden Ways, that does not mean he can also travel them. I think—I could be wrong, of course—but I think that because Lady Lea is such a radiant creature of light she could adversely affect his powers."

"Can she get away, free herself?" Hervan asked.

"That, I do not know. If we wait here, it's possible they will emerge, at or near this point, bringing the lady with them."

"And if they don't?" Thirbe asked.

Poulso shook his head sadly and said nothing.

"There's nothing to be done in this field except guard it?" Hervan asked.

"I believe so."

Hervan gestured. "Then that's what we'll do. Sergeant Taime, send the men to quarters. See that they're fed and given a measure of mead."

"Yes, sir!"

Hervan gave the priest a nod of dismissal and turned back to his tent. Thirbe, however, gripped his good arm and held him fast while the others dispersed. When Barsin tried to intervene, he was waved back.

"Hold on," Thirbe growled. "That's not all you're going to do?"

"What else?" Hervan asked, trying to keep his temper. "The priest can't perform the miracle you've asked for. Can you?"

"I can do better than swallow tripe from that paper-skulled priest. He's lying to save his cowardly hide."

"You may not like the Reformants, but—"

"I got nothing against the order itself, just this lazy fool," Thirbe said. "I'd rather he defied me on his honor and conscience than lie. We'd have done better with a Penestrican along."

"Gault forbid," Hervan said uneasily. "Those women are—"

"What? Competent?"

"I was going to say formidable."

Thirbe uttered a short, mirthless laugh. "At least they'd know whether our good lady had any chance right now."

Hervan was thinking. "Bandits wearing legion armor," he said slowly. "Led by a . . ."

"Oh, say it and be done," Thirbe said. "A *donare*. What are you scared of?"

"I still don't believe that."

"Why not? Because we're standing here as survivors?" Thirbe scowled at him. "They can't cut threads of life in close-quarter fighting. And if they'd wanted to slaughter us to the last man, they would have."

"Do you think the army has rebelled?"

"An uprising?" Thirbe shot him a sharp look, but shook his head. "Doubt it. Weren't carrying standards, so they're renegades certain. Some of the trade caravans have reported trouble from that kind. Bound to be some of the riffraff swept out of service in the reforms. Plenty hire themselves out as mercenaries, too."

"Their attack was skilled and swift, almost as though they were lying in wait for us."

"Of course they were waiting for us!" Thirbe said in

loud exasperation. "Gault's mercy, but any bafboy could see it was a planned attack. If they'd been after money or plunder, they'd have gone for the supply wagons. No, they took exactly what they wanted."

"Women."

"No, noddy! Our good lady, alone. And they let us live, like they knew we couldn't catch 'em afterward. A professional job, start to finish."

"The report said Thyrazene weapons—"

"That old ploy!" Thirbe snorted. "Wouldn't fool a blind idiot."

"But how could they have known we were taking this route?" Hervan asked. "I chose this road on the spur of the moment, and—"

"And you don't think that fire supposedly sweeping Brondi was anything but a ruse to turn us onto this road, where we could be caught?"

Startled, Hervan stared at him hard before dismissing the idea as too fanciful. "I think my scouts can tell the difference between a real fire and one set in trickery."

"Why? Fire is fire, ain't it? If part of the town is burning, does it matter if it was an accident or set? We came wandering this way just the same, and got caught easy as fish in a barrel."

Hervan frowned, uncomfortably aware that Thirbe had a point.

"Just look how we were attacked," Thirbe continued, "from three sides, guaranteed to send Lady Lea fleeing right across yon fields into a trap. I'm certain it was a legion commander carrying her off. I saw his eagle when I was fighting him."

"Legion commander?" Hervan said in disbelief. "That knock in the head has addled your wits. More likely the blackguard stole a legion commander's breastplate somehow—"

"Impossible! Now whose wits are addled? I tell you I know eagle rank when I see it and when I fight against it."

"No officer of such high rank would stoop to outlawry."

"Why not? There were four legions disbanded, officers and soldiers alike, all those who wouldn't change allegiance. Kalthunda is dead. Which leaves three other commanders, Osthel and—"

Despite himself, Hervan said, "Osthel is an old man, said to be living on the coast and exiled from his family. They want nothing to do with him."

"In combat, it's odd what you notice and what you don't," Thirbe said thoughtfully. "The black Eighth was commanded by a praetinor named Shadrael tu Natalloh."

"No praetinor would stoop to this villainy!" Hervan said in outrage. "You cannot seriously accuse *him*."

"Do you know the man?"

Flushing, Hervan looked away. "No, not—not personally. But he's not the man."

"Well, then, that leaves Maxivim, no, Mavnim. Something like that."

"Mardico."

"Aye, Mardico Tohn. A Beloth-loving scoundrel if ever there was one. The stories about him would turn your hair white to hear 'em."

"I heard he'd bought a farm and was living simply."

"False rumor," Thirbe said. "Gone over to the Madruns, more like. As for Shadrael, he's Ulinian by birth and—"

"And of the patrici," Hervan broke in. "You can't possibly suspect someone of his noble birth and achievement. His brother is warlord of Ulinia."

"Aye, a province that wants to break loose from the empire," Thirbe said thoughtfully. "Saw Shadrael once, years ago, when he was maybe a cohort leader. A fierce one already, even before the Madrun campaign."

"Where he distinguished himself with tremendous honors," Hervan said. "I saw his triumph when I was a boy. He was a hero, riding through the streets of Imperia to meet Emperor Kostimon. I watched his chariot go by from our window."

"But definitely *donare*," Thirbe said.

"Great gods, man, nearly all the very best legion commanders are."

Thirbe held up his hands. "Easy, lad. Time you learned that war can make even bad men heroes. Mardico was always bad, through and through, indulging in every vice imaginable. But Shadrael risked the Kiss of Eternity and *lived*." Thirbe tapped the side of his nose. "You know what that means."

Doubt flooded Hervan before he shoved Thirbe's gossip away. He'd always admired Lord Shadrael and as a schoolboy he'd studied the man's battle strategies in the Madrun campaign. Battle strategies . . . he remembered reading about a tactic similar to what they'd encountered today. A strange feeling sapped his convictions. Maybe—but, no, he still could not believe a man whom he admired so as a boy would commit the infamy of stealing the emperor's sister.

Once again in his mind's eye, Hervan saw Commander Shadrael tu Natalloh ride by in a processional triumph, wearing full armor, but carrying no weapons, his helmet tucked under his arm to show his submission to the emperor. His profile had been one of arrogant self-assurance, the face of a man who has achieved great things, and will accomplish even more—oh yes, seeing him that day, Hervan had vowed that one day he, too, would achieve military honors and be awarded a triumph by his grateful emperor. He would follow family tradition and enter the cavalry, of course, but he would rise as high in distinction as Lord Shadrael, or higher. For of course he was Itierian, not Ulinian, and born superior in every way.

"What a triumph he was given!" Hervan said. "An extraordinary sight I've never forgotten. That was the day he was named to the ranks of praetinor. My father told me there were wagers laid on how quickly he'd make general."

Thirbe grunted. "Instead, he's an exile, stripped of honor and rank, discharged without pension. Why defend a man like that?"

"In those days, Protector, everyone was shadow sworn. It meant little."

"Don't talk to me about the old days, whelp. I lived through them. You didn't. Officer or foot soldier, you couldn't serve your legion without swearing oaths to Faure and—and the others."

"That's what I just said. Why do you judge Lord Shadrael so harshly? Did you serve under him?"

"Not me," Thirbe said emphatically. "But there were things we had no choice about, Gault help us, things we were forced to do. And then there were choices. Shadrael chose to risk his soul committing *shul-drakshera* on a wager."

"I've heard of that!" Hervan said. "The Kiss of Eternity."

"It ain't nothing to get excited about," Thirbe said.

"Only the most courageous—"

"Ain't courage playing games like that. Just stupidity. No one made him. Not even the rites of Alcua went that far. And to my mind, he's the one we want."

"It could be him," Hervan admitted reluctantly. Thirbe, he thought, was like most old men who disapproved of *drakshera*, forgetting how important it was to prove your bravery. Hervan supposed that becoming elderly meant losing heart and courage. What a pity. "If so, Lord Shadrael would be the most ruthless renegade of all."

Thirbe nodded. "Whether it's Mardico or Shadrael, we've got our good lady taken for a pawn in whatever plot's afoot."

"Ransom?"

"Maybe. Or the stakes could be higher."

Hervan blinked at that. He hadn't expected Thirbe to be so astute about political matters.

Thirbe drove a fist into his palm. "Damn! I hate being helpless like this. Her, so dainty and young, so innocent and kind and good, held by some band of evil swinegullets. The idea of it twists my guts until I can't think. I should have protected her better, instead of getting walloped off my horse like a green boy."

The raw emotion betrayed in his voice caught Hervan's sympathy. "Thirbe—"

The protector gestured. "Ah, don't mind me. My head feels like a split melon, that's all. And I'm about dead with shame at that fiend letting me live."

"What?"

"He could have killed me in the first exchange of blows, and didn't," Thirbe said fiercely. "As soon as my shield went to pieces, I was done for. Toying with me, insulting me, when he could have snapped my life at any time."

Hervan stared at him, amazed he would admit such a thing. "You should be grateful you're alive, not insulted."

"Grateful! I spit on him. If he's hurt her . . . if he's touched her . . . ah, shadows smite me." Thirbe passed his hand across his eyes and fell silent.

Hervan cast about for some way to offer comfort and couldn't think of anything. "Come dawn, we'll be tracking her—"

"Where? Are you daft? They've gone—*whoosh*—into thin air."

"And the priest said they can't travel the Hidden Ways. When they come out, I shall be waiting for them," Hervan said grimly.

"What if that itty-witted priest is wrong?"

"What he said made sense."

"To you, maybe. Not to me. I don't think Poulso's ever gone into the shadow world. It ain't for the fainthearted."

Hervan drew a deep breath, trying to find patience. "We'll attack as soon as they emerge."

Thirbe grunted skeptically. "Have you sent to Brondi yet for reinforcements?"

"I don't need reinforcements," Hervan said. "My men are valiant and well trained."

Thirbe scowled. "You've lost half of them."

"Not quite."

"Aye, by all means, let's quibble over the tally. Today, you were outnumbered, outmaneuvered, and outflanked by someone a lot smarter than you. Might as well admit it, and get on with sending word to the emperor immediately for instructions and reinforcements."

"Who are you to be telling me what to do?" Hervan demanded in a rage. "You're no officer, and never were."

"Nope. I marched for twelve years in my legion, and after my hitch was up, my tailbone pounded leather riding from one end of the empire to the other, guarding tax collectors."

"A predlicate," Hervan said with scorn. "A common guard."

"Guard, aye. Common, no. As well you know. I've seen plenty of field battle, and more tours of duty than you. I know your regulations, same as I know army ones and most of the others. But say you ignore orders and make a stand, what in Gault's name do you expect to accomplish if you should meet these devils again? Your men couldn't handle them today."

His bluntness kindled a sullen blaze in Hervan's chest. "We were surprised, that's all."

"Surprised? Aye. The understatement of the year. And now your men are tired and hurt, less capable than before. Even you're not fit."

"I can still ride," Hervan said. "I can issue orders, even if I can't fight."

"If all this is to impress the lady—"

"I know my duty," Hervan said. "I will not shirk it."

"Your *duty* is to send a courier to the emperor, then retreat and gather reinforcements as needed."

"Crimsons do not retreat. We fight to the death."

"If you can find the enemy, which you can't."

Hervan fumed for a moment. The last thing he intended to do was inform the emperor of his failure. No, it was imperative that he keep any news of this disaster contained until he could rescue Lea.

"Lost your nerve, Protector?" he asked at last with a sneer. "A short time ago you were striking the priest because he would not open the Hidden Ways. Now you want to run away for help."

Thirbe gripped him by the front of his cloak and pulled him around, seemingly oblivious of Hervan's bitten-off cry of pain. "Damn your eyes! If Poulso had found us a way to the shadows, I'd be there," he said hoarsely. "Now you listen to me, you puppy! We're less than a day's ride from Brondi. There's a garrison there, with men enough to supply those you've lost, and more!"

"Foot soldiers," Hervan said with contempt, trying to pull free of Thirbe's grip without jarring his collarbone. Barsin approached him, but Hervan waved his adjutant back lest he overhear too much. "A legion camp hardly better than an outpost."

"It's got men, ain't it? And maybe dragon couriers to send word fast to New Imperia."

"And I tell you that we'll handle this matter ourselves, without interference."

"You calling the emperor interference?"

Hervan swallowed. "No, of course not. But he's too far away to be of use. Lady Lea needs us *now*."

"Aye, I'll agree with that. But we send for reinforcements from Brondi, as required."

"No. My men were caught unprepared once, but I assure you that in a rematch they'll more than hold—"

"Rematch?" Thirbe said with scorn. "This is battle, not a game of terlio."

"I know that. But you do not command this force, Protector. I do. And my decisions stand."

"You'll get the girl killed, if she ain't dead already."

"Her safety was entrusted to me. If she's alive, and I can reach her, I'll do everything in my power to save her," Hervan said. "Everything. I'm sworn to this duty, and the Crimsons do not fail."

"Seems to me the Crimsons already have."

Furious, Hervan stood nearly nose to nose with the protector. "Hear this," he said in a quiet, rigidly controlled voice. "As soon as we're done, as soon as the lady is safe, and my shoulder is mended, I'll see you eat that remark. Name the day. Name your weapon. Am I clear?"

Thirbe stepped back from him and stood in silence before shaking his head. "You pathetic little . . . don't you know reality from games, boy? Don't you?"

"Of course I do!"

But Thirbe shook his head again, and limped away, leaving Hervan's challenge unanswered.

Chapter 11

Slowly Lea regained her wits, blinking open her eyes to find herself still trapped in a nightmare. Dark, pervasive gloom surrounded her, illuminated by a sickly gray light that made her think of the pale underbellies of fungus found in woods. The icy cold and snow did not intrude here. No wind blew. The air carried a tang of stone and soil and cold ashes. And everywhere could she feel evil's oppressive breath.

Malevolent *jaiethquai* pervaded stone, mist, and shadow. She felt swallowed by it, suffocated, and remembered that her abductor had taken her necklace of *gli*-emeralds away, as though he'd known exactly what they were. Without their protective shield of magic, she felt vulnerable indeed. But not helpless, she reminded herself.

She was still on horseback, riding sitting up and propped against her captor's breastplate. Her elbow was pinched uncomfortably between his armored body and the saddle, for he held her close. A portion of his black cloak had been pulled forward to cover her. Even with its protection, she felt cold, as though she'd gone and lain in a wintry stream. Her mouth started to tremble, but she compressed her lips very hard and forced her *quai* to be strong. At the moment she might be a mouse pinned by a predator's paw, but she would remain still and silent in order to gain opportunity. It was *not* weakness, she assured herself, to be prudent.

Obviously they were *between*, inside what the shadow folk called the Hidden Ways. Lea had gone *between* a few times in her life, escorted by the earth spirits and later by the Choven mystic Moah, but those had been experiences of shining, ethereal light and a mist as soft and refreshing as spring water. This passage—*this* reality—between the physical and spiritual worlds was like something broken and perverse. Everything about it was so very wrong.

Tears pricked her eyes, but she held them back. *Stay strong,* she thought. *Breathe normally and have faith in the teachings.*

They moved at a slow, steady, almost cautious pace. She wondered if the men had any sense of time passing, if they realized how long they'd trudged through what seemed to be a cave passage.

It was not, of course. Lea—if she squinted—could see the illusion of stone and dirt walls fade. In their stead she saw jutting fingers of rock, and dead trees split into jagged stumps. They passed through the shadow of forest. She suspected these might be the woods she'd aimed for in the small valley before her capture. Or perhaps not. If her captor was strong enough to move quickly through the Hidden Ways, they might have left the valley far behind, be well beyond the hills, or even farther. She did not know how long she'd been unconscious.

An eerie quiet surrounded them, unnatural and unsettling. The men did not talk among themselves as they marched behind the commander's horse, following where he led. Even the cadenced tramp of their feet seemed muted. They had been trained, she supposed, to stay silent and not distract his concentration.

For it was not easy, Lea knew, to traverse the ways of

between. Landmarks were illusory and what seemed to be real might not exist at all. Distance was the most difficult element of all to gauge. Perhaps this warrior was counting, as some did, or perhaps he was heeding a guiding force. But let him falter or stray, and they could become lost forever.

Although tempted to interfere, she did not. She did not want to be lost with him and his small army. *Wait,* she told herself. *Wait.*

At last her abductor raised his hand, and they halted. In the sudden stillness, punctuated here and there by a cough or the scrape of a boot sole on stones, she heard a faint trickle of running water.

Thirst assailed her, and her tongue felt glued to the roof of her mouth. Suddenly she felt so parched she could barely swallow, yet she knew to drink here would be an illusion. Shadow water would not sustain her.

He shoved her slightly forward. "Sit up, and stop pretending to sleep."

Startled, she sat very still while he swung out of the saddle with a creak of leather and reached up for her. Instinctively she shrank back, but he gripped her slim waist and set her on the ground effortlessly, as though she weighed little more than a feather.

"Walk. Stretch," he said. His voice was gritty and rough with strain. "You can't escape, but don't wander far."

The light was too dim for her to see him clearly. Tall though he was, in his black armor he became almost invisible in the gloom. Now and then he moved in such a way that the pallid light glimmered on the medal at his throat. His posture, even his quiet gestures showed him plainly to be no ordinary soldier, no common ruffian. His armor fit him too well to have been stolen, and his gear was neither cheap nor ordinary. His helmet visor remained down, concealing most of his face, but she saw that his eyes no longer glowed red the way they had before. She did not walk in *severance,* yet in this place she could see the threads of life, as ugly and sometimes as frayed as worn ropes, floating up from the heads and shoulders of the men. Only, there were none visible around her captor. It frightened her. If he was *casna*—demon spawn—then she had no chance of escaping him.

Yet some instinct in her could not believe him such a creature. He did possess *quai*. She sensed it now, although it was so bleak that she had been unaware of it at first. She frowned. Perhaps . . .

He lifted a gloved hand in repudiation. "Don't."

Although he spoke softly, there was a warning in his tone that she heeded at once. Hugging herself, she drew back without a word, yet made no effort to walk away as he'd suggested.

"Commander."

It was one of his men, the scarred centruin with the ruined voice, the one that had killed Rinthella.

No, Lea thought with an inner sob. *I killed her.*

The centruin came up, clutching a short whip, and here in the Hidden Ways, his face between the leather cheek guards of his helmet looked skeletal, flesh worn away to reveal pale bone. His cruel eyes held neither compassion nor pity when he glanced at Lea, and his teeth were rimmed black with rot. The mark of Beloth was burning in tiny flames on his left cheek. His threads of life looked charred and frayed in clumped knots. Lea saw that his *quai* was very dark, darker even than her abductor's.

"Commander," he said again, his voice a harsh croak.

As the two men began to converse in low, almost inaudible voices, Lea hurried away, not caring where she ventured as long as she left their proximity.

Within a few steps, stumbling a little on ground that she could almost see clearly yet never was quite what she expected, she reached the stream. The water sounded very shallow and fast. Seeing and hearing it made her thirst burn so intensely that, although she knew better, she knelt and tried to dip her hand into the liquid.

Her fingers passed through nothing.

Miserably she licked dry lips and sat back on her heels,

bowing her head. On her left, the men began taking turns approaching the stream, scooping up a cup of illusionary water, and moving away. They did this in a disciplined, orderly fashion, as soldiers would. *Renegade soldiers,* she thought. Lawless men, no longer in her brother's service. She watched them drink, wondering if they realized no real water was passing between their lips.

Even if under orders to stay quiet, they should have been grinning, bright with triumph, but they weren't.

Maybe, she thought, they were as afraid of this evil place as she was.

Concerned that she seemed to be the only prisoner, Lea stood up and craned her neck, looking over the men in search of anyone she might consider friend. But, seeing no one she knew, she felt terribly alone.

At that moment, something tugged at the hem of her skirts.

Startled, she turned around but saw nothing next to her. She frowned, knowing she hadn't imagined it, and her heart began to thud a little faster.

Again, there came a sharp swift tug at her skirts, this time from the side. She twisted her head, but still saw nothing.

But she heard a faint, almost inaudible, hissing. She swiftly moved only her eyes, and glimpsed a pale, slim creature about the size of a cat except that it walked upright. It vanished before she got a good look at it.

A splash in the water made her turn. She saw the liquid gleam of two eyes on the water's surface as something small came swimming across the stream. Emerging, the creature lay flat and shimmering on the pebbles before it swelled into a three-dimensional shape with legs and arms and talons and fangs. Its head was misshapen and narrow, and its shiny little eyes glared at her fiercely before it scuttled sideways into the darkness.

The hissing noise came again from beside her. Lea bit her lip, but stayed otherwise motionless, letting the cat-sized creature tug at her skirts. It grew bolder, creeping around her, prodding the cloth with its talons and sniffing a long while before it paused to stare up at her. Its sly eyes glowed like yellow flames.

Another of its kind joined it, crawling out of the shadows to venture closer. This one, she saw from the corner of her eye, was malformed, its head misshapen and its spine contorted. It was as pale as soured milk, and the sight of it made her swallow hard.

The hissing sounded louder, accompanied now by a muted clicking. She saw more yellow eyes glowing at her from the shadows, and could endure no more.

Her courage slipped, and she crouched swiftly, causing the creatures to scatter back into hiding. Yet they did not go far. She could hear them hissing and clicking, watching from all around her. More and more of them were gathering. Demons, she thought, unnerved. Shadow spawn that should not exist. Never mind that they displayed deformities, scars, or even missing limbs; their very survival, along with the fact that it was still possible for men with magical powers to open the Hidden Ways, meant that Beloth's vile influence remained far stronger than common knowledge believed. There was still enough evil lingering in the world, still enough malevolence, to keep these remnants of shadow going.

Why feel surprised? she asked herself angrily. Had she not witnessed enough pettiness, greed, and misspent fervor at court these past three years? Were there not even now misguided wretches in New Imperia who sought to worship and deify her, to form a cult of adulation around her, to seek her wisdom on every matter as though she were an oracle? It was why, when Caelan had asked her to travel to Trau in his place, she had seized the opportunity so eagerly. To get away . . . to fulfill her last official function and then vanish into the mountains near the glacier. Yes, she intended to return to the Choven and abide among her mother's people, safe and isolated in a proper balance of *jaiethquai* thereafter.

Now, as she crouched on the ground with the little demons watching her, she groped about for pebbles and

swiftly rowed them in the shape of a square before stacking
more in a simple pattern.

As she worked, the boldest of the creatures crept up to
stare at what she was doing before it bleated a cry and re-
coiled, slashing the air with its claws and hissing. Glad, she
reached for another pebble just as a booted foot stamped
the abacus-like pattern she'd made, grinding some of the
stones into the dirt and knocking the rest awry.

Startled, Lea had no time to react before the commander's gloved hand gripped the front of her cloak and yanked
her bodily to her feet.

"Stupid," he snarled at her.

She hardly heard what he said, for he stood before her
without his helmet. For the first time she saw his face.
Lean, chiseled features . . . the high cheekbones and slightly
tilted dark eyes of a Ulinian aristocrat. Slim black eye-
brows knotted angrily over an aquiline nose. A jaw firm beneath its stubble of beard, surprisingly youthful. A mouth
refined and mobile, with perhaps a touch of sensitivity at
the corners, although at the moment it was clamped in a
thin line. Handsome, he might be, but cruelty and impatience formed his expression. He glared at her without
mercy.

"Don't you know better than to work your magic here?"
he asked.

Lea's small chin lifted. "They're demons. I won't have
them gathering around me."

"Leave the little ones be," he said, his tone harsh and
flat. "They've suffered enough."

"They could never suffer enough. They shouldn't even
exist."

He barked a brief laugh that held no amusement. "Stupid
and naive. Light Bringer may rule the empire, but we have
not all curled up into dust and ashes just to please him."

"You—"

He gave her a shove. "Move."

She tried to jerk away, but he caught her hand with
crushing strength and wrenched her around. It was the first

time he'd touched her without his glove, and the involuntary *sevaisin* between them caught her by surprise.

With an oath, he released her, jerking back his hand as though burned. Overwhelmed by a tide of emotions she could not begin to understand, much less control, Lea tried to retreat from him, but sank to her knees instead. Tears spilled down her cheeks.

He stood over her, a dark silhouette. "Stop that. Get up!"

Grief and fear engulfed her. Seeing inside him, knowing some part of him, was too terrible to endure, for he was . . . he was . . . With a wrench she managed to break *sevaisin*, but she felt pain rip through her, as though she'd torn her flesh. She cried harder.

"Hear me," he said, gripping her shoulder. "You must show no weakness here. Get up. Stop your sniveling at once."

But she could not obey him. All of it, the shocking brutality of the ambush, the death of men sworn to protect her, Thirbe lying unmoving on the ground, Fyngie's death and Rinthella's worse fate, the evil of this place, and now the involuntary joining with someone like this man—this creature—who was . . . who was . . . It all overwhelmed her. Crumpling over, she buried her face in her hands and wept.

The commander gripped her arms and pulled her to her feet, shaking her when she swayed. "Stop this!" he said. "I can hold back only so much, can protect you only so far. If you do not control yourself, they'll attack."

As he spoke, he pulled her hands away from her face, and pearls that had formed from her tears went spilling everywhere. He frowned, staring at her in amazement. "You—"

Lea flung down the rest of the pearls. They rolled in all directions, glowing briefly in the gloom before turning dark. Wrenching free from his slackened grasp, she hurried away, wanting to get as far from him as she could. In two strides he caught up with her, steering her past the watching soldiers with repeated prods to her back.

At one point, she stumbled and would have fallen but for the quick hand of a soldier, who steadied her back on her feet.

His eyes, set in a homely face, looked kind. He almost smiled at her—until he glanced at his commander and stepped back with all expression wiped hastily from his face.

Still, that small show of humanity was enough to help Lea regain her self-control. She drew in a breath, sending the soldier a look of gratitude.."Thank—"

The commander shoved her forward. "Move."

She was lifted up onto his huge black warhorse, where she sat stiff and horrified while he climbed into the saddle behind her. Drawing on his gauntlets and gathering his reins, he gestured at his men before hesitating. That was all the warning Lea had before he sagged forward heavily against her, bracing his hand on the pommel. She could hear him breathing raggedly, and at first she thought he was about to fall.

Resisting the temptation to push him out of the saddle and flee on his horse, Lea struggled to support his heavy weight. The others were too close for her to try anything. Already the centruin was riding up, starting to speak, then choking back words as the commander abruptly straightened. A muscle knotted in his jaw as he grimaced, his features contorting. Lea saw red fire blaze briefly in his eyes.

Gasping, she shrank back, but his arm went around her and pulled her close as he kicked his horse forward.

The centruin rode beside him, stirrup to stirrup. "Commander," he said in a rasping whisper. "We're far enough away. Let us drop out of the Hidden Ways and—"

"Not . . . yet."

Puckering his mouth, the centruin dropped back. In silence, they all trudged onward.

Fresh tears blurred Lea's eyes, despite her attempt to control them. Her emotions churned in chaos, driving all inner harmony away.

It could not be true. She did not want it to be true. Yet the vision she'd involuntarily seen, however brief, could not be brushed aside. *Sevaisin* did not lie, and what she'd glimpsed inside this man had to be faced, whether she wanted to or not.

For in him she'd seen her future, a destiny she'd never planned on, and one she did not want.

Chapter 12

In the dead of night, Hervan awakened, feeling restless and half-caught in a dream he couldn't remember. Fiery embers glowed balefully in a pile of ash, filling his tent with orange light. Lying down had proved impossible, so he was propped up on several rolled blankets. Damned uncomfortable they were, too. His hand had gone numb from the awkward way his arm was trussed to his side, and his broken bone ached miserably.

Next to his cot, his servant Crox lay knotted up in a blanket on the ground, uttering soft snores. Atop Hervan's campaign chest, his cuirass gleamed with polish, his leather gauntlets had been scrubbed with pumice and ash to restore their white perfection, and his boots shone with a fresh application of blacking—all readied for the morrow. Hervan frowned. There should have been a full cup of wine within reach, but obviously the lazy knave hadn't thought to provide it for him.

A faint sound from outside distracted him from rousing his servant. Curious, Hervan struggled up, nearly stepping on Crox, who should have risen to serve him. Slinging a blanket awkwardly around his shoulders, Hervan ventured outside.

It had stopped snowing. Overhead, the clouds had parted to allow a full moon to shine down on pristine white ground. The ruins cast strange shadows in the pale landscape, and the world held a still, hushed quality. The hair prickled uneasily on the back of his neck.

He heard a distant sound of male voices. They paused, then murmured again, paused, and murmured.

Recognizing the pattern, Hervan swore softly beneath his breath and ducked back inside his tent. He found Crox sitting up, hair wild and eyes staring.

"My dagger and boots," Hervan ordered.

"Are we breaking camp? Are we under fresh attack?"

Hervan snapped his fingers impatiently, and Crox scrambled to do his bidding, even fetching a thick cloak for him to wear instead of the blanket.

"Shall I go with you, sir?"

"Gods, man, I don't need your help to piss," Hervan said. "Go back to sleep."

He stepped outside, drawing a deep lungful of the frigid air to wake himself up, and made note of the sentry positions before slipping into the shadows between the tents. In moments, he'd left camp and was picking his way cautiously through the snow, stumbling a bit over the rubble concealed beneath it. His breath misted white about his face, and soon he was panting and hurting, wishing he'd stayed in his tent where he belonged.

A shape loomed out of the darkness before him with a suddenness that made him reach for his dagger. Recognizing his lieutenant in the moonlight, Hervan eased out his breath.

"Rozer," he said quietly.

"Captain. We didn't expect you to join us." Rozer glanced around. "Have you come alone?"

"Of course."

Rozer nodded and escorted him past a corner where two walls stood nearly intact. On the other side, four men sat on large, rectangular stones, holding steaming cups. They stared at Hervan in unfriendly silence before getting up.

Something tight eased in Hervan's chest. Conscious of Rozer at his back, he went forward.

"Men," he said quietly, well aware of how clearly sound could carry over snow.

Sergeant Taime stepped forward. "Come you as friend or foe?"

It was a loaded question, full of all that had been left unsaid two years ago when Hervan—on the urgent advice of his father—had withdrawn his membership in the Talon Cadre. There was no harm in the brotherhood, of course. Hervan knew that every officer belonged to some secret society or other, sometimes several. Such memberships were expected, especially in the Household Regiment. Even the rank and file, notoriously superstitious, had their groups. All now officially forbidden, of course, by the reforms.

"Well?" Taime demanded.

"I come as—as your captain."

"That's no answer."

"Taime," Rozer said in rebuke, and the sergeant shut up. "Well, Captain, if you're curious, we're drinking toasts to our fallen comrades."

"And calling the dead."

Rozer drew in a sharp breath, and the others exchanged glances.

"What of it?" the lieutenant asked.

Hervan was glad Rozer didn't deny it. He'd known the lieutenant since they were boys, growing up on adjoining estates. They took their commissions on the same day, had trained together. Not until Hervan dropped out of the cadre had their paths grown apart. But it was good to know that Rozer still cared enough not to lie to him.

"A fine old tradition, honoring our dead," Hervan said now. "Did they come?"

"Not yet," someone replied, and was elbowed sharply by Taime.

"We'd just started," Rozer said. "There's a lot of old

death in this valley. We don't want to call forth the wrong ghosts."

Hervan swallowed hard, forcing himself to nod. He'd never been enamored of the rituals. The fellowship was fine, and the drinking marvelous. To this day he remembered a birthday celebration they'd thrown for him. Giddy with wine, he'd gone blindfolded into a chamber containing a haggai—smuggled in Gault knows how—and no pleasure he'd known since then had equaled that experience. Most of the rituals, however, were boring recitations or chants and responses from rote. The words meant nothing to him. Only a few ceremonies—usually the most important ones—proved unnerving. Twice had he stood in a circle that called the dead; twice had he toasted their shimmering pale images with blood-spiked wine. It was a bit hair-raising, but he knew of nothing darker that went on in the cadre. Despite his father's nervous fears, they were not using shadow magic, not really.

"I, too, would like to honor our dead," Hervan said now.

Rozer moved closer. "Would you? What else do you want?"

Hervan shoved prickles of doubt aside. He'd made his decision before he came out here. "Ask them to open the Hidden Ways to us."

Some of the men gasped aloud. Another started to laugh, but swiftly hushed.

Rozer ducked his head, and through the shadows and moonlight, Hervan saw him smile.

"That's my Oli," Rozer said in low-voiced approval. "That's the friend I remember, full of courage to the rattle, not afraid of light *or* shadow."

They gathered around him then, clapping him on his good shoulder and leading him over to sit down on one of the stones. It felt like a block of ice under his rump, but he perched there just the same, trying not to shiver, and felt the reckless delight of illicit conduct.

Taking the flagon for himself, Rozer handed Hervan one of the cups. The contents smelled quite dreadful to

Hervan. He lowered the warm steam away from his face, knowing it was not time yet to drink. *No one has to know,* he assured himself. *Least of all Father. His spies can't report on me out here.*

"I must say, Captain, you played your part very well by asking the priest to do this," Rozer said. "Taking the officially safe route, when all the time you knew we could do more. Is the protector satisfied?"

"No, but the priest is. We've scared him enough, I think," Hervan replied with bravado. "And if he is a spy, he'll report that I did everything in the approved manner."

"Damned Reformant," Taime muttered. "Ain't his job to go around preaching to the men. Some of what he says is culled straight from Vindicant text, but some of it is pigwash."

"We'll have to get rid of him before we venture into the Hidden Ways," Rozer said.

"That's easy," Hervan told them. "The wounded will be left here in camp. He'll stay behind to minister to them."

Rozer hesitated. "Er, yes, if that's the way you want it done."

Hervan stared at him in surprise, suddenly wondering if Rozer had meant that the priest should be killed.

"I heard the protector yelling about sending for Brondi reinforcements," Rozer said. "Will we wait for them?"

"No."

The men stiffened, and Hervan said quickly, "By the time they arrive, the trail will be too cold. I don't know about the rest of you, but I don't want to ride back to New Imperia like a whipped dog. Considering the proud history of our regiment, do you want to be known for a failure like this?"

They exchanged looks in the moonlight, and he knew he had their complete attention. "No word to Brondi," he said, his voice firm. "We make do without reinforcements, and we don't send a courier to report what's happened."

A grim silence fell over them, broken by Taime. "We could be hanged for dereliction of duty."

"Only if we fail," Hervan said.

"It's still a risk, sir."

"I know that. But if we go strictly by the book and sit here on our duffs waiting for reinforcements, we'll never find her."

"What if we go after her now and still fail to find her?" another man asked.

"We mustn't fail."

"But, Captain, if we do?"

Hervan frowned, impatient with their doubts. "Then we'd have to desert."

Rozer grinned, his eyes alight at the challenge, but some of the others looked alarmed.

"That's dishonor!" Taime said, squinting and hostile. "Never been done in the Crimsons. I ain't going to be the first."

"Then we don't fail."

They still looked unconvinced.

"See here," Hervan said. "Aside from the lady's plight, think of ours. If we follow regulations now, our careers are finished."

A murmur went around the group. Several nodded.

Rozer leaned forward. "It's either get her back or serve out the rest of our days patrolling a salt island off the Madrun coast."

"That's right," Hervan said.

"Those whoreson renegades have us outnumbered," Taime said. "And if they've got magic on their side, real magic for battle, how—"

"They caught us by surprise this time," Hervan said. "They won't do it again. And they won't expect us to go after them. Poulso says their magic is weak. It must be, since they haven't the shadow god to support them."

"Seemed strong enough today," a man chimed in.

"It doesn't take strength to open the Hidden Ways," Hervan said. "There's a trick to how it's done."

"Do you know it?" Rozer asked.

"Of course not."

They grinned at Hervan's answer, and he grinned back. "We'll need a guide," he said.

That sobered them.

Taime glanced around at the others. "I've put in ten years of service. And I had to unswear my secret oaths to stay in. Some of you have done that, too. Some of you"— he glanced at Hervan—"are new enough you don't know what that required."

"Damned Reformants," a man named Aszondal muttered in the dark.

Taime nodded. "Going into the Hidden Ways unprotected by Alcua is risky. And if we do get through, and live to tell about it, it'll be called treason."

"No one has to know but us," Hervan said.

"Once we go through we're in this together to the finish," Rozer added. He grinned fearlessly. "I'm willing to take the risk. Gault knows I have no choice. If I lose my commission—or my head—my lady betrothed will never forgive me for the shame of it."

"Be serious," Hervan said.

"I am! I dare not risk losing her fortune to pay off my gambling debts."

The men chuckled at his joke but refused to meet each other's eyes.

"This is no game, men," Hervan said. "And nothing to boast about in the barracks later."

"We'll have to swear each other to strict secrecy," Taime said. "Or face the hanging rope."

Hervan frowned, wishing the man would stop talking about executions.

"A blood oath!" Rozer said in delight. "I haven't sworn one of those since Light Bringer took the throne."

"Forbidden, ain't they?" Taime said gloomily.

Anxious not to lose their support, Hervan lifted his hand. "We'll risk all for the lady. Are you with me on that?"

"Aye," Aszondal said with a sigh. "She's worth my life. I'll say that."

"Aye," said another.

"Aye."

Hervan's heart swelled with pride and relief. They were good men, brave fellows, every last one of them.

"She could be dead already," Taime said. "Like Lady Fyngie with her neck broke."

Rozer broke into a fit of coughing, and Hervan could have cheerfully strangled the sergeant at that moment.

"Then we take home her corpse," he said. "I can't face Light Bringer empty-handed."

Glumly they nodded agreement.

"So we'll do it?" Hervan asked.

"We must," Rozer said.

"We'll still need a guide," Hervan insisted. "Who can do it? You, Taime?"

"Not me," the sergeant said. "I been through often enough, Gault help me, but I'm no guide. Ain't trained for it."

Hervan exchanged a look with Rozer. His friend, to his knowledge, had never been inside the Hidden Ways, nor had Hervan. "Who, then? Fishul?"

"Perfect for the job!" Rozer declared. "I know he's been through many times. He used to talk about it in barracks when I was a—"

"Fishul's dead," Taime said.

"Narge?"

"Dead, also."

"Gods," Hervan said in exasperation, "haven't we anyone?"

"What about the predlicate?" Rozer asked. "They're trained for it, trained for anything."

"The pred—" Hervan's mouth went dry. He swallowed hard, frowning into Rozer's gaze, which was steady. "You mean Lady Lea's protector?"

"Thirbe," Rozer said. "He'll do it. He's keen to go after her."

Someone chuckled. "Whose head rolls first when there's trouble? The protector's."

They grinned at that, but Hervan was scowling. The unfinished challenge between him and Thirbe festered like a barb that could not be pulled out. "*I* sent for the priest, you know. I was the one to call for—"

"All the predlicates have the training, don't they?" Rozer asked, paying no heed. "Perfect."

In the background, Aszondal was shaking his head. "He's not one of us. We dare not trust him."

"Exactly," Hervan said.

"So we'll make him swear a blood oath of secrecy," Rozer began.

"He'll never do it," Taime said. "And I'll bet you my boots, sir, that Aszondal's right. We dare not ask."

"He will," Rozer insisted, while Hervan kept silent. "Didn't you see him hit the priest for refusing?"

"He's too close to the throne," Taime said. "Much too close."

"That's true," Aszondal chimed in. "It wasn't until Poulso refused to help that I heard Thirbe ask the captain about sending for reinforcements. He's given up. He has no intention of overstepping the priest's ruling."

"He's a coward," Hervan muttered.

"I don't think so," Rozer said. "So he's wary about going too far, too publicly. So are we, or we wouldn't be meeting in secret now."

"But, sir," Aszondal said, his gaze shifting between Hervan and Rozer, "having the official sanction of a priest is one thing. Doing this without authority is forbidden."

"So's calling up the dead to honor them," Rozer said. "When have you let that stop you?"

Aszondal fell silent, and no one else spoke.

"Captain?" Rozer asked.

Hervan scowled, his mind desperately seeking another solution, any solution other than having to ask Thirbe for help.

Rozer leaned forward. "Captain, we need him, and I'm certain he'll not refuse. The man's in love with her."

Hoots of derision, swiftly muffled, went up.

Even Hervan snorted in disbelief. "That old man? He could be her father."

"So?" Rozer asked. "You think old men don't lust for young maidens?"

Hervan felt appalled, even disgusted by the idea of Thirbe wanting to touch Lea. "But—"

"Come now, sir, don't say it's forbidden for a protector and his—" Rozer cleared his throat suggestively. "We know better."

Muted chuckles broke out from some of them, while Hervan glowered at the snow.

Rozer shot him an impatient look. "I didn't say the lady reciprocated. Gods, Captain, she doesn't even give *you* a second look, and you've been pouring the famous Hervan charm over her like syrup since we set out."

Swift grins flashed around, while Hervan burned with embarrassment. There was a certain amount of latitude in the cadre that permitted men to speak their opinions freely, regardless of rank, but Hervan thought Rozer was going too far now, crossing the line of discipline and taking advantage of their friendship. It was not seemly for the commanding officer to be teased in front of his men under any circumstances.

"Then we agree," Rozer said. "Thirbe should be asked. The risk is justified. I think you should approach him, Captain."

Hervan's annoyance grew. Thirbe would believe he was seeking reconciliation, perhaps even making overtures of apology if he went asking for help now. "Think whatever you please," Hervan said with a snap. "It's not up to you, Lieutenant, to issue orders to me."

"And this is no time to let personal grudges stand between us and what needs to be done," Rozer said.

Hervan jerked as though prodded, and the sudden movement sent a stab of pain through his shoulder. By the time he caught his breath he'd reconsidered what he'd been about to say to Rozer. After his bravado and fiery urging for them to take these risks, he saw how impossible it was for him to back away now. *They will think me afraid of the man if I do,* he thought. *Damn Rozer.*

"I'll ask Thirbe," he agreed, seething at the necessity for it. "But only at the right time. Not before."

"Very wise," Rozer said in approval, and the others nodded.

"And if the lieutenant's wrong? If the protector won't agree?" Aszondal asked.

Rozer mimed the motion of a knife thrust and raised his brows at Hervan. "Eh?"

The captain nodded grimly. "We'll give him no choice. And when we're done with his help, he'll be silenced before we return to New Imperia. That way, we never have to worry about him bleating to the emperor."

"Very sensible," Rozer said. "No more doubts, men. If our valiant captain is willing to silence an imperial protector, he'll leave no other loose ends to betray us later."

They all nodded except Taime. "What about the lady herself?"

Hervan had been expecting this question. He didn't know the answer. "Gault willing, she'll never know."

But Taime was like a dog worrying a bone. "It's said the emperor can't be lied to. Is she not the same? Could you lie to the lady, Aszondal? Could you, Lieutenant? Captain?"

Hervan's fist clenched in his lap. "Leave that to me, Sergeant."

"Ah yes, our dear captain has the gift of making ladies grateful," Rozer said, winking.

Taime didn't smile with the others. "She ain't warmed to him so far."

"But if he rescues her, she'll change her mind," Rozer said. "Eh, Captain?"

In no mood to hear Lea's name bandied like a barracks joke, Hervan shot him a quelling look. "It's the emperor's gratitude we'll need more."

Aszondal spoke up. "We'll have it, for he's fair besotted with her. I'm thinking he won't care what we do, as long as she's delivered safe. Won't ask too many questions."

"Exactly," Hervan said. "If the lady's brought home

alive, we'll live and prosper. If not, disgrace and desertion, as I said before."

Rozer lifted his cup in a mocking toast. "The Crimsons never fail," he said. "We live by that motto."

"Or die for it," Taime grumbled under his breath.

Rozer breathed out the ghost of a chuckle. "Stabbing the failures and covering up the rest. Who am I to break tradition? I'm with you, Captain."

"Aye," Aszondal said. "Yours to the last."

Hervan raised his cup in salute. The others did likewise.

"Call forth the dead," Hervan said. "Summon forth our comrades and the ghosts of this benighted place. Do it quickly, and do it well!"

He quaffed the foul contents of the cup, choking down the drink before he could spew it from his mouth.

As he did so, he seemed to hear his father's voice lecturing in the back of his head: *Treason in drinking from a blood cup. Treason in defying the emperor's orders. Treason. Treason. Treason.* Hervan shut it away, refusing to listen. Feeling a mixture of recklessness and dread knotted in the pit of his stomach, he told himself it was courage. The risks had to be taken; there was no other way. He'd gone too far already to back out now.

For the first time since assuming his command, he saw more than approval in these men's faces. He saw respect there as well, even from Sergeant Taime.

It did not feel as good as he'd expected. *That I should have to agree to murder and treason to gain it,* he thought.

Chapter 13

$\mathfrak{E}$xhaustion burned inside Shadrael by the time he finally spoke the word that had been sawing through his mind forever, and led his men out of the Hidden Ways back into the reality of cold, stinging air and moonlight shining over snow-covered ground.

Hills and woods surrounded him. He inhaled the scents of pine laced with pungent toklar bush. This cold and snow, the trees, the terrain were *not* what he'd been aiming for. Everything was wrong, and he knew a burst of alarm, sharp and sour, before he controlled it.

"Commander—"

"Have the men fall out and rest," Shadrael broke in before Fomo could ask questions. Fomo knew where he'd planned to take them, but the rest of the men did not. "Half rations—cold—and a full measure of water each."

Saluting, the centruin set to work.

Pushing away the headache buzzing in his temples, Shadrael kicked his horse through a thicket of trees, riding uphill into the clear to take his bearings.

Overhead, the hands of the gods had brushed the night

sky with a spangle of lights. Above the fat milky moon, the star Kelili shone hard and bright inside the circle of her four lesser sisters. He knew that north constellation as well as the back of his hand, for it had guided him through the night hunts of his boyhood. Five years past, he'd followed it in leading his battered legion to safety from the Madrun wilderness. Now, gazing up at it, he gave the bright star a tiny Ulinian salute, touching his lips and forehead. With Kelili to guide him, he could never be lost.

To the east lay a dark jumble of foothills descending to forest. To the west lay the narrow valley once known as Falenthis, the valley of ruins and ancient tragedy where he'd abducted Light Bringer's sister this afternoon.

Stunned, unable to believe it, Shadrael stared hard at the landmarks. Moonlight gleamed stark and white, reflected by the snow. It illuminated the landscape with such clarity there could be no mistake.

From this vantage he could see nearly the entire valley. *There* stood the crumbling pillars of its imperial arch. *There* ran the black line of the stream near the base of the opposite hills. And *there* lay the distant heaps of fallen buildings. A handful of fires, flickering like tiny beacons, showed him where the lady's escort made their camp tonight in the narrow flat betwixt stream and road.

Disappointment sagged through him, and he bowed his head. All that effort to magically fold distance and time, all that sacrificing of his precious reserves to cross this wretched province and reach Ulinia by dawn, and to what result? They'd gone scarcely farther than a half day's normal marching could have taken them.

Mortified, shocked, he looked again, telling himself that in his weariness he must be mistaken. But Falenthis it was. A place cursed through history, and evidently so tainted still that its bad luck had afflicted him and his men.

Or was the accursed valley to blame?

He glared at the girl shamming sleep in his arms. *She* was to blame for this, he thought. *She* was why he'd come so pathetically short of his objective. Of course shadow magic no longer worked as it once had. Never again could it do so, but as long as the Hidden Ways could be opened, they were there to be used.

Unless a creature like this girl skewed everything.

He gave her a fierce shaking. "Wake up."

She pulled herself erect. "Is it over?"

Even the fatigue dragging through her voice could not stifle how musical it was. *A pretty voice,* he thought. Then he frowned at his own fancies.

She twisted about so that he could see her profile. Moonlight reached down through the bare tree branches to finger her face. Her pale skin seemed to glow in the delicate light. Tangles of golden hair, curling in ringlets with the soft sheen of silk, spilled across her shoulders. Finding it painful to gaze at such innocence and purity, Shadrael shifted his gaze.

"Look over there," he said, pointing at the valley. "See the fires of your friends, who camp at their ease rather than search for you."

She frowned, her features half-concealed in the play of luminous light and shadow. "Do you think such a lie will torment me? Do they not need rest and time to attend the injured?" She hesitated, half-turning away. "I—I thank you for not killing them all."

Surprised, he almost laughed. "Lady, I did not spare them to please you."

"What do you want with me? You've slaughtered half my escort, killed my handmaidens, and carried me off like some kind of prize. Why steal my necklace while leaving the wagons untouched?"

"So you noticed that despite a raging battle."

"What do you want with me?"

"None of your business."

She drew in her breath in a sort of gasp and bowed her head. "I see. A political hostage. We thought the—there would be someone else at risk."

"It would take a bolder army than mine to abduct the empress."

Lea's gaze widened. "By whose order am I taken?" she asked.

"You think I'm not acting on my own initiative?"

"No. Who is behind you?"

"Does it matter?"

"Of course! What is this about? What does your master seek to force my brother to do?"

Shadrael had to admire her directness, even if he felt slightly miffed by her assumption—however true—that he served someone else.

"Will you not answer?" she persisted. "Why keep it secret?"

"If you knew, how would that satisfy you?"

"Do you know whom you serve?"

"Yes."

"Then who?"

"None of your business."

Although her eyes were veiled by night he could feel their direct stare. "Will you please return my necklace?" she asked.

"No."

"Is Captain Hervan in your employ? Is that why he brought me into your trap?"

"Gods, why so many questions?" Shadrael burst out.

"Would you rather I screamed and cried?"

Frowning, he touched a dried tear track on her cheek with the tip of his gloved finger. "Do you always shed pearls when you cry?"

She drew back, lifting her hand to brush at where he'd touched her face. "None of your business."

He nearly laughed, but curbed his amusement. Abruptly he lifted her off his horse and set her on the ground. "Walk about. Stay quiet and keep well away from the men. I don't need to explain why."

She stood in the snow, shivering a little under her cloak, and hesitated, her face a pale oval moon in the darkness. She stared at him a long while, silent and intent. Finally she turned and stumbled away through the snow.

Aware that he could recapture her easily if she chose to run or hide, Shadrael nevertheless watched until she entered a stand of scrubby pines and left his sight. He'd expected a pampered, hysterical princess, one who would scream at the sight of him or perhaps offer coy wiles in a bribe for her freedom. Instead, what kind of maiden was this, he wondered, to spin magic inside the bleak ruin of the Hidden Ways, to thwart his own spellwork, to withstand the terror of her abduction and the murder of her attendants with calm courage? She had even dozed for a while in his arms, displaying a kind of trusting innocence—or stupidity—that disconcerted him.

A ploy to gain your sympathy, he warned himself. She was the clever, unpredictable kind of captive who would cause as much trouble as possible. Already she'd certainly knocked his plans awry. It was bound to happen again, perhaps several times, before he delivered her and collected his payment. Then she could lead Vordachai a merry chase, and good riddance.

The soft sound of approaching hooves muffled by the snow caught his attention. Without turning his head, he flicked his hand in permission for Fomo to join him.

The centruin reined up at his side and drew in a sharp breath at the sight of the valley spread before them. "Faure's hell!"

"The valley's old curse clutches at us," Shadrael said, lying to save his pride. "See how we've scarcely left it."

"Demon's luck," Fomo said hoarsely, and spat in disgust. "We've gained almost no distance. How far must we go to escape it?"

Shadrael did not answer.

Fomo pointed at the camp. "Looks like the curse is glued to those poor morts we left alive. Figured by now they'd have tucked tail and run to Brondi for help, bleating all the way."

There was no hesitation in Fomo's tone, no indication that he was picking his words with care. Shadrael, on edge and ready to strike, realized that his centruin had swallowed the lie. A bleak, mirthless smile curled Shadrael's lips. So here he was, obliged to dance along a precipice of artifice and trickery, pretending they must journey to Ulinia the hard way, in quick march, for sound strategic reasons.

"Fine joke on them if they can't leave," Fomo said.

"Better if they do," Shadrael said.

"Maybe they're too stupid to run. Think they've sent for reinforcements?" Fomo asked. "That why they're waiting?"

"They're required to report their situation to the nearest imperial official."

"Regs." Fomo spat. "Can't do nothing in the army without some rule about it. But it don't look much like they're doing anything they should. Maybe things are different for cavalry, what with their fancy ranks and pretty uniforms."

Something touched Shadrael, a fingering of darkness, featherlight in touch. He frowned. "Someone in that valley is using magic."

Fomo uttered a hideous wheezing sound that passed for laughter. "What for? Are the light eaters doing a little prance to their—"

"Quiet." Shadrael felt that elusive touch again, weak but a definite summons. Someone was weaving a spell, its tracings like the crisscrossed slime tracks left by a slug on garden leaves. Involuntarily he glanced over his shoulder at his men. "It's *necria* magic. They're calling the dead."

"The hell they are. To track us?"

"Perhaps. Better watch the men. Some of the *casna* may be affected enough to answer that summons."

"Is it that strong?"

"No, it's weak and crude, but if I felt it, some of the others will, too."

The centruin turned his head to stare at Shadrael through the moonlight. "I'll see no one obeys it. If they're coming after us, you want us to set up another ambush?"

"Did you plant the false trail?"

"Three dropped swords of Thyrazene make, and a pouch with orders to take her to the Viermar himself."

Shadrael frowned. "I told you to name a lesser dragon lord, not the chieftain."

"Viermar sounds better." Fomo shrugged. "More threat of war that way."

"Anyone who's met the Viermar knows he's senile and toothless, with no intention of starting a war."

"Got sons, ain't he? Sons chafing to fight, and seize power and glory for themselves. Those bleating sheep in the Imperial Council won't take time to think this through."

Shadrael grunted. In his opinion, Vordachai's simple little plan to abduct the girl and point the blame at his neighboring province, the always unpopular Thyrazenes, was the kind of naive tactic anyone could see through. Might as well write VORDACHAI OF ULINIA IS BEHIND THIS in the mud. Only, Fomo was right, Shadrael thought. Who on the council was going to put reason before emotion with a girl like Lea at stake? Simple, crude, naive little plan. Either it would work perfectly or it would lead the Imperial Army right to Vordachai's portal. *You keep on wishing for war, elder brother,* he thought. *The odds are improving that you'll have one.*

"Could have done a better job of it if we'd killed all of them," Fomo said. "Could have torched a few corpses, made it look like dragon burns. Set it up real nice."

"I suppose you'd be happier if I'd let the men wear Thyrazene gear and come leading a dragon on a chain."

Fomo grinned, his scarred face hideous in the moonlight. "Now, there's a thought. Have a little fun with them, eh? But, gods, I wouldn't have taken that pretty-boy captain for a shadow user. Very clever, sir, bringing us out of the Hidden Ways as soon as he started trying to track us through them. Very clever."

Shadrael said nothing. If that's what Fomo wanted to believe, it served his purpose well enough.

"You want us to set up camp here, sir? We can kindle some bright, pretty fires, really visible to any lookout in the valley, and lure them up. Finish 'em off, and be done."

"If I'd wanted a complete massacre, it would have happened at the time of ambush," Shadrael said coldly.

"This plan of the warlord's is muck," Fomo complained. "And watching you, m'lord, having to stick to it, even when we know better ways, fair makes me sick. Better to have killed 'em all and taken the girl straight on through the Hidden Ways. Hard on the men, sure, but quick and tidy. No messing about with false trails and planted evidence."

Shadrael drew a deep breath, tired of Fomo's chatter that kept prodding the sore spot of his failure with the Hidden Ways. The furies and whispers buzzed inside his head. He craved more killing, wanted to slaughter every living creature around him. In an effort to control himself he tried to *sever*, but there was only rending pain and a flash of vertigo that made him slump forward and clutch at his horse's mane to keep from falling.

Quick as thought, Fomo was off his horse and helping Shadrael dismount. When Shadrael sank to his knees, Fomo scooped up handfuls of snow and pressed them to his commander's burning face.

"Easy, m'lord," he whispered hoarsely. "Easy now. Let it go out of you. Let it go."

The snow seared Shadrael's flesh at first, then felt blessedly cool. The furies died down, muttering in the deepest recesses of his mind, and he drew a breath of relief. Full awareness of the world came back to him. He blinked his vision back into focus and drew an unsteady breath.

"You'll do now," Fomo said, giving his shoulder a little pat. Then the centruin stiffened. "Here!" he rasped out. "What're you looking at?"

Shadrael jerked up his head, his face dripping with melted snow, and saw Lea standing a short distance away. She was staring at him with a troubled face, and undoubtedly she'd seen it all.

Humiliation flared through him, and at that moment he hated her.

"Ain't you ever seen *donare* shakes before?" Fomo asked, his voice harsh and challenging.

"Is he ill?" she asked. "Is he wounded?"

Shadrael could not bear it. He struggled to his feet, despite Fomo's restraining hand, and glared at her. "Go over there!" he said, his voice strained and unnatural. He pointed toward the trees. No longer did he care that he'd told her not to go near the men.

She obeyed, walking slowly toward the trees, pausing once to glance over her shoulder at him. When she was finally out of sight, he lowered his hand and bit back a groan. The pain in his chest was like a knife twisting around and around.

Fomo steadied him. "It'll pass," he said in reassurance. "It'll pass."

Eventually, it did. Shadrael pulled away from his centruin's support and turned to fiddle unnecessarily with his horse's tack, tugging at buckles and checking the saddle girth. He felt hollow inside, drained dry, dissatisfied, and restless.

"A bad one," Fomo said, offering gruff comfort. "Not the worst, though."

"No," Shadrael forced himself to say. "Not the worst."

He remembered it involuntarily, that day in the midst of a ferocious fight against Madruns, when the world had gone black and he'd been so lost in killing madness that he nearly had not emerged again. He'd been told that he'd killed five of his own men who tried to pull him away from hacking his dead foes into pieces. That, he did not remember. Only the queer, shaking aftermath and nausea, the burning, almost uncontrollable urge to keep killing and killing until his body failed him and his brain bled dry.

This, he assured himself, was not that bad. But someday, he feared, he would no longer be able to come back from the madness. Some *donare* died of seizures. Others went slowly insane and had to be killed. Others managed themselves well and lived long, successful lives. Before the destruction of Beloth, Shadrael had walked a sure, very controlled edge. Now, struggling without shadow support, he felt himself teetering, losing his balance. One day soon, he would fall into the abyss.

I need a soul, he thought, struggling against desperation. *I need it to quell this, to give me a chance of survival.*

Contempt for such a weakling thought filled him, and he shoved it away. *There is no going back,* he reminded himself. *What's done is done.*

Wiping his face with the crook of his elbow, he slowly grew aware that Fomo was talking.

"Could split the men at dawn, with you and our main force taking the girl on to Ulinia as planned," the centruin said. "Me and the rest could make big tracks toward Thyrazene, lead those fools a good, long chase." He paused a moment to give Shadrael a sly look. "Of course, the men would want to be paid up front, but I'd see that they didn't abandon the job."

Shadrael spun around, striking Fomo in the face with the back of his hand.

The centruin went to the ground, catching himself on one knee and hand. "Commander, I was—"

Shadrael kicked him, knocking him onto his side. "Did I ask you to plan strategy?"

"No, Commander. I just—"

Not daring to use magic to punish him, Shadrael picked up Fomo's dropped whip and lashed him with it. Three vicious strokes, effectively placed.

Fomo flinched under each blow, but he didn't cry out. And when Shadrael stepped back, breathing hard, and flung down the whip, Fomo made no move to rise or fight back.

Had he been a dog he would have been exposing his belly. Shadrael could feel the fear and resentment mingling in the man, a man loyal to him not through any genuine affection or respect but only because Shadrael had once saved his life and more than once saved his career.

Now Shadrael stood over him, trembling in anger, afraid the madness might return, yet not quite caring if it did. He wanted to kick Fomo again, smash his ribs and

kidneys and leave him puking in the snow, but fought off
the temptation. As yet, he needed the centruin with him,
unreliable or not.

"So you'll see the men don't abandon the job." Coldly
he echoed Fomo's words, while the rim of Fomo's eye
showed white. "So they'll want to be paid first. Oh, very
clever. I suppose you were going to next suggest that I
leave the division of our force to you. That way, you could
pick the best of the group, leaving me the dregs, take your
payment, and scamper off." He gestured. "On your feet!"

Warily, the centruin obeyed. His scarred face wavered
between expressions of appeasement and the desire to
draw a dagger and fight.

"Did you think me so ill, so *weak*, that I'd agree to such
a scheme?" Shadrael demanded.

"Commander, I—"

"Silence!"

Glaring, Shadrael watched while Fomo slowly straightened himself to attention. The harsh discipline of army
training was holding, but Shadrael could see that discipline
and training would not control this man forever. Despite
his pretenses of concern, Fomo was like a dog, loyal only
to strength, and ready to take advantage of any weakness.
If Fomo ever, *ever* suspected that Shadrael could no longer
utilize shadow magic effectively, he would attack, stealing
the girl for himself.

*Great Beloth, just keep him useful until I finish this mis-
sion,* Shadrael thought. After that, he did not care what became of the ungrateful wretch.

"I wasn't aware that I had to discuss my strategy for this
mission with you," Shadrael said, his voice raw with all he
was suppressing. "Especially beyond what you need to
know."

"No, sir."

"I've given you no permission to make suggestions."

"No, sir."

"We'll waste no more time with the Crimsons. No ambush, no leading them on false trails. They don't know

which way we've gone. The clues we've planted are enough to give them ideas. If luck shines on us, they'll report back to the emperor or desert."

Fomo started to grin at that, then hastily wiped all expression from his face. "And if they don't give up?" he asked.

Shadrael curled his fists, and Fomo flinched.

"Is this a discussion, Centruin?"

"No, sir."

"We'll continue to the top of that hill." Shadrael pointed, ignoring Fomo's indrawn breath. "If the men keep up a good pace, we should be able to take cover there in the forest well before dawn. Detail two men at the rear to brush out our tracks as we go."

Fomo hesitated, and Shadrael expected him to protest about how far the men had come and how tired they were, but the centruin wisely did not. "Got two, maybe three men won't make it," was all Fomo said.

"When they drop, kill them and hide the bodies."

Fomo saluted. "Shall I bring the girl back to you now, sir?"

"Let her walk."

Saluting again, Fomo picked up his whip from the snow cautiously, as though he half-expected Shadrael to strike him with magic. Moments later, Shadrael heard him cracking his whip and rasping out commands to get the men started. They groaned and grumbled. By the time Shadrael pulled himself into his saddle and joined them, the men were on their feet but not yet in order. Some were still munching on handfuls of grain, swigging water, ignoring Fomo's commands.

Shadrael drew rein in the trees, watching them, vigilant for any sign of mutiny. The girl was standing a short distance away from the men, staying sensibly concealed in the shadows beneath a tree. Apparently they hadn't noticed her presence yet.

Shadrael looked around, gauging how much moonlight they had left. Sniffing the air, judging the amount of wind, he scowled at the depth of snow. It would not be easy for his men to make the next hill in their present mood and condition. They were worn out from having marched that morning, lain in wait, fought a hard battle, and marched all this time by magic—exhausting in itself. If they weren't allowed to rest soon he'd get nothing from them if they had to fight again, not that he planned for more combat to happen.

If they had to march the whole distance to Vordachai's stronghold without magic converting their steps into league-long strides, the *casna* would be the first to desert. The rest could be kept going, provided he didn't lose Fomo's cooperation. Just thinking about such a long, arduous journey sank Shadrael's spirits, but he fought off discouragement. It was always best to prepare for the worst, while expecting the best. He would rest himself, gauge the right opportunity in a day or so, and if he could suppress the girl's talents sufficiently, he would try again to take them through the Hidden Ways.

By now Fomo had the men trudging forward. Not just any centruin could have accomplished it.

That is why I keep you, Shadrael thought in approval and kicked his horse forward to take the lead.

As he rode past the girl's hiding place, he gestured. She emerged into the moonlight, floundering a little through a drift of deep snow. When he made no move to pull her up before his saddle, she fell into line behind his horse. The men closest to her murmured lewd suggestions, and Shadrael heard her shocked intake of breath. She did not say a word.

Fomo moved along the line, cracking his whip, and within a short time the men sank into the misery of marching and left her alone.

Their descent downhill proved to be slow and sometimes hazardous. A man slipped off the trail and fell crashing through undergrowth. Shadrael did not rein up or issue orders for anyone to go to his aid. When Lea began to stumble and falter, however, the voice of reason warned Shadrael to take care. He dared not risk her tumbling off the trail and breaking her neck. A dainty thing, as delicate as glass that could shatter in his hands, she could not endure much harsh treatment. Alive, she was an invaluable hostage. Dead, she was only carrion to be abandoned in the forest.

Halting, he had the girl lifted up in front of his saddle. The man who performed this task managed a sly caress that made her flinch and slap at him.

Shadrael's dagger stabbed his hand. Howling, the man stumbled back, catching himself just before he could topple off the narrow trail. A hunchbacked lurker came to his aid, pulling him upright before shuffling over to Shadrael and patting Lea's booted foot.

"Pretty. Pretty," it mumbled.

She shrank back, and Shadrael kicked it away. "Get back in line, both of you!"

Riding on, Shadrael could feel the girl shaking, either from cold or fear. Clearly she was miserable and tired. Well, so were they all.

Ahead, a pair of scouts barely visible in the tree-dappled moonlight searched out the trail. Behind him, the men stumbled along, swearing to themselves at times, but otherwise quiet.

"I wouldn't have told," she whispered eventually, breaking the silence between them. "You didn't have to punish me for what I saw."

Unexpectedly, Shadrael felt ashamed of himself. She was right, but that didn't matter. He quelled his emotions. "The first lesson for a hostage to learn is to keep quiet and do exactly as you're told."

"Haven't I?"

He did not answer her. If he suppressed her too much, he thought, he might render her unconscious or even kill her. *Take care,* he warned himself.

Lea twisted to look up at him. "What is it you fear so, Commander?" she asked softly.

Surprised, he met her eyes for a moment. The moon glow shimmered in their depths, and he felt again that swift, stabbing pain from the light inside her. He wanted to look away, but somehow she held his gaze.

"Can you tell me?" she asked. "*Will* you tell me?"

Frowning, he flicked her chin with the tip of his gloved finger, making her flinch. "Don't meddle with what you cannot understand."

"I understand more than you think. And I see—I see . . ." Her voice grew noticeably shaky before she allowed her sentence to trail off. "Oh, who are you, to take me away like this?"

"My name is nothing."

"That's not true. But I didn't ask for your name. I asked who you *are*."

He was too tired for cryptic conversations. He reached down and squeezed her pale, slender hand hard enough to make her wince. He could have snapped her delicate bones, and he made sure she knew it.

When he released her, she made a muffled little sound, averting her face, and he suspected she was crying again.

"Time for you to be silent," he said harshly.

"You don't have to hurt me when you make a request."

"I give orders, not requests. And pain will teach you obedience."

"Will it? A crueler man than you tried to teach me such lessons long ago, only he did not succeed. Nor will you. I think the inflicting of pain makes you feel as cruel and wicked as you're pretending to be. But why do you try so hard to be what you are not?"

Opening his mouth, he breathed shadow magic over her. She turned pale as snow and slumped over as though he'd struck her physically. A quick grab kept her from tumbling to the ground, and as he drew her against him, her head lolled over his arm, hair hanging in a sheet of gold.

Alarmed, he drew off his glove and touched her throat to see if he'd killed her. Ah, her pulse fluttered against his fingertips, strong enough. In relief, he took his hand away, yet he could not resist one surreptitious stroke of his palm across her hair. It was as soft as he'd imagined.

"Little fool," he growled, his anger still hot inside him.

"Don't tempt me. Don't spark my temper, for no matter what you think, you are safe from everyone but me."

The night seemed cold and endless. Finally they made their way to the summit of the next hill and took cover under the sheltering trees. The men burrowed like wild dogs into piles of leaves, curling their backs against rocks, fallen logs, or any protective ground they could find. Most of them fell asleep with their rations still in their hands. Yawning sentries took their positions with reluctance.

Fomo was waiting when Shadrael dismounted with the unconscious Lea in his arms, and let a man lead his horse away to be unsaddled. If the centruin noticed that the girl was now wrapped in Shadrael's cloak, he said nothing about it.

"One scout found a cave of sorts," Fomo rasped, rubbing one bleary eye with his fist as he spoke. "More an overhang of rock, but it's sheltered enough to allow a fire."

"Good. She's far too cold," Shadrael said.

As he turned in the direction Fomo pointed, the girl's dangling foot brushed the centruin's arm. Fomo flinched like he'd been branded and hurried ahead of Shadrael to lead the way.

Shadrael found the overhang less sheltering than was needed for the girl's comfort, but it would have to do. His body ached, and once pine boughs had been cut and piled up for him to lay the girl on, he was glad to loosen the buckles of his breastplate and sink down on the cold ground with his back against rock.

Fomo and a helper bustled around, bringing Shadrael food and water, kindling a small fire that soon popped and crackled in welcome warmth. "Should be you in that bed, not the likes of her," Fomo muttered.

Shadrael unrolled a blanket and tossed it over the girl before wrapping himself in another one. Its thin wool provided scant protection against the numbing cold, but he made no demand for an extra one. Army issue was one blanket per soldier, two per officer. He would rob no man of that small comfort. Faure knew they had little else.

Weary to the depths of his bones, Shadrael leaned his head back yet doubted that sleep would come. He was too tired for it, too keyed up by the presence of the girl, and too troubled by what lay ahead. Unwilling to be mesmerized by the flames, he watched instead clouds reaching long, wraithlike fingers for the moon, veiling its bright radiance. The star Kelili was fading as well.

Dawn would come late, he realized, for more clouds were massing on the horizon, no doubt ready to drop rain, snow, or sleet. A dozen plagues on the girl, he thought, for traveling this late in the year.

For the first time today, he allowed himself to relax and feel satisfaction. All he had to do now was deliver his hostage alive and collect his reward. But of course it wasn't that simple.

Turning his head, he watched Lea sleep while the firelight glinted on her hair and cast flickering shadows across her face. Her lashes lay curled on her cheeks, and he saw that she was younger than he'd first supposed.

No, he thought grimly, it wasn't that simple at all.

Picking up his left glove, he shook out the pearls he'd kept, pearls made by her tears. Cupping them in his hand a moment while the firelight turned them golden, he grimaced and flung them out into the snow.

Chapter 14

Whispered chanting surrounded Hervan, sending strange little prickly sensations through him. He knelt shoulder-to-shoulder with the others, uneasy about what he was doing yet consoling himself by keeping silent while his companions spoke forbidden words of the old rite. Thus did they weave a spell back and forth, until its pattern eventually began to glimmer faintly in their midst. He found himself shivering. The snow under his knees was damp and very cold. He wished he had stayed in his tent, wished he'd accepted disaster and let his family's fortunes sink with his own. Instead, here he was, participating in a ritual that—if discovered—could bring him under charges of treasonous spellcraft, with penalties of death, all to save Light Bringer's sister.

There was an irony in that somewhere, he thought, biting his lip to keep his teeth from chattering. Still, if he did manage to rescue the girl, she would regard him as her hero. Her indifference thus far to his good looks, lineage, and captaincy had piqued him considerably, for, sister to the emperor or not, she was not that lofty and he not so low in estate. Had she been in love with someone else, he could have understood better his failure to attract her. Still, all of that would change soon, for she would be grateful for his rescue.

Brother-in-law to the emperor, Hervan fantasized sleepily while the chanting continued. *Uncle to the emperor to come.*

He envisioned himself wealthy beyond imagining. Never again would he have to worry about gambling debts and wine merchants' bills. He would give his parents a new villa and sneer freely at his sister's pompous husband. And every day when he strode in from hunting, Lea would be waiting for him, dressed in shades of blue to match her magnificent eyes, and offering her sweet kisses in welcome.

"Sssst!"

The warning came from Taime, on his left. Snapping from his dream, Hervan blinked at the apparitions forming slowly atop the glowing spell lines. At first he thought himself dreaming. He blinked hard, but the spectral figures of three short, wizened men did not fade. They cringed and writhed, wringing their hands all the while. Never were they still, and their faces contorted as though in agony.

"Speak to us, shades of Falenthis," Rozer said sternly.

"Plague!" one of the ghosts wailed in a thin, barely discernible voice. "Come not among us, for the mark is on our doors. Flee while you can!"

"We care nothing about your plague," Rozer said.

"Shadows gather around us. We are doomed, doomed!" sobbed another.

"Leave your troubles. We have questions for you. Important questions," Rozer said.

"Mael's eye has seen us, and we perish," moaned the third.

Shifting impatiently, Rozer raised his hand. "Be still, shades of Falenthis, and listen. Blood was shed on this ground today."

"Much blood," agreed the ghosts. "Blood of men. Ashes of shadow. Dust and ruin lie over us."

Hervan frowned at all this, impatient with the ghosts' lack of cooperation. Intending to interrupt with demands of his own, he started to his feet, but Sergeant Taime gripped his sleeve in warning, and Hervan remained still.

"The men who came here today," Rozer said to the ghosts. "Killers. Lovers of shadow. Where are they now?"

"Where?" a ghost echoed plaintively.

"Where?"

"Where?"

"Show us where they are. We command you. We are of the world corporeal, with authority over you. Speak!"

One of the ghosts sank back into the ground. The second one followed him. But just as Hervan thought they were all going to vanish, the third turned and pointed across the valley with one wavering, translucent hand.

"Open the paths of death to us that we may follow them," Rozer said. "So do we command."

But the third ghost faded from sight, his tormented face disappearing last of all.

The glowing lines of the spell flickered and vanished. Beside Hervan, Taime exhaled heavily, letting his body slump. Despite the cold, the sergeant was perspiring, and the others seemed equally exhausted, subdued, dark silhouettes against the snow. Stars glittered overhead, as hard and bright as diamonds. Hervan waited, his annoyance growing.

"Is that all?" he finally asked. "I thought you could command them, Rozer."

The lieutenant lifted his head and wiped his brow with his sleeve. "We've got a direction."

"Have we?"

They all stared at him.

"Yes, northeast," Rozer said. "You saw the ghost point that way."

"Did he point, or wave us farewell? To my mind, he was useless."

Anger twisted Rozer's weary face. "Did you expect a chorus of shades reciting precise directions? Sir."

His insolence frayed Hervan's temper. "I expected the Hidden Ways to open."

The men exchanged glances.

"We *tried*, Captain," Taime said. "We—"

"The ghost pointed northeast," Rozer said stubbornly. "It's not everything we hoped for, but it's a start."

Fuming, Hervan stared at the distant dark mass of hills. Was he now to roust the sleeping camp and set out on a wild-goose chase with no more information than this? Having steeled himself to commit an act of tremendous courage by entering whatever might be left of the shadow world, he found himself deflated, disappointed, and feeling rather foolish. The Talon Cadre was no fierce, secret society, he thought. It was nothing but a group of charlatans, pretending powers they did not have.

"We can set out now," Rozer said. "Perhaps catch them."

"Are you mad?" Hervan scowled at him. "Catch them *where*? Northeast, perhaps, if you insist. But how far away?"

The bite in his voice silenced the lieutenant.

"Your orders, sir?" Taime asked.

Hervan's frustration intensified. How in Gault's name did he know what orders to give? Suddenly all he wanted was his bed and a fire.

"Captain, look!" Aszondal said suddenly, pointing.

Hervan swung around in that direction and saw a pair of translucent, wavering faces peering at them from atop a broken wall. No bodies were attached to the faces, and before he could react those tormented countenances faded from sight.

"And there!"

Turning, Hervan saw more ghosts flitting about the ruins, passing from shadow into moonlight, fading and appearing. Some writhed and flailed their arms. Others calmly performed mundane tasks. None of the ghosts seemed to be aware of the others, or of the living men staring at them.

Icy chills prickled down Hervan's spine. "What in Gault's name . . . have we called forth all of them?"

"Surely not," Rozer said, but his voice sounded shaken.

"This can have nothing to do with us. Perhaps the shades always walk this valley at night."

A sensation between his shoulder blades, the certainty that someone was watching him made Hervan turn around. That's when he saw a distant, upright figure draped in black robes, a figure that did not waver or fade. It looked as solid as life.

"What is that?" Aszondal whispered.

Dry-mouthed, Hervan swallowed and kept staring in near panic, unable to look away. A traveler? he wondered. A stranger? Someone spying on them from camp? If it should be a witness to what they'd done . . .

"It's coming this way," Taime whispered.

And so it was, although Hervan didn't see it move. Yet it was closer, surging toward them like a puppet dangling from a string. Its face was veiled in black. *Shadow,* Hervan thought. His heart thudded faster, and only the sudden weakness in his legs kept him from running.

Another figure, garbed in tatters of once-fine garments, long hair flowing in a wind not of this world, appeared between the men and the approaching figure in black as though to hold them apart. Recognizing the shade of Lady Fyngie, Hervan wanted to avert his gaze, yet found himself frozen. Her heart-shaped face, always so merry in life, now contorted in sorrow. Her eyes were huge pools of shock.

When she beckoned to the men, Rozer shoved Hervan forward. "She wants you, Captain."

He wasn't sure about that. His heart seemed to have found its way into his throat, choking him. Telling himself to be stalwart in front of the others, he drew a shallow breath and forced himself to walk toward Fyngie's ghost.

At closer range, she seemed to grow until she was larger than he and terrifying. The wind he could not feel stirred her rags and hair as she floated in the air before him. Her pallid face and mournful eyes regarded him with tenderness. He realized she must still know him and his companions. Her death was so recent, so sharp an experience, that perhaps she'd not yet forgotten her former ties.

Grief for her, this pert, pretty maiden, stung him. He was furious on her behalf, at the waste of her life, at the brutal way she'd been slain. He yearned to say something, but what comfort could he offer? "Lady Fyngie," he began, feeling awkward, "will you help us? Will you show us where to look for Lea—"

Fyngie's ghost waved pale hands in agitation. As yet she did not speak.

The figure in black loomed up beside her, so close that Hervan stumbled back a step before his knees locked. His heart was thunder in his chest. Black-shrouded hands lifted, and he saw that the creature was going to draw away the veil concealing its face.

He gasped for breath, mesmerized despite his terror. He didn't want to see, didn't want to know.

But it was only Rinthella. Her beautiful, dead-white visage stared down at him. With the black hood thrown back, her dark hair escaped to writhe about her pale features. Her eyes held a dark fury that made him quail. She pointed to him with a hand glowing white.

"You have it," she said.

Her voice was awful to hear, no longer vibrant with laughter, no longer alive. "You have it."

Some instinct made him reach into his pocket and draw out the opal he'd taken from her dead hand. How pale it shone, as though the moon had somehow been captured inside it and fought to escape. He held it up. "This?"

"The stone of sorrow," she said. "The stone of despair."

"I'm sorry I took it," he told her. "You can have it back."

But of course he could not touch her. Nor had he any way to move the jewel from his world into hers. Her eyes, fiery and insane, glared into his, and he feared that baleful look would somehow petrify him into rock. Yet no matter how hard he tried he couldn't tear his gaze away.

"Rinthella," he whispered, "what do you want?"

She pointed at his hand. "The stone of mourning. She warned me what it was, but I did not heed her. Put it back. Put it back!"

"Lady Lea," he said eagerly. "You mean Lady Lea. Where is she? Which way have they taken her? Show us, Rinthella. Guide us through the world of shadows and help us save her."

"Put it back."

"Yes, yes, I shall. I promise. Only tell me where to search for her. Please, Rinthella. Help us."

As Rinthella turned her head, her dark hair blew toward him. He flinched, but the strands never touched his face.

"Why did you bring us here?" Fyngie asked, startling him. "Why? Why? The valley of sorrow. The valley of death."

"I'm sorry. But if there's any chance at all to save Lea, help me. Both of you, please."

"Before dawn, Vineena will join us," Fyngie said, her voice growing shrill. "Her soul will scream to the heavens. Why did you bring us to the valley of death?"

He shook his head. "I can't help you now. I'm sorry. Guide us to Lea. Please!"

"Vineena is afraid to join us," Fyngie continued as though he hadn't spoken. Her enormous, shocked eyes stared at Hervan in rebuke. "She suffers. Death comes not easily to her."

"I'm sorry. But where is Lea?"

"Our blood lies on you, Olivel Hervan. Our blood lies on you!"

"Let me avenge you," he said earnestly, extending his hand to show her the glowing opal. "I swear on this stone that I'll make the blackguards pay for what they've done. But show me where to go. In Gault's name, guide me to them."

"Put it back!" Rinthella screamed.

"Avenge us!" Fyngie said.

They circled him, faster and faster, screaming words he couldn't understand until he was nearly deafened. After a few moments, the sound reached a crescendo of noise that became a shrieking gale of wind, a storm blowing him in all directions. Buffeted, half-blinded, his ears ringing, he

staggered to keep his balance, throwing his arm across his
face in defense.

"Lea!" he shouted.

Fyngie reappeared, her heart-shaped face forming in
the wind, her hair streaming wild. "Look to the stone."

"What?"

"Look to the stone," she said, and pointed northeast. "It
will guide you."

Rinthella had shed her black robes, reappearing as tattered as Fyngie. "No, no, no!" she screamed. "Put it back!
Its curse will strike you down. Put it back!"

And then both were gone, along with the wind that had
buffeted him so violently. Dazed, he sank to his knees, his
grip tight around the opal. He was panting for air, his
senses swimming, his mind still filled with the sight and
sound of them.

He realized that Rozer was holding him, clamping a
hand across his mouth. Hervan tugged at it weakly, and
Rozer took his hand away.

The men lifted Hervan back on his feet. He swayed and
might have fallen if Rozer hadn't steadied him.

"Captain," Sergeant Taime was saying urgently. "Captain, are you all right? Can you hear me? Are you all right?"

Rozer patted Hervan's face. "Snap out of it. And for
Gault's sake, don't scream like that again. You'll rouse the
whole camp."

Hervan stared at them blankly, struggling to regain his
wits. "I—I—"

"Give him this."

A flask, warm from someone's pocket, was shoved at
him. He could not hold on to it with his numbed fingers.

Impatiently, Taime pressed it to his lips.

Smoky mead. Hervan drank, choked, sputtered, and
drew in the first truly deep lungful of air he'd inhaled since
the ghosts of Fyngie and Rinthella appeared.

"What did they say to you?" Rozer demanded. "Did
they tell you where to look? Will they take us through the
Hidden Ways?"

Hervan wiped his brow with the back of his hand, then unclenched his fingers and stared down at the opal. It had stopped shining brightly, but when he stared hard at it he thought he saw a tiny spark of light in its center. *Thank you, Fyngie,* he thought.

"Can't you hear what I'm saying?" Rozer said. "Captain, do you still have your wits? Did they tell you where to look?"

"Yes," Hervan replied, and cleared his throat. "Yes. They—they did. Northeast." He pointed. "Those hills."

Triumphant looks of relief flashed around him.

"As we thought," Rozer said. "As I said before."

Hervan ignored him. "Does anyone have a map?" he asked. "I don't want to rouse Barsin for the map case. Rozer, what about yours?"

"Pawned."

Hervan gestured awkwardly. "Then try to get mine. Inside my—"

Rozer reached beneath his trussed arm, digging around to the pocket inside Hervan's tunic. He drew out a supple doeskin map, Mahiran made and frightfully expensive. In the moonlight the beautiful coloration of its drawings and illustrations were muted to inky shadows.

Hervan gestured for him to unroll it atop a stone. The men gathered around close as Hervan held the opal over the map approximately where the valley was located. "Lea," he said. "Lady Lea E'non."

At first nothing happened, and he felt Rozer fidget impatiently at his shoulder. Hervan moved the opal diagonally across the map, northeast from the valley, and the stone began to glow as though lit from within.

Taime stepped back with a muttered oath, and even Rozer seemed startled.

"As close as that?" he asked. "But why? If they can use the Hidden Ways, why not go straight to their destination? What are they waiting for?"

"Us," Hervan said. "Clearly it's a trap."

"Shall I rouse the camp?" Taime asked.

"No," Hervan said, trying to make his voice sound brisk and assured. "We've no fight left in us tonight."

"They might not either," Rozer said.

"True. But I'm not going into their ambush. We'll break camp at dawn. Leaving behind the wounded and all nonessentials, including servants. Barsin can be left in charge, told to bury the dead and prepare reports. That will get him out of the way."

"What about the protector and priest?" Rozer asked.

Hervan frowned. "We may need them. Taime, I want the archers assigned to remain as guards."

"Sir!"

His confidence growing quickly, Hervan glanced around. "We'll come at them in a way they don't expect. With this guide, we can't lose them now."

"Unless they use the Hidden Ways again," Rozer said.

"That's a risk we'll have to take. But I think Poulso may be right about their magic being weak."

"Didn't look so weak this afternoon," Taime said sourly. "Not when the jaws of hell opened right before you. My heart fair stopped, Captain, when I thought you might ride straight inside after them."

So that's what had happened, Hervan thought. He nodded as though he faced such dangers every day. "We've sworn to use the Hidden Ways, should it become necessary. At the moment it isn't, and that's what the ghosts you raised were trying to tell us. If Gault is with us, this"—he held up the stone—"should be sufficient."

The men nodded approvingly, looking rather relieved.

Grateful to Fyngie for turning the opal into a talisman for finding Lea, Hervan pocketed it and lifted his fist in salute. "Trust in Gault and do our damnedest."

They laughed, returning the salute. "Our damnedest!"

But there was no laughter the next day when, just after noontide, they found the corpses of three men, stripped naked and stacked like firewood. All three showed battle wounds, dark gaps in gray, half-frozen flesh. All three had more recent stab wounds to the heart.

"Killing their own wounded," Thirbe muttered, stumping away from the bodies to rejoin Hervan. "Looting their own dead."

The captain sat atop his horse, watching while his men searched for tracks. If the renegades had waited for them, they'd long since given up and moved on. Cold, tired, and aching despite the haze of smoky mead in his head, Hervan squinted grimly, longing for some confirmation that he was right and Thirbe wrong.

"These bodies are proof that we're on the right trail," he said now.

"Who's to say they were among those lawless bastards we fought yesterday?" Thirbe muttered, climbing onto his horse with a grunt of effort. "Could be anyone."

Hervan shot him a look of exasperation. "Must you always see the wrong side? Of course they're who we're looking for. They have army tattoos. And I know battle wounds when I see them."

"Not good enough," Thirbe said. "What sign of *her*?"

"Sir." It was Taime, saluting at Hervan's stirrup.

"Well?"

"There's been a camp, over there." The sergeant pointed at the nearby trees. "They've brushed out their tracks, but the scouts are searching now to pick up their trail." He paused, his gaze steady on Hervan's. "And we found a sheltered spot, where a fire was built and pine boughs cut fresh, to make a bed."

Thirbe leaned forward. "For m'lady?"

"Anything else?" Hervan asked.

"Only this." The sergeant handed up a small pebble.

Turning it over in his fingers, Hervan rubbed some of the soil away and saw the gleam of an emerald. Very poor quality, pale in color and flawed, but it told him that Lea had been there. When he held it next to the opal, both stones sparked light.

Startled, Hervan nearly dropped them both. But already they'd stopped glowing and looked like inert jewels once more.

"What in the name of—what *was* that?" Thirbe asked.

Hervan carefully stowed away the opal before he handed over the emerald.

Thirbe peered at it, turning it over and over in eager fingers. "Not one of hers. Not off her necklace."

"But there *because* of her. Great Gault, man, can't you be grateful for this evidence?"

"Slim evidence." Thirbe kept the emerald. "I won't be grateful till I see her safe and sound."

Hervan frowned, and Rozer caught his eye with a meaningful little tilt of his head in Thirbe's direction. Hervan swiftly shook his head, dropping his gaze from Rozer's.

"To think she was here, this close to us all night, and we've come too late," Thirbe muttered.

Hervan flinched, but held his tongue. His own frustration was enormous, and he didn't need the steady reproach in Rozer's and Taime's eyes to remind him that he'd made a mistake in not moving out last night as they'd suggested.

As predicted by Fyngie's ghost, Lady Vineena had died at dawn, delaying their departure and putting all the men into an ugly mood. Now there would be no battle to avenge her and the others.

Caught between the excitement of the ghosts, the pain of his aching shoulder, and worry about Lea, Hervan had slept very little. His eyes were sore and gritty from lack of sleep, and his head felt stuffed with wool. The smoky mead was slowing his wits more than it numbed his shoulder.

He needed to devise another plan and quickly, but he couldn't think of anything except to follow his quarry's tracks, if there were any to be found.

"Come on," he muttered beneath his breath. Last night, caught up in the excitement, his senses stirred by the blood potion he'd drunk, he'd been willing enough to enter the Hidden Ways. In the bleak light of day, half-frozen and hurting, he found himself hoping for tracks. He did not feel up to the task of coercing Poulso to open the Hidden Ways, if the priest could even do it, much less going inside.

"Captain!" Sergeant Taime returned. His cheeks were flushed red with cold and excitement, and his eyes were snapping. "Compliments of the scouts, sir. They've found tracks."

"Excellent!"

Relieved, Hervan kicked his horse forward too eagerly. It bounced into a trot that jolted his shoulder and sent pain lancing through him. Reining up with an oath, he gritted his teeth hard until the agony subsided.

"Young fool," Thirbe said gruffly beside him. "You've no business out here. Ought to be back in camp, bedded, and mending that shoulder."

Hervan's eyes were watering. As soon as he could find his voice, he sniffed and lifted his head. "I have vowed to save her."

"Oh, aye. Of course you have. But you're no war hawk, boy. Just a chicken with one wing."

If that was his notion of sympathy, Hervan thought furiously, he could damned well keep it to himself.

"I was right about pursuing her!" he said through his teeth. "And now we've found the trail and—"

"The one they've left for us," Thirbe said, and spat. "Might not be the one we ought to take."

Hervan glared at him, tired of his constant pessimism. "I'll find her."

"Unless they vanish back into the Hidden Ways, damned shadow spawn that they are. They can play cat and mouse with us all they like."

"If you want, turn back now. You can send for your reinforcements and toast by the fire until they arrive, for all the good it will do you, or Lady Lea, or anyone. I intend to take action!"

"So I see," Thirbe said in a dry, unimpressed voice. His gaze raked Hervan up and down. "Still playing the hero, with no notion of what you're doing."

"Enough." Hervan tightened his reins. "You are dismissed!"

Thirbe's gray eyes narrowed. "Try to force me back, and

it's the last thing you'll do. My duty's here, same as yours. You've got no authority over me."

They glared at each other, while Hervan longed to be fit and well, able to run his sword through the old man's gullet. *No duel,* he thought resentfully, still smarting from Thirbe's contemptuous refusal of his challenge. *When the time comes I'll cut you down like a sick Madrun and leave you in the road.*

In the silence, a scornful little smile quirked the corners of Thirbe's mouth. Seeing that, Hervan felt his resentment blaze hotter than ever.

But he was the first to drop his gaze. "If you're to stay with us, then stop complaining."

It sounded weak and churlish the moment he said it, but it was too late to retract his sullen remark.

Thirbe leaned back in his saddle and grinned. "I'll say what needs saying as long as you keep making mistakes."

"I—"

"And I got no intention of leaving you to go after her on your own. You're likely to get her killed with your bumbling."

"Insult me no further, old man. I warn you now to take care."

Thirbe nodded, cocking one gray brow. "Oh? Going to have someone knife me in the back and leave me for the crows, like these?" He gestured at the bodies, his expression harsh. "Don't try it, son."

Hervan stared at him coldly, haughtily, refusing to answer although he hated the old protector's wily knack of seeming to know just what he was thinking.

"That's enough, now," Thirbe said, his voice unexpectedly kinder. "You're trying, I suppose, but you ain't up to this job with your shoulder—"

"Spare me your sympathy. I'm in command, and we'll catch them soon. Then I'll fight that bastard in black armor until he—"

"Sure," Thirbe broke in. "Let's hear you jabber about how you're going to whip a praetinor one-handed with a broken shoulder. You can barely sit that horse. Seems to me, it's *you* who ought to return to camp. Leave this business to those capable of doing the job."

"Leave it to you!" Furious, Hervan found himself almost sputtering. "Abandon my command to you? Impossible! *You?* I'd sooner cut my throat than put you in charge."

"You'll find *her* throat cut if you don't cool down and stop yelling at the top of your lungs," Thirbe said. "Sound carries far in hills like these. You want them to know how close we are?"

"I know what I'm doing," Hervan muttered, hot-faced at the reprimand, which this time he knew was deserved. "You can stop treating me like a child and remember I'm in command here."

"Ain't fit for command, no matter how many times you boast that you are. Not today."

"That's for me to decide, not you." Hervan turned to the impassive sergeant, waiting at his stirrup with one hand resting casually on his sword hilt and his gaze steadily on Thirbe. "Sergeant, pass the word. Let's move out."

Chapter 15

Finished with his council for the day, Emperor Caelan strode through his recently completed palace, passing bowing courtiers, messengers, idlers, and the curious. Wearing his sun-streaked hair loose on his shoulders and clad in a scarlet tunic edged with imperial purple, his tanned, muscular arms bare save for wide gold bracelets on each forearm, he towered head and shoulders above nearly everyone else. His eyes—once blue, but altered to a light silvery hue after his battle with Beloth—were keen and quick, missing little that went on around him.

In his wake came his lords of service, his chamberlain, his priest adviser, attendant scribes and pages, and his armed protector. Unlike Kostimon, the old emperor, who'd ambled along, taking time to acknowledge those who greeted and flattered him, and giving people in the palace sufficient time to prepare for his arrival, Caelan moved in a whirl of activity. He never strolled, never dawdled. When a meeting ended, he was the first out of his chair as though propelled on springs, whisking out the door before some of his councilors had finished bowing and murmuring their appreciation of his presence. There was no lolling in the shade on a hot autumn day, drinking chilled wine and nibbling on candied figs. Caelan was busy, always busy. He had endless ideas and wanted to set them in motion, and the most frequent complaint he uttered was that his days were too short.

"Give him time," the older courtiers murmured sagely to each other. "A young, enthusiastic emperor will settle eventually and delegate duties to his officials and minions. The court will calm down into a more pleasant, enjoyable atmosphere. There will again be afternoon revels and banquets lasting all night. Give him time."

But at the moment, as he strode along so quickly his portly chamberlain was having to trot to keep pace, puffing for breath and growing red in the face, Caelan knew he was behind schedule. The arguments waged today within his privy council had been unexpectedly fierce, making the meeting run far too long.

It was nearly dusk. Long indigo shadows were reaching deep into the palace through the tall windows, and gathering beneath the loggias. Link boys in palace livery were darting about, lighting the countless torches, lanterns, and lamps of scented oil. There was to be a banquet tonight in honor of the new Gialtan ambassador, just arrived at court. Elandra's home province was a firm ally, but Caelan did not want to jeopardize that relationship or take it for granted.

"Your Excellency," his scribe was saying, "the appointments with Lord Merstirk, General Ulth, and the merchants of—"

"Send them all my apologies," Caelan said, interrupting this list of unfinished tasks. If he ever paused to think about all that needed doing and all that never quite got accomplished, his head would ache. Elandra had taught him never to permit clerks and underlings to rule his schedule, and she was right.

Caelan tossed the scribe a smile. "Make new appointments."

"New . . . yes, of course, Excellency," the man said, then

muttered under his breath, "How in Gault's name am I to fit
them elsewhere?"

Ignoring the grumble, Caelan quickened his stride.

Ahead, the passageway turned, dropped down a flight of
shallow stone stairs, and so brought Caelan to a pair of tall,
elaborate gates wrought with the warding symbols of
Choven protections. Imperial Guards stood in front of
them, but already word of Caelan's approach had been sent
ahead.

"The emperor! Make way for the emperor!"

These warning shouts from the pages caused an instant
flurry. Flunkies bowed low. The Guards stepped aside
smartly, saluting in unison. The gates to the women's
pavilion swung open. Most of Caelan's entourage, permitted no farther, fell back. He swept in, appreciative of per-
fumed air cooled by enormous punkahs suspended from
the ceilings, creaking lazily as small boys pulled their
ropes. Carpets in an array of hues and patterns covered the
floor. On all sides, maidservants and ladies-in-waiting
stopped whatever they were doing to curtsy low to him.

He was conscious of entering a place of feminine allure
and mystery. Every part of the pavilion had been fashioned
to further that mystique. The walls were curved and flowing. Small passageways branched off on all sides, leading
to the private quarters of the ladies of the court. Ahead of
him, the enormous atrium formed a sort of common room
open to the evening sky. It was furnished with numerous
small tables inlaid with capiz shellwork and cushioned
chaises. A vast circular pool of water rippled like molten
silver beneath the pattering shower of a fountain. Fish in
rainbow hues flashed and darted just beneath its surface,
gathering in anticipation as the serving girls in loose silk
trousers brought large bowls of food and scattered it across
the water's surface. Some of the fish had been trained to
leap up to take food from a steady hand.

Caelan cast the serving girls an appreciative glance before climbing the steps of polished alabaster that led to the

empress's private apartments. Lamps had been lit beneath each step, so that the translucent stone glowed with golden light beneath his feet. Ahead stood more gates bearing Choven protections. And behind them rose a set of double, solid bronze doors sculpted with the Imperial Crest and Elandra's initials in bas-relief.

As these swung open, only Caelan and his protector walked through the portal into an enchantment of flickering lamplight, cool air, exotic perfume, and a mix of vivid colors in the hangings and silk cushions. The empress's sitting room epitomized comfort and luxury.

Rumasin, the Gialtan eunuch who ran Elandra's household, glided forward in greeting. He was old, although few wrinkles marred his skin. His complexion was the shade of undyed linen with a smattering of pale freckles across his nose and cheekbones. Wise green eyes looked respectfully into Caelan's, and he bowed low with his palms pressed together.

"May I take Your Excellency's boots?" he asked.

Caelan nodded, allowing the tranquility of his surroundings to wash over him and tame the hectic buzz of his day. Eager to discuss the meeting with his wife, he looked past the eunuch, but Elandra was not yet present.

Rumasin beckoned to a servant, who came forward with a stool for Caelan to be seated upon. Kneeling, Rumasin drew off Caelan's boots and handed them to the servant, who bowed and carried them away. They were already clean and polished, but Caelan knew that when they were brought back to him for his departure, they would shine even more. Another servant brought embroidered slippers lined with Mahiran cloth. The moment Rumasin slipped them on his feet, Caelan felt a tingling sensation of refreshment travel up his legs.

He sighed in contentment, accepting a cup of delicious fruit water brought to him on a tray of silver, and felt the last of his day's tension drain away. Smiling at Rumasin, he sipped more of the beverage, and asked, "The empress?"

"She has bidden me to greet Your Excellency and ask for your patience in waiting."

"Ah," Caelan said, draining his cup. "There must be some uproar in the nursery."

Rumasin smiled and glided away.

When his son was born, Caelan had ordered the establishment of a separate household for Prince Jarel. The infant had begun life with his own apartments within the women's pavilion, possessing fifty servants and highborn attendants to revolve around his small needs.

At first, it had been customary for the baby to be brought to his doting parents each evening at dusk, to be admired and played with briefly before their evening banquets and entertainments. A few months ago, Jarel had begun walking. Now he was running, his clever little hands getting into everything. The calm, well-ordered nursery routine had been shattered, and chaos broke out frequently. Jarel was said to have his maternal grandfather's temper, his father's strength, and his mother's determination. Although this sitting room remained elegant and welcoming in every detail, it had been stripped of its most fragile and precious breakables, for little Jarel was as lively as a *jinja* and as destructive as a wind spirit.

An earsplitting squeal in the distance told Caelan that his son and heir was coming. From its cushion in a corner of the room, the empress's golden-hued *jinja* shot upright with a hiss, pointed ears quivering.

Caelan laughed and saluted the creature with his cup. "Hide, while you still can."

Another squeal, much closer, came from the passageway, accompanied by the rapid thud of small feet. Hissing, the *jinja* whirled around and bolted out of sight just as the door burst open and a naked toddler ran in, shouting, "Fa! Fa!" at the top of his lungs.

Hastily, Caelan put down his cup and made a grab for his son, who was trying to climb up his legs. The child was dripping wet and as slippery as a river eel. Red-haired and blue-eyed, he had a chubby little freckled face full of guile

and mischief. Beaming from ear to ear, he yelled in delight
as his father lifted him high in the air, and flung himself
bodily at Caelan's neck.

"Fa!" he yelled, grabbing fistfuls of Caelan's hair and
yanking hard.

Still laughing, Caelan hugged him close. "That's my big
boy."

"Oy!" Jarel shouted, pounding his father with chubby
fists. "Me Fa's oy!"

Caelan blew a loud raspberry on his son's bare stomach,
and the boy screamed and kicked with laughter.

"Welcome, my lord and husband," Elandra's voice said.

Looking up, Caelan smiled at his lady wife. Her Imperial Majesty Empress Elandra, Queen of Itieria and Star of
Gialta, wore a gown soaked from waist to hem. Her hair
was half-pulled from its pins, with a lock straggling loose to
her shoulder. Still, her beautiful face was serene, and only
the maid standing behind her with a towel in one hand and a
child-sized set of sleeping robes in the other showed fluster.

Curtsying, Elandra walked up to Caelan and lightly ca-
ressed the back of his head.

Quickly he caught her hand and kissed her palm. As always, the sight of her stirred him. He'd loved her from his
first glimpse of her as a tense, beleaguered bride of the old
emperor. Each day, Caelan counted her presence in his life
as his greatest joy and blessing. Without her, he could not
have ruled this empire, for he was not trained to the position as she'd been by her first husband. Without her, he
would not have survived the aftermath of his fight with Beloth or the chaotic early days of his reign. He owed her his
life and his heart. And she had given him this madcap,
squirming son who was now kicking wildly in an effort to
get down.

"Leggo, Fa!" Jarel shouted.

When Caelan released him, Jarel darted over to his
mother, hurling himself into the soft billowing fullness of
her skirts, then darting away with a laugh before she could
catch hold of him.

The maid, still flapping her towel, set off in pursuit, saying ineffectually, "Now, that's enough, Your Highness. That's enough, sir."

Caelan and Elandra exchanged happy smiles. He rose to his feet and kissed her thoroughly. "You look beautiful."

"I'm sure I look a fright," she said calmly, tucking back her errant lock of hair. "How did the council go? Have they approved plans for healing arts to be added to our university as a course of study?"

Caelan's smile faded. "It wasn't discussed. There's been an attack on the northern border. The Fifteenth and Sixteenth Legions are marching out to support the troops already stationed there."

Her hands stopped tidying her hair, and she grew quite expressionless. "Then it's definitely war."

"No, not definitely. A few skirmishes, maybe nothing more."

"They're testing you."

He nodded calmly. "Of course."

"What else happened in council?"

"More provincial protests about high taxes."

She shrugged, a warlord's daughter, unafraid of anything. "I told you that's what Oucred of Ulinia would say."

"Aye, a dozen times at least. It's what they *all* kept saying. And it seemed to be all they would say." He sighed. "I'm told that Ulinia is certain to rebel if I tax them more. They're in a drought—"

"Ulinia is always in drought," she said. "Or they suffer from famine, or a pestilence has just swept the villages. If that warlord can find an excuse to get out of paying you, he will. His father, I've been told, was worse. A thorough scoundrel."

Caelan raked back his long hair with his fingers and sat down. "So do I placate the Madruns or the Ulinians? I don't want war from either at the moment. There's too much else that needs doing. But if it comes down to one versus the other—"

"It won't," she said. "Not unless you let Oucred and

Bavriol negotiate the empire's interests foolishly into that kind of corner. There's always another way, my darling. Remember that when they pressure you with their silly ultimatums."

He grunted, far from convinced. She hadn't sat through the arguments today, or heard the bad reports streaming in from the Madrun line. He wasn't sure he wanted to tell her yet about the mutiny in one of the legions. It had been suppressed already, brutally, the rebels executed swiftly without trial. The one thing Caelan absolutely could not allow to escape his control was the army. Without it, he could not hold this empire.

Gods, he'd far rather wade into a battlefield with a blade in his fist than sit through these long afternoons of sword rattling from old fools who were more theory than practicality.

Standing behind his chair, Elandra rubbed his tight shoulders. "You're thinking of the mutiny."

Surprised, he caught one of her hands and kissed it. He loved the shape and scent of her fingers. "So you know."

"Of course. I pay my informants well."

Tipping back his head, he gazed up at her. "It could spread rapidly."

"But it won't. You can count on General Turmikian's loyalty. There are bound to be traitors who escaped the initial reforms. They'll be cleaned out, given time and patience."

"But if these shadow lovers infect the rest of the army—"

She bent and kissed him. "Have faith, Light Bringer."

A squeal came from the opposite end of the room, accompanied by a ferocious spitting snarl and an explosion of cushions in all directions. The *jinja* clawed its way up a tapestry and leaped atop a cabinet of intricately carved fyr wood, hissing down at Jarel, who patted the base of the cabinet and laughed.

The maid pounced, swathing His Imperial Highness in the towel and lifting him despite his struggles. His laughter became a howl, and then wails of rage filled the air. The

maid brought him back to his parents to be kissed and pet-
ted despite his red face and huge tears of fury. Still howling, he was carried away to bed, and peace settled over the
room.

Elandra smiled in that special way she reserved for Caelan alone. "I must go and dress for this evening. We want to
make a good impression, don't we?"

"What sort of man is this ambassador?" Caelan asked.

"I'm not sure. I've never met him, but my reports say
he's very proud, very haughty."

Her expression had not changed, but Caelan knew her
well enough to discern a fleeting shadow in her eyes.

"Too proud to bow to a former slave and the illegitimate
daughter of his warlord?" he asked.

She uttered a rueful laugh, her eyes wise as they met
Caelan's. "How do you always know what I'm thinking?
He's a Pareve. That family has always thought itself very
superior, even to the House of Albain. He'll be a snob."

Caelan shrugged. He no longer worried about the past,
and experience had taught him that snobbery could not
break down the unassailable fact that he was emperor and
everyone else was not. "Are you going to wear cloth of
gold and all your topazes?"

Elandra shook her head. "That would be trying too
hard. He doesn't rate that much ceremony."

Kissing his cheek, she vanished into her bedchamber,
where he heard the babble of women's voices as the mysteries of his wife dressing for dinner began. Caelan had to
smile at her tactics, for she'd deliberately neglected to tell
him what she was wearing. He'd learned that it was a
woman's way to weave mystery and little surprises through
a marriage. If that's what she wanted, if that's how she
thought she kept her allure vital, then he was content to let
her do so. In fact, he cared not what she wore or how she
fastened up her hair. She was his, and together they were
happy. That was all that mattered.

Yet as he accepted a fresh cup from the servants, a sudden sense of uneasiness crawled through him. Frowning,

he put the cup down untasted. Such feelings had come to him with increasing frequency this week. He could not trace them, had at first dismissed them as political worries.

Now, feeling less sure, he beckoned to his protector.

The man strode over, alert and calm. "Yes, Majesty?"

"As we leave for the banquet," Caelan said quietly, his gaze resting on Elandra's closed door, "inform the Imperial Guards that I want extra men posted for the protection of the empress and my son."

The protector frowned. "Is there a problem, Majesty?"

Caelan looked at him. "Let's just say I want to avoid one."

Chapter 16

Lea crouched in the bushes near a trickling stream, uneasily aware of the guard watching her from atop a rock a short distance away. Bandy-legged and so covered in tattoos that his skin looked blue, he was the one she liked the least, the one who had a habit of staring at her while licking his mouth and sniggering. His gaze gave her the chills, but she tried very hard to ignore him. She did not want him to realize how much they frightened her, especially with the commander gone from camp.

Warily she put a garment in the water to soak, weighting it down with stones while she scrubbed another. She had positioned herself in a way to block the guard from seeing what she was cleaning, but doing so made it difficult to keep an eye on him.

"Spirits, come to me," she murmured.

Thus far, she'd sensed neither water nor earth spirits nearby. She tried to clear her mind and center herself, but each time the guard snickered, fresh alarm shot through her, scattering her concentration.

During the past seven days, they'd left snow country for

a warmer, rockier clime. The land lay dry and golden under an autumn sun. Sparse grasses were turning brown, and slender trees shivered yellow-tipped leaves in the wind while birds flitted among their branches. In the rocks across the stream, a beady-eyed chippaqui stared at her, too wild and shy to come entirely into the open. Had it not been for the guard, Lea would have enticed the small animal with acorns and pine nuts, but she did not try. The guard was likely to kill it for fun.

This was the first day they'd camped in idleness. Some of the men had gone hunting while the rest lay sprawled about, dicing with low-pitched laughter and much wagering, or just snoring on their backs. It was the first day the commander had let Lea out of his sight, and she was determined to seize the opportunity.

"Spirits," she whispered again, calling harder with her mind. "Spirits, come!"

They did as they pleased, of course. She could not be sure they would answer at all, and indeed it was risky to call element spirits in strange country, for she did not know whether they would prove to be benign or malevolent. After Rinthella's death she'd been leery of trying, but now she felt desperate. There had been plenty of night marches lately when she wished with all her heart that the dreadful wind spirits of Trau would appear and scour these brutes to mere heaps of bone.

"Tylik!" a voice shouted.

Startled, Lea dropped the dainty scrap of underlinen she was washing and had to lunge quickly to keep it from floating down the stream.

"Yo," her guard replied lazily.

"Got anything to bet? Cleef wants to play Serpent's Tongue."

From the corner of her eye, Lea saw Tylik stand up on his rock to talk to the man who'd joined him.

"What? He find a snake's nest?"

"Pretty little striped ones, all wrapped up in a cozy knot. You in?"

Tylik licked his mouth and glanced at Lea. "On duty."

"You can still bet, can't you?"

"Dunno." Tylik glanced at Lea again while she kept at her washing, pretending not to listen. "Cleef's got a hide like a beetle. What would bite him?"

"Said he'd put his hand in the nest and pull one out. Challenged Brofy to do the same."

"Brofy?" Tylik howled with laughter, slapping his leg. "I want to see *him* holding a snake's tail. Bet you fifty he'll squeal and dance around like a Penestrican witch."

"Done!" the other man said. "Come on."

"Can't. Got duty."

"Watching her? That ain't duty. That's a pleasure."

The way he said the last word made both men snigger. An icy chill prickled along Lea's spine. She tensed, her fingers tight around a stone.

"Got sentries posted, Tylik. She can't get away. Hurry and let's see this. With any luck, the commander will never know you took your eye off her."

"Wish I had more of me on her than that," Tylik said, as he followed the other man away.

As they left, Lea eased out her breath and ducked her head in an effort to master her anger. She slammed the stone once, very hard, against the ground. "Earth spirits!"

One came, as though it had been waiting for Tylik to leave her. She felt, then saw, the ripple in the ground, and the soft dirt at the stream's edge bulged slightly next to her.

At once she pressed her palm to the soil, feeling the sun-warmed surface, then the coolness beneath that. Rough and gritty to her touch, the earth spirit trembled like something half-wild.

With her mind, she soothed it, even as she calmed herself. With her *quai* gathered around her, she saw the spirit's brown face peering up at her.

"You are Lea," it said into her mind.

"I am," she whispered.

"Lea, queen of us, welcome. Many treasures have we to share."

"Thank you, but not now, please," she whispered urgently, knowing she had little time. "I accept your tribute with thanks, but do not bring it to me now."

"It is brought already."

And she saw the soil's surface sparkle, as though diamonds were catching the sunlight. Disappointment caught at her throat, but she made herself say, "How lovely."

"You do not like," the spirit said flatly. *"This tribute offends you."*

"No, I accept it with thanks." Anxious to make amends, she scooped up the diamonds and held them cupped in her palm. They were all very small and rough-edged, but their centers held fire. She only wished they were *gli*-diamonds, but these possessed no magic to help her.

"I need *gli*-stones." She knew it was wrong to ask for a gift, for anything specific. The earth spirits bestowed on her whatever they wished, and could not be directed. "Forgive me, but I am in trouble. That is why I ask. *Gli*-stones could help me."

"There is no gli *here. You ask for what cannot be given."*

Disappointment unbalanced her *quai*, and she struggled to maintain it. "Can you take me from here? Can I ride your back *between*?"

Tiny nuggets of gold gleamed in the soil before her. She picked them up, one by one, mixing them with the diamonds.

"You ask for what cannot be given," the earth spirit said. *"Our tribute is small."*

"I accept your tribute with gratitude," she replied formally. "I am in trouble. Will you tell the Choven I am here?"

The spirit stared at her, brown and impassive, but it did not speak.

She felt her heart beating faster, and tried to stay calm. "Please tell the Choven I am here."

"What is Choven?"

"Wanderers. People of the—"

"No." Another diamond appeared, larger than the others

and yellow in hue. *"You ask for what cannot be given. There are no wanderers."*

In the distance, the men whooped with laughter, and wild oaths rose above the noise. Lea lost her concentration, and the earth spirit vanished with a faint rumble of disturbed soil.

Dismayed, she curbed her impulse to call after it, for she knew it would not return. Had she been wearing her *gli*-emeralds, it might have obeyed her. Without them, she was lucky it had come to her at all. She knelt there, fighting back tears, and wished she could summon a dozen spirits to shake the very ground, destroying the camp and her captors with it.

They roared with fresh laughter.

"What are you doing?"

She jumped, her heart in her throat, and saw the commander in his black armor looming over her. Refusing to remain kneeling before him, she scrambled to her feet. Her face burned, and she would not look at him.

His dark gaze swept her, the meager amount of washing, and the setting itself. Without his helmet, he looked younger but no less formidable.

Clean-shaven, his black hair cropped extremely close to his skull, he stood before her now with bleak eyes, thinned mouth, and a jaw of granite. For a guilty moment she wondered if he'd seen her communicating with the earth spirit. But then he always looked at her with suspicion. Laughter rarely lit his face. No gentle manner ever softened him. His force of will was a hammer that beat his ruffians into submission day after day, so that they marched where he led them, made do with short rations when he gave them no time to hunt, and obeyed him without question.

Bending over her, he took her clenched hand and forced her fingers to uncurl. The diamonds and nuggets were revealed, bright in the sunshine.

His gaze sharpened. "Where did you get these?"

Haughtily she lifted her palm to him, offering him the jewels and gold without answering his question.

He did not take them. "Where did you get these?"

"Does it matter? You want them. Have them."

Still he did not move. His dark eyes narrowed on her. "You are generous with your wealth today. Why?"

"Would it matter if I wanted to keep my belongings?"

A muscle twitched in his jaw, telling her the insult had registered. Slowly he took the diamonds and gold from her hand and pocketed them, his eyes daring her to protest.

She dusted off her hands, despising his arrogance, and transferred her disappointment with the earth spirit into anger at him.

"Where is your guard?" he asked.

Shrugging, she gathered up her small amount of washing. He dashed it from her hand. "I asked you a question!"

Furiously, she picked up the two pieces of damp white linen and snapped them to shake off the dirt and mud. "I'm not responsible for your men."

"You are, if you've spirited one into thin air."

"Is that what you think I can do? Why haven't I spirited myself away, then?"

"You will," he said grimly. "Given the chance, that's exactly what you'll do."

Fresh guilt crawled through her. She felt as though her thoughts were branded on her face for him to read.

"What have you been up to?" he asked.

"Nothing!" She shook her head. "My washing. That is all."

"Liar. If you've harmed—"

"I wish I *could* harm him! And you!" she said, losing her temper. "I wish I had these magical powers you think I possess. Then I would show you. I would teach you—"

Realizing what she was about to say, horrified by her loss of inner harmony, she choked back the words and bent to immerse her garments in the stream.

He remained silent behind her for a few moments, then strode away. Shortly afterward, she heard the men's laughter cut off and his voice, as cold and level as a frozen pond, speaking to them.

Tylik came scurrying back through the trees, scowling as he took up his position on the rock. He clutched his money purse in one blue-tattooed hand and was mumbling and cursing to himself. Catching her looking at him, he shouted an insult that burned her ears.

Trembling, she gathered up her things quickly. As she left, heading back to camp, Tylik followed her, his eyes insolent and insulting.

There had to be a way to escape these brutes, she thought. If only she could get her necklace away from the commander. If only she could just run. However, she dared try nothing foolish, for if ever opportunity came to her it would do so only once.

In camp, a man lay sprawled on the ground among their makeshift tents and rickety shelters made from cut tree branches. He was twitching and moaning, clutching his hand that had swelled to twice its normal size. The others stood around him, watching him suffer. No one went to his aid.

Appalled by the sight, Lea stumbled to a halt.

She saw an enormous, thick-shouldered brute with a shaved head kneel beside the snakebit man and grasp the front of his tunic.

"Pay up, Brofy," he said. "Where's your stash?"

The injured man moaned and thrashed. Lifting his head, he tried to speak, but could not utter any coherent words.

"Come on! You owe me good. Pay up before you die."

Unable to bear more of this, Lea hurried forward. "Help him!" she cried. "Give him water. Cut the wound and let the poison out. Don't—"

A rough hand caught her shoulder and pulled her back just before she could shove her way into their midst. It was the commander, grim-faced, who held her. His dark eyes glittered with an expression she did not understand. Despite her efforts to twist free, he would not let her go.

"Stay out of this," he said.

"But he'll die if he isn't treated quickly."

"It's *drakshera*. The game of fate."

"Why won't you help him?"

"It's nothing to do with you. He chose to play. Let him alone."

She stared up at the commander, seeking some hint of mercy or compassion in his hawkish face. "Please. *Please*."

Brofy screamed and thrashed, then lay still. A bestial howl rose from the throat of the last lurker in their company, and the creature—terribly malformed and awful to see—burst into the open and darted back and forth in a kind of dementia. The men cheered, shrieking Brofy's name, while his competitor ripped open the dead man's pockets and even gashed the soles of his boots. It was there that he found two large coins. Jumping to his feet, he held them aloft in triumph and began dancing a jig.

Lea thought they'd all run mad. How, she wondered, could they view death like this? How could they celebrate it?

The man with the shaved head whirled around, grinning hugely to reveal rotted teeth. "Who's on for another go? You, Armar? You, Tylik? Come on, Tylik! Play Serpent's Tongue with me."

Tylik yelled back an insult, and then they were all shouting, egging each other on in a kind of frenzy. Lea drew back from them, instinctively moving closer to the commander.

"Come." He led her away, and she went with him willingly to the camp's edge.

"Why—why—" She paused for breath, swallowing hard. "Why do you not stop them?"

"Why should I?" he asked.

She stared up at him in consternation. "But you are their leader. Don't you care what they're doing?"

"Not much." His black eyes held little patience. "It's the way of soldiers, something to pass time."

"There are plenty of other ways to do that."

For an instant the commander almost looked amused. "What? Reading to improve their squalid minds, perhaps?"

"Now you're making fun of me."

"Because you are naive, a child ready to tell the world

what to do when you've lived cloistered behind safe walls all your life."

"That's untrue!" she said sharply.

"Is it?" His voice was flat and uninterested.

She opened her mouth to persuade him and then stopped herself. There was nothing she needed to explain, she thought. Nothing he needed to know.

For days he'd pushed them all at a difficult pace. Branch-whipped and bruised, scarcely allowed time to eat, forced to sleep on hard ground or a pile of prickly pine boughs with only her cloak and blanket to keep out the cold, denied the opportunity to wash or change her travel-stained clothes, Lea had ridden day after day on the withers of her abductor's warhorse, her shoulder bumping into his breastplate, her booted feet dangling by his armored knee. For days she'd found his proximity unbearable, yet she'd had no choice but to endure it, to endure his arm holding her close. Day after day, she prayed for enough strength to suppress her tears before his dark, critical eyes, to reveal as little of her shaken emotions as possible, to stay strong.

How, she wondered, could he be a part of her destiny? From that shocking moment of inadvertent *sevaisin* inside the Hidden Ways, she'd known her future to be tied to his. Yet how could her fate be entwined with this brutal war monger? This thief and kidnapper? This mercenary who dared wear the medal of praetinor, a medal he'd probably stolen from a true hero?

She'd never doubted her own powers of insight before, never doubted one of her visions or glimpses of the future. Since meeting him, she'd prayed with all her heart to be wrong, just this once. To be completely mistaken and in error.

On this bright day, he seemed to blot the sun from her world, and no matter how many times she closed her eyes and chanted in her mind, "It cannot be true. It cannot be true. It cannot be true," she had only to steal a peep at his stern face to feel the cold shudder of certainty.

He could not be wished away. He could not be ignored. That's why she was trying desperately to find some trace of good in him, some element that was salvageable.

But at this moment, when he stood here cold and unmoved after watching one of his men die, it did not matter that he watched over her safety or made sure she was given adequate food, a fire for her comfort at night, her hands never tied, or his cloak thrown over her in shelter from rain or pelting sleet. Such acts of kindness were motivated by his goal of delivering her as a living hostage, in good health, and still of value. *He cares for nothing and no one,* she thought.

He swung about to face her now, and one of his brows lifted in a quizzical way she hadn't seen before. Contempt tightened his face. "Have you stared your fill?"

Embarrassed heat swept up and over her, making her ears roar. She saw his mouth curve in a mocking little smile, but she was unwilling to back down, no matter how mortified he might be. Steeling herself, she struggled to meet his sardonic gaze.

A few times, she'd tried to fight back against his sarcasm, but it was like prodding a scorpion. She never knew what he might do, this man who constantly strove to control himself, a man so fierce, so violent, so guarded inside with a thicket of iron root and brambles covering his innermost secrets that she could not see his heart. There were very few people or creatures that she could not see straight through.

Whatever his secret, she knew it to be too terrible to accept. A man who cast no shadow *was* himself shadow. Not just shadow sworn, but actually a physical manifestation of Beloth's evil. How he could exist with the shadow god destroyed she did not understand. How he could stand here in the sunlight and speak to her as though he were still a man, she did not know.

And how, how, *how* could he be part of her future? Was she to be corrupted by the people who had hired him to abduct her? Was her soul going to be smashed, her morals broken, her life reduced to ruin? Or did the vision mean something else?

"Why," he said, breaking the silence so abruptly that she flinched, "will you not leave this alone? Why do you keep probing and asking your damned questions?"

"I've asked nothing," she said quickly.

He frowned. "You never stop trying to sense what lies inside me. Am I supposed to be flattered? I'm not. There is nothing for you to see, Lady Lea. Nothing!"

The violence and self-loathing in his voice made her eyes widen. "I'm sorry," she whispered, "but I think there must be. I hope so."

"Keep your hopes to yourself. Keep your questions to yourself. You've been docile enough thus far, and I've given you as much liberty as I dare, but continue with this and I swear you'll ride the rest of the way gagged and bound."

She remembered that first night, when she'd defied him, and he'd forced her to walk half the night through ankle-deep snow.

"Yes," he said as though reading her thoughts. "You know I don't make idle threats."

"I know you are harsh and sometimes cruel, but you are also fair. You have treated me kindly as your prisoner."

"Honeyed words will gain you nothing."

"The more mystery you make of yourself, the more curiosity you provoke," she said, although reluctant to admit it. "That's all."

He grunted as though he didn't believe her. "Curiosity and hope do not mix well together. Frequently they bring disaster."

"Riddles?"

In two strides he was on her, gripping her arm so hard she gasped, and shoving her backward to pin her against a tree trunk. "I don't play games," he growled, his voice rough with a savagery barely under control. "This is no court flirtation."

"Stop it!" she said in angry shock. "How dare you!"

"I'm trying to protect you, girl. You're too stupid to see

it, but the less you know, the better chance you have of being ransomed out of this."

Bewildered, she frowned up at him. "But once I'm delivered, will I not know my captor? Will I not know who holds me for ransom? What does it matter? Politically, I am—"

"There's more at stake here than money," he broke in. "Your brother's empire will stand or fall because of you."

Stunned by what he was saying, she rallied. "I have not that much importance."

"You hold a brother's heart in your hands."

"But—"

"Mael's eye! Will you not see? He's generous, weak, and inexperienced. He should have gutted his council and planted his foot on the empire's throat while everyone was stunned. Mercy and timidity do not keep a throne."

"Caelan is *not* timid! And how would you know how to rule?"

"To begin with, I'm no ex-slave, crawling out of the gladiator's pit to cuckold the true emperor and steal his throne."

Lea slapped him hard. Her hand stung from the blow, and the red imprint of her hand glowed briefly on the pallor of his cheek. For a moment he didn't move. They glared at each other, black eyes clashing against blue; then he gripped her arm so hard she thought he would crush it.

She felt sick with pain, but she wouldn't cry out. "Liar. Slanderer," she said, gasping out the words. "Nothing you say is true."

"You know only his court. You never saw him prancing around the empress as her so-called protector."

Anger made Lea struggle, but he held her pinned. "Elandra isn't like that. She wouldn't! And my brother is the best of men. You don't know him!"

"Don't I?" The commander's low laugh drove a chill through Lea. "I've been served a dish of his mercy. I've eaten well of his cankered reforms, and I will spit on his name as long as I have breath."

Understanding flooded her. She stared at him, feeling a
horrible kind of pity. "You're one of those driven from the
army. You would not swear your oath to him, and you were
discharged."

"Oh, that's a pretty way to phrase it," he said savagely.

Her chin went up. "A commander of brutes and lurkers,
a man who takes amusement when his own men die in
agony, a servant of the shadow god—why should you be
treated kindly? Why should you be kept in the army, to
work your evil unchecked? The reforms were necessary
and right!"

"If I were not being paid hundreds of ducats to bring
you in safely, I'd break your neck for that."

She heard the rawness in his voice and believed him.
Appalled by what she'd said to him, by the risks she'd
taken, she dared say nothing else.

"You're worth a fortune to me," the commander said.
"But how much more will your brother pay to free you?"

"Do you plan to ransom me for yourself? Cheat your
employer?"

For a fleeting instant the commander looked amused,
but then he sobered. "No. I'll do what I'm hired to do.
Nothing more."

"Are you so sure?"

His gaze narrowed. "Do you think this is only about
money? Do you really think the emperor has only to toss
his treasury down in payment, and you'll be released?"

She met the commander's black eyes, so close, blazing
into hers. Her mouth trembled, and this time she could not
answer. He kissed her, hot and hard, then stepped back
from her in abrupt release.

She hardly knew what to think. The kiss had been violent, not tender. Even so, it had robbed her of breath, of
thought. She hated him and all that he'd said. She hated his
masculine arrogance that believed he could control her
with lust.

His fingers, she saw, had left angry red marks on her
wrist, like brands. Those would fade, but not his words, not

his brutal possession of her mouth. She wiped her lips with the back of her hand, and despised herself for trembling.

"I warn you, for your own good," he said, his voice sounding more normal now. "Keep quiet, and do what you're told. Make an effort to see and know as little as possible. There's nothing you can do for your brother and his court, no warning you can give, no escape you can attempt. Stay a pawn, Lea. Obey their instructions."

"Whose instructions?" she cried. "Who dares this?"

"Take no larger part than what they ask of you," the commander continued grimly as though she hadn't spoken. "Perhaps you'll survive this. Perhaps. Gault knows your brother won't."

Chapter 17

Boiling with rage, Shadrael strode away from the white-faced girl. As he crossed the camp, the men stopped their foolery and scrambled out of his path. Ignoring them, Shadrael quelled Fomo's attempt to speak to him with a stony look, and plunged through the undergrowth toward the stream.

Bushes plucked at his cloak and scraped across his armor. He shoved his way into the clear and paced up and down beside the shallow rivulet, his boots crunching over a gravel bar before sinking into soft dirt beyond it. There, almost in the water, he halted, glaring sightlessly at the golden-leafed trees dotting the hill on the other side.

What in Beloth's name had possessed him to kiss her? Furious with her, furious with himself, Shadrael clenched his fists in a desire to strike something, anything. It was the kind of thing a fool would do; a green, untried recruit was trained better than this. Hostages destined for ransom were to be left strictly alone. Gods above, if he couldn't control himself, how could he demand it of his men? The lust in them for her was like a constant stink in his nostrils, while he—he was no better.

All he'd wanted to do was smash that gentle innocence of hers, strip her of her calm little brand of courage and show her . . . show her . . .

What? he wondered bleakly. What had he to teach her? She knew he was evil, knew his men were worse than beasts.

For days, she'd defied his expectations by being a model prisoner, docile and obedient, making no complaints, no demands. The pace he'd set was a brutal one, and there were evenings when he'd lifted her off his horse and seen the purple shadows of exhaustion beneath her eyes. Even then, she'd not whined or begged him for anything. Nor had she played any tricks, such as casting spells or bashing his skull with a rock in the dead of night.

So why this furious need to shock her, goad her, and punish her? Why? Because she was pretty, and gentle, and good? He'd brought desperate unhappiness to her blue eyes, and left her pale and shaking—not in fear of him, but in disgust. He'd driven her to lose her temper; he'd cornered and harried her gentle spirit until she fought him, even struck him, this girl who'd probably never spoken an unkind word before in her life. What kind of pride could he take in that?

Gault above, but she was even trying to find good in him, depending on him at least to remain a civilized officer and man of honor in her presence. And now he'd smashed that as well.

He'd not wanted her friendship, or even her liking. But that look of horrified revulsion in her gentle eyes was worse than anything she could have said. He felt like a whipped dog, yet despite his remorse he could not turn back and undo his cruelty. An apology was unthinkable, however much his upbringing, his very honor, demanded it of him.

If I had a soul, I might be worthy enough to kiss the hem of her robe, nothing more, he thought. *But I haven't even that.*

Resolutely he shut off such thoughts. There could be no turning back, ever. To harbor even a single regret was to unbolt the door to insanity.

A harsh croaking sound caught his attention. Looking up, he saw the gray raven of the Vindicants sitting on a nearby tree branch. His bitterness turned against the priests. Still spying . . . still shadowing his every move in hopes that he might yet deliver his hostage to them.

Well, he'd taken Vordachai's gold—although it was but a fraction of the promised payment—and given his bond.

The priests had offered him nothing at all . . . yet everything.

Snarling, he abruptly picked up a stone and hurled it at the raven, frightening the ghostly bird away.

He could not believe them capable of giving him another soul. They were not gods. They had no such power. Yet he wanted to believe. Because he'd met Lea, he wanted to believe it desperately.

"M'lord Commander?"

It was Fomo's rasping voice, almost a whisper, sounding very cautious indeed.

Startled, Shadrael swung around with his dagger drawn, but when he saw his centruin standing there with hands held up in appeasement, he relaxed and sheathed his weapon.

"A good way to find my blade in your heart," he said.

Fomo's small eyes were wary. "Didn't come on you by stealth," he said hoarsely. "Swear it."

It was a lie, but Shadrael nodded as though he accepted it.

"Permission to speak, sir."

"What is it? Scout report?"

Fomo shook his head. "The hunters are coming in. They've bagged several wild goats and a few hares."

"So we'll eat well tonight," Shadrael said impatiently. "Is that all?"

"There will be more than enough food for tonight. Do we pack the extra meat with us, or leave it behind?"

"Gods, Fomo, since when must I to tell you how to carry out your own duties?"

The scarred centruin held his ground. "No, Commander, that's not what I'm asking. If we're about to return to the Hidden Ways, we can't take meat with us."

Shadrael bit back another reprimand. Fomo was right. The raw flesh would spoil instantly, and it would draw every demon and creature subsisting there straight to them, probably in attack.

Of course, Shadrael knew that Fomo really wanted to know something else, and this was his oblique way of asking.

"I'm waiting for the scout's report," Shadrael said. "Meanwhile, feed the men, and give the extra to the lurker."

"It won't fight unless it's starved," Fomo said.

"I know."

"Brute's got no sense. It'll gorge until it's unable to move. We supposed to carry it with us?"

"No."

Fomo grinned, showing his bad teeth. "The men won't kill it. No one wants lurker stink on his sword blade."

"It should have deserted with the others," Shadrael said. "We're better off without it."

"Might follow us in a day or two."

"Not with the Crimsons on our trail."

Fomo's amusement faded. "Those damned *harwots*." He spat. "Staying close as leeches."

Unable to shake them off, and unwilling to lead them straight to his brother's stronghold, Shadrael had instead turned up into these rocky hills of Kovria, where the flinty ground made tracking next to impossible. Short of killing the girl, there was no way he could think of to negate her effect on the Hidden Ways. Twice more had he opened them and led his men through, and both times they'd emerged far short of their mark, with Shadrael so exhausted from the effort that he could barely function. And much to his astonishment, pursuit had always caught up with them. Necria magic could not reach this far, which meant the Crimsons were using some other kind of guide, perhaps even Lady Lea herself, as a means of following them.

The rest today had been ordered because the men needed it, but also for Shadrael to determine if his latest trick had finally lost their pursuers.

"Sir! Centruin Fomo! Commander!"

Both Shadrael and Fomo turned as one of the scouts came running up to them. Winded, the man stumbled to a halt, struggling to catch his breath.

"Your report," Shadrael said impatiently. "Quickly, man!"

"Yes, sir. They've made the pass, and they're coming up from that direction." He pointed.

Shadrael grimaced to himself while Fomo swore.

"How fast are they moving?"

"Pretty fast." The scout considered. "I think they'll reach us by nightfall."

Shadrael and Fomo exchanged involuntary looks. "That's faster than I expected," Shadrael admitted.

"Unless you're planning to lead 'em straight to the war-lord's gates, we'll never have a better place for ambush," Fomo said.

Shadrael swept him an arrogant look. "Why do you think I've waited?"

"Aye, that's what I've been waiting to hear!" Grinning, Fomo saluted him. "I'll give the orders."

"Get the men fed and strike the camp. We'll attack just before dusk. From the lookout point I showed you earlier."

"Yes, Commander!" Fomo grinned happily. "Old times, ain't it?"

"Centruin."

"Yes, sir?"

Shadrael met Fomo's gaze. "This time, we leave no survivors."

Lea knew something was afoot from the moment the centruin came striding back through camp and issued orders to the men skinning the freshly killed goats. The dice games were rolled up and tucked away. Tents and shelters came down. Packs were stacked neatly. Everyone seemed

to be ignoring her as she made her own small preparations
for departure by gathering her damp articles of laundry
where she'd spread them on a bush to dry and folding her
heavy cloak in a way that would make it easy to carry.

She knew, of course, that her valiant cavalrymen had
not deserted her, but were following doggedly despite the
commander's efforts to lose them. Perhaps they were closing in today, or perhaps the commander was preparing
some new trick against them. Too many disappointments
already had taught her not to hope too much, but she
sensed the approach of opportunity. When it came her way,
she intended to be ready.

Her fraught emotions had been folded as neatly as her
cloak and would be dealt with later. The commander's cruelty, his slurs and threats against Caelan, her most beloved
brother, had hurt especially. Determined to thwart him and
hoping to avert more bloodshed, Lea intended to escape,
however she could.

The smell of bloody meat thrown on the fire repulsed
her. She retreated deeper into the bushes, moving slowly to
attract no suspicion. Someone would notice her absence
soon, but if searching for her delayed them, so much the
better.

Her plan, simple and rather desperate, was to head for
the stream, walk in it for a while to hide her tracks, then
emerge onto one of the gravel bars and climb up into the
rough hills and gullies if possible. Even without her *gli-*
emeralds, she would try to call on the air spirits to conceal
her. She believed that if she could simply hide for a while,
that might distract the commander and his men long
enough to give the cavalrymen a chance to reach her.

Taking cover near the stream, she cautiously watched
the clearing. In the near distance she could hear the men
calling out orders and questions, their voices cheerful as
they urged the meat to cook faster and laid wagers on who
could eat it the rawest.

Lea swallowed back her disgust. They would bet on
which cloud could outrace another, she told herself, but if

their foolery made them careless in watching her, so much the better.

Still wary, she kept looking all around but saw no one, not even Tylik. Gathering her courage, she darted away from the brush and into the open, running into the icy waters of the shallow stream with a splash and heading upstream as fast as the ankle-deep water would permit. It was awkward, carrying her cloak and trying to hold her skirts out of the water, but she forged onward, her spirits rising with every step.

The water ran scarlet with the dye from her red boots, as though stained with blood, and worriedly she hopped out onto a patch of gravel sooner than she would have liked to. The woods before her were thin, offering less cover than she wanted, but she sprinted toward them just the same.

A shape glimpsed from the corner of her eye was all that warned her before she was tackled and knocked to the ground. A man's weight slammed on top of her, heavy, bruising her against the unyielding soil. She cried out, despite her intentions; then his dirty hand clamped across her mouth, and she heard heavy breathing and a low-pitched snicker that made her go rigid with fear.

"That's right, Princess," Tylik's voice said in her ear. "You been watching me watching you all day now. Time we had us some fun."

Her outstretched hand caught up dirt, and she threw it in his face. Squalling, he reared back and dug at his eyes, and she flung herself away from him.

She got only to her hands and knees, however, for her skirts hampered her. Tylik caught her by her long hair, yanking her back cruelly into his arms.

His embrace was unbreakable, despite her struggles. His sour breath panted hot on her ear and cheek. When he tried to turn her around to kiss her and tear at her bodice, she slapped at him, getting in a glancing clout on his ear that made him yelp. Her fingernails raked him, and he flinched back.

Swearing, he glared at her, his eyes narrowed and mean. "If you want it rough, you can have—"

A sword blade cut off his head, slicing through neck sinew, bone, and muscle in one swift blow. Blood splattered across Lea in a hot spurt, and Tylik's head went rolling across the gravel like a grisly ball. Too stunned to scream, she looked up.

The commander towered above her, silhouetted against the sky, his gory sword held aloft in his gloved fist. She feared he meant to strike her dead as well.

Instead, he crouched before her, his black eyes murderous, his face raw with anger. "Are you hurt? Tell me! Are you hurt?"

It registered then, how close she'd come to losing her head with Tylik, how close his sword tip had passed before her face.

Shudders ran through her. She couldn't catch her breath enough to speak. Her heart was racing hard, making the blood pound in her ears.

"Lea! Answer me."

Something in his voice reached through her shock. She managed to shake her head.

The commander gripped her hand and pulled her to her feet, steadying her when her knees dipped and wobbled.

The barbed *quai* of death and killing engulfed her, and so potent was this man's aura of violence that she felt dizzy, unable to regain her wits. Her gown was soaked with Tylik's blood. The hot, fresh stench of it made her gasp for breath. She sank to the verge of a swoon, and the commander's arm slid around the small of her back, holding her up.

"You *are* hurt," he said roughly, lifting her in his arms and carrying her farther up the bank. He laid her on a drifted pile of soft leaves, away from the gore, and crouched beside her. A crease etched his brow. When he smoothed her hair back from her eyes and brushed dirt from her cheek, his touch was gentle.

"Lea. Lea," he whispered.

Her eyes opened fully, and for a moment she found herself looking into his unguarded gaze. His eyes were those
of a normal man, one who cared. She blinked, and he drew
back from her at once.

"I could have killed you," he said gruffly.

"I thought you had." Her face puckered as she saw again
in her mind Tylik's head flying through the air, spraying
blood as it went. "Why didn't you just hit him? You could
have punished him without—why did you kill him like
that?"

Anger slammed a door between them. "Little fool!" the
commander said. "Leading a blackguard like that to a tryst."

His unjust accusation rallied her. She sat up. "I didn't. I
didn't!"

"What did you expect, running off from camp? You
knew you'd be followed. This offal was bound to seize his
chance."

The unfairness of his blame stung her. She bit back her
denials, too proud to defend herself further, and stared up
at him through tear-filled eyes. That's when the *sevaisin*
came again, without warning, involuntarily, and just as
powerfully as before.

Alarmed, she tried to break the connection, but he was
quicker in slashing it. He jumped away from her as though
arrow-shot and clenched the hand that moments before had
been smoothing her hair. His breath came as short and
raggedly as hers. But while her head was filled with marvel, he was glaring, as red as fire.

"Damn you," he breathed out. "Damn you!"

She reached out her hand. "So that is what you—"

He whirled away, slamming his bloody sword into its
sheath without cleaning it and drawing a war axe from his
belt. It was short-handled, more of a hatchet, and its steel
head caught the sun in gleaming reflection as he seized a
sapling and chopped it off in a single blow. Another blow
cut off its leafy crown. Tossing it aside, he chopped down
another, and another, working fast until he had an armload
of pike-length stakes.

Pointing with his axe, he said, "Over there."

Confused, unsure at first of what he meant to do, Lea walked over to the stream. Inside, she was a messy confusion of impressions stolen from his mind during that brief joining of *sevaisin*. Thoughts of jealousy and betrayal and fury and guilt and concern and cold intention tumbled about until she could barely think. As they faded, however, one thing clarified in her mind.

"You're going to fight," she said in a whisper. "Are the Crimsons here?"

A grim smile touched his mouth. "The Crimsons are going to die."

"No, please!"

Without looking up, he thrust the crudely cut stakes one by one into the ground, making a sort of tall fence that encircled her. She did not understand what he was doing. The soil was soft. She could pull these stakes out and escape easily. Yet when she put out her hand to grasp one, he spoke a curt word of magic.

The wood sparked power against her hand, flinging it off. She retreated instinctively, although her enclosure was so small she could take no more than two or three steps in any direction.

"Don't do this," she said, pleading with him. She tried to step through a gap, tried to reach for his arm, but he thrust her back. "All this time we've stayed ahead of them. Why attack them now?"

He pushed the last stake into the ground and stepped back. His eyes burned like black holes in the pallor of his face. "I let them live once, most of them."

"Yes, yes, you did. I thanked you for it. Why change that decision?"

"Because they do not quit."

Her chin lifted high. "Of course not. They are the Household Regiment and sworn to keep me safe."

"Better they had never dogged my trail," he said, looking unimpressed. "They should have accepted the trickery laid before them and turned back at Falenthis."

"Is that your only reason?" she asked. "That they refuse to follow your plan? Is that your only reason for attacking them now, from ambush like a barbarian?"

He frowned. "How do you know—" With a curt gesture, he cut himself off. "I see that you made swift use of *sevaisin*, reading my mind."

"And you're evading my question. Have you no good reason for what you do?"

"I have excellent reasons for everything I do."

His contempt made her feel like a child who cannot win a reasoned argument and so wants to scream in frustration.

"How can you condemn them for trying to save me?" she whispered.

"How can you expect me to do otherwise?" His gaze seared her. "Am I to welcome them into camp and hand you over with a smile?"

"Trick them!" she insisted. "You have wiles you haven't begun to use. Throw them off. Use whatever means you must, but don't slay them."

He gave her a mocking little bow. "I'm flattered that you believe my fighting prowess is superior to theirs. Or do you see the future and know the outcome of this little battle already?"

She bit her trembling lip. "Yes, I see it. I know its ending."

Her admission seemed to surprise him, but he recovered quickly. Raising both hands, he spoke words of shadow magic in a low, gruff voice.

The *jaiethquai* of this place—already disrupted by his slaying of Tylik—shattered completely before the assault of his magic. Biting off a cry, Lea stumbled back as far from him as the enclosure would permit. The words he spoke hurt her. She pressed her hands to her ears, whispering words of a different kind of countermagic, but she was too late. The glowing force of his spell held her trapped, like an insect in a bottle.

"In Gault's name, you don't have to do this," she said.

He lowered his hands, looking strained by the effort

he'd made. "It goes too far. They follow you too well. That stops now. For the sake of my br—it stops now."

"Shadrael!" she cried.

He jerked to a halt and spun around, eyes blazing. "You know? How dare you address me as though we are—"

He broke off, but fiery embarrassment was already spreading through Lea. He did not have to complete his sentence for her to understand. An unmarried woman did not address a man unrelated to her so intimately unless they were betrothed. She had used his name without thinking, used the knowledge gained through *sevaisin* as naturally as drawing breath. Horrified, she struggled not to show her mortification.

"I—I—Commander Shadrael," she said, fumbling to correct her error by speaking more formally, "I beg you not to—"

"My name is not for your use!" he shouted. "I warned you not to seek knowledge of me beyond what I've shown you!"

On some level, it touched her that he could be so upset by her knowledge. She understood that he was protecting her from himself, in his own misguided, terrible way, just as he'd protected her from Tylik.

"You are not as evil as you believe yourself to be," she said now in kindness. "You—"

His curt gesture cut her off. "You were not to know," he said as though to himself. "You were not to know! Everything can now be linked to—"

"As soon as we've broken camp, we'll ride away. You can lose the cavalrymen in these hills. Don't, please don't do this. Let them go. You don't have to kill them."

"My name is death," Commander Shadrael said, staring into the distance. "My mouth holds a killing breath. My eye is blight, as fierce as Mael's. I was born to destroy, trained to—"

"Mael is destroyed. Beloth is destroyed," she said urgently. "Their reign is broken, and the world is free to grow

and rebuild. You're free, too. Don't you see? You need not
serve them anymore."

His gaze snapped to hers. "Don't bleat your assurances
to me. I was a doomed man long before Light Bringer
came to break the world. As for liberty, there is no such
thing. I am chained to stone for all time, and one day the
demons will feed on my entrails."

So bitterly did he speak, so raw and exposed was his
inner anguish that she faltered. She did not know how to
comfort him, did not know how to make him believe or
hope.

He stepped closer to her magical cage. "You understand
nothing, Lea. Nothing! The Crimsons are using magic to
track you. Shadow magic, the kind your brother has forbidden."

"No," she whispered, shocked anew. "I don't believe
you."

"That's because you think the world spins all new and
fresh, balanced on the triad of harmony. You forget that as
long as men crawl in the mud and breathe the wind they
will know hatred and enmity. Resentment dies hard, little
girl. Betrayal and guilt and evil do not fade away just because you wish it. Your friends use forbidden magic in *your*
cause. They have broken your pretender brother's express
law, to save *you*. Who is to blame for their treason, if not
you?"

"But—"

"Because of *you*, they will die."

Tears slipped down her cheeks before she could brush
them away. "I have not asked this of them. I haven't!"

"Haven't you?" He walked over to Tylik's corpse, heedless of the blood he stepped in, and nudged it with his toe
before glancing back at her. "Are you not divinely beautiful? Divinely attractive? Your face is reason enough for any
man to sacrifice his last breath. You don't have to ask with
words, Lea. Your very existence calls out the question, and
we all answer it, fools and puppets that we are."

Stabbed by his comments, she forced herself to meet his

eyes, so bright with scorn. She did not know how to answer him. The brittleness of his voice warned her to stay silent.

He went on glaring, his face pinched and white. The hem of his cloak was wicking up a dead man's blood. His armor looked like night in the blazing corona of late afternoon sun. He started to say something else, but her lacerated heart cried out in defense.

As though he heard that silent cry, he mercifully closed his mouth instead, his lips compressing tight. Abruptly turning on his heel, he walked away from her without looking back.

Chapter 18

Riding along a rocky trail too narrow at times for two horses abreast, Hervan felt perspiration trickling down his scalp beneath his helmet. His shoulder no longer ached unless his horse did something to jolt it hard, but he'd grown gaunt and tough from these days of pursuit, driving himself beyond the limits he once thought he had. This was terrible country, all low hills and little canyons. The ground was mostly gravel and stone, the undergrowth stunted shrubs full of thorns that scratched his boots and the horses' legs.

He found it impossible to see far enough ahead in such broken terrain to shake the sense that they were being watched and perhaps about to be attacked. And although he was crowding his scouts, riding almost at their heels instead of waiting, he no longer cared about the risks he ran.

A sort of dogged obsession had gripped him, fed by misery and physical hardship. The fact that the mercenaries had so far not been able to elude him kept him going. Every night and dawn he checked the opal against his map, and he felt certain now that he knew where Lea was being taken. By his estimate, they were less than ten leagues from Kanidalon, where the Ninth Legion was stationed. Help was within reach, yet he stubbornly refused to seek it.

"Sir!"

One of his scouts—bearded, ragged, filthy—jumped into the path of Hervan's horse, startling the animal so much it reared up. Hervan curbed it at once, but the jolt to his healing shoulder was painful.

Swearing, he sawed at the reins enough to back his mount away from the man and issued orders for the squadron to halt.

"Gods, are you mad?" he asked, glaring down at the scout. Only then did he notice that the man had blood running down the side of his face and looked more disheveled than usual. Throttling his temper, Hervan asked, "What's happened? What is it?"

"Captain," the scout said, out of breath. "They must be close by. Their scouts . . . we've been seen."

Rozer squeezed his horse up beside Hervan's and tossed the scout a water skin. Hervan fidgeted impatiently while the man drank.

"Report," he commanded.

"Well, sir. We were looking at some old tracks, trying to make sense of them, when these men came up from behind us. Moving fast. Blundered right into us. We did our best to fight, but one got away." The scout paused to rub the back of his wrist across his lips and handed back the water skin.

Hervan asked, "Are you sure they're with the men we're looking for?"

"Had army tattoos," the scout said. "The pair of 'em carried no water, no food on their belts. They're camped somewhere close, no doubt of it."

"Damn," Hervan mumbled. "They'll run like—"

"Unless they set up a trap for us," Rozer said.

At Hervan's nod, Rozer pulled out the map. The pale doeskin had grown grubby from much handling, but the bright inks glowed richly in the afternoon sunlight. Hervan held the opal over the map, and where it started to glow, Rozer scraped a small X with the point of his dagger.

"We're a hard day's ride, maybe two, from the Ulinian border," Rozer said.

A gruff voice cleared its throat behind them. Hervan looked over his shoulder to see Thirbe coming up, grizzled and gaunt, his face as seamed as old leather.

"What's all this?" the protector demanded. "News? We in Ulinia yet?"

"Not according to the map."

"The map," Thirbe said with scorn. He spat. "Feels like Ulinia. Looks like Ulinia. Going to stumble over a baron's boundary mark any time now." He scowled past Hervan at the scout. "You found anything?"

"They've spotted us, sir."

Thirbe's expression turned grim, and his eyes narrowed. "Have they, now? So they're waiting for us to catch up, are they? This country is built for ambush. The worst terrain in the empire."

"We're going to trick them first," Hervan said.

Rozer's expression grew eager and keen. Rolling up the map, he backed away, making room for Thirbe to come closer.

The protector never took his gray eyes off Hervan. "You got something in mind, son, spit it out."

Hervan turned to the scout. "Get out there and find their camp. Don't let them see you this time, understand?"

"Yes, sir."

Rozer lobbed his water skin back to the scout, who caught it with a grateful grin and melted into the undergrowth as though he'd never been there.

"I'll bet you a ducat he's not going to the warlord," Rozer said to Hervan, "but to that Vindicant hideout no one can find."

Hervan frowned at him. "You have no evidence that the Vindicants are in Ulinia, only hearsay."

"Be a coup for us if we found it, though."

"The lady comes first!" Thirbe said sharply.

Hervan and Rozer exchanged looks, and Hervan didn't bother to hide his exasperation. "Obviously," he said.

"Which is why we have to attack them *before* they go over the border."

"Or is it that you'll have to report to the Ninth?" Thirbe asked harshly.

Hervan stared at him, feeling the heat of his skepticism, not wanting to answer.

"Aye," Thirbe said. "That legion commander has jurisdiction, and his authority will supersede yours."

"It's not about who gets the glory of saving her," Hervan said quickly. "But prying her loose from Lord Vordachai will require a siege."

"And I still put my money on the Vindicants," Rozer said.

Hervan glared at him. "Will you forget the Gault-forsaken priests? If we are following Lord Shadrael, we mustn't forget that he's related to the warlord. His brother, in fact. His loyalty will be there."

Rozer gave Thirbe a nudge with his elbow. "Would you please remind the captain that the army doesn't permit family ties? Any mercenary worth his sword will work for the highest bidder. I say the priests."

"Ex-priests," Hervan snarled. "They haven't money anymore. Besides, he's—"

"Hold! The pair of you!" Thirbe broke in. "I've listened to this brangling long enough. Act like officers, damn you, and remember what we're here for."

Anger swept through Hervan, but he managed to curb what he really wanted to say. "No one's forgotten anything."

Thirbe grunted. "You been following someone who may just be one of the best strategists in the army for how many days now, and you ain't figured out that he's never going to do the obvious? He's got some devious plan up his sleeve, bound to, leading us around these hills, and if we don't look sharp we're going to lose him."

Hervan glanced at Rozer. "Get the priest."

As the lieutenant backed his horse away, Hervan drew a deep breath and turned to Thirbe. "Haven't you wondered how I've been tracking these blackguards so closely? Even when they've left a cold trail?"

"Got my opinions about it."

"You're so sure the man ahead of us is going to ambush us. Only I'm going to surprise him first." He showed Thirbe the opal. "This is our guide. Lady Fyngie showed me how to use its powers."

"Have you taken sunstroke?" Thirbe asked. "I ain't gut-snapped enough to believe that. The lady's dead, and that's just a stone."

"No, no, and no," Hervan said, enjoying seeing the protector flustered. "Lady Fyngie's ghost haunts my dreams nightly, making sure I'm going to avenge her. And . . . the others, of course."

"Maybe you'd better rest a bit," Thirbe said. "Or go easy on the mead."

Despite himself, Hervan grew hot under his cheekbones. Thirbe's sarcasm was like a thorn prick, always painful. No matter how much he steeled himself, Hervan was never quite prepared for it.

"Look at the opal, damn you! It was given to Lady Lea by a water spirit just before she was taken."

"Aye, I remember that. And I remember her putting it back." Thirbe scowled. "How come you by it?"

"Never mind," Hervan said. "Just know that it is our talisman and our guide to her. Do you want to see it glow?"

Thirbe's horse suddenly flung up its head as though he'd tightened the reins. "There'll be none of that," he said sharply. "Talking to ghosts and calling up spirits. You're no—is the priest in league with you?"

Hervan laughed. "No. But you're in league with me, predlicate."

"I ain't a predlicate now," Thirbe began, then clamped his mouth shut and glared at Hervan with suspicious, angry eyes. "So that's it. You've found a way in? You want to get ahead of them?"

"Exactly," Hervan said. "Use the Hidden Ways to jump ahead of our quarry and give those devils the surprise of their lives."

But Thirbe was already shaking his gray head. "That'll put the lady right in the heart of battle. No good."

"Stop thinking like a protector, damn you, and remember your predlicate training!"

"Does no good to track the lady all this way if you're going to see her caught on someone's sword."

Hervan's temper flared hot and violent inside him, but he curbed it, clamping his jaw so hard he could feel his teeth grinding together. "Then, once we're through, it will be your job to protect her."

"Still risky. He could slit her throat the moment we appear."

"Are you going to throw this opportunity away?" Hervan asked. "Just refuse to help her now that we're—"

"Could have done this any number of times," Thirbe broke in. "Why now? Why today?"

"We've been through all that. I must rescue her before we cross the border."

"Who's going to know?"

"Stop acting stupid. We've been seen by his scouts. We've got to act now before he turns on us, or flees."

Thirbe glanced behind him. "Priest's coming. He said before he couldn't do it. Think you can change his mind for him this time? Or is this ghost that's haunting you going to do it for us?"

"That's enough," Hervan said, his voice low and mean.

They locked eyes, and Thirbe seemed to see the fury that Hervan could barely control. His weathered face went bland.

"Maybe it is," he said mildly. "You really believe the priest can do it?"

"A former Vindicant priest has to know how." Hervan set his jaw. "I'll force him to do it this time, Protector, but I need to know you're with me all the way."

"Listen, running through the Hidden Ways ain't as easy as you seem to think it is," Thirbe began. "If you don't—"

Hervan frowned. "You can't be afraid to go in there!"

"You ain't never gone through. Ain't never come face-to-face with shadow."

"Gods, man, what does that matter? The shadows are gone. The Hidden Ways hold nothing to harm us now. Don't try to frighten us with old stories about lurking demons and the breath of Beloth."

"This ain't a stroll through a garden," Thirbe said, his voice sharp. "There's danger yet, and you got no experience."

Somehow Hervan held on to his temper. "That's why I'm asking—no, telling—you to guide us through. Leave the rest to me. Here's Poulso."

He swung away from Thirbe to smile broadly at the priest. Poulso had lost weight, making his jowls sag. His ugly wart had grown even more prominent and unsightly. A terrible rider, he'd suffered miserably on this hard journey, but so had Hervan with a broken collarbone. The captain wasted no pity on him.

"We've come to a crisis, priest, and need your help."

Poulso looked eager. "I will be glad to say prayers for the men—"

"Not that," Hervan broke in. "We've little time if we're to save Lady Lea. Open the Hidden Ways for us now, and be quick about it."

"What?" Poulso's prominent eyes bugged farther. "What are you saying, Captain?"

"You heard me."

The priest looked swiftly from Hervan to Rozer to Thirbe. "But—but I can't! I thought I'd made that clear."

"You did," Thirbe said grimly.

"Then—"

"We're no longer asking," Hervan said. "We're telling you. We have one chance to save her, and we're taking it right now."

"But—but this is impossible. Quite impossible! It's forbidden."

Swift as thought, Rozer put his dagger to the priest's throat.

Poulso's face drained of color. He sat frozen in his saddle,

his mouth open and gasping for air. "Light of Gault, pre-
serve me from—"

"Shut up!" Rozer said while a thin trickle of blood ran
down Poulso's throat. "None of that. Do as the captain has
ordered you."

"No, no! I won't!"

"You haven't a choice," Rozer said.

Poulso rolled his eyes toward Hervan. "Do you know
what you're asking? To enter shadow, to partake of evil
willingly? Do you realize what it will cost you?"

"If you refuse us now, then you condemn Lady Lea to
death," Hervan said, uttering the lie with such conviction
he saw a flicker of uncertainty in Poulso's brown eyes.

Hervan gave Rozer a nod, and Rozer took his dagger
away from the priest's throat.

Poulso lifted his hands to the cut and shut his eyes. He
started trembling. "Merciful Gault, guide me now," he whispered.

"Don't you care about her?" Hervan asked. "Can you
live with the guilt of having failed her when she needed
you most? Look at me, damn you, and stop sniveling your
prayers! It's got to be done."

The priest's eyes looked wet and terrified. "You would
do this? Unswear yourselves, jeopardize your souls?"

Hervan lifted his hand. "For the lady, I will do it gladly."

"And I," Rozer said.

Poulso's gaze shifted to Thirbe. The protector hesitated
long enough to make Hervan's stomach clench before he
gave the priest a straightforward look.

"These are hard times, priest. I can't let her go to the
clutches of Vindicants and worse. Can you?"

"Vindicants," Poulso whispered. "I thought mercenaries
had—"

"Who do you think has hired these scoundrels?" Hervan
asked.

"But I have renounced my oaths. I have sworn anew."
Poulso clasped his thick hands together. "Gault will not
forgive me for this. I am afraid, afraid!"

Hervan exchanged a glance with Rozer. "Then you're going to die here and now, for condemning Lady Lea to torture and agony in the hands of evil men. Gault may forgive you for remaining loyal at her expense, but on my honor, *I* will not."

Rozer lifted his dagger, and the priest cried out, twisting as though to fend off the blow.

"All right! All right!" he gasped out. Tears ran down his cheeks. "I'll do it. But who will guide you? I can't do that. I—I—"

"That's for me to take on," Thirbe said, his voice quiet and steady. "You're doing what's right. Think of the lady's sweet good nature. She's worth all we can give her."

"Yes," Poulso whispered. He wiped his face with the back of his hand. "Yes. She walks in harmony. What is my honor, in exchange for her safety?" He sat a moment, staring at nothing, before pressing his fingers to his lips. "We shall need fresh blood for the cups. Those of your men, Captain, who have never gone through the Hidden Ways must be prepared."

Hervan frowned impatiently. "There's no time for that."

"Better do as he advises," Thirbe said. "This ain't—"

"I tell you there's no time!" Hervan struck the pommel of his saddle with his fist. "Gods, must the pair of you raise objections to everything? Let's get it done before we lose what scant advantage we have!"

Poulso gave him one last glance, his eyes like a whipped dog's, before moving his horse forward, a little apart from the others. He took off his Reformant ring, started to kiss it, but then did not. As he tucked it away, his face held shame and despair. Bowing his head, he spread out his arms and began to mumble a chant that sent an uneasy prickle through Hervan.

The horses nickered nervously and shifted about.

"By Gault," Rozer said in excitement, his eyes alight, "we're finally going to do this!"

"Hush," Hervan cautioned him, although his heart was thudding fast. "Tell Taime to pass the word among the men. When we come through, we must be ready to attack immediately."

Rozer nodded but Thirbe caught his sleeve before he could turn his horse. "Tell them they must unswear their oaths to Gault," he said in warning. "They cannot enter in a state of Light."

"Done."

Rozer rode off, and Thirbe turned back to Hervan. His weathered face looked grim indeed, while Hervan was drawing in deep breaths, feeling a swell of anticipation.

"I'll need that stone of yours, that opal," Thirbe said. "And your map."

Suspicious, Hervan drew back. "Why?"

"Not to keep, noddy! I have to have some clear idea of where I'm leading us."

Hervan hesitated, finding himself reluctant to entrust Thirbe with either.

"Come on. Be quick about it, or he'll have the Ways open before we're ready." Thirbe glared at Hervan. "I ain't going in if I don't know where I'm coming out."

Hervan nodded and produced his doeskin map one-handedly, but he did not give Thirbe the opal. "We've marked the spot," he said.

"I see it," Thirbe muttered, peering at the markings. "Thank Gault it'll be a short passage. I don't want anyone panicking and bolting off once we're inside. There's no coming back from that, you hear? And no hope of searching for the lost ones later."

"I understand," Hervan said, tired of his warnings. "We're not green recruits, old man. We do know what we're doing."

Thirbe grunted, squinting at him as he handed the map back. "Some of your veterans will do fine. As for you, I think you'd better stay behind, or at least ride up this trail with part of the men to cut off their line of retreat."

"What?" Furious, Hervan stuffed the map back into his pocket. "I've told you before that I'll never surrender command to you—"

"Hold that temper! Give the command to the lieutenant if you don't trust me. I don't care, only you can't fight like you are and—"

"I won't be left behind! I can't believe you expect it of me, not now, when we're so close."

Thirbe cocked his head to one side. "Is it the lady's well-being you want, or glory in battle for yourself?"

Hervan bit back his retort. A roar of shame went through his ears, and he couldn't meet the protector's gray eyes.

"Thought so," Thirbe said.

At that moment Hervan had never hated anyone as much as he hated this old man.

"Going to order me left behind now?" Thirbe asked, mocking him softly. "Going to let that fine temper get the better of your good sense? You know we need a contingency to cut them off, someone to hold this trail if I should miss with the Hidden Ways."

Hervan's head lifted. "I know nothing of the kind. We'll surprise them, turn their own tricks against them, and catch them flat-footed. And I'm going through, no matter what you say."

Exasperation flashed across Thirbe's face. "Then unswear your soul, boy, because the Ways are opening *now*."

Chapter 19

In the palace, Caelan had for once shaken off his duties and was sitting at his ease with Elandra. Musicians were playing softly in the adjoining antechamber, but he and his wife were alone, discussing the festival that had taken place earlier that afternoon.

He was reaching for a scroll Elandra was handing to him when he felt a strange, unsettled sensation pass through him. Frowning, he let the scroll drop while the room went dim around him.

"Caelan," whispered Lea's voice. It reached his ears so softly he thought at first he was imagining it. *"Caelan."*

Forgetting Elandra, oblivious of where he was, Caelan rose to his feet. All his senses were alert. "Lea?"

"Caelan, help me!"

Alarmed, he *severed* and stepped *between*, finding himself in a pale, mist-shrouded place. He thought there might be trees behind him, but he could not truly see them. Before him rippled a stream of water, so faint and misty he could barely make it out. On the opposite bank stood Lea. Her clothing and hair shone with pale radiance.

Delighted to see her, aware that she was very far away, he started to call out, but she was stretching forth her hands in a gesture of warning.

"Caelan," she called so faintly he had to strain to hear, *"I have been taken hostage."*

"Who?" he demanded. "Who's done this?"

It was as though she couldn't hear him. Her message came again: *"I have been taken hostage. I am held prisoner. I need your help!"*

"Lea!" he said sharply. "Where are you? Who has you?"

She wavered and almost faded from sight. His heart nearly stopped, and he took a step forward, although it brought him no closer. "Lea—"

"Caelan, help me! I am held by Commander . . ."

Her voice grew inaudible. He couldn't hear her at all. "Who? Lea, tell me again."

". . . a trap for . . . going to massacre the entire . . . beware, dear brother. Don't believe what they . . . I can't escape him. The shadow magic . . . strong . . . taken my necklace. Help me!"

Then she was gone. Frantic, Caelan called her name twice more, but there was no response.

Releasing himself from *severance*, he came back from *between* and found himself on his knees in Elandra's sitting room. His head was bowed, and he was breathing hard as though he'd been running. A cold sweat chilled him beneath his clothes.

Elandra was kneeling beside him, holding a cup in one hand, her fingers digging into his shoulder. "Caelan?" she asked anxiously. "Caelan, beloved? Can you hear me? Can you tell me what afflicts you?"

Expelling his breath, he brought up his hands to rub his face. "I'm well. I'm not ill."

"You nearly swooned. Are you still dizzy? Drink this."

Pushing the cup away impatiently, he got to his feet. On some level he was aware of Elandra's anxiety, but he had no time to reassure her. Lea needed his help, and immediately. But how was he to reach her? Where *was* she? If she

could not slip across *between* and elude her captors, she
must be in terrible jeopardy.

"Caelan!" Elandra said sharply, breaking through his
frantic thoughts. "Speak to me! Tell me what is happening!"

He swung around and gave his wife a blank stare, finally
noticing her pallor and the worry in her eyes. Contrite, he
gripped her hands. "I'm sorry," he said. "It's Lea. She's in
trouble."

"What kind of trouble? What's befallen her?"

Caelan beckoned to his protector, who crossed the room
to him at once. But before issuing orders to the man, Caelan turned to Rumasin, on duty as usual. "I need armed
men, my horse, weapons," he said to the eunuch who ran
Elandra's household. "Summon the Imperial Guards and
tell them so."

"Yes, Excellency." A swift flick of the eunuch's finger,
and a servant hastened out the door.

Another servant brought Caelan his boots, while a third
took the elaborate overrobe he was flinging off.

Elandra hovered over him. "Can you tell me nothing
more? Please!"

"She's been captured, abducted, held hostage. I don't
know by whom. I don't know where she is. She said it's a
trap, and that she's in danger and cannot escape." He raised
troubled eyes to Elandra's. "They've taken her emeralds."

"Her necklace?"

"Yes. Which leaves her vulnerable." He stared down at
his weaponless belt with exasperation. "Where's my lackey?
I'll need a cloak and provisions. Better—"

"Dear one." Elandra dared interrupt him. "Where are
you going with your horse and men?"

He shrugged a trifle ruefully. "I don't know that either.
I must take action."

"Of course. But sensible action."

He frowned, standing there with fists clenched, muscles
rigid with the need to *go*. And he knew Elandra was right.
A terrible weight began to press on his heart. Feeling
damnably helpless, he swallowed hard.

Elandra gripped his sleeve. "I beg you to take care," she said. "Are you certain it really was Lea and not some trickery put into your mind?"

"I don't know. I don't know!" He struggled to master his emotions and think. "The voice was right. She looked right. But . . ."

"Yes?"

Doubt trickled through him. "How could she reach me at all without her necklace?"

"Didn't she call out to you like this when you were children, and separated?"

Grimly he shook his head. "She had her emeralds then, but she hadn't been taught how to use them."

"So you don't think she could reach you without the *gli*-stones enhancing her natural powers?"

"Perhaps." He shrugged. "If this message *is* a trick, why mention her necklace at all?"

"True." Fresh worry puckered Elandra's face, and she turned away.

He knew that tense line of his wife's back very well. Elandra seldom admitted her concerns; she tended to hold them inside and let them gnaw at her. He pulled her close against him in comfort. "I had no sense of a lie," he murmured. "I believe it was really Lea. Yet something was wrong. I can't put my finger on it, but it wasn't quite like the Lea I know."

"Do you think she was afraid? Did you sense fear in her?"

"Not that. More . . ." Sighing, he gave up. "I can't explain it."

"And what if it *wasn't* Lea at all?"

Anger swept him. "Am I supposed to ignore her call for help? Pretend it could not possibly be her? What if it is? What if she needs me desperately right now, as she said? Why do I stand here discussing it, when I need to go to her?"

"Caelan, hear me," Elandra said. "If you jumped on the fastest horse in your stables you could not reach her for days, possibly weeks. A dragon—even if you consented to

ride one—could not fly you there fast enough. You don't
know where to begin your search. Be calm, beloved. *Think*
this through. This is no time for you to be gone from the
palace."

"Don't you think I know that?"

She flushed. "I'm sorry. I don't mean to sound heart-
less. If she can guide you to her, then I shall hand you your
sword and wish you a speedy journey. Until then . . ."

A muscle was twitching in his clenched jaw. He nodded
agreement, knowing Elandra was giving him sensible advice. He hated being helpless like this, but Elandra was
right.

After a moment, he said grimly, "She told me a commander had taken her."

Elandra drew in her breath audibly. "Which one?"

He shook his head.

"The army again!" Elandra said. "An officer!" She
turned suddenly pale. "Do you think it's Captain Hervan?"

"No, she said commander, quite clearly. That's an army
rank, not cavalry."

"Yes, of course. Do you suppose this plot is part of the
latest legion mutiny? Or someone discharged in the reforms, trying to take revenge against you?"

Too frustrated to speculate, Caelan spread wide his
hands.

"You need answers. Until you have them—"

"I must wait," he said. "Damn and damn and damn."

Commotion sounded outside, and a centruin of the Imperial Guards rushed inside. He saluted the emperor and
empress smartly.

"Centruin Lucrux, Excellency. Yours to command!"

"Thank you, Centruin. I've received a message from my
sister, saying she's in danger and taken captive."

Shock paled the centruin's face. "Sir!"

"I do not know as yet if it's a true message or false,"
Caelan said. He wondered now if the prior feelings of uneasiness he'd experienced had also been Lea's attempts to
reach him. Yet what good did frantic speculation do? He

reminded himself to not let his boiling emotions cloud his judgment.

Studying the centruin's young face, he found no guile there. "Has any report of trouble come in her escort's dispatches? No matter how trivial or insignificant. Any indication of something gone awry?"

"Their weekly report is now two days overdue, Excellency."

It was like being hit with a war hammer. Caelan took an involuntary step forward. "Why wasn't I informed?"

"The reports have been delayed before, Excellency. Hazards of travel, and so forth." The centruin's gaze wavered briefly. "It's procedure to take no action unless a report is delayed by a week at—"

"A *week*!" This time, Caelan could not restrain his outburst. "She could be in the hands of Gault knows what kind of scoundrels, and we are to wait a *week* before we grow concerned? Who issued such a stupid order?"

The centruin looked like he'd been carved of wood. "Official procedure, Excellency."

Quelling the urge to strike him, Caelan began pacing back and forth. Several moments passed before he trusted himself to speak. "What did the last message say?"

When the centruin hesitated, Caelan spun around to glare at him. "Well?"

"I cannot tell you, Excellency. I—I am not privy to Captain Hervan's reports."

"Get them!" Caelan roared.

Saluting, the man fled.

Caelan resumed pacing, fuming with every step. His suspicions were on fire. "It's a plot," he muttered. "Not road bandits at work. Has to be a plot. The palace in league with—"

"Perhaps," Elandra broke in. "Let us assess this cautiously, and not mistake inefficiency for treason."

"Inefficiency!" He felt like he was choking. "If she's—"

"Caelan, you must stay calm. You are not thinking, dearest. You are far too upset. I know this is hard, very hard. I love her, too, but a web is growing around us, and we must take care."

Troubled, he blew out his breath and nodded. "Vindicants at work?" he asked. "Hiring mercenaries to abduct her, perhaps?"

"Led by a disaffected officer swept out of the army by the reforms?" Elandra said thoughtfully. "Perhaps. Such a large convergence of woes is coming at us too quickly to be accidental."

"Agreed. The Vindicant brotherhood reached deep into the army. Its influence isn't going to be easily erased."

Elandra hesitated. "If it *is* Vindicants who hold her hostage, they will ask you an awful price for her ransom."

Caelan sighed. He needed no such warning from Elandra to see the implications Lea's abduction would have. His sister was as precious to him as his wife and Jarel, and who in the empire did not know this? Who in the empire, who among his numerous enemies and detractors hated and resented him more than the priesthood he'd abolished along with the shadow god?

If the Vindicants haven't abducted her, they will take her from the one who has, he thought. *They will hurt her, as they long to hurt me.*

The thought of Lea being mistreated almost unmanned him. He knew she would be used as leverage to bring him down, and he did not know how he would be able to withstand their terms.

Too late now to tell himself he shouldn't have sent her to Trau as his representative in the upcoming *holdenthal,* a festival where, by Trau tradition, the hold masters gathered to forge trade and property agreements with each other and renew fealty to their emperor. Their loyalty oaths had of course been sworn at his coronation, according to imperial law. But the *holdenthal* was an old custom, as old as the ancient kings of Trau.

When the invitation came, he'd listened to his council's wishes that he not attend in person lest he be seen conferring too much favoritism on his home province. Lea had begged so prettily to go as his representative, and at the time it had seemed like a harmless expedition. Lea was homesick, although she didn't complain, and he'd enjoyed seeing her so excited and full of anticipation.

Against his better judgment he'd sent her back to that cold, forbidding land of their birth, but how could he have refused her? Had he not sworn to himself that he would grant her anything she wanted for the rest of her life? Even that would never make up for those years of separation, of not knowing what had befallen her, of thinking her dead and torn to pieces in the forest by wolves.

Guilt slammed against his conscience. He told himself now that he should have protected her better, should have sent an entire army cohort to safeguard her journey, no matter what she said. Left to her own devices, Lea probably would have set forth with her protector and a cheap cloak as a disguise—unaware that no artifice could mask her beauty or inner radiance. She hadn't wanted the army with her, and so Caelan had chosen a squadron of cavalry instead, seeking officers slightly more refined, less violent and battle-worn than army professionals.

You fool, Caelan thought harshly, condemning himself. *You have put her in jeopardy a second time, as bad as when you abandoned her to perish in the ice caves.* He wished with all his heart that he'd refused to let her leave the palace gates.

"Beloved." Elandra touched his hand. "If you really do think this trouble comes from a Vindicant plot, shall I send for the Penestricans? We'll need every ally we've got."

Fighting back the stinging in his eyes, Caelan nodded. "Yes. I think you'd better."

Chapter 20

Intent on setting up his ambush, Shadrael had chosen a location where the trail narrowed through a slender gulch. Standing atop a rock, he was busy deploying his men. Pointing them here and there along the top of the gulch, he watched critically while they took cover in the thorny scrub. Satisfied, he was about to take his position when he felt a shift between the spirit world and reality.

Startled, he broke off in midword to Fomo and spun around. As always, his reactions were faster than those of his men. Fomo was still frozen, gaping at him, while Shadrael saw the air ripple and shred apart.

He drew his sword. "The Hidden Ways are opening. Men! To me!"

Fomo squawked a hoarse cry of his own, cracking his whip in warning.

Already horses and riders in the short red cloaks and plumed helmets of the Crimsons were pouring out of the darkness. As their bugler sounded a battle charge, they galloped through the trees straight at Shadrael.

The narrow gulch was behind him, cutting off retreat.

On his right, the ground dropped off steeply. The only maneuvering room lay to his left, but he had no chance to reach his mount, no time to do anything other than tear off his cloak and brace his feet. His helmet was strapped to his saddle, out of reach, along with his war axe. All he had to hand were his sword, long dagger, boot knives, and throwing stars.

Beside him, Fomo drew his sword, cursing fiercely. "How'd they—"

Too late for chatter; the charge was upon them. Shadrael stood his ground coolly, aware of his men pouring down the hillside behind him in great, stumbling leaps, just that much too slow and too far away to meet the first onslaught. To his credit, Fomo stood shoulder to shoulder with Shadrael, and did not run for his life.

At the last moment, just before a shouting cavalryman plunged his sword through Shadrael's chest, he *severed* and twisted aside just enough to avoid being run down. As the rider swept past him, Shadrael snapped his threads of life and saw the man go tumbling from the saddle. Quick as thought, Shadrael snapped the threads of life of three other men before the rest veered off, milling in the confined space. By then, Shadrael's men had joined the fight in a screaming melee of clashing swords. They were all too tangled together now for him to cut any more threads of life without risking the lives of his men.

He came out of *severance*, staggering slightly to keep his balance, and saw Fomo deflect a cavalryman coming at him. Fomo's blow was clumsy and desperate, serving its immediate purpose but failing to bring down his foe.

Shadrael spun as the big horse passed him, and ruthlessly cut a tendon in the horse's leg. With a scream, the horse stumbled and went down, flinging off its rider in a crashing fall. Skipping around the kicking, struggling horse, Shadrael pounced on the fallen rider and drove his long dagger through the man's throat.

Freeing his weapon, he whirled to meet another opponent bearing down on him, and from the corner of his eye saw a Crimson in officer's braid sitting apart from the action. The officer was wounded, with one arm bound awkwardly in a sling. Clearly he was unable to fight, and Shadrael's eyes narrowed with calculation.

Then Shadrael was fending off attack, ignoring his disadvantage in fighting horsemen from the ground. He parried a blow, the blade of his shorter, heavier sword scraping against the serrated edge of a cavalry weapon, and drove his dagger into his foe's leg.

A hot spurt of blood nearly hit Shadrael in the face. He slashed the girth of the man's saddle and shoved hard, dumping his opponent onto the ground while the startled horse bolted out of the way.

Flailing for balance, desperately trying to raise his weapon, the cavalryman had no time to hold off Shadrael, who was already on him, cutting a great gash through the man's shoulder and nearly taking off his arm.

Something hit Shadrael hard in the back, almost driving him to his knees. Catching his balance, Shadrael jumped aside. This new opponent was on foot. Reaching behind him, Shadrael grabbed a helmet plume and dragged his attacker forward as he spun around. The move pulled the man onto his dagger with a shock of impact that numbed Shadrael's hand. The tempered black steel of his blade pierced the other's cuirass, and Shadrael yanked up hard to drive his dagger even deeper.

Blood bubbled from the cavalryman's mouth. He stared at Shadrael in astonishment, trying to speak, and crumpled.

Climbing over him, Shadrael saw Fomo cornered, outnumbered, and in trouble. Shadrael flung a throwing star into the back of one of Fomo's opponents, then found himself face-to-face with a large, thick-chested cavalryman wearing lieutenant insignia. On foot and brandishing his longer sword with a ferocious grin, the lieutenant gave Shadrael a quick, mocking salute.

Panting a little, Shadrael balanced on the balls of his feet and drew his dagger again, holding it loose and ready in his left hand to balance the sword in his right. He did not bother to return the salute, knowing his foe was trying to distract him by any means possible.

"Come on!" the lieutenant shouted.

Their swords clashed hard, ringing out over the noise, and for a few moments they fought well matched. There was a dancing light in this Crimson's eyes, a reckless laugh in his throat. He fought dirty, like a seasoned veteran, and he was quick for his size.

The rapid exchange of blows tired Shadrael. He could find no chance to use his dagger, and his shorter sword made it difficult to take the advantage that he wanted. Still, a cavalryman on foot was but half a fighter, and no match for regular army.

Yelling, Shadrael feinted right, then left, saw his opponent prepared for such an easy trick, and dropped to his knees, skidding under the lieutenant's sword so close he felt its blade lightly graze his brow. The Crimson jumped to one side, evading Shadrael's quick dagger slash at his legs, and swung his sword with two hands at Shadrael's unprotected head. Shadrael ducked just in time, caught the sword with his own, and tried to flip it out of his opponent's hand, but without success.

"Ha-ha!" the man yelled. "Come on!"

Blood was already running in Shadrael's right eye from the cut he'd taken. He squinted, making adjustments for its effect on his vision, and lunged again from his knees, slashing hard to hamstring the lieutenant.

The tip of his long dagger caught target, while he took a hard blow to his shoulder in return and heard the scrape of steel across his armor. The double shoulder plating held, however, saving Shadrael from losing his arm. He saw, to his irritation, that he'd slashed boot leather only, not tendons.

Shouting, the lieutenant kicked at him, stumbling back in an effort to get out of reach. Shadrael wrapped his arms around the man's legs and brought him down. Locked together, they rolled over and over in the dust and confusion. Something kicked Shadrael in the back, but he paid no heed as he tightened his hug on the Crimson's legs and jerked his shoulder to drive its spike deep into the back of the man's thigh.

The lieutenant howled with pain and struggled harder. Shadrael twisted the spike deeper, then yanked backward, using the spike to hamstring the man. Flailing and kicking, screaming oaths, the lieutenant struggled away from him, but could not gain his feet. Shadrael loomed up over him, plunging his sword into the man's groin.

A great gout of blood gushed forth, and shock quivered through the lieutenant's face. "Hervan!" he shouted. "I'm done!"

The sound of galloping hoofbeats made Shadrael whirl, bracing to meet a mounted charge, but the officer in the sling rode past him without engaging.

Surprised, Shadrael stared past the struggling bodies and flash of weapons, but caught only a glimpse of scarlet cloth in the trees as the man rode away.

Coward? Shadrael thought, fending off someone who blundered into him. No. The officer was riding off in the direction of the mercenary camp, riding toward Lea.

A murderous fury swept through Shadrael, and for a moment he knew nothing but a frantic urgency to go after the man.

"Here's death from Rozer," snarled a hoarse voice.

A blow struck him in the side, making him stagger. Shadrael turned, realizing too late that he hadn't finished the lieutenant after all.

Grimacing in triumph, the dying officer sank down. Clutching his wound, unable to stanch the flow, Rozer slowly let the hilt of his weapon fall from slack fingers. He tipped back his head to stare up at Shadrael while a look of puzzlement filled his eyes. "I—I'm unsworn," he said in a voice of wonder, and died.

Pain began to shoot through Shadrael's side, but he *severed* it, disregarding the injury as unimportant, and fought his way through the shifting crowd of men to the nearest riderless horse.

He caught its dangling reins and jumped into the saddle. For a moment he felt oddly breathless as though he might pass out, but *severance* held. Shouting at Fomo, who brandished his sword in acknowledgment, Shadrael galloped after the officer in the sling.

Only now, as he ducked low to avoid the sweeping slap of tree branches, did Shadrael allow himself to think. How had the Crimsons found them? How had they opened—and *used*—the Hidden Ways? In that, they had completely surprised Shadrael, who hadn't anticipated such a move. Who among them was still practicing shadow magic? Was it this officer, now on his way toward Lea? How did the knave know where to find her?

He's the one using magic, Shadrael thought.

In Shadrael's mind, Vordachai's orders no longer mattered. He'd left survivors the first time, taking his one prisoner and letting the rest of the squadron go. But this time, he would see them all slain. And no one was going to take Lea from him. No one.

Chapter 21

With the palace looming behind her, Empress Elandra was making an official promenade across the east gardens. She wore a gown of Mahiran cloth, the threads an intricate weaving of spun gold and pale umber silk. Elaborate embroidery on the skirt made it stand out stiffly around her. A delicate spell sewn through the seams of the garment enhanced her beauty in a subtle way, dazzling the onlookers. Her long auburn hair was coiled neatly beneath a headdress studded with pearls and topazes. A necklace of fat yellow pearls strung on chains of gold hung about her neck. In the newest fashion, a hammered gold chatelaine dangled from her waist.

A narrow carpet had been unfurled across the grass to protect her slippers, and diminutive pages carried her train. Her attendants, led by Lady Avitria, followed her at a decorous distance, preening in their best gowns, enjoying the chance to air their finery.

The empress made slow progress, for she took time to speak to various courtiers and their ladies, who were likewise parading along the longest axis of the gardens. The flowers, reviving in the cooler weather brought by recent autumn showers, were blooming profusely in drifts of magenta and yellow. And beyond the intricate fretwork of the fence, thronging crowds pressed close to the bars to gaze at the empress and her fine court. They cheered and called out to her, and now and then Elandra paused with a smile to wave in return.

A Reformant priest escorted her, chatting with her earnestly about acquisitions for the palace library, a place once used as a repository for Kostimon's collection of pornography and odes to Beloth. Lord Nardeth was a learned man with a quick and agile mind, but although she favored his plans Elandra felt too distracted today to pay close heed to them.

She was too worried about Lea. Adding to her concern was the fact that so far the Magria had not responded to her summons. This was so discourteous, so unusual that it alarmed Elandra.

Even if the Magria were too busy to come immediately, it was her custom to send a message explaining the circumstances behind a delay. Instead, there had been only silence. Elandra feared her message had perhaps been intercepted, or tampered with. She was trying to decide whether to send members of the Imperial Guard to make sure all was well with the sisterhood.

"And so you agree to these arrangements, Majesty?" Nardeth asked. "You feel they are suitable?"

Blinking, Elandra realized she'd heard almost nothing he'd said. She bestowed a gracious smile on him. "Most suitable. Everything is as I would wish."

Delight and relief lit his thin face. He bowed deeply to her. "Your Majesty is kind indeed. Thank you. I shall commission purchase of the texts immediately, subject to your final approval, of course."

"Of course," she murmured.

From the corner of her eye she glimpsed a messenger approaching rapidly. More bad news? she wondered. She kept her expression calm, but it was difficult.

"The emperor and I appreciate your hard work," she said to the priest in dismissal.

Respectfully he bowed, retreating just as the messenger strode up.

"Speak," Elandra said to the man.

He swept her a bow. "By your leave, Majesty. A Penestrican is at the gates and says she has your summons."

"Has she been kept waiting outside like an errand girl?" Elandra asked in astonishment. "Does the gatekeeper not understand the Magria is always allowed admittance?"

"It's not the Magria, Majesty."

Perplexed, Elandra held back a frown. A messenger from Anas, she decided in disappointment. Another delay.

Although she knew she should, for the sake of appearances, continue her promenade, Elandra was too impatient. With Lea's welfare at stake, the rules of protocol could wait.

"Order the gatekeeper to admit the Penestrican at once," she commanded. "Have her conducted into the women's pavilion. I shall receive her shortly."

The boy bowed and loped away to do her bidding. Elandra turned to her ladies and announced the end of her promenade, dismissing them to do as they wished for the remainder of the afternoon. While everyone was looking baffled or curious, she twitched her train from the hands of her pages, caught her protector's eye, and left the carpet to make her way across the grass to a stone path leading to one of the canals. Descending the shallow steps leading to the water's edge, she jumped lightly onto one of the large silver disks floating on its surface without waiting for her protector's assistance.

Someone behind her gasped aloud. "She'll be drowned!"

Elandra paid no heed. Keeping her balance, she even managed to avoid wetting the hem of her ample skirts and was intrigued by how the disk supported her weight, bobbing only slightly beneath her.

"To the palace," she commanded.

At once, the disk glided forward, bearing her along on the water's surface without a splash or even a ripple. There was no rush of speed, only a slow, steady motion; just the same, Elandra found it rather exhilarating. This was the first time she'd used a canal disk, although she knew Caelan made a habit of utilizing this newest gift of Choven magic.

Now, as she glided through the gardens toward the palace, standing serene and dignified on this amazing form of transport, she smiled and nodded graciously to the people she passed on the banks. Most of them looked too startled, too dumbfounded to respond, although a few managed to give her obeisance. She promised herself that, when Lea was safe again, and some of the empire's troubles quieted, she would bring little Jarel to the canals and cross the water like this with him. How he would love it.

Reaching the opposite end of the central canal, the disk beneath her feet slowed to a gradual stop and bobbed at the base of the stone steps. She climbed them, sweeping past the astonished pair of palace officials who had been chatting there, and made her way indoors.

Guards were waiting to escort her. Alone, without the rest of her abandoned entourage, she went swiftly to the women's pavilion and settled herself in a rather austere public chamber, instead of her more comfortable and exotic personal sitting room. With Lea in trouble and Caelan nearly beside himself with worry, this was not a time for sipping fruit water and nibbling delicacies.

When the doors opened to admit a young woman in long black robes, Elandra was sitting erect and quietly in a tall-backed chair carved from Mahiran satinwood. Her *jinja* crouched beside her chair, busy fingering the elaborate embroidery on her skirts and chittering softly beneath its breath. Two of her ladies-in-waiting, who had not accompanied her to the garden, stood nearby, their expressions pleasant and without expectation. A chamberlain hovered near the door, and Elandra's protector prowled about before taking a stance behind her chair.

The woman who entered alone wore a stole of black cloth draped over her head, and walked forward with eyes cast down and head slightly bowed. She was short of stature and plump, yet her movement held a hint of seductive grace not usually found among the sisterhood.

As she drew near, Elandra's *jinja* suddenly twitched its pointed ears and jumped upright to stare hard at the priestess. Hissing in fury, it flung its brimless fur cap away and jumped off the dais toward her.

The priestess halted, shrinking back, but at that moment Lady Avitria hurried in by a side door. Her own *jinja*—a small, cowed creature with unhealthy blue coloring and a small dark blue cap—rushed past her to dart into the path of Elandra's *jinja*. Suddenly there was vicious snarling from both creatures, and they swirled into a fight.

"Bronzidaec!" Lady Avitria said. "Bronzidaec, stop at once!"

Gasping, the priestess backed away, pressing a corner of her stole to her face, her enormous eyes peeping over its edge.

Elandra jumped to her feet. "Send for Rumasin!" she said. "Hurry! They must be parted before one is killed."

Snarling and snapping, the two *jinjas* clawed and bit until magic began flashing in green bursts about them. As her ladies scattered in alarm, Elandra took a prudent step back, agonized with worry for her golden. Only Lady Avitria held her ground, watching the battle coolly without expression on her haughty face.

By the time Rumasin came hurrying in with two bulky servants carrying a large square of canvas and a net, Lady Avitria's *jinja* was squealing in agony.

Helplessly, Elandra pressed her fists together. She had not called commands to her own *jinja*, for she knew it would neither hear her nor obey. Occasionally in her childhood, she'd seen *jinjas* fighting. Such battles were vicious and sometimes both combatants perished, even if they were parted in time. *Jinja* bites made awful, poisonous sores and could be lethal.

"Hurry!" Elandra called to Rumasin.

The eunuch clapped his hands, and the menservants

rushed forward to throw their net over the fighting creatures. Using long rods, the men expertly forced the *jinjas* apart. While one man held the net in place, the other deftly snared Elandra's *jinja* in the canvas and rolled it up.

Furious squalling and much thrashing went on, surprising Elandra, for she'd expected her golden to quieten immediately. It had served her well and during the Terrors it had been quick to sense shadow magic and the approach of evil. Elandra was extremely fond of it.

"I'm sorry, Majesty," Lady Avitria said. "My blue is always causing trouble. I don't know why."

Elandra nodded unhappily. She knew that most of the *jinjas* in the palace were walking bundles of jealousy, quick to lose their tempers, show their teeth at each other, and snap at the air in warning. For some reason, none of them liked the blue. Elandra had no idea where Lady Avitria had acquired it, but by all accounts it was not well trained.

Now it lay on the carpet, whimpering as it was rolled in the net and carried out. Lady Avitria watched it go without making any effort to touch it. "Oh, Bronzidaec," she said sadly.

Quiet fell over the room. The other ladies fanned themselves, still looking scared. The chamberlain cleared his throat. Elandra's protector relaxed beside her and stepped back.

Lady Avitria walked over the torn parts of the carpet and curtsied low to Elandra.

"I beg Your Majesty's forgiveness for my *jinja*'s behavior. It was very wrong to attack your golden. It knew better than to start a fight."

Shaken, feeling a little sick now that the incident was over, Elandra sat down without paying much attention. "I thought it was the other way around. My *jinja* attacked yours."

"Oh no." Lady Avitria smiled fleetingly, although her eyes looked cold. "Your Majesty is too kind, too gracious. No, no, my Bronzidaec was to blame. If it survives, I assure Your Majesty that it will be punished."

Frowning, Elandra said, "You do not need to flatter me

by holding your creature to blame. I saw clearly what happened."

"Majesty—"

"Enough." Elandra lifted her hand in dismissal of the matter.

It was only a *jinja* spat, more violent than usual, nothing more. Elandra beckoned to the priestess, who'd retreated nearly to the door. "Come here."

Hesitantly, the priestess obeyed. "Majesty, thank you for your summons."

Elandra's slim brows lifted. "I sent for the Magria, not you. What message do you bring?"

"One of apology, deepest apology, and a plea for your pardon." The priestess pulled away her stole to reveal the brassy blond hair and rounded face of Elandra's half sister, Bixia.

Astonished, Elandra could only stare. She had not seen Bixia in years, not since her half sister was led away from the sandpit inside the Penestrical stronghold, screaming in rage and promising revenge. Bixia, pampered and spoiled, had been their father's legitimate daughter, born of his first wife. Elandra had been Count Albain's natural-born daughter, a product of his passionate affair with the wife of another man. Raised together in Albain's palace, the two girls had never felt any bond for each other. Bixia's cruel and jealous aunt had made Elandra a servant within the household and abused her without Albain's knowledge. And Bixia, believing herself destined to marry Emperor Kostimon, was indifferent to Elandra's plight. Instead, it was Elandra who had gone to the imperial palace while Bixia had vanished, never to be found . . . until now.

It was too great a surprise . . . so completely unexpected that Elandra found herself with nothing to say at all.

Bixia's eyes searched hers for a moment, bold and defiant until Elandra said nothing, did nothing. Then Bixia's expression grew unsure. She frowned, stepped back, and sank into a curtsy.

"Majesty," she said softly.

If any resentment lingered in her voice, Elandra could not hear it. Rising to her feet and waving back her protector, Elandra moved to the edge of the dais.

"Well, Maelite," Elandra said finally, her tone brittle. "What brings you to me?"

Someone in the room gasped aloud, and everyone stared suspiciously at Bixia, who jerked upright. Her face turned very pink. Her eyes were both wary and indignant. "I'm no Maelite, Majesty. I swear it to you."

"Swear what you please. Why should I believe you?"

"Majesty, please—"

"Your aunt was a witch who practiced her evil for years undetected. She raised you. Did she not train you well in her ways?"

"No, Majesty. I—"

"My *jinja* just tried to attack you, did it not?"

"No, Majesty!"

Lady Avitria stepped forward. "Your golden went for Bronzidaec, Majesty. I saw it clearly from where I was standing."

Elandra swept her attendant a look of impatience. "Do not interfere," she said coldly, and Lady Avitria retreated in chastened silence.

"Well, Bixia?" Elandra asked coldly. "The last time I saw you, you cursed me and swore revenge. Is that why you're here now, to execute it?"

"No, Majesty. I was angry that day. I have repented since then."

"Have you?" Elandra looked her up and down. "What proof do you bring?"

Bixia touched her robes. "I wear the black of the sisterhood. I have joined them and trained hard."

"You wear the robes," Elandra said, still suspicious. "But you bring no Penestricans with you."

"The Magria sent me alone today. It is part of my penitence before I can achieve the next level of training." Bixia hesitated, then quoted, " 'The past must be unchained, the future abandoned. The now is all that matters, for now is all the gods provide.' "

Some of Elandra's sharpest suspicions subsided. Sitting down, she looked her half sister over. It remained difficult to think of indolent, vain Bixia willingly embracing the austere rigors of the sisterhood. "So you can now quote Penestrican text. When did you decide to join the order?"

"I never left the sisters," Bixia said. "I never left the stronghold from the day I entered it."

"Nonsense! You were taken out."

"Taken from the sand and snakes. But I remained inside the walls."

Elandra frowned. The Magria had never mentioned Bixia's presence there, but strangely enough that made sense. The Penestricans were full of secrets and mysteries. They did many inexplicable things for their own purposes and seldom bothered to explain. On the other hand, in the city there had been an occasional rumor of a buxom, blond-haired tavern dancer called Beesia, who always disappeared before any imperial agents could question her.

"Why," Elandra asked, "have I heard nothing from you before?"

Bixia bowed her head. "I wasn't ready."

Elandra's frown deepened. That, at least, had the ring of truth.

"Please," Bixia said. "It hasn't been easy for me. I was angry for a very long time. I thought you robbed me of a glorious future. That reversal of destiny was—was very hard to accept."

"And have you accepted it?"

"Yes."

Staring into her eyes, Elandra saw no guile in them. But Bixia had always lied when it suited her purposes. She could exert charm, or tears, at the snap of fingers. She was not to be trusted.

"So you've come, as part of your training," Elandra said coolly. "Do you bring me a message from the Magria?"

"Oh yes. I am to say for her that she regrets not attending Your Majesty today, as requested. She will come soon."

"When?"

Bixia blinked. "I don't know. She has seen a—a disturbing vision and I am supposed to escort Your Majesty to the serpent pit for its interpretation."

"You just said she was coming to me."

"Soon," Bixia said, looking confused. "Soon, but not now. It would be better if Your Majesty could go to her."

The chamberlain puffed up in outrage. "Her Majesty does *not* go forth like a common—"

"Enough," Elandra said, and he fell silent, breathing hard.

She leaned back in her chair. If what Bixia said was true, she thought, then Caelan's vision of Lea had not been false. Perhaps Lea had also reached out to the Magria for help. Aware that no one save for Caelan and herself as yet knew of his vision, Elandra found herself starting to believe Bixia.

"Tell me more of the Magria's vision."

"I cannot, Majesty." Ducking her head, Bixia simpered a little. "You know that no one is permitted to discuss them."

"No one in this room will gossip," Elandra said coldly. "Tell me what you know."

"I'm sorry, Majesty. I witnessed nothing."

"You were not present? You did not assist in the ritual?"

"No."

Elandra waved dismissal. "Then you've spoken your message, and wasted too much of my time. You may go."

The chamberlain bustled forward, but Bixia dodged him to rush to the dais edge. Elandra's protector moved to intercept her, but she was already sinking to her knees in supplication.

"Please, please don't send me away," she pleaded. "Please don't be cold to me. I have suffered much. You have no idea. And now if you don't come, the Magria will be angry."

Elandra stiffened.

Lady Avitria stepped forward. "How dare you speak to

Her Majesty this way? It's not your place to rebuke the empress!"

Bixia's gaze darted back and forth. She turned pale with alarm. "I beg Your Majesty's pardon. I didn't mean it that way. The Magria will be angry with *me*, Majesty. Not with you. Never with you."

"Don't grovel," Elandra said in cold disgust.

But Bixia crept even closer, reaching out as though she would dare touch Elandra's slipper. The protector's sword point stabbed the floor right in front of her fingers, and she pulled back her hand with a gasp.

"Oh." She stared up at Elandra with big eyes. "Will you please come, as the Magria has requested? It's urgent, Majesty. Very urgent."

If it was an urgent matter, Elandra thought, still annoyed, then Bixia had shown no hurry to deliver the Magria's message. As usual, Bixia seemed to be centered on her own concerns more than any others'.

"I do not choose to leave the palace today," Elandra said formally. "I shall communicate with the Magria later. You may tell her that I am disappointed, and you have my permission to—"

"Oh, please, please don't make me go yet!" Bixia cried. "I know I've offended you, but I want your forgiveness! I beg you, Elandra, don't be cold to me now. Hecati was so mean to you, so cruel, and I didn't care. I understand now what you went through. I've been hungry and mistreated. I've been beaten. I understand, truly I do. I'm sorry, very sorry. Please don't send me away."

As she spoke, she parted her robes slightly to show scars on her shoulders next to a very tiny tattoo of a serpent. "You see?" she whispered. "I do know."

Elandra's heart was touched by those ugly scars. She saw the memories of hurt and humiliation in Bixia's eyes, and remembered her own ordeals.

The Guards were coming in now, summoned by the chamberlain, but with a frown Elandra gestured for them to wait.

"I pity you those lessons, Bixia," she said in compassion.

Lifting a tearstained face, Bixia sniffed dolefully. "The Penestricans are not kind," she whispered.

"No."

"But—but they've given me a place, a shelter, a—a home of sorts. Else I would have had nothing."

"Our father would have housed you, married you elsewhere."

Something—either cynicism or scorn—twisted Bixia's features briefly before it vanished. "You were his favorite. When Hecati's true affiliations were discovered, he abandoned me. He did what you're doing now, judging me by what she was. I had nowhere to go, nothing I could do except stay inside the order." She wrung her hands together. "It wasn't fair!"

How often had Elandra heard her half sister wail that complaint? But how much of life truly was fair? She wished she could believe Bixia's change of heart. She wanted to, quite intensely. But Elandra remembered the lie Bixia had told their father about how her expensive Mahiran wedding robe came to be torn, and how she'd done nothing when Elandra was blamed for the damage and punished. Every stinging blow of Hecati's stick remained branded on Elandra's memory. The humiliation of Hecati's foot on her neck, grinding her face into the carpet, returned as sharp and vivid as the moment it happened. Elandra's fingers dug hard into the wooden arms of her chair.

"What do you want of me, really?" she asked.

"Can you never forgive me?" Bixia asked softly, tilting her head to one side. "Can we never again be sisters?"

Elandra had sometimes imagined what she would do or say if Bixia were ever found. The idea of Bixia being safe all this time, with never a message sent, never a single attempt at communication made, was disturbing. *I was foolish to worry about her,* Elandra told herself now. *Bixia is the sort who always survives.* Elandra was not a person to hold grudges, but she supposed Bixia wanted a place at court.

Elandra would have believed her more readily if Bixia had come begging for money.

"Oh," Bixia said now as the silence lengthened. Her expression grew bleak with disappointment. "I see. I am too late for reconciliation. You are too great in estate and position, and I am too low."

"That's absurd," Elandra said, stung. "You cannot accuse me of such snobbery."

"I beg Your Majesty's pardon. I do not presume to make any accusation at all."

Elandra frowned, debating over whether to send for a truth-finder. The Penestricans were the best at it, but her most recent summons to the sisterhood had resulted in this sudden, completely unexpected visit from Bixia. *They are testing me,* Elandra thought with a spurt of resentment. *Just as they did long ago before my marriage to Kostimon. They are trying me in some mysterious way to suit their own purposes.*

Annoying though they were, the Penestricans were staunch allies to the throne, and Elandra did not want to damage that alliance. Furthermore, although she might not like Bixia, she knew she should not appear so cold, so unsympathetic that people said she'd become a haughty empress, too arrogant to reach out to members of her own family. Bixia, she saw, looked unhealthy. There was strain in her eyes when she wasn't casting all her charm at Elandra, a sort of exhaustion in the droop of her shoulders that said perhaps she was still ill-treated. Whatever lay in the past between them, her half sister was plainly in need.

"We shall see, Bixia," Elandra said. "I must consider what you've said to me."

Relief lit Bixia's face, and she looked pretty again. "Thank you!" she cried eagerly. "I know it's hard for you—for Your Majesty to believe that I've changed. I was never good to you before. I was selfish and vain. I know that now."

"So you've said."

"Let me do something for you, something to show you the worth of my intentions."

"That isn't necessary."

"Oh, but I want to! I have a talent, a very small gift. The Penestricans discovered it during my training." A shadow flickered in her face, then vanished swiftly. "A little gift of seeing."

This time, Elandra could not conceal her astonishment. "You? Capable of visions?"

Bixia laughed. "Oh no! Not visions, and I cannot cast truth. I can't even be trained. I just glimpse what the great Magria is seeing in the rituals." She shrugged helplessly and gave Elandra a small smile. "It causes trouble, so I'm not allowed to participate or even enter the serpent pit."

Confused, Elandra sat back, not sure she believed such a tale.

Lady Avitria caught her eye. "I have heard of such people, Majesty," she murmured helpfully. "They are called latents."

"Oh yes." Elandra nodded. "The naturals who are sometimes found in villages and brought into the orders for . . . training?"

"More likely to protect them from ignorant peasants." Lady Avitria glanced at Bixia and said cautiously, "I have always heard latents are not trainable."

"I'm not," Bixia agreed blithely. "I'm of no use to the sisters. I can't even manage to be a dream walker. So I am a service sister. I clean and mend. Sometimes I see what the great Magria sees, and sometimes I don't."

Distracted by the unwelcome—although just—image of her highborn sister scrubbing and fetching for the sisterhood, Elandra heard a strong hint in Bixia's voice.

She sent Bixia a sharp look. "And you've seen the latest of the Magria's visions?"

Bixia nodded. "She'll be angry with me for telling, but how can it hurt if I show it to you?" Hesitating, she tilted her head and sent Elandra a most beguiling little smile.

Elandra found herself smiling back. How often had she

seen Bixia turn such a look on their father? He had melted every time beneath Bixia's charm. Elandra remembered how amusing Bixia could be in their father's presence, how she used to make him roar with laughter, how she used to coax anything from him that she wanted.

Still, Elandra remained cautious. Tempting though it was, she was about to refuse Bixia's offer when her half sister said, "I thought it might please you to see how the emperor's sister does on her journey."

Everyone came to attention. Even Lady Avitria smiled, and the chamberlain stepped closer.

"Lady Lea is well?" he asked eagerly, forgetting it was not his place to interrupt the empress during an audience. "She has reached Trau safely?"

Bixia hesitated, and Elandra lifted her hand to recall the chamberlain to his duty.

Turning red, he mumbled an apology, bowed, and retreated.

Swiftly Elandra reconsidered her decision. As yet the court was unaware that Lea might be in difficulties. Her young sister-in-law's immense popularity had not waned since her departure from the palace. If anything, people talked about her more.

The overwhelming desire for news made Elandra set aside her caution. How could Bixia know about Lea unless she really had seen something, perhaps even the same vision Caelan had seen? Elandra dared not throw away this opportunity to gain more information. With her guards and attendants in the chamber, she felt safe enough.

"You won't tell the great Magria, will you?" Bixia asked with some apprehension. "I mean, she hasn't given me permission to do this, and only she is supposed to share visions with Your Majesty. I just wanted to prove to you that I've changed."

It was rather pathetic, Elandra thought. Poor Bixia, plumper, not as pretty now, not as young. Elandra saw the same lazy defiance of rules, the same willingness to do whatever it took to get what she wanted.

I'll give her anything, Elandra thought, although she had no intention of saying so, or of looking too eager. "What payment do you ask for this defiance of the Magria's rules?"

Bixia looked shocked. "Nothing!"

"You don't expect a place at court? The emperor's sister is much favored here. Do you want the same status?"

Greed flickered in Bixia's eyes, but she bowed her head quickly. "No, Majesty. I ask for nothing."

Elandra heard the lie in Bixia's voice and knew the request would come, if not today, then soon. Bixia must be wild to escape the strict austerity of the sisterhood. No doubt her eyes had been filled today with the grandeur and magnificence of the women's pavilion. *They could never beat the love of luxury out of her,* Elandra thought.

Warning herself not to expect too much from this unreliable source of information, Elandra stepped off the dais to join her half sister. When her protector tried to accompany her, she waved him back.

"Very well," she said to Bixia. "Cast your vision if you can."

"Majesty," the protector said, "take care."

Nodding, she watched Bixia, still not believing her capable of much.

Bixia raised her hands into the air and tilted back her head, mouthing something in silence. Then she reached into her robes and brought forth a handful of pale sand. She dribbled it onto the floor in a pattern that did not resemble the usual Penestrican symbols. Indeed, these looked like harmless squiggles, and the sight of them made Elandra frown in disappointment, certain that this was charlatanism after all.

Bixia beckoned Elandra to step onto the sand. "Look, Empress," she whispered, holding her hands before Elandra's face and spreading them wide.

At first there was nothing to see, but then a glimmer appeared in the air between Elandra and her half sister. Elandra saw the air darken before her as a swirling cloud of inky mist formed.

"Look," Bixia said, her voice taking on the crooning persuasion of a professional hustler. "Come closer. Look deep and *see*."

Frowning a little, Elandra refused to lean forward as she was urged, but she did look.

And she saw a shape, very small, very dim, taking form within the dark swirling mist. It looked like a girl. It looked like Lea. Amazed, Elandra reached out.

Quick as a striking cobra, Bixia grabbed her wrist and twisted it hard, jerking her forward into the mist. Instinctively, cursing her own gullibility, Elandra pulled back, lifting her topaz pendant for protection as she did so.

Fire shot from the mist, right at her face, but struck the pendant instead and glanced off. Although most of the magic shot missed Elandra, as she ducked she felt the edge of it burn across her temple. People were shouting around her, and she heard Bixia cursing in a shrill, frantic voice.

Elandra's pendant exploded. Knocked backward by the blast, Elandra was torn from Bixia's grasp. Her ears were ringing. Her whole body felt numb. She could see nothing. And then she hit the floor with a jolting impact that knocked the breath from her lungs. The back of her head hit something hard and sharp, flaring white pain through her head, and all went dark.

Chapter 22

With a groan, Thirbe came to, and found himself lying with his face in the dust. He shifted his head, which weighed as much as a boulder, scraping his cheek through the dirt before he managed to rest it on his outflung arm.

Memory stirred in his muddled thoughts, confused impressions of shouting and violence exploding around him, the thunder of galloping hooves, a stab in the back, steel—alien and cold—piercing his armor and ribs, the jolting impact of hitting the ground, then nothing.

Until now.

Merciful Gault, but he hurt.

All was quiet around him, save for some birds squawking in the trees and the song of insects in the grass. He'd fallen into a small fissure of rock down below the trail, and extracting himself was awkward. Sitting up nearly made him pass out, but he sucked in his breath to keep from yelling and endured until the pain subsided. Nauseated and trembling, clammy with sweat, he felt certain he might as well lie down and die right there.

He did neither.

The wound was midway up his back. He was losing blood, and when he tried to lift his left arm the agony left him doubled over and gasping.

So here he was, sitting trailside, with a sharp piece of rock digging into his rump while he slowly bled to death. Thirst burned his throat. Someone had stolen his cloak, but he still had his boots and weapons, probably thanks to having fallen into these rocks.

Betrayal was a sour thing, a rotten evil, and he cursed Hervan in all ways possible. He cursed the Crimsons and their fool ideas that had jeopardized the emperor's sister and brought him, Rafin Thirbe, to being left to die in a dusty ditch.

"May you find hell, Hervan," he swore aloud. "May you rot there for a thousand eternities with Mael's breath charring your bones and Beloth's claws digging out your entrails. May your flesh burst from pustules and your privates shrivel up and burn with fire. Damn you!"

A soft sound down the slope from him caught his attention away from angry self-pity. He drew his dagger, gritting his teeth in an effort not to moan, and leaned forward as much as he dared to see what was coming. A sorrel horse with a white blaze came into sight. It was grazing with its bridle on, the reins dragging the ground, a saddle twisted askew on its back. Thirbe stared in disbelief. It was his horse, and he'd never loved an animal more than at that moment.

He licked his dry lips and gave a low whistle. The horse lifted its head, pricking its ears in Thirbe's direction and staring at him while Thirbe held his breath and dared make no movement that might frighten it off.

"Come on. Come on," he said under his breath.

The horse put its head down to graze again, cropping the sparse tufts of grass growing from rocky ground.

"Here, you lazy rack of bones," Thirbe said. He whistled again, holding out his hand.

The horse snorted and climbed the hill to him with some tail switching and head tossing. It hesitated just out of reach, and Thirbe forced himself not to lunge for the dangling reins.

"Come on," he crooned, and the horse walked up to him and blew hot breath in his hair as it nuzzled him. Its velvety mouth lipped his fingers.

Thirbe closed his hand over the reins and felt profound thankfulness.

Using his horse as support, he made it to his feet, gasping and fighting off the tiny black spots dancing in his vision. It wasn't easy, but he righted the saddle and fumbled in his supply pouch for cloth and a spare sword belt. Eventually he got a crude bandage cinched around himself, and then he sat down for a while, the reins firmly knotted around his wrist so the horse couldn't wander off while he slept.

When he awakened, feeling more parched and terribly weak, he found the sun going down.

His head had cleared, and although his anger burned a steady flame in his heart, he felt grateful that he'd not died unsworn; Gault had been merciful to him there.

Feeling decidedly shaken by his close call, he bent his proud neck and humbly gave thanks, seeking forgiveness for his actions and renewing his vows. Maybe the gods would accept his prayer and maybe not. He would have to perform an act of atonement for taking the Hidden Ways. When he found a priest he'd have to pay for a sacrifice and full cleansing rites.

For the first time since regaining consciousness, he allowed himself to wonder about Lady Lea.

Hervan, the damned little pox mark, had been right when he'd said Thirbe loved her, aye, he did. But like a daughter. He'd felt the brittle shell around his heart soften from the first day he entered her service, when her blue eyes had stared at him with such warm understanding and her smile had lit up his dour world.

Gritting his teeth, Thirbe climbed into the saddle and set his horse picking its way slowly through the battle site. Men lay sprawled in death, flies buzzing around them,

stripped of boots and gear, their protections and personal
effects scattered, their fine uniforms bedraggled or stolen,
their helmet plumes trampled in the dirt. Vultures already
wheeled lazily in the sky, waiting for the feast to come. The
unnecessary waste of lives made Thirbe scowl grimly.

He found Lieutenant Rozer, lying gray and still in an
enormous pool of blood. He found Sergeant Taime crumpled near the gulch wall, so hacked and battered he was almost unrecognizable. Nearby lay Aszondal's body, tangled
with the corpse of a mercenary. And over in the bushes, as
though he'd been hiding, lay Poulso the priest, stabbed in
the back.

"Like me," Thirbe muttered with a fresh wave of anger.

Bad enough to see his comrades slain like this, but it
was the betrayal that burned Thirbe worse than his wound.

The insult of it, the dirty cowardice of Rozer's sneaky
blow just as they poured out of the Hidden Ways, left a bad
taste that Thirbe could not spit out of his mouth.

"Knifed and left for dead," he said. "But I ain't dead,
Captain Fancy-Me-Lad, and since you ain't here, I figure
you've slipped off and let your men die without you."

He circled around, counting carefully, but Hervan was
not found. At the edge of the trampled ground, Thirbe finally found a track, a hoofprint he recognized as belonging
to the captain's horse. Thirbe had been trained to always
know the tracks of his officers in case of trouble; the skill
had come in useful during his army years, even more useful when he was a predicate, and now he stared in the direction Hervan had taken and narrowed his eyes.

"I ain't letting you get away with attempted murder,
shadow magic, and whatever the hell else you're doing," he
said aloud. "Using the shadows always carries a reckoning.
I don't know what'll be coming to me for it, but I'm *your*
reckoning, boy. I'm your reckoning."

He knew he hadn't a prayer of saving Lady Lea now.
Gault help the poor maiden, for he'd failed her. But he could
hunt down Hervan and take vengeance on him. Young Captain Hervan of the Household Regiment—blessed with

good looks and the vanity to go with them, a young man favored at court, favored in life, raised to do anything he pleased and damn the consequences—was not going to be saved this time, Thirbe thought grimly.

"Papa can't buy you out of this trouble," Thirbe muttered, his voice hoarse as he tightened his reins. "Thanks to you, my sweet lady is lost. For that, and this hole in my back, I'll be your shadow. I'll track you, chase you through the very gates of hell, if I must. I'll see you eat steel, even if I die for it."

With his vow spoken, he kissed the knuckles of his sword hand and held his fist weakly in the air for Gault to witness. Then, grimacing in pain, he kicked his horse forward.

At the palace in New Imperia, Caelan rushed through the galleries and passages, strode down a loggia without seeing the astonished or worried courtiers who backed out of his way. Someone called out, but he paid no heed.

The sentinels snapping salutes at the gates barely had time to step aside as he swept into the women's pavilion and made his way into Elandra's private apartments. Inside, he was met by the backs of a crowd of onlookers, all craning their necks and whispering.

"The emperor!" a page shouted belatedly. "Make way!"

His escort of Guards was already pushing people aside. Caelan strode past them, past a line of stern sentries at the inner doors, through her personal sitting room, an antechamber, and finally into Elandra's private bedchamber.

His beloved wife lay curled on her side, either asleep or unconscious. Her long auburn hair glinted fire on her pillows, its highlights reflecting the lamplight and candle flames. Bareheaded women in Penestrican robes tended her, bathing her arms and bare feet with water, gently applying compresses of damp linen to the small wound on her brow.

The sight of her like this unmanned him. Caelan jerked

to a halt and stared, his throat working, his powerful hands clenching helplessly at his sides.

"Excellency."

The stern, almost cold voice that spoke to him belonged to a woman with keen blue eyes and a shining curtain of straight blond hair that hung down her back in pale contrast to her somber black robes. Anas, young Magria and leader of the Penestrican order, seer of visions, stepped forward from the gloomy edges of the chamber. Her beautiful face held no expression.

She smelled of herbs, and their pungent combination of scents flung Caelan back in time to his father's infirmary, a place with bare stone walls and a long battered worktable. He remembered himself as a young boy, standing at the table with a mortar and pestle, resentful of having to grind herbs for potions when all he wanted was to go fishing with Old Farns.

"The empress will live," the Magria said before he could ask. "Be not afraid for her. She is stunned, but not fatally injured."

So coldly, so emotionlessly did the Magria speak that Caelan didn't believe her at first. But he realized there was no reason for her to lie.

A massive wave of relief rolled over him. Shutting his stinging eyes a moment, he tried to breathe. "Gault be praised," he murmured.

But when he attempted to go to Elandra's side, the Magria intervened.

"Do not disturb her now."

His alarm came back. "You said she's not hurt."

"No, I said her injury is not fatal. She needs rest and quiet."

With a gesture, the Magria led him away into a smaller chamber. The ladies-in-waiting scattered away from them with frightened faces, leaving them alone except for Caelan's grim protector and the Imperial Guards at the door.

"I've had the report," Caelan said impatiently before the Magria could speak. "I know the attacker was her half sister,

Bixia. She fled, tried to hide in the palace, but she's already been caught and taken by the guards for questioning."

"Your torturer will learn nothing from her," the Magria said.

"Then *you* question her."

"No need, Excellency." The Magria's blue eyes blazed with anger. "A Maelite puppet, lacking powers of her own. They used her as a weapon. She knows nothing of value."

"A Maelite," he breathed. A muscle jumped in his clenched jaw. He burned to order the entire palace turned inside out, with every person questioned and put to the lash. The place was riddled with spies and traitors, despite all efforts to keep them out. *Elandra could have died,* he thought and felt chilled.

"Bixia dared call herself a Penestrican," the Magria said with suppressed fury. "Dared pretend she could cast a vision. When your torturer is finished with her, give her to me, Excellency. Not for questioning, but to pay dearly for her lies."

It occurred to him that the Magria was angrier about the slander done to her order than the actual attack on Elandra, but he shoved that thought away. "Done," he said. "Although I doubt even you can punish her as much as she deserves. But how was Elandra tricked? She's too clever to be caught unawares. She would never trust Bixia."

The Magria nodded, her delicate nostrils flaring as she drove her anger back under control. "I believe there must have been a spell working to cloud her mind, to make her more susceptible to trickery."

"Who could work such a spell inside the palace without detection?"

"Maelites."

"Gods, how did a witch get in here? How did our protections fail?"

"Let that question be put to Lady Avitria."

"Avitria? Is she—"

"Yes."

Shocked, he remained silent for a few moments, staring

at the door leading to Elandra's chamber. His dear Elandra, whom he'd sworn to keep safe, lay hurt, struck down inside her pavilion with Imperial Guards and her protector around her. The sense of safety they'd all relied on had been an illusion. First Lea, now Elandra, he thought.

"My son?" he whispered.

"You are wise to take extra precautions there," the Magria said. "But do not fear for the child. We shall watch over him."

Caelan inclined his head in acknowledgment of the offer, even as his more skeptical side wondered if the Magria could keep her promise. "As for my wife . . . her sister, her chief lady-in-waiting . . . how many more are involved in this plot to harm her?"

"Let that question be put to Lady Avitria."

"Elandra's *jinja* should have sensed the use of magic. What good are the creatures if they don't do their job?"

"Even a *jinja* can be fooled. These enemies were clever, Excellency. Her *jinja* tried to protect the empress, but it was tricked, deflected." The Magria frowned. "It managed to slay Avitria's blue *jinja*, which was not a *jinja* at all."

"What was it?"

"A *desticrir*. A small woods demon."

Again he stared at her in shock. "How—"

"Come, Excellency," the Magria said impatiently. "Surely you know that not all creatures of shadow have perished yet."

The cold, cutting contempt in her voice made him think of his father. "Yes, I know," he said, controlling his temper. "But I do not expect to be told that a demon has been living in the palace for months undetected. And don't tell me to ask Lady Avitria about this, too!"

"Avitria acquired it from another woman. Although it wore a disguising spell, Avitria must have recognized what it was immediately and put it to use. How it came to be here is another matter, which perhaps your agents will want to trace. You are surrounded by numerous plots, Excellency. This attack on the empress is but one of them."

The Magria stared at him. "And the one on your sister is another."

"Then you know about Lea."

"Oh yes," the Magria assured him. "And you have been wise not to go in search of her, despite strong temptation."

He brushed the compliment aside. "Who has her, Magria? Who threatens her with harm?"

The Magria opened her fist, and a tiny serpent with an emerald glittering in its mouth slithered across her wrist and up her sleeve to her shoulder. It vanished in her hair. "The answer you seek is not easy to provide."

"A pox on your riddles and mysteries! Where is she? Who has abducted her? How much danger surrounds her? Where am I to ride to gain her rescue?"

"Ride?" For a moment the Magria looked alarmed. "You must not leave your throne unguarded, Excellency. I thought you understood that."

"As soon as I know where to find her," he said grimly, "I shall take action."

"But not you personally. Your enemies seek to draw you away from the center of your power, away from the emerald throne. Resist. I urge you most strongly. War is coming to your empire."

Caelan frowned. She was not telling him anything he didn't already know. "Right now, this is not about my empire. It's about my wife and sister. Their safety."

"You have forgotten the second part of your destiny, Light Bringer."

He sighed, in no mood for prophecy. "I've seen the end of Kostimon, Beloth, and Mael. Isn't that enough destruction?"

"You have begun your destined task. You must finish it."

"Later. Now, I want—"

"Does it matter what any of us want?" she asked sharply. "Is not what we *are* more important?"

"For the last time, I ask you to tell me where to find Lea. Who has taken her?"

"Several enemies converge on her, Excellency."

"Then it's as I thought. The Vindicants will take her from—"

"Perhaps. The readings are . . . difficult." The Magria's gaze searched his before she lowered her eyes. "You will not like what I have to say."

Believing she was going to foretell Lea's death, he felt dread sink through him like a stone. Suddenly he wished he hadn't asked, but of course he had to know. Steeling himself, he said, "I must have the truth. Tell me."

"You will be betrayed, Excellency."

"By Hervan? Is the captain responsible for Lea's situation?"

"No, *you* will be betrayed. By one you hold dear."

"What are you saying?" For a moment intense anger swept him. "Not Elandra! In Gault's name—"

"No," the Magria said, her gaze steady on his. "The empress is faithful in all respects."

"Who, then? Why do you—" He frowned, shaking his head. "Lea is the one in trouble," he said carefully, as though explaining the matter to a simpleton. "She would never do anything against me."

"Are you so certain?"

"Completely! She's incapable of doing wrong."

"People are capable of many things, Excellency. People do change."

"But not my sister, my—*no!*" Furious, he swung around for the door.

"Excellency," the Magria said quietly, her voice penetrating his anger. "Please, wait."

He glared over his shoulder. "Why should I? If *slander* is all you can give me—"

"The visions do not lie."

"This one is *wrong*."

Anger burned in the Magria's blue eyes. She reached into her sleeves with both hands and threw a pair of serpents on the floor between them. At once the snakes began crawling, and it was all Caelan could do to stand his ground and not back away.

His protector came forward, but Caelan stopped the man with a gesture.

The Magria pointed at the writhing snakes. "See what I have seen, Excellency, and judge for yourself. If you dare!"

Chapter 23

The sun was sinking low, its fiery rays blazing through the trees and turning the surface of the stream molten gold. Lea sat on the ground, hugging her knees tightly and feeling cramped from the small confines of her cage. With the sun going down, the air had grown cool. Shivering, she strained to catch some sound, yet all she heard was the wind quaking the trees. A shower of golden leaves fell suddenly, startling her. She watched them tumble into the stream and be carried away.

By now, the battle should be over, she thought, unable to stop worrying. She refused to hope, for no matter who won there would be death and *na-quai*, the destruction of spirit.

For the third time since the commander had caged her here, she put out her hand to touch the stakes. This time, no magic repulsed her fingers.

Unable to believe it, she touched a stake again. There was no hindrance. The spell had ended.

Shadrael is dead, she thought.

A little pang went through her, one she chose not to examine. She yanked the stake from the ground. It came easily from the soft dirt, and she flung it away before pulling out another and another, until she could squeeze out of the circle and run.

Without hesitation, she headed for the stream, her breath loud and ragged in her ears. She stumbled several times until, muttering, she gathered her long skirts up in one hand and slapped angrily at her tears with the other. She was *not* going to cry, she told herself sternly. She was *not* going to be a fool.

At all costs she intended to avoid the camp for—no matter what might have happened to the commander—some of his men might yet return. She splashed across the stream for the second time that day, intent on getting away. If the Crimsons came searching for her, she could leave her hiding place and rejoin them.

The approaching sound of galloping hoofbeats made her freeze in her tracks, her heart thumping uncertainly. *Who?* she wondered. Lifting her arms, she cast forth her senses. "Oh, kind spirits of the air, guide me in this," she whispered. "Who comes to me?"

The wind blew harder, whipping around her and sending her hair tangling across her face. As she dragged her tresses back, she caught a scent of something charred and musty . . . the unmistakable stink of the Hidden Ways.

Not Shadrael, she thought. If it should be Fomo or one of the others . . . fear flashed through her. "No!" she breathed, and ran for her life.

Crossing the bank of gravel, she reached the bottom of the nearby hill and plunged into the gully cut into its base. Brush snagged her hair and clothing, but she kept going until she tripped on a root, stumbled, and fell. Jolted hard, she managed to keep from crying out and scrambled forward on her hands and knees to collapse at last in a small depression behind a thick bush. She curled up small and still, her heart hammering hard.

The hoofbeats were louder now, coming toward the stream. Holding her breath, Lea sank lower into the leaves and made sure her bedraggled skirts covered her red boots.

The dust she'd stirred up tickled her nose, but she fought not to sneeze. Like a mouse, she dared make not the slightest movement in hopes that she would blend into the cover.

Her straining eyes glimpsed red among the trees beyond the stream, just before a horse and rider emerged into the open. Although the sun was sinking low, it was not yet dusk, and she could see the man clearly. Her eyes widened in astonishment, for Captain Hervan's distinctive manner of sitting a horse could not be mistaken. With his left arm bound in a sling, his short cloak swinging from his shoulders, his long helmet plume blowing behind him in the breeze, he reined up his horse and looked all around before he slowly approached the enclosure of tall stakes that had held her prisoner. Looking at the tracks she'd left in the dirt, he turned his head and stared at the woods.

He seemed to be looking right at her.

Lea did not move. She did not jump from her hiding place, call out to him, or wave. At first she was astonished at herself, yet some instinct kept her cautious. She felt danger around her, danger of a kind unknown to her.

A ripple nearby in the ground warned her that an earth spirit had come. Not daring to turn her head, she shifted her eyes to one side to peer down at it.

"Beware," it said in her mind. *"Danger. Be still."*

Even as the warning pushed through her thoughts, she heard the sound of another horse, approaching very fast.

The urge to shout a warning to Hervan filled her throat, yet she choked it back. Ashamed and confused, she blinked her stinging eyes and made no sound.

Hervan needed no warning, however, for he'd obviously heard the approaching horse. He spun his mount around to face whoever was coming, and drew his sword awkwardly in readiness.

Run, Lea thought urgently. *You're hurt. You cannot fight.*

And then her senses felt the brush of *sevaisin*, involuntary and unmistakable. A swift rush went through her, and her eyes widened in surprise.

The commander—a grim, unmistakable figure in black

armor—burst from the trees, bearing down on Hervan. He
was riding a cavalry mount instead of his own black horse,
and he'd lost his helmet. Blood streaked his face. When he
saw Hervan waiting for him, he let out a hoarse, savage cry
and spurred his lathered horse even faster.

Hervan kicked his mount forward. The two men galloped straight for each other, both shouting at the top of
their voices. Just as it seemed to Lea that they would crash
headlong, Hervan leaned over very low from the saddle in
a feat of daring horsemanship and whacked the flat of his
blade against the throat of the commander's mount. Shying
sideways, the horse bucked in a twisting corkscrew move
that jerked the commander off balance.

Even so, he stayed in the saddle, his horsemanship obviously equal to the captain's. He even managed to parry
Hervan's fierce blow.

The clang of steel echoed loudly, covering Lea's involuntary gasp. Hervan was almost standing in his stirrups, his
reins loose on his horse's neck as he hammered blow after
blow at the commander, who had still not fully recovered
his balance on his shying horse.

Then unexpectedly the commander kicked free of his
stirrups and jumped to the ground, landing heavily and
awkwardly, going to his knees. His horse dodged away
with a kick that missed him. With a whoop Hervan spurred
his mount right at the commander.

The horse reared up and leaped in a maneuver Lea had
seen demonstrated on the palace grounds, its forefeet striking out with lethal force.

She shot to her feet. "No!" she screamed. "Shadrael!"

Miraculously, he scrambled aside before a hoof could
smash his skull to pieces, and slashed at the horse's belly.
Thinking he was going to stab the animal, Lea screamed
again, but he'd only cut the saddle girth.

Hervan went flying through the air and hit the ground
hard. Tumbling over, the captain groaned and lay still.

Aghast, Lea pushed her way through the brush, running
now to reach the men. As she drew near, she could hear the

commander gasping for air. He stood near Hervan, bent double with his hands braced on his knees, his sword still clutched in one hand. The captain writhed a moment as though he would rise, then collapsed again. He was still groaning piteously.

Her heart wrung by them both, Lea came up just as Shadrael straightened. His black eyes were like bottomless holes in the pallor of his face. Seemingly unaware of her presence, he lifted his sword as though to finish Hervan. The captain, his handsome face gray and twisted with pain, raised a feeble hand in surrender.

The violence in the air was a tangible, horrible thing. Lea felt as though she were drowning in it.

Ignoring Hervan's gesture, the commander prepared to strike.

Sickened, remembering how he'd sent Tylik's head rolling with a single blow, Lea cried out, "Stop! Stop it now! He asks for mercy."

Shadrael slowly lowered his weapon. When he turned to stare at her, for one terrifying moment there was no recognition in his dark eyes.

Lea's heart felt squeezed by an awful pressure. "Please, please," she whispered.

Blinking, Shadrael seemed to regain his wits. "I cannot grant him mercy," he said, his voice raw. He swiped absently at the blood and sweat running down his face. "Cannot."

"You must. You must," she said, going to her knees beside the hurt captain and clutching his good arm as he tried to roll over. "Captain Hervan, let me help you."

Hervan's face was drawn and perspiring. The agony in his eyes wrung her tender heart, yet something in them gave her pause. He looked mad, obsessed. Ignoring her, he glared up at Shadrael. Warily, she allowed her hand to fall from Hervan's sleeve.

"Get back from him," Shadrael said.

"Why? So you can kill him? He has surrendered to you. Let him be."

"I need no prisoners."

"But—"

"He has not given me his sword. For your own sake, Lea, get back from him!"

"I'll get the sword for you," Lea said.

"No! Take care!"

Although it should have seemed bizarre for her abductor to be warning her against her rescuer, she did not have to be told there was something very wrong with Hervan. He was shuddering, his eyes burning with a haunted malevolence that alarmed her.

Before she could lose her nerve, she gently took the sword from Hervan's hand. To her relief, he did not resist. Even so, touching the weapon brought her into contact with its aura of bloody violence. Nearly dropping it in reflex, Lea eased herself away from Hervan and threw the sword into the water.

The captain laughed a little, never taking his gaze from Shadrael.

"There," Lea said, brushing off her hands. "Help him sit up, please, so I can tend to his injury."

"Don't touch him," the commander said. "Can't you see he's gone mad? He'll turn on you when you least expect it."

She frowned. "Captain Hervan! Olivel? Can you hear me? Do you know me?"

"Don't bother," Shadrael said. "He's come through the Hidden Ways unprepared. What a fool!"

"We must help him," Lea said. "I have none of the true healing arts, but perhaps a—"

"Nothing will help. I know the signs. Better to kill him and put him out of his misery."

"No!" Lea cried. "If that's your idea of mercy—"

Another low, insane chuckle from Hervan silenced her.

She saw the two men glaring at each other with naked hatred. Shadrael looked alert and keen for more fighting. But never had she seen such a feral, savage expression on Hervan's face. Gone was the suave, charming young man who'd so exasperated her on her journey, and in his place crouched a—a beast.

In that instant she understood why soldiers in the army were so brutal and wicked, why they wasted their free time in stupid, dangerous games and depravity. It was the only way to hold the madness at bay, the madness wrought in them by traveling the Hidden Ways. How, she wondered, had Shadrael managed to retain the amount of humanity he had?

"Defiler!" Hervan snarled. "Seducer! Fiend! I'll have you yet!"

As he spoke, he threw a small jeweled dagger right at Shadrael's face. The commander ducked, plunging his sword into Hervan's throat. And there, at Lea's feet, the captain sank down, gurgling and gasping as his life ran out of him.

Some of the madness drained from his features. His eyes rolled up as though straining to take one final look at her shocked face, and he struggled to smile. "Lea . . ."

With her name on his lips, he died, his eyes still staring sightlessly at her.

She sensed the fleeting rush and chaos within her *jai-ethal* as his soul departed, passing unsettled into *na-quai*. The swift destruction of his spirit told her that he'd died unsworn. Horrified, she took a step back and another before she lost her balance and sat down hard.

The commander straightened up with a grunt, absently cleaning his sword and sheathing it. Lines of weariness carved his face and his eyes were bleak. He seemed unaware of the new cut now bleeding down his cheek.

"Don't waste your grief on this one," he said. "It takes some men that way, the first time through. They're useless afterward, like rabid dogs that have to be put down."

Lea flinched. "Is this your idea of comfort? No one deserves such a death."

Shadrael's expression turned grim. "Was he your lover? Is that why you care so much?"

She closed her eyes, too tired to go on fighting him. What did explanations matter now? Hervan—poor, misguided man—lay dead. She could not imagine what lengths of desperation had driven him to travel the Hidden Ways in pursuit of her . . . to *unswear* himself in order to do it. She'd not asked for such a sacrifice. She was not worth such devotion.

Had Hervan thought she would love him in gratitude for his bravery? That she would appreciate or even approve of his throwing away honor and damning himself for eternity, for her?

"The rest of the Crimsons should be slain by now," Shadrael said into the silence. "My men will catch up with us soon, once they've looted the bodies and caught the horses."

Lea did not bother to reply. She felt numb and battered. What chance had she now of rescue? She did not believe her message had reached Caelan. She'd glimpsed a dim image of him, but that was all. Without her necklace of *gli*-emeralds, so weak had been her powers that he could not possibly have seen her in return, much less heard her plea. If he'd spoken to her, she hadn't heard him. *No,* she thought dully, *it was hopeless.*

"How did you get out of *kwaibe*?" Shadrael asked now, finally gaining her attention. "I put you there. I contained you. How did you escape?"

She did not care. She did not want to talk about such trivial things. Angrily she turned her face away.

"Answer me! How did you escape?"

"What does it matter now?"

"Did you break the spell? Are you that strong? It's bad enough that you've misaligned the Hidden Ways when I try to take you through, and now this. Can I do nothing with you?"

She almost let him believe the lie, but her honesty compelled her to face him. "The spell faded away, and I came out. I could not break it without my—" She broke off, annoyed with herself.

He seemed not to notice what she left unsaid. "Faded," he said bleakly, staring into the distance. Then, in fresh suspicion, he turned on her. "What have you been doing?"

"Nothing."

"Don't lie to me." He gave her a shake. "I can tell you've used magic. What have you been doing? What have you done?"

The anger in him buzzed around her, far more dangerous than hornets. She knew his temper, knew how brutal and unpredictable he could become, especially if he'd been killing. The thick, coppery smell of Hervan's death filled the air between them, making her swallow hard.

I will not cry, she told herself. *I will not let him see me cry.*

Afraid, she drew a sharp breath and held it, refusing to answer.

Swearing, Shadrael bit off his gauntlet and gripped her face with his bare hand. His fingers dug into her flesh. "Tell me what you've done! I have to know the full range of your powers if I'm to hold you prisoner!"

Before she could speak, he used *sevaisin*, and this time the joining of her senses with his was brutal, invasive, painful. She struggled to resist, but he forced the connection, hurting her so much she cried out.

His mind filled hers with a stormy torrent of suspicions and savagery, and then she saw deeper . . . saw a fleeting glimpse of his true character . . . saw beyond it to his secret. In her shock, she stopped fighting him.

Abruptly he released her, breaking *sevaisin*. She collapsed to her knees, weeping in sheer reaction, pressing her hands to her face while he turned away, clenching and unclenching his fists, rage and humiliation coming off him with such force it felt as though they were still linked together.

"Damn you. Damn you!" he shouted. "Don't look at me like that! What do I care if you know? My men know. My brother knows. Everyone in the legion knows!"

She looked up at him through a blur of hot tears and saw him pacing.

"I have no soul," he growled, glaring at her. "There, I have said it to you, little innocent girl with your big eyes and your stupid belief that everyone is good. I am not good! You should know that by now. I am not! And my men are not. We are damned, as damned as this man." He gave Hervan's body an impatient kick. "And every moment I am in your presence I hurt, as though you are a hot blade set to cauterize me."

Lea gulped back her tears. "What is unsworn can be set to rights while life remains."

"Unsworn!" He unleashed a bitter laugh. "If that were all . . ."

"You can—"

"Shut up! I won't listen to that. I won't be pitied and I won't be preached to." He marched up to her as though he would grab her and hoist her to her feet, but he did not touch her. "Don't you dare patronize me with your damned piety."

The raw pain in his voice betrayed him. So she held her tongue, seeing that he could not bear comfort, could not listen to the truth, could not even accept hope. He was too lacerated, too damaged to believe anything she might say.

Besides, why should she bother to explain that she already knew about his wounded soul? What had shocked her just now was to discover his yearning to take someone else's soul instead of his own. Who had told him such a wicked thing? How had he come to believe something so wrong, so blasphemous, so misguided was even possible?

Feeling pity and compassion mingled, she watched him pacing.

"So," he said finally, his voice less strident and defensive. "So you've broken through all the barriers and reached your brother, have you?"

"Why ask, since you have forced your secrets upon me and taken mine in return?" she asked.

He frowned, looking momentarily ashamed. "I hurt you."

"Yes."

"It was . . . necessary." His frown deepened. "You lied to me."

"Did you think me incapable of it?"

"Yes."

She averted her gaze and said nothing. She could have told him that he was to blame for that, too, but it would not help either of them.

"So the emperor knows now," Shadrael said. "Despite my putting you in *kwaibe*, despite my taking away your *gli* necklace, you still managed to tell him what has befallen you. Which means I can't take you to—"

Breaking off, he grimaced in pain and pressed his hand to the side seam of his breastplate.

She remained kneeling like a beggar at his feet and told herself, *He is ill after he uses shadow magic. He is weakened by his violence. I can escape him now before his men come back.*

But when she tried to climb to her feet, her legs refused to support her. She sank down again, trembling all over, the taint of death and the effects of forced *sevaisin* making her run hot and cold.

Her necklace landed in a heap before her.

Astonished, she looked up at Shadrael, but he was turned away, still hunched and breathing hard.

"Go," he said with an angry gesture. "I cannot keep you. Get away. Take your chances that my men don't find you in the woods."

Lea lowered her gaze to the necklace of *gli*-emeralds. She wanted to pick it up so desperately that her hands shook with yearning. Yet she curled them into fists and pressed them hard together to withstand the temptation.

If she took them and fled, she would be able to hide in the woods until the mercenaries were gone. And then what would befall her? She could survive on her own despite the coming of winter. And Caelan would find her.

But her childhood memories of when Caelan had abandoned her came back so sharply that she could almost hear her screams after him. She felt the icy snow around her and that frantic sense of despair as she'd watched him run out of sight, straight toward disaster. On that terrible day, Caelan had thought he was doing the right thing in trying to help their father and the others at the hold. But he'd been wrong, and he'd paid a harsh price for his mistake.

Now, as she stared at Shadrael, she knew he was making an even bigger mistake, no matter how kind. He understood nothing, yet he was trying—in his own way—to apologize to her.

Beneath his harshness and bad temper he was not truly, not wholly an evil man or he would not suffer so. What had it cost him to set her free when the last obstacle to completing his mission lay dead at his feet?

She understood now why the gods had brought them together, but she did not want the responsibility of trying to salvage a man like him, a man trapped in shadow. She did not want to *care* about Shadrael tu Natalloh.

But it was too late for what she wanted. She already *did* care.

And she foresaw the future—his, if he let her go—and hers if she went with him. But if she picked up her necklace and ran, everything would change. She would be safe while he . . .

She stared at the emeralds, and could not bring herself to touch them.

Appalled, she doubled over in a knot of painful distress. She wept for all that she was losing. Because of him.

"Lea," Shadrael said finally, his voice so quiet and flat with exhaustion it sounded almost gentle. "It's no trick. Just go."

She turned away, aching, refusing to look at him.

Crouching stiffly, he picked up the *gli*-emeralds and put them away. She felt a tremor, wanting them and the strength they gave her, wanting anything to reassure her right now.

Shadrael placed his hand gently on her shoulder. She flinched, and he withdrew it as though burned.

"More pearls," he said, scooping some off the ground. "You are crying pearls again."

"Yes. Pearls of sorrow," she whispered bleakly.

"For your friends? The cavalrymen? This captain? Are you crying pearls for him?"

For myself, she wanted to say. *For what I've lost. For what I must become. I am giving up everything for you, and I do not know if you are worth it.* Frowning, unable to articulate what she was thinking, she stayed silent.

Shadrael weighed the pearls in his palm. "I had to kill him. You must realize that."

"You don't answer to me for your actions, Commander."

"Don't I?" he asked softly. Then he cleared his throat. "Now that the emperor knows of your plight, he'll head straight here, to Ulinia. I have led the imperial jackal, despite my care, right to Vord—" Wincing, he broke off and pressed his hand harder against his side. "I cannot do this."

The agony in his voice made her look up as he staggered a few steps away from her. He swayed and braced his feet apart to hold his balance.

Watching him, suddenly aware of how pale he'd become, Lea rose to her feet. She did not go to him. She did not run away. She seemed held in place, like a moth caught in a spider's web. She could not leave him, and she was afraid.

Catching her staring at him, Shadrael bared his teeth. "We're not supposed to care about our families," he burst out. "The army grinds it out of us in the first year. No allegiance to home or kin. There is to be nothing but our legion, our standard." He flung a bloodstained hand to the north, pointing. "But *that* is home."

She said, choosing her words with care, "You're taking me to the warlord of Ulinia."

"Vordachai. His name is Vordachai."

"Lord Vordachai hired you to abduct me."

"I did not want you to know, for his protection." Scowling, Shadrael dabbed some of the blood from his face. "You would not like him. I do not like him. But I do not—I do not want the emperor to crush him to dust. And so I will betray my brother to save him. Do you understand?"

"No."

Shadrael nodded, looking sad. "He will not understand either. He will say I'm doing this for myself, that I value my own selfish concerns over his. He's right."

"What does this matter?" Lea cried, out of patience. "Why can't you take me there and have your wounds tended? Let Lord Vordachai send word to my brother that I am safe. Let this end, here and now."

He stared at her as though perplexed. "You didn't go when I gave you the chance. You haven't fought me on our journey. You've done almost nothing to escape, nothing I expected of you . . . End this? No. The game has barely started."

She heard him through a sort of daze. Exhaustion sapped her, drained her dry. How could she continue this? she wondered. How could she endure what was to come?

"You, Lea, are the wind, the water, the ground I stand on," he said in an odd voice. He hefted the pearls in his hand and sighed. "You are light brought to this world and made into something so fine, something so . . ."

Swaying, Shadrael let his voice trail off. The sun was setting now. Indigo shadows gathered around them, and the air had turned so cold it made her shiver. His wild talk might be delirium, she thought. He might die. Even so, there was no going back to what she'd been before she met him. She had changed too much.

Another pearl rolled down her cheek and she caught it, holding it in her cold hand as though she did not know what to do with it.

The night gathered closer, wrapping her in a blanket of darkness. She felt as though she were stepping into a chasm of shadows, falling forever, with no knowledge of how to get out.

A bird flew at them, its wings flapping close over her head. Lea ducked but Shadrael watched it fly over and inexplicably laughed.

"Yes, raven!" he shouted. "You have your answer! Tell your master to await us."

Lea felt a shiver go through her that had nothing to do with the cold air. Suddenly afraid, she turned away, but Shadrael caught her, moving faster than she'd believed him capable, and gripped her wrist when she would have pulled free.

"You had your chance, and you didn't take it," he said. The strange moodiness was gone from his voice. "Come on."

"But you're hurt—"

"I'm not dying, if that's what you're hoping for," he said. "And I'm not too weak to deliver you, as hired."

She stumbled along, unable to quite keep up with his long stride. "But you just said you wouldn't take me to your brother."

"The highest bidder has won," he said and laughed without mirth.

He led her across the stream to where the horses were grazing. Warily lifting their heads, they were skittish about being caught, but Shadrael drew them to him.

He pulled the bridle off Hervan's horse and released it before boosting Lea onto the other one.

"You're strengthened by the dark, aren't you?" Lea asked.

"Lady Lea, I *am* darkness."

"That's not true," she said. "I know better now."

"You know nothing about it," he said angrily. "I've warned you not to try to redeem me. It can't be done."

He climbed into the saddle behind her with a grunt of pain, his breath hissing between his teeth a moment until he recovered.

She thought he would turn south to find his men, but instead he swung the horse northward, toward the rough mountains. Surprised, Lea looked back. "Your men! Aren't you—"

"They'll catch up," he said indifferently. "Why didn't you run when you had the chance?"

She lifted her hand to brush her cheeks. There were no

more pearls to weep. Not now. "You don't really want to know. You said not to talk about it."

He stared at her, his gaze temporarily honest and unguarded. "I am not worth it," he said softly.

She nodded, not hiding her sigh. "It doesn't matter what you believe now. It's what I know."

Chapter 24

In New Imperia, the vision faded before Caelan's disbelieving eyes. He turned away, scowling, feeling a little dizzy from the lingering effects of the Magria's magic. "That bird," he said, puzzled by the last thing he'd seen clearly. "Was it an omen? What did it mean?"

The Magria looked grim. "The gray raven is a symbol of the Vindicants."

"Great Gault!" Caelan said in horror. "He's taking her to them?"

"It appears so. I beg your forgiveness for the weakness of this vision. It would be stronger in our place of—"

"If only we could have heard what they were saying." Fretting, Caelan began to pace back and forth. "Can you not follow them, discover where they are going now?"

"No."

"I've heard rumors that the Vindicants took refuge in Ulinia, but it's not proven. If we knew for sure, knew where to dig them out."

The Magria's gaze flickered. She looked almost plain in

her weariness. "I cast the visions I am given, Excellency. I do not conjure them up to order."

"But a dream walker, can it not follow her? Find her? Isn't there some way to know where she is?"

"Lady Lea's thoughts are not open to us, Excellency. I have shown you all there is. Should another vision come to me, I will of course offer it to you."

Frustrated, he flung up his hands. "How am I to help her?"

"Clearly she does not wish your help."

"She reached out to me, Magria. She asked me to come to her. I heard her most clearly."

The Magria seemed not to believe him. "And you have seen for yourself in *this* vision that she did not flee her so-called captor, not even after he killed her rescuer. She went with him willingly, and she is staying with him. She has made her choice."

"But before—"

"Do you still trust your vision over mine?" the Magria asked sharply. "You are no trained seer, Excellency. Do you believe you alone understand the correct interpretation of these sightings? Will you not admit that what you saw before was born of your worry and desires and what I have shown you now is the truth?"

Furious and offended, Caelan bit back what he really wanted to say. "You may withdraw, Magria. I've heard enough of your suppositions."

The Magria matched him angry look for look. "Be warned, Excellency. I spoke to you before of betrayal. I told you that you would not like what I had to show you."

"But Lea would never . . . he has coerced her somehow. He must have."

"His magic is weaker than hers. And with her necklace, she—"

"Why didn't she take it?" Caelan asked, clenching his fists. "Why?"

The Magria said nothing. Her blue eyes held steel.

After a moment he forced himself to meet the woman's gaze. Sadly he nodded.

"The portents of war are clear," the Magria said. "Prepare yourself for it. The betrayer has been revealed to you. Accept it. There is no more to be said."

She walked out then, leaving him baffled by what he'd witnessed and angered by what he'd been told.

"Ah, Lea, Lea," he said aloud in heartache. "What are you doing, little one?"

In the steel-hued light of dawn, a solitary horse and rider came out of the trees into a clearing where a mountain stream ran shallow and clear. The corpse of an officer in black boots, white gauntlets, and a crimson cloak lay sprawled on the trampled gravel. Animals had been at the body in the night. A vulture took lazy flight now, its dark wings lifting into the air.

Dismounting stiffly, Thirbe knelt beside the stream to drink thirstily of the sparkling cold water. He had fever, and the throbbing ache of his wound made him lightheaded. He'd ridden all night, pausing now and then to prop himself against a tree trunk and doze a little before his horse shifted and roused him. He'd dared not dismount and take a good rest for fear of being found by roaming mercenaries and killed in the woods. Dying alone and unburied, his body fodder for carrion eaters, was not how Thirbe intended to go.

This morning, he felt stiff and incredibly sore. The dew falling on him was icy cold, and he shivered as he drank some more, then sat back on his heels to stare at Captain Hervan's ravaged gray face. Handsome no longer, Thirbe thought, but then death was never pretty.

Angered, he tossed a pebble into the water with a little plop. "Cheated, by Gault," he muttered. "I make a vow of revenge, and what do I get? Beaten to it."

His voice made the birds rise from the trees, flying about before settling into the branches once more. He hurt and he hungered, and his thirst could not be quenched. His little quest had kept him going through the night, kept him alert and wily until the last straying mercenaries had passed him by, moving fast through the dark woods like the devils they were.

So his quest was over. He felt empty and too tired to think. Was he to perish in this Gault-forsaken forest, the wolves and vultures to gnaw on his bones?

The light was growing stronger, and the last sigh of night seemed to lift above the trees and breathe itself into day. The first rays of glittering sunlight rose above the hills, shining on something small and white near Hervan's torn hand.

Thirbe frowned, hesitating only a moment, before he crossed the stream and bent down for it.

A stone, smooth and pale, shimmering iridescent in his fingers. "The opal," he muttered in wonder.

As his fingers closed on it, he felt his despair shift inside him, fading into new determination and energy. The stone began to glow, milky white, as though it had life of its own.

He knew what it was, all right. He'd seen Hervan hold it over the map as they tracked Lady Lea. He'd heard the talk among the cavalrymen, knew from Poulso the priest that it was a cursed stone and that the ghosts of Lady Fyngie and Lady Rinthella had haunted the captain's sleep, with one urging him to avenge them and the other urging him to turn back.

But Thirbe had seen Lady Lea's hand draw this stone from the waters of that little stream in the valley. And there was nothing cursed about the maiden, nothing evil that could touch her hand.

His heart leaped in hope, and he straightened, swinging his gaze north toward the Ulinian badlands. There was still a chance of finding her.

It was all the purpose he needed. He searched Hervan's body and found the doeskin map, and tucked both it and the opal carefully away.

Kneeling there on the graveled bank, he held his sword hilt to the heavens and vowed before Gault that he would not surrender this quest to see Lady Lea safely found and restored to her family.

This mission was his penitence, his punishment, and perhaps his future glory. He would not, he swore on all he held sacred, fail her again.

THE ULTIMATE IN FANTASY!

From magical tales of distant worlds to stories of those with abilities beyond the ordinary, Ace and Roc have everything you need to stretch your imagination to its limits.

Marion Zimmer Bradley/Diana Paxon

Guy Gavriel Kaye

Dennis McKiernan

Patricia McKillip

Robin McKinley

Sharon Shinn

Katherine Kurtz

Barb and J. C. Hendees

Elizabeth Bear

T. A. Barron

Brian Jacques

Robert Asprin